TEMPTED

ALSO BY P. C. CAST and KRISTIN CAST

TEMPTED

A House of Night Novel

P. C. CAST and **KRISTIN CAST**

ST. MARTIN'S GRIFFIN

NEW YORK

TEMPTED. Copyright © 2009 by P. C. Cast and Kristin Cast. All rights reserved. Printed in the United States of America. For information, address St. Martin's Press, 175 Fifth Avenue, New York, N.Y. 10010.

www.stmartins.com

ISBN 978-0-312-56748-4

First Edition: November 2009

10 9 8 7 6 5 4 3 2 1

Kristin and I would like to dedicate this book to our fabulous editor, Jennifer Weis, who is a pleasure to work with and who makes rewriting bearable. We heart you, Jen!

ACKNOWLEDGMENTS

Kristin and I want to again acknowledge our wonderful team at St. Martin's Press. We've come to think of them as family, and appreciate their kindness, generosity, creativity, and belief in us. Thank you thank you thank you: Jennifer Weis, Anne Bensson, Matthew Shear, Anne Marie Tallberg, Brittney Kleinfelter, Katy Hershberger, and Sally Richardson. We also want to send XXXOOO to our brilliant cover design team, Michael Storrings and Elsie Lyons.

Thank you, Jenny Sullivan, for your excellent and scarily accurate proofreading skills.

As always, we thank our amazing agent and friend, Meredith Bernstein, who changed all our lives with three little words: vampyre finishing school.

And, of course, thank you to our fans! Especially those of you who contact us and tell us how much the HoN has touched your hearts.

TEMPTED

CHAPTER ONE

Zoey

The night sky over Tulsa was alight with a magical crescent moon. Its brilliance made the ice that coated the city, and the Benedictine Abbey where we'd just had our showdown with a fallen immortal and a rogue High Priestess, shimmer so that everything around me seemed touched by our Goddess. I looked at the moonlight-bathed circle that stood in front of Mary's Grotto, the place of power where not long ago Spirit, Blood, Earth, Humanity, and Night had been personified and then had joined to triumph over hatred and darkness. The carved image of Mary, surrounded by stone roses and nestled within a ledge high in the grotto, appeared to be a beacon for the silver light. I stared at the statue. Mary's expression was serene; her ice-covered cheeks glistened as if she wept in quiet joy.

My gaze lifted to the sky. *Thank you.* I sent a silent prayer up to the beautiful crescent that symbolized my Goddess, Nyx. *We're alive. Kalona and Neferet are gone.*

"Thank you," I whispered to the moon.

Listen within . . .

The words swept through me, subtle and sweet like leaves touched by a summer breeze, brushing my consciousness so lightly that my waking mind barely registered them, yet Nyx's whispered command imprinted itself into my soul.

I was vaguely aware that there were a lot of people (well, nuns, fledglings, and a few vampyres) around me. I could hear the mixture of shouting, talking, crying, and even laughing that filled the night, but it all felt distant. At that moment the only things that were real to me were the moon above and the scar that sliced from one shoulder all the way across my chest to the other shoulder. It tingled in response to my silent prayer, but it wasn't a tingle of pain. Not really. It was a familiar warm, prickling sensation that assured me Nyx had, once again, Marked me as hers. I knew if I peeked under the neck of my shirt I would find a new tattoo decorating that long, angry-looking scar with an exotic filigree of sapphire—a sign that proved I was following my Goddess's path.

"Erik and Heath, find Stevie Rae, Johnny B, and Dallas—then check the perimeter of the abbey to be certain all the Raven Mockers fled with Kalona and Neferet!" Darius shouted the command, snapping me out of my warm, fuzzy prayer mode, and once I'd been shocked out, it was like an iPod had been cranked too high as sound and confusion flooded my senses.

"But Heath's a human. A Raven Mocker could kill him in a second." The words burst from my mouth before I could clamp it shut, proving beyond all doubt that being moonstruck wasn't my only moronic skill.

Predictably, Heath puffed up like a cat-smacked toad.

"Zo, I'm not a damn pussy!"

Erik, looking very tall and full-grown, kick-your-butt vampyre-like, snorted sarcastically and then said, "No, you're a damn human. Wait, that *does* make you a pussy!"

"So, we defeat the big baddies and inside five minutes Erik and Heath are banging their chests at each other. How totally predictable," Aphrodite said with her patented sarcastic sneer as she joined Darius, but her expression completely changed when she turned her attention to the Son of Erebus Warrior. "Hey there, Hotness. You doing okay?"

"You need not worry about me," Darius said. His eyes met hers, and they practically telegraphed the chemistry between them, but instead of going to her like he usually would and doing some very gross kissing, he remained focused on Stark.

Aphrodite's gaze went from Darius to Stark. "Okay, eew. Your chest is totally crispy crittered."

James Stark was standing between Darius and Erik. Okay, well, *standing* wasn't exactly what he was doing. Stark was swaying and looking extremely unsteady.

Ignoring Aphrodite, Erik spoke up. "Darius, you should probably get Stark inside. I'll coordinate the reconnoitering with Stevie Rae and make sure everything runs smoothly out here." His words seemed okay, but his tone was all I'm-the-big-guy-in-charge, and when he followed up with a condescending "I'll even let Heath help out," he really sounded like a pompous butt.

"You'll *let me* help out?" Heath snapped. "Your *mom* will let me help out."

"Hey, which one of them is supposed to be your boyfriend?" Stark asked me. Even in the terrible shape he was in, he caught my glance with his. His voice was scratchy, and he sounded scarily weak, but his eyes sparkled with humor.

"I am!" Heath and Erik said together.

"Oh, for crap's sake, Zoey, they're both idiots!" Aphrodite said.

Stark started to chuckle, which turned to a cough, which changed again to a painful gasp. His eyes rolled back and, like a slinky, he collapsed.

Moving with the quickness that came naturally to a Son of Erebus Warrior, Darius caught Stark before he hit the ground. "I need to get him inside," Darius said.

I felt like my head was going to explode. Sagging in Darius's arms, Stark looked well on his way to being dead. "I-I don't even know where the infirmary is," I stuttered.

"Not a problem. I'll get a penguin to show us," Aphrodite said. "Hey, you, nun!" she yelled at one of the nearby black-and-white–clad sisters who had scurried out of the abbey after the night had gone from battle chaos to aftermath chaos.

Darius hurried after the nun, with Aphrodite following him. The warrior glanced over his shoulder at me. "Aren't you coming with us, Zoey?"

"As soon as I can." Before I could deal with Erik and Heath, from behind me a familiar twang saved the day.

"Go on with Darius and Aphrodite, Z. I'll take care of Dumb and Dumber and be sure there's no booger monsters left out here."

"Stevie Rae, you are the Best Friend of All Best Friends." I turned and hugged her quickly, loving how reassuringly solid and normal she felt. Actually, she seemed so normal that I got a weird twinge when she stepped back and grinned at me and I saw, as if for the first time, the scarlet tattoos that spread out from the filled-in crescent in the middle of her forehead and down either side of her face. A sliver of unease threaded through me.

Misunderstanding my hesitation, she said, "Don't worry about these two dorks. I'm gettin' used to jerking them apart." When I just stood there staring at her, the bright smile she'd been wearing dimmed. "Hey, you know your grandma's okay, right? Kramisha got her back inside right after Kalona was banished and Sister Mary Angela just told me she was goin' inside to check on her."

"Yeah, I remember Kramisha helping her into the wheelchair. I'm just . . ." My voice trailed off. I was just what? How could I put into words that I was haunted by a feeling that everything wasn't right with my best friend and the group of kids she'd allied herself with, and how do I say that *to* my best friend?

"You're just tired and worried 'bout a bunch of stuff," Stevie Rae said softly.

Was that understanding I saw flicker through her eyes? Or was it something else, something darker?

"I get it, Z, and I'll take care of things out here. You just be sure Stark's okay." She hugged me again, and then gave me a little push in the direction of the abbey.

"'Kay. Thanks," I said lamely, starting toward the abbey and totally ignoring the two dorks who were standing there staring at me.

Stevie Rae called after me, "Hey, remind Darius or someone to keep an eye on the time. It's only about an hour until sunrise, and you know me and all the red fledglings gotta be inside out of the sun by then."

"Yeah, no problem. I'll remember," I said.

The problem was it was getting harder and harder for me to *forget* Stevie Rae wasn't what she used to be.

CHAPTER TWO

Stevie Rae

"All right, you two, listen up. I'm only gonna say this once—*act right*." Standing between the two guys, Stevie Rae put her hands on her hips and glared at Erik and Heath. Without taking her eyes from them she yelled, "Dallas!"

Almost instantly the kid jogged up to her. "What's up, Stevie Rae?"

"Get Johnny B. Tell him to take Heath and search around the front part of the abbey over by Lewis Street and make sure the Raven Mockers are really gone. You and Erik take the south side of the building. I'll go down along the tree row by Twenty-first and check it out."

"All by yourself?" Erik said.

"Yes, all by myself," Stevie Rae snapped. "Are you forgettin' I could stomp my foot right now and make the ground under you shake? I could also pick you up and toss you on your silly jealous butt. I think I can handle checkin' out those trees by myself."

Beside her, Dallas laughed. "And I'm thinking red vamp with an earth element affinity trumps blue drama vamp."

That made Heath snort and laugh; and, predictably, Erik started to bow up again.

"No!" Stevie Rae said before the stupid boys started throwing punches. "If y'all can't say anything nice, then just shut the heck up."

"Did you want me, Stevie Rae?" Johnny B said, coming up to stand beside her. "I saw Darius carrying that arrow kid into the abbey. He said I should find you."

"Yeah," she said with relief. "I want you and Heath to check out the front part of the abbey over by Lewis. Make sure those Raven Mockers really are gone."

"I'm on it!" Johnny B said, giving Heath a pretend punch on the shoulder. "Come on, quarterback, let's see what you got."

"Just pay attention to the dang trees and shadowy stuff," Stevie Rae said, shaking her head as Heath ducked and dodged and struck Johnny B's shoulder with a few quick punches.

"No problem," Dallas said, starting to move off with a silent Erik.

"Make it quick," Stevie Rae called to both sets of guys. "The sun'll be up soon. Y'all meet me in front of Mary's Grotto in half an hour or so. Holler loud if you find anything and we'll all come runnin'."

She watched the four guys to be sure they were really going where she'd sent them, and then Stevie Rae turned and, with a sigh, started on her own mission. Dang, talk about annoying! She loved Z more than white bread, but dealing with her BFF's boyfriends was making her feel like a toad in a tornado! She used to think Erik was the hottest guy in the world. After spending a couple of days with him, she now thought he was a big ol' pain in the butt with a super-sized ego. Heath was sweet, but he was just a human, and Z had been right to worry about him. Humans definitely died easier than vamps or even fledglings. She glanced over her shoulder, trying to catch sight of Johnny B and Heath, but the icy darkness and the trees had swallowed her and she couldn't see anyone.

Not that Stevie Rae minded being by herself for a change. Johnny B would keep an eye on Heath. The truth was that she was glad to be rid of him and jealous Erik for a little while. The two of them made her appreciate Dallas. He was simple and easy. He was her kinda-sorta boyfriend. The two of them had a *thing,* but it didn't get in the way of stuff. Dallas knew Stevie Rae had a lot to deal with, so he let her deal. And he was there for the off times. Easy-peasy, cute and breezy! That was Dallas.

Z could learn a thing or two about handling guys from me, she thought as she trudged through the grove of old trees that ringed Mary's Grotto and buffered the abbey's land from busy Twenty-first Street.

Well, one thing was for sure—it was definitely a crappy night. Stevie Rae hadn't gone a dozen paces before her short blond curls were soaked. Dang, water was even drippin' off her nose! She backhanded her face, wiping off the cold, wet mixture of rain and ice. Everything was so weirdly dark and silent. It was freaky that there were absolutely no streetlights working on Twenty-first. Not one car was on the street—not even a cruising TPD squad car. She slipped and slid down the incline. Her feet met road and only her super-good red vampyre night vision kept her oriented. It seemed like Kalona had run away and taken sound and light with him.

Feeling skittish, she backhanded the sopping wet hair from her face again and pulled herself together. "You're actin' like a chicken, and you know how stupid chickens are!" She spoke aloud and then got double spooked when her words sounded bizarrely magnified by the ice and darkness.

Why in the world was she so jumpy? "It could be 'cause you're keepin' stuff from your BFF," Stevie Rae muttered, and then clamped her lips shut. Her voice was just too loud in the dark, ice-filled night.

But she was gonna tell Z about the other stuff. Really she was! There just hadn't been time. And Z had enough on her mind without more stress. And . . . and . . . it was hard to talk about it, even to Zoey.

Stevie Rae kicked at a broken, ice-covered branch. She knew it didn't matter if it was hard. She was gonna talk to Zoey. She had to. But later. Maybe a lot later.

Better to focus on the present, at least for right now.

Squinting and cupping her hand over her eyes to try to shield them from the sting of the icy rain, Stevie Rae peered up into the branches of the trees. Even with the darkness and the storm her eyesight was good, and she was relieved not to see any big dark bodies lurking above her. Finding it easier to walk on the side of the road, she made her way down Twenty-first Street heading away from the abbey, all the while keeping her eyes up.

It wasn't until she was almost at the fence line that divided the nuns' property from the upscale condo beside it that Stevie Rae smelled it.

Blood.

A wrong kind of blood.

She stopped. Looking almost feral, Stevie Rae sniffed the air. It was filled with the wet, musty scent of ice as it coated earth, the crisp, cinnamon smell of the winter trees, and the man-made tang of the asphalt beneath her feet. She ignored those scents and instead focused on the blood. It wasn't human blood, or even fledgling blood, so it didn't smell like sunlight and spring—honey and chocolate—love and life and everything that she'd ever dreamed of. No, this blood smelled too dark. Too thick. There was too much of something in it that wasn't human. But it was still blood, and it drew her, even though she knew the wrongness of it deep in her soul.

It was the scent of something strange, something otherworldly, that led her to the first splashes of crimson. In the stormy darkness of the sunless predawn, even her enhanced vision saw it only as wet splotches against the ice that sheeted the road and covered the grass beside it. But Stevie Rae knew it was blood. A lot of blood.

But there was no animal or human lying there bleeding.

Instead there was a trail of liquid darkness thickening in the sheeting ice, moving away from the street and into the densest part of the grove behind the abbey.

Her predator's instincts kicked in instantly. Stevie Rae moved stealthily, hardly breathing, hardly making a sound, as she tracked the blood path.

It was beneath one of the largest trees that she found it, hunkered down under a huge, newly broken branch as if it had dragged itself there to hide and die.

Stevie Rae felt a shudder of fear pass through her. It was a Raven Mocker.

The creature was huge. Bigger than she'd thought they'd looked from a distance. It lay on its side, head tucked down against the ground, so she couldn't see its face very well. The giant wing she could see looked wrong, obviously broken, and the human arm that lay beneath it was weirdly angled and covered with blood. Its legs were human, too, and curled up like it had died in a fetal position. She remembered hearing Darius firing a gun as he and Z and the gang had ridden like bats outta hell down Twenty-first to the abbey. So, he'd shot it from the sky.

"Dang," she said under her breath. "That must've been one heck of a fall."

Stevie Rae cupped her hands around her mouth and was getting ready to holler for Dallas so he and the other guys could help her drag the body somewhere when the Raven Mocker twitched and opened its eyes.

She froze. The two of them stared at each other. The creature's red eyes widened, looking surprised and impossibly human in the bird face. They flicked around her and behind her, checking to see if she was alone. Automatically, Stevie Rae crouched, putting her hands up defensively and centering herself to call earth to strengthen her.

And then he spoke.

"Kill me. End this," he gasped, panting in pain.

The sound of his voice was so human, so completely unexpected that Stevie Rae dropped her hands and staggered a step back. "You can talk!" she blurted.

Then the Raven Mocker did something that utterly shocked Stevie Rae and irrevocably changed the course of her life.

He laughed.

It was a dry, sarcastic sound, and it ended in a moan of pain. But it was laughter, and it framed his words with humanity.

"Yes," he said between gasps for breath. "I talk. I bleed. I die. Kill me and be done with it." He tried to sit up then, as if he were eager to meet his death, and the movement caused him to cry out in agony. His too-human eyes rolled back and he collapsed to the frozen ground, unconscious.

Stevie Rae moved before she remembered even making the decision. When she reached him, she only hesitated for a second. He'd passed out facedown, so it was a simple thing for her to move his wings aside and grab him under his arms. He was big, really big—like, as big as a real guy, and she'd braced herself for him to be heavy, but he wasn't. Actually, he was so light that it was super-easy to drag him, which was what she found herself doing while her mind screamed at her: *What the hell? What the hell? What the hell?*

What the hell was she doing?

Stevie Rae didn't know. All she knew was what she *wasn't* doing. She wasn't killing the Raven Mocker.

CHAPTER THREE

Zoey

"Is he going to be okay?" I tried to whisper so I wouldn't wake Stark and was, apparently, unsuccessful, because his closed eyelids fluttered and his lips tilted up slightly in a painful ghost of his cocky half smile.

"I'm not dead yet," he said.

"And I'm not talking to you," I said in a much more irritated voice than I'd intended.

"Temper, *u-we-tsi-a-ge-ya*," Grandma Redbird rebuked me gently as Sister Mary Angela, prioress of the Benedictine nuns, helped her into the little infirmary room.

"Grandma! There you are!" I hurried to her and helped Sister Mary Angela ease her into a chair.

"She's just worried about me." Stark's eyes were closed again but his lips still hinted at a smile.

"I know that, *tsi-ta-ga-a-s-ha-ya*. But Zoey is a High Priestess in training and she must learn to control her emotions."

Tsi-ta-ga-a-s-ha-ya! That would have made me laugh out loud if Grandma hadn't looked so pale and frail, and if I hadn't been so, well, worried in general. "Sorry, Grandma. I should watch my temper, but it's kinda hard when the people I love most keep almost dying!" I finished in a rush and had to draw a deep breath to steady myself. "And shouldn't you be in bed?"

"Soon, *u-we-tsi-a-ge-ya*, soon."

"What does *tsi-ta-ga-a-s*-whatever mean?" Stark's voice was thick with pain as Darius spread a thick cream over his burns, but in spite of the wound he sounded amused and curious.

"*Tsi-ta-ga-a-s-ha-ya*," Grandma corrected his pronunciation, "means rooster."

His eyes glimmered with humor. "Everyone says you're a wise woman."

"Which is less interesting than what everyone says about you, *tsi-ta-ga-a-s-ha-ya*," Grandma said.

Stark barked a quick laugh and then sucked air painfully.

"Be still!" Darius commanded.

"Sister, I thought you said you guys had a doctor here." I tried not to sound as panicky as I felt.

"A human doctor cannot help him," Darius said before Sister Mary Angela could respond. "He needs rest and quiet and—"

"Rest and quiet are fine," Stark interrupted him. "Like I said before: I'm not dead yet." He met Darius's eyes and I saw the Son of Erebus shrug and nod his head briefly, as if he'd conceded some point to the younger vampyre.

I should have just ignored the little interplay between them, but my patience had evaporated hours before. "Okay, what aren't you telling me?"

The nun who'd been assisting Darius shot me a long, cold look and said, "Perhaps the injured boy needs to know his sacrifice was not made in vain."

The nun's harsh words gave me a jolt of guilty shock that closed my throat and didn't let me respond to the hard-eyed woman. The sacrifice Stark had been willing to make was his life for mine. I swallowed past the dryness in my throat. What was my life worth? I was just a kid—barely seventeen. I'd messed up over and over again. I was the reincarnation of a girl created to trap a fallen angel, and that meant deep inside my soul I couldn't help loving him, even when I knew I shouldn't . . . couldn't . . .

No. I wasn't worth the sacrifice of Stark's life.

"I already know it." Stark's voice didn't waver; suddenly he sounded strong and sure. I blinked my vision free of tears and met his eyes. "What I did was just part of my job," he said. "I'm a Warrior. I've sworn my life into the service of Zoey Redbird, High Priestess and Beloved of Nyx. That means I'm working for our Goddess and being knocked to the ground and burned a little really doesn't mean shit if I helped Zoey beat the bad guys."

"Well said, *tsi-ta-ga-a-s-ha-ya,*" Grandma told him.

"Sister Emily, I relieve you of your infirmary duties for the rest of the night. Please send Sister Bianca here in your stead. I believe you should, perhaps, spend some time in quiet contemplation of Luke 6:37," said Sister Mary Angela.

"As you wish, Sister," the nun said and hurried from the room.

"Luke 6:37? What's that?" I asked.

"'Judge not, and ye shall not be judged: condemn not, and ye shall not be condemned: forgive, and ye shall be forgiven,'" my grandma said. She was sharing a smile with Sister Mary Angela when Damien knocked softly on the half-open door.

"Can we come in? There's someone who really needs to see Stark." Damien glanced over his shoulder and made a *stay-there* motion behind him. The soft *woof!* that came in response told me the some-*one* was really a some*dog.*

"Don't let her come in." Stark grimaced in pain as he abruptly turned his head away so that he couldn't see Damien or the doorway. "Tell that Jack kid she's his now."

"No." I stopped Damien as he began to back away. "Have Jack bring Duchess in."

"Zoey, no, I—" Stark began, but my raised hand stilled him.

"Just bring her in," I said. Then I met Stark's eyes. "Do you trust me?"

He looked at me for what seemed like a really long time. I saw his vulnerability and pain clearly, but finally he nodded once and said, "I trust you."

"Go ahead, Damien," I said.

Damien turned and murmured something over his shoulder and then he moved aside. Jack, Damien's boyfriend, came into the room first. His cheeks were pink and his eyes were suspiciously bright. He stopped after a couple of feet and turned back to the door.

"Come on. It's okay. He's in here," Jack coaxed.

The blond Lab padded into the room and I was surprised by how quietly she moved for such a big dog. She stopped briefly by Jack's side and looked up at him, wagging her tail.

"It's okay," Jack repeated. He smiled at Duchess and then wiped away the tears that had escaped his eyes and were slipping down his cheeks. "He's better now." Jack made a motion to the bed. Duchess's head turned in the direction he'd pointed, and she looked directly at Stark.

The injured boy and the dog just stared at each other while I swear we all held our breath.

"Hi, pretty girl." Stark spoke hesitantly, his voice choked with tears.

Duchess's ears perked up and her head cocked.

Stark held a hand out and made a beckoning motion. "Come here, Duch."

Like his command had broken a dam inside the dog, Duchess surged forward, whining and wriggling and woofing—basically sounding and acting way more like a puppy than her one hundred plus pounds said she could no way be.

"No!" Darius commanded. "Not up on the bed!"

Duchess obeyed the warrior and contented herself with stuffing her head against Stark's side and sliding her big nose under his armpit while she wagged her entire body, and Stark, face glowing with happiness, petted her and told her over and over again how much he'd missed her and what a good girl she was.

I hadn't realized I'd been bawling, too, until Damien handed me a tissue.

"Thanks," I muttered, and wiped my face.

He smiled briefly at me, and then he moved to Jack's side, putting his arm around his boyfriend and patting his shoulder (and handing him a tissue, too). I heard Damien tell him, "Come on, let's go find the room the sisters have ready for us. You need to rest."

Jack made a sniffling, hiccupping sob sound, nodded, and let Damien begin to lead him from the room.

"Wait, Jack," Stark called after them.

Jack looked at the bed where Duchess still had her head pressed against Stark, who had his arm wrapped around the Lab's neck.

"You did good taking care of Duch when I couldn't."

"It wasn't any trouble. I've never had a dog before, so I didn't know how really great they are." Jack's voice broke only a little. He cleared his throat and went on. "I'm—I'm glad you're not, uh, evil and awful and stuff like that anymore so she can be with you again."

"Yeah, about that." Stark paused, grimacing as the pain of his movements caught up with him. "I'm not exactly one hundred percent yet, and even when I am, I'm not sure what my schedule's going to be. So I'm thinking that it would be a big favor to me if you and I could maybe share Duchess."

"Really?" Jack's face lit up.

Stark nodded wearily. "Really. Could you and Damien take Duch back to your room, and maybe bring her to see me again later?"

"Absolutely!" Jack said, and then he cleared his throat and continued. "Yeah, like I said before. She hasn't been any problem."

"Good," Stark said. He lifted Duchess's muzzle in his hand and looked into the Lab's eyes. "I'm okay now, pretty girl. You go with Jack so I can get all better."

I knew it must have caused him agony, but Stark sat up then and bent to kiss Duchess and let the dog lick his face. "Good girl . . . that's my pretty girl . . ." he whispered, and kissed her again and said, "Go on with Jack now! Go on!" and he motioned to Jack.

After one last lick of Stark's face, and a single reluctant whimper, she turned from the bed and trotted to Jack's side, wagging her tail at him and nuzzling him in greeting while he wiped his eyes with one hand and petted her with the other.

"I'll take really good care of her and bring her back to see you as soon as the sun sets today. Okay?"

Stark managed a smile. "Okay, thanks, Jack." Then he collapsed onto the pillows.

"He needs rest and quiet," Darius told all of us, and he continued to work over Stark.

"Zoey, perhaps you can help me get your grandma to her room? She, too, needs rest and quiet. It has been a long night for all of us," said Sister Mary Angela.

Shifting my worry from Stark to Grandma, I looked back and forth between the two people I cared so much about.

Stark caught my gaze. "Hey, take care of your grandma. I can feel that the sun will be rising soon. I'm going to go out like a light about then."

"Well . . . okay." I went over to the side of his bed and stood there awkwardly. What was I supposed to do? Kiss him? Squeeze his hand? Give him a thumbs-up and a dorky smile? I mean, he wasn't my official boyfriend, but he and I had a bond that went beyond just friends. Feeling confused and worried and basically out of my comfort zone, I put my hand on his shoulder and whispered, "Thank you for saving my life."

His eyes met mine and the rest of the room faded away. "I'm always going to keep your heart safe, even if mine has to stop beating for that to happen," he told me softly.

I bent and kissed his forehead, murmuring, "Let's try not to let that happen, 'kay?"

"Okay," he whispered.

"I'll see you when the sun sets again," I told Stark before finally hurrying over to Grandma. Sister Mary Angela and I eased her to her feet, almost carrying her out of Stark's room and down a short hall to another hospital-like room. Grandma felt tiny and fragile under my supporting arm and my stomach twisted anew with worry for her.

"Stop fretting, *u-we-tsi-a-ge-ya*," she said as Sister Mary Angela propped pillows around her and helped make her comfortable.

"I'm going to get your pain medication," Sister Mary Angela told Grandma. "I'm also going to be sure the blinds in Stark's room are closed and the drapes drawn tight, so you have a few minutes to chat, but when I come back I'll insist you take your pain pill and sleep."

"You're a hard taskmistress, Mary Angela," Grandma said.

"It takes one to know one, Sylvia," said the nun. And she hurried from the room.

Grandma smiled at me and patted the bed next to her. "Come sit close to me, *u-we-tsi-a-ge-ya*."

I sat beside Grandma, tucking my legs up under me, trying to be careful not to jostle the bed too much. Her face was bruised and burned from the airbag that had saved her life. Part of her lip and her cheek had stitches darkening them. She had a bandage on her head and her right arm was swathed in a scary-looking cast.

"Ironic, isn't it, that my wounds look so terrible, but they are far less painful and far-reaching than the invisible wounds inside of you," she said.

I started to tell Grandma I was really okay, but her next words sliced through what was left of my denial.

"How long have you known you were the reincarnation of the maiden A-ya?"

CHAPTER FOUR

Zoey

"I felt drawn to Kalona from the first second I saw him," I said slowly. I wouldn't lie to Grandma, but that didn't mean telling her the truth would be easy. "But almost all the fledglings and even the vampyres were drawn to him—actually, it was like they were under some kind of spell he was able to cast."

Grandma nodded. "So I already heard from Stevie Rae. But it was different with you? More than just this magical allure he has?"

"Yeah. With me it wasn't so much that I was under his spell." I swallowed past the dryness in my throat. "I wasn't tricked into thinking he was Erebus come to earth, and I knew he planned evil with Neferet. I saw his darkness. But I also wanted to be with him—not just because I believed he might still be able to choose to be good, but because I *wanted* him, even though I knew it was wrong."

"But you fought against that desire, *u-we-tsi-a-ge-ya.* You chose your own path, that of love and goodness and your Goddess, and thus the creature was banished. You chose love," she repeated slowly. "Let that be balm to the wound he has rent in your soul."

The tight, panicky feeling in my chest began to loosen. "I *can* follow my own path," I said with more conviction than I'd felt since first realizing I was A-ya reincarnated. Then I frowned. There was no denying that she and I were connected. Call it essence or soul or spirit or whatever—it tied me to an immortal being as surely as the earth had imprisoned him for centuries. "I'm not A-ya," I repeated more slowly, "but I'm not through with Kalona. What do I do, Grandma?"

Grandma took my hand in hers and squeezed. "As you said, you follow your path. And right now that path is leading you to a soft, warm bed and a full *day's* sleep."

"One crisis at a time?"

"One *thing* at a time," she said.

"And it's time you followed your own advice, Sylvia," Sister Mary Angela said as she bustled into the room with a Dixie cup of water in one hand and pills in another.

Grandma smiled wearily up at the nun and took the medicine from her. I noticed that her hands were shaking as she placed the pills on her tongue and drank the water.

"Grandma, I'm going to let you rest now."

"I love you, *u-we-tsi-a-ge-ya*. You did well today."

"I couldn't have done it without you. I love you, too, Grandma." I bent and kissed her forehead, and as she closed her eyes and settled back against her pillows with a contented smile, I followed Sister Mary Angela from the room and fired questions at her as soon as we were in the hall. "Did you find rooms for everyone? Are the red fledglings doing okay? Do you have a clue if Stevie Rae got Erik and Heath and whoever else together to check out the area around the abbey? Is everything safe out there?

Sister Mary Angela held her hand up to stop my word flood. "Child, take a breath and let me speak."

I suppressed a sigh but managed to stay quiet as I followed her down the hallway while she explained that she and the nuns had set up a cozy dormlike area for the red fledglings in the basement, after Stevie Rae had told her they'd be most comfortable down there. My gang was upstairs in the guest dorms, and yes, the kids had given an all clear on the Raven Mockers outside.

"You know, you really are incredible." I smiled at her as we paused outside a closed door at the end of a long hall. "Thank you."

"I am my Lady's servant, and you are most welcome," she said simply and held the door open for me. "This is the stairwell that leads down to the basement. I've been told that most of the kids are down there already."

"Zoey! There you are. You have to come check this out. You will not believe what Stevie Rae did," Damien said as he hurried up the stairs toward us.

I felt my stomach clench. "What?" I immediately started down to meet him. "What's wrong?"

He grinned at me. "Nothing's wrong. It's incredible." Damien took my hand and pulled me with him.

"Damien's right about that," said Sister Mary Angela, coming down the stairs after us. "But I think incredible is the wrong word for it."

"Is the right word more like terrible or horrible?" I asked.

He squeezed my hand. "Stop being such a worrier. You beat Kalona and Neferet tonight; everything's going to be okay."

I squeezed his hand back and made myself smile and look less worried, even though I knew deep in my heart, deep in my soul, that what had happened tonight had not been an ending or even a victory. It had been a terrible, horrible beginning.

"Wow." I stared around in shocked disbelief.

"Wow squared is more like it," Damien said.

"Stevie Rae really did this?"

"That's what Jack told me," Damien said. He and I stood side by side and peered into the darkness of the newly hollowed earth.

"Okay—creepy." I spoke my thoughts aloud.

Damien gave me an odd look. "What do you mean?"

"Well," I paused, not entirely sure what I did mean, even though the tunnel definitely made me feel uneasy. "Um, it's, uh . . . *really dark.*"

Damien laughed. "Of course it's dark. It's supposed to be dark. It's a hole in the ground."

"To me it feels more natural than a hole in the ground," said Sister Mary Angela as she joined us at the mouth of the tunnel, peering with us down its black length. "For some reason it comforts me. Perhaps it's the way it smells."

The three of us sniffed. I smelled, well, *dirt*. But Damien said, "It smells rich and healthy."

"Like a newly plowed field," the nun agreed.

"See, it's not creepy, Z. I'd definitely hide down here during a tornado," Damien said.

Feeling overly sensitive and kinda silly, I blew out a long breath and peered into the tunnel, trying to see it with new eyes and feel it with a more accurate instinct. "Could I use your flashlight for a second, Sister?"

"Of course."

Sister Mary Angela handed me the big, square, heavy-duty flashlight she'd carried with us from the main basement into this little side section she'd called their root cellar. The ice storm that had encased Tulsa for the past several days had knocked out the abbey's power—as it had most of the city's power. They did have gas generators, so in the main part of the abbey a few electric lights were on, along with the zillions of candles the nuns liked so much, but they hadn't wasted electricity in the root cellar, and the only illumination came from the nun's flashlight. This I shined into the hole in the ground.

The tunnel wasn't very big. If I spread my arms, I could easily touch both sides of it. I looked up. It only cleared my head by about a foot. I sniffed again, trying to find the sense of comfort the nun and Damien obviously felt. My nose wrinkled. The place reeked of dark and dampness, roots and things that had been stirred up from under the surface. I suspected those *things* slithered and crawled, which automatically made my skin shiver and crawl.

Then I mentally shook myself. Why should a tunnel in the earth seem so gross? I had an affinity for earth. I could conjure it. I shouldn't be afraid of it.

Gritting my teeth, I took one step into the tunnel. Then another. And another.

"Hey, uh, Z, don't go too far. You have the only light, and I wouldn't want Sister Mary Angela to be left back here in the dark. She might get scared."

I shook my head and, smiling, turned around, shining the flashlight toward the entrance and illuminating Damien's worried face and Sister Mary Angela's serene one.

"You wouldn't want the *nun* to be afraid of the dark?"

Damien shifted guiltily.

Sister Mary Angela rested her hand on his shoulder for a moment. "It is kind of you to think of me, Damien, but I have no fear of the dark."

I was giving Damien a *don't be such a sissy* look when the feeling hit me. The air behind me changed. I knew I wasn't alone in that tunnel anymore. Fear fingered its way up my spine and I had a sudden urge to run—to get out of there as fast as I could and to never, ever come back.

And I did almost run. Then I surprised myself by getting mad. I'd just faced a fallen immortal—a creature I was connected to on a soul-deep level—and I hadn't run then.

I wasn't going to run now.

"Zoey? What is it?" Damien's voice sounded far away as I whirled around to face the darkness.

Suddenly a flickering light, like the glowing eye of an underground monster, materialized. The light wasn't big, but it was bright, temporarily causing spots in my field of vision and partially blinding me so that when I looked up the monster appeared to have three heads, with a wild, waving mane, and shoulders that looked mismatched and grotesque.

Then I did what any sensible kid would do. I sucked air and let loose with my very best girl scream, which was instantly and creepily echoed by the three mouths of the single-eyed monster. I could hear Damien shrieking behind me, and I swear Sister Mary Angela even squeaked a startled gasp. I was starting to do exactly what I'd just promised myself I wouldn't do—run like hell, when one of the heads stopped screaming and stepped forward into the beam of the flashlight.

"Shit, Zoey! What is wrong with you? It's just the Twins and me. You scared us crapless," said Aphrodite.

"Aphrodite?" My hand clutched my chest over my heart, trying to keep it from pounding out of my body.

"Of course it's me," she said, marching past me in disgust. "Goddess! Get a grip."

The Twins were still standing in the tunnel. Erin was holding a thick pillar candle so tightly her knuckles were white. Shaunee was standing next to her, so close their shoulders were smashed together. They looked frozen and big-eyed.

"Uh, hi," I said. "I didn't know you guys were down here."

Shaunee thawed first. "Ya think?" She wiped a shaking hand delicately across her forehead and turned to Erin. "Twin, did she scare me white?"

Erin blinked at her BFF. "I don't think that's possible." She squinted at Shaunee. "But no, she didn't. You're still a gorgeous cappuccino." Erin's hand that wasn't holding the candle flew up to her thick, golden hair and patted through it frantically. "Did she make my hair fall out or turn unattractively and prematurely gray?"

I frowned at the Twins. "Erin, your hair is not falling out *or* turning gray, and Shaunee, you cannot be scared white. Jeesh, you guys scared *me* first," I said.

"Look, next time you need to chase off Neferet and Kalona, just scream like that," Erin said.

"Yeah, it makes you sound like you lost every bit of your damn mind," Shaunee said as they swept past me.

I followed them out into the root cellar where Damien was fanning himself and looking gayer than usual, and Sister Mary Angela had just finished crossing herself. I set the flashlight butt end down on a table crowded with stuff in glass jars that looked eerily like floating fetuses in the murky light.

"So, really, what were you guys doing down here?" I said.

"That Dallas kid told us this is how they got here from the depot," Shaunee said.

"He said it was cool down here and that Stevie Rae had made it," Erin said.

"So we thought we'd come down here and see for ourselves," Shaunee said.

"And why are you down here with the Twins?" I asked Aphrodite.

"The Dynamic Duo needed protecting. Naturally they turned to me."

"How did you guys suddenly appear like that, anyway?" Damien asked before Twin bickering could start.

"Easy-peasy." Erin walked quickly back down the tunnel, still carrying her candle. She turned to face us after she'd gotten just a few feet farther in than I'd been. "The tunnel makes a sharp left here." She stepped to the side and her light disappeared, then she stepped back and reappeared. "That's why we didn't see each other till the last second."

"It really is amazing that Stevie Rae somehow did this," Damien said. I noticed he didn't move any closer to the tunnel, but stayed by the flashlight.

Sister Mary Angela approached the entrance. She touched the side of the newly hollowed out hole with reverence and said, "Stevie Rae did this, but she did it with divine intervention."

"By 'divine intervention,' are you talkin' 'bout more of your the-Virgin-Mary-is-just-another-form-of-Nyx stuff?" Stevie Rae's twang coming from the other side of the root cellar made us all jump.

"Yes, child. That is exactly what I mean."

"I don't wanna offend you, but that's just about the weirdest thing I've ever heard," Stevie Rae said. She walked over to us, and I thought she looked pale. As she got closer to me I smelled something strange, but her grin made her face change to her cute, familiar self. "Z, did that big ol' girl scream I heard come from you?"

"Uh, yeah." I couldn't help grinning back at her. "I was inside the tunnel and I didn't expect to run into the Twins and Aphrodite."

"Well, that makes sense. Aphrodite is kinda booger monstery," Stevie Rae said.

I laughed, and then, grabbing the opportunity to change the subject, I said, "Uh, speaking of monsters, did you find any Raven Mockers left up there?"

Stevie Rae's eyes shifted from mine.

"It's all safe. Nothin' for you to worry about," she said quickly.

"I'm so glad," Sister Mary Angela was saying. "Those creatures were such an abomination—mixing man and beast." She shivered. "I'm relieved we are rid of them."

"But it wasn't their fault," Stevie Rae said abruptly.

"Pardon me?" The nun looked more than a little confused at Stevie Rae's defensive tone.

"They didn't ask to be born like they were—all mixed up because of rape and evil. They really were victims."

"I don't feel sorry for them," I said, wondering why Stevie Rae sounded like she was standing up for the nasty Raven Mockers.

Damien shivered. "Do we have to talk about them?"

"Nope, we sure don't," Stevie Rae said quickly.

"Good, and anyway, the reason I brought Zoey down here was to show her the tunnel you made, Stevie Rae. I have to tell you—I think it's astonishing."

"Thanks, Damien! It was seriously cool when I figured out I could actually do it." Stevie Rae took a few steps past me and into the mouth of the tunnel, where she was instantly surrounded by the total darkness that stretched behind her like the insides of a huge ebony snake. She raised her arms so that her palms pressed against the dirt walls of the tunnel. Suddenly she reminded me of a scene from *Samson and Delilah,* an old movie I'd watched with Damien a month or so ago. The image that flashed through my memory was when Delilah had led the blind Samson to stand between massive pillars that held up the stadium filled with awful people taunting him. He'd gotten his magical strength back and ended up pushing the pillars apart and destroying himself and . . .

"Isn't that right, Zoey?"

"Huh?" I blinked, disturbed by the sad, destructive scene I'd been reliving in my mind.

"I said, Mary didn't move the earth for me when I made the tunnel; the power Nyx gave me did. Jeesh, you're not payin' attention to me at all," Stevie Rae said. She'd taken her hands from the side of the tunnel and was giving me her *what's going on inside your head now?* look.

"Sorry, what were you saying about Nyx?"

"Just that I really don't think Nyx and the dang Virgin Mary have anything to do with each other; Jesus' mama definitely didn't help me move the earth to make this tunnel." She shrugged a shoulder. "I don't want to hurt your feelings or nothin' like that, Sister, but that's what I think."

"You're entitled to your own opinion, Stevie Rae," said the nun, looking as calm as usual. "But you should know that saying you don't believe in something doesn't make it any less possible that it exists."

"Well, I've been giving this some thought, and personally I don't find it such an odd hypothesis," Damien said. "You should remember that in your *Fledgling Handbook 101*, Mary is illustrated as one of the many faces of Nyx."

"Huh," I said. "Really?"

Damien gave me a stern look that clearly said *you really should be a better student* before he nodded, and in his best schoolteacher voice continued, "Yes. It is well documented that during the influx of Christianity into Europe, shrines to Gaea, as well as Nyx, were converted to shrines for Mary long before people converted to the new . . ."

Damien's droning on and on was a soothing background as I peered into the tunnel. The darkness was deep and thick. Just inches behind Stevie Rae I could see nothing. Absolutely nothing. I stared, imagining forms hiding there. Someone or some*thing* could be lurking mere feet from us and we'd never know it, not if they didn't want to be seen. And that scared me.

Okay, but that's ridiculous! I told myself. *It's just a tunnel.* Still, my irrational fear pushed at me. Which, sadly, pissed me off and made me want to push back. So, like every moronic blond extra in a horror movie, I took one step into the darkness. And then another.

The dark swallowed me.

My mind knew I was only a couple of feet from the root cellar and my friends. I could hear Damien blabbing about religion and the Goddess. But my mind wasn't what was beating in terror against my chest. My heart, my spirit, my soul—whatever you want to call it— was screaming soundlessly for me to *run! Get away! Go!*

I felt the pressure of the earth as if it wasn't a hole in the ground, but instead it had filled in, covering me . . . suffocating me . . . trapping me.

My breath was coming faster and faster. I knew I must be hyper-ventilating, but I couldn't stop myself. I wanted to back away from the hole that snaked away from my feet into the darkness, but all I could manage was a stumbled half step back. I couldn't make my feet do what I was telling them to do! Dots of lights sparkled in my eyes, blinding me, while everything else started to go gray. Then I was falling . . . falling . . .

CHAPTER FIVE

Zoey

The darkness was unrelieved. Blinding more than my sight, it wiped away all of my senses. I thought I was gasping for breath and flailing around, trying to find something—anything I could touch, hear, or smell—anything that would give me a handhold on reality. But I had no sensation at all. The cocoon of darkness and the fluttering of my frantic heartbeat were all I knew.

Was I dead?

No, I didn't think so. I remembered that I'd been in the tunnel under the Benedictine Abbey, only a few feet away from my friends. I'd been freaked out by the darkness, but that couldn't have made me drop dead.

But I'd been afraid. I remembered being very afraid.

Then there had been nothing but this darkness.

What's happened to me? Nyx! My mind screamed. Help me, Goddess! Please show me some kind of light!

"Listen with your soul . . ."

I thought I cried aloud at the sweet, reassuring sound of the Goddess's voice in my mind, but when her words were gone, there was only the unrelenting silence and darkness.

How in the hell was I supposed to listen with my soul?

I tried to calm myself and hear something, but there was just silence—a soul-sucking, black, empty, utter silence like nothing I'd ever before experienced. I had no framework to guide me here, I only knew—

The realization struck me and my mind reeled with understanding.

I did have a framework to guide me. Part of me had experienced this darkness before.

I couldn't see. I couldn't feel. I couldn't do anything but turn within myself, questing for the part of me that might be able to make sense of this, that might be able to guide me out of here.

Memory stirred again, this time taking me back long before the night in the tunnel under the abbey. The years fell away with my resistance until finally, finally I felt again.

My senses returned slowly. I began to hear more than my own thoughts. There was a drumbeat that pulsed around me, and within it were woven the distant voices of women. The sense of smell returned to me, and I recognized the dank scent that reminded me of the abbey tunnel. Finally, I could feel the earth against my naked back. I only had an instant to sift through the flood of my returned senses before the rest of my awareness was jolted awake. I wasn't alone! My back was pressed against the earth, but I was being held tightly in someone's arms.

Then he spoke.

"Oh, Goddess, no! Do not let this be!"

It was Kalona's voice, and my immediate reaction was to cry out and struggle blindly away from him, but I wasn't in charge of my body and the words that came from my mouth were not my own.

"Sssh, do not despair. I am with you, my love."

"You trapped me!" Even as he cried the accusation, his arms tightened around me, and I recognized the cold passion of his immortal embrace.

"I saved you," my strange voice responded as my body settled more intimately against his. "You were not meant to walk this world. That is why you have been so unhappy, so insatiable."

"I had no choice! The mortals do not understand."

My arms wrapped around his neck. My fingers twined

through his soft, heavy hair. "I understand. Be at peace here with me. Lay down your sad restlessness. I will comfort you."

I felt his surrender before he spoke the words. "Yes," Kalona murmured. "I will bury my sadness within you and my desperate longing will finally be spent."

"Yes, my love, my consort, my Warrior . . . yes . . ."

It was that moment that I lost myself within A-ya. I couldn't tell where her desire ended and my soul began. If I still had a choice, I didn't want it. I only knew that I was where I was destined to be—in Kalona's arms.

His wings covered us, keeping the chill of his touch from burning me. His lips met mine. We explored each other slowly, thoroughly, with a sense of wonder and surrender. As our bodies began to move together I knew complete joy.

And then, suddenly, I started to dissolve.

"No!" The scream was wrenched from my throat and my soul. I didn't want to leave! I wanted to stay with him. My place was with him!

But, again, I wasn't in control, and I felt myself fading away, rejoining the earth, as A-ya sobbed, her broken voice echoed one word in my head: REMEMBER . . .

The slap burned against my cheek, and I sucked in a big breath that cleared the last of the darkness from my mind. I opened my eyes and the beam of the flashlight caused me to squint and blink. "I remember." My voice sounded as rusty as my mind.

"You remember who you are, or should I smack you again?" Aphrodite said.

My mind was slow to function because it still screamed *no* at being wrenched from the darkness. I blinked again and shook my head, trying to clear it. "No!" I cried the word with so much emotion that Aphrodite automatically moved away from me.

"Fine," she said. "You can thank me later."

Sister Mary Angela took her place, bending over me and smoothing my hair back from my face, which was sweaty and cold. "Zoey, are you with us?"

"Yes," I said in a broken voice.

"Zoey, what is it? What caused you to hyperventilate?" the nun asked.

"You're not feeling sick, are you?" Erin's voice was a little tremble-y.

"Not getting the urge to cough up a lung or anything?" Shaunee asked, looking as upset as her twin sounded.

Stevie Rae shoved the Twins aside so she could get close to me. "Talk to me, Z. Are you really okay?"

"I'm fine. I'm not dying or anything like that." My thoughts had reordered themselves, though I couldn't seem to shake off the last traces of the despair I'd known with A-ya. I understood my friends were scared that my body had begun rejecting the Change. Forcing myself to focus on the here and now I held my hand out to Stevie Rae. "Here, help me up. I'm better now."

Stevie Rae pulled me up, careful to keep her hand under my elbow while I swayed slightly before finding my balance.

"What happened to you, Z?" Damien asked as he studied me.

What was I supposed to say? Was I supposed to admit to my friends that I'd had an incredibly vivid memory of a past life where I'd given myself to our enemy of today? I hadn't even had time to wade through the maze of new emotions the memory had caused within me. How was I going to explain them to my friends?

"Just tell us, child. The truth spoken is always less frightening than supposition," said Sister Mary Angela.

I sighed and blurted, "The tunnel scared me!"

"Scared you? Like, there's something in there?" Damien had finally quit staring at me and was peering nervously into the dark opening.

The Twins took a couple steps farther into the root cellar and away from the tunnel.

"No, there's nothing in there." I hesitated. "At least I don't think so. Anyway, that's not what scared me."

"You expect us to believe you fainted because you were scared of the dark?" Aphrodite said.

They all stared at me.

I cleared my throat.

"Hey, y'all. Maybe there's stuff Zoey just doesn't wanna talk about," said Stevie Rae.

I looked at my best friend and realized if I didn't say something about what had just happened to me I wouldn't be able to face what I needed to do about her.

"You're right," I told Stevie Rae. "I don't want to talk about it, but you guys deserve to hear the truth." I let my gaze take in the rest of the group. "That tunnel freaked me out so much because my soul recognized it." I cleared my throat and went on, "I remembered being trapped in the earth with Kalona."

"You mean because there really is some of A-ya inside of you?" Damien asked softly.

I nodded. "I'm me, but I'm also, somehow, still a part of her."

"Interesting . . ." Damien breathed a long sigh.

"Well, what the hell does that mean for you and Kalona today?" Aphrodite asked.

"I don't know! I don't know! I don't know!" I burst out, the stress and honest-to-goddess confusion about what had just happened boiled over inside me. "I don't have the damn answers. All I have is the memory and zero time to process it. How about you guys back off just a little and let me get the mess inside my head straight?"

Everyone shuffled around and mumbled okays, sending me *she's lost her mind* looks. Ignoring my gawking friends, and the unanswered Kalona questions that were almost visible in the air around me, I turned to Stevie Rae. "Explain to me exactly how you made the tunnel."

I could tell by the question mark in her blue eyes that she was worried about my tone. I hadn't sounded all "Crap! I just fainted and need to change the subject 'cause I'm embarrassed by being a reincarnated chick." I'd sounded like a High Priestess.

"Well, it wasn't really that big of a thing." Stevie Rae looked nervous and uncomfortable, like she was trying too hard to be nonchalant because she was feeling the exact opposite. "Hey, are you sure you're okay? Shouldn't we go up out of here and maybe get you a brown pop or somethin'? I mean, if this place gives you flashbacks, talkin' someplace else sounds like a good idea."

"I'm okay. Right now I just want to hear about the tunnel." I met her gaze steadily. "So tell me how you did this."

I could sense the other kids, as well as Sister Mary Angela, watching us with curiosity mixed in with their confusion, but I kept focused on Stevie Rae.

"'Kay, well, you know the Prohibition tunnels are practically everywhere under the downtown buildings, right?"

I nodded. "Right."

"Also, remember that I told you I'd been doin' some reconnoitering to see where they all went?"

"Yeah, I remember."

"Okay, so, I found that kinda half-covered tunnel entrance that Ant told y'all about the other day—the one that branches off away from the others that go under the Philtower Building and stuff." I nodded again impatiently. "Well, it was filled in with dirt, but when I felt around the little hole left in the middle of it, I knocked a bunch of dirt away, stuck my arm through, and felt a bunch of cool air. That made me think there was probably more tunnel on the other side of it. So I pushed, with my mind and my hands and my element. And earth responded."

"Responded? Like it shook or something?" I asked.

"More like it moved. Like I wanted it to. In my head." She paused. "It's kinda hard to explain. But what happened was the dirt that had sealed the tunnel ended up crumbling and I stepped through the new bigger opening into a really, *really* old tunnel."

"And this old tunnel was made of dirt, not lined with concrete, like the tunnels under the depot and downtown, right?" Damien said.

Stevie Rae smiled and nodded, her blond hair bouncing around her shoulders. "Yeah! And instead of heading downtown it pointed to midtown."

"It came all the way here?" I tried to guesstimate in my head how many miles that was and could no way do the math. Of course, I am math impaired, but still, it was a ways.

"Nope. What happened was that once I found the dirt tunnel and kinda opened it up, I went explorin' in it. Okay, it starts as one of the offshoots of the Philtower Building. I thought it was weird and kinda cool that it headed away from downtown."

"How could you tell that?" Damien interrupted her. "How could you even guess where you were heading?"

"Easy-peasy for me! I can always find north, you know, the direction of my earth element. Once I find it—I can find anything."

"Hmm," he said.

"Go on," I said. "Then what?"

"Then it ran out. Just, well, stopped. Before you slipped me the note about meeting you here at the sisters' place, that's where I stopped, too. I mean, sure, I was plannin' to go back and check it out some more later, but it really wasn't a high priority to me. When you told me I might have to move the kids here, I couldn't quit thinkin' about the dirt tunnel. I remembered that it had been headed in this direction before it ran out. So I went back there. I thought about where I wanted to go and how I wished the tunnel would go there. Then I pushed again, like I'd done to get the opening bigger, only more so. Then, well, presto-chango, the earth did what I told it to do, and here we are! Ta-da!" She finished with a big smile and a flourish.

Into the silence that surrounded Stevie Rae's explanation, Sister Mary Angela's voice sounded utterly normal and reasonable, which made me heart her even more than I already did. "Remarkable, isn't it? Stevie Rae, you and I may disagree upon the source of your gift, but I am nonetheless in awe of its vastness."

"Thank you, Sister! I think you're pretty awesome, too, 'specially for a nun."

"How did you see down there?" I asked.

"Well, I really don't have a problem seeing in the dark, but the other kids aren't as good at it as I am, so I brought some lanterns from the depot tunnels." Stevie Rae pointed to a few oil lanterns that I hadn't noticed before in the dark corners of the root cellar.

"Still, it was a long way," Shaunee was saying.

"Seriously. It must have been dark and creepy," Erin said.

"Nah, the earth really isn't creepy to me, or to the red fledglings." She shrugged. "Like I said, it was no big deal. Actually, it was super-easy."

"And you managed to get all the red fledglings here safely?" Damien said.

"Yep!"

"Which all?" I asked.

"What do ya mean, which all? That doesn't make any sense, Z," she said. "I brought all the red fledgings y'all met before, plus Erik and Heath. Who else are ya talkin' about?" Her words sounded normal, but she ended with a weird, nervous laugh and wouldn't meet my eyes.

My stomach clenched. Stevie Rae was *still* lying to me. And I didn't know what to do about it.

"I think maybe Zoey is feeling confused because she's exhausted, as she should be after the experience she's had tonight." Sister Mary Angela's warm hand on my shoulder felt as reassuring as her voice. "We're all tired," she added. Her smile took in Stevie Rae, the Twins, Aphrodite, and Damien. "Dawn is not long off. Let's get you settled with the rest of your friends. Sleep. Everything will seem clearer when you're well rested."

I nodded wearily and let Sister Mary Angela shepherd us out of the depths of the root cellar and up the staircase we'd come down not too long ago. But instead of continuing up and into the hallway of the abbey, the nun opened a door off the landing I hadn't noticed when I'd been hurrying after Damien earlier. A shorter staircase led into the main basement area, a big but normal-looking cement basement, which had been transformed by the nuns from a giant laundry room to a temporary dorm. There were a bunch of cots spread out along two walls opposite each other, made up with blankets and pillows and looking cozy. There was a kid-sized mound in one of the beds, and the poof of red hair that was sticking out of the blanket he'd pulled up over most of his head told me that Elliott had already crashed. The rest of the red fledglings were clustered around the washer-dryer area, sitting on those folding metal chairs that always make my butt cold, watching a large flat-screen TV that was perched on top of one of the washers. There was a lot of yawning going on with them, which meant it really must be almost dawn, but they seemed mesmerized by whatever was on TV. I glanced at the screen and felt my tired face break into a big grin.

"*The Sound of Music*? They're watching *The Sound of Music*?" I laughed.

Sister Mary Angela lifted one eyebrow at me. "It's one of our favorite DVDs. I thought the fledglings might enjoy it, too."

"It is a classic," Damien said.

"I used to think that Nazi kid was cute," Shaunee said.

"Except he rats out the Von Trapps," Erin said.

"Which is when he turned not so cute," Shaunee continued as the Twins grabbed folding chairs and joined the other fledglings in front of the TV.

"But everybody likes Julie Andrews," Stevie Rae said.

"She shoulda smacked them damn spoiled kids," Kramisha said from her place in front of the TV. She glanced over her shoulder and gave Sister Mary Angela a tired smile. "Sorry 'bout the 'damn,' Sister, but they is brats."

"They just needed love and attention and understanding, like all children do," said the sister.

"Okay, barf. Seriously," Aphrodite said, "before any of you break into a chorus of 'How Do You Solve a Problem like Maria?' and I have to gnaw through my slender wrists, I'm going to find Darius and my room." She waggled her brows and started to twitch out of the basement.

"Aphrodite," Sister Mary Angela called. When Aphrodite paused and looked back at her, the nun continued. "I imagine Darius is still with Stark. Saying good night to him would be just fine, but you'll find your room on the fourth floor—you'll be sharing it with Zoey and not with the warrior."

"Ugh," I said under my breath.

Aphrodite rolled her eyes. "Why does that not surprise me?" And, muttering to herself, she continued to twitch away.

"Sorry, Z," Stevie Rae said after she rolled her eyes at Aphrodite's back. "I'd be your roomie again, but I think I should stay down here. Being underground really feels better to me after the sun rises, plus I need to stick close to the red fledglings."

"That's okay," I said a little too quickly. *So now I didn't even want to be alone with my BFF?*

"Is everyone else still upstairs?" Damien asked. I saw him glancing around, and I was pretty sure he was looking for Jack.

I, on the other hand, hadn't been looking around for *any* of my boyfriends. Actually, after their stupid, testosterone display outside, I was thinking that being boyfriendless sounded better and better.

And then there was Kalona and the memory I wish I'd never had.

"Yeah, everyone else is upstairs in the cafeteria or already in bed. Hey, Earth to Zo! Check it out. The nuns have a massively big selection of Doritos, and I even found some brown pop for you—full of caffeine *and* sugar," said Heath as he jumped down the last three steps into the basement.

CHAPTER SIX

Zoey

"Thanks, Heath." I suppressed a sigh as Heath walked over to me and, grinning, offered me some nacho cheese Doritos and a can of brown pop.

"Z, if you're really okay I'd like to find Jack and be sure Duchess is okay, then I'm going to sleep for a little bit of forever," Damien said.

"No problem," I said quickly, not wanting Damien to say anything about my A-ya memory to Heath.

"Where's Erik?" Stevie Rae asked Heath as I chugged the can of brown pop.

"He's still outside being all king of the castle."

"Did you find anything after I left?" Stevie Rae's voice suddenly got so sharp that several of the red fledglings glanced over from watching Maria and the Von Trapps sing "My Favorite Things."

"Nah, he's just a butt and rechecking what Dallas and I already checked."

Dallas looked up from his place in front of the TV at the sound of his name. "Everything's cool out there, Stevie Rae."

Stevie Rae made a *come here* motion at Dallas, and he hurried to join us. She lowered her voice and said, "Fill me in."

"I already told you outside before you came down here," Dallas said, his eyes wandering back to the TV screen and cream-colored ponies . . . crisp apple strudel . . .

Stevie Rae gave his arm a smack. "Would you pay attention? I'm not outside anymore. Now I'm in here. So fill me in *again*."

Dallas sighed, turned his full attention to her and gave her a cute, indulgent smile. "Okay, okay. But only 'cause you asked so nice." Stevie Rae frowned at him and he continued. "Erik, Johnny B, Heath here," he paused and nodded at Heath, "and me—we searched like you told us to, which was no fun 'cause the ice is really slick and it's super-cold out there." He paused. Stevie Rae stared silently at him until he continued. "Anyway, *like you already know,* we were doing that while you were searching down by Twenty-first Street. After a while we all met back at the grotto. That's when we told you we found those three bodies at the Lewis and Twenty-first Street corner. You told us to take care of them. Then you left. So we did what you said, and then me and Heath and Johnny B came inside to dry off, eat, and watch TV. I guess Erik's still out there looking around."

"Why?" Stevie Rae's voice was sharp.

Dallas shrugged, "Could be like Heath said. The guy's a butt."

"Bodies?" said Sister Mary Angela.

Dallas nodded. "Yeah, we found three dead Raven Mockers. Darius shot them out of the sky 'cause they had bullet holes in them."

Sister Mary Angela lowered her voice. "And what did you do with the dead creatures?"

"Put them in the Dumpsters behind the abbey like Stevie Rae said. It's freezin' out there. They'll keep. And no garbage trucks are gonna be picking up anytime soon, what with the ice and everything. We thought they could stay there till y'all decided what to do with 'em."

"Oh! Oh, my!" The nun's face had gone pale.

"You put them in the Dumpsters? I didn't tell you to put them in the Dumpsters!" Stevie Rae practically yelled.

"Sssh!" Kramisha told her while the TV watchers gave us the stank eye.

Sister Mary Angela motioned for us to follow her, and the five of us went quickly out of the basement, up the stairwell, and into the abbey hall.

"Dallas, I can*not* believe you put 'em in the Dumpsters!" Stevie Rae rounded on him as soon as we were out of earshot of the others.

"What'd you expect us to do with them, dig a grave and say Mass?" Dallas said, then he glanced at Sister Mary Angela. "Sorry, I didn't mean to blaspheme, Sister. My folks are Catholic."

"You meant no offense, I'm sure, son," said the nun, sounding a little shaky. "Bodies . . . I—I hadn't thought about the bodies."

"Don't worry about it, Sister." Heath patted her arm awkwardly. "You don't have to mess with them. I get what you're feeling. This whole thing: the winged guy, Neferet, the Raven Mockers, well, is all hard to—"

"They can't stay in the dang Dumpsters," Stevie Rae spoke over Heath as if she hadn't even heard him. "It's not right."

"Why not?" I asked calmly. I'd been quiet until then because I'd been studying Stevie Rae, watching closely as she became more and more upset.

Stevie Rae suddenly didn't seem to have any problem meeting my gaze. "Because it's not right, that's why," she repeated.

"They were monsters that were part immortal who would have tried their best to kill us all in a split second if Kalona had given them the word," I said.

"Part immortal and part what?" Stevie Rae asked me.

I frowned at her, but Heath answered before I could. "Part bird?"

"No." Stevie Rae didn't even look at him. She kept staring at me. "Not part bird, that's the immortal part. In their blood they're part immortal and part human. *Human,* Zoey. I feel sorry for the human part, and think it deserves more than being stuck in the trash."

There was something about the look in her eye—about the sound of her voice—that really bothered me. I answered her with the first thing that came into my mind. "It takes more than an accident of blood to make me feel sorry for someone."

Stevie Rae's eyes flashed and her body jerked, almost like I'd slapped her. "I guess that's one difference between you and me."

All of a sudden I realized why Stevie Rae was able to feel bad for the Raven Mockers. In a weird way, she must be seeing herself in them. She'd died and then, due to what I supposed she could call an "accident" she'd resurrected *without* most of her humanity. Then, due to another "accident," she'd gotten her humanity back. Looking at it that way, I guess she felt sorry for them because she knew what it was like to be part monster, part human.

"Hey," I said softly, wishing she and I were back at the House of

Night and could talk as easily as we used to. "There's a big difference between an accident causing something to be born messed up, and something terrible that happens *after* someone's born. On one hand you're made the way you are—on the other, something tried to change you into someone you're not."

"Huh?" Heath said.

"I believe what Zoey is trying to say is that she understands why Stevie Rae might empathize with the dead Raven Mockers, even when she really has nothing in common with them," said Sister Mary Angela. "And Zoey would be right. Those creatures are dark beings, and even though I, too, am disconcerted by death, I understand that they needed to die."

Stevie Rae's gaze left mine. "You're both wrong. That's not what I'm thinkin', but I'm not gonna talk about it anymore." She started down the hall, walking quickly away from us.

"Stevie Rae?" I called after her.

She didn't even look back at me. "I'm gonna find Erik, make sure everything's really okay out there, and then send him inside. I'll talk to you later." She turned and disappeared through a door I assumed led to the outside, slamming it behind her.

"That's not usually how she acts," Dallas said.

"I'll pray for her," Sister Mary Angela whispered.

"Don't worry," Heath said. "She'll be back inside pretty soon. The sun's getting ready to come up."

I swiped my hand across my face. What I should've done was follow Stevie Rae outside, corner her, and make her tell me exactly what was going on. But I couldn't deal with one more problem just then. I hadn't even dealt with my A-ya memory. I could feel it sitting there in the back of my mind like a guilty secret.

"Zo, are you okay? You look like you need some sleep. We all do," Heath said, yawning.

I blinked and gave him a weary smile. "Yeah, that's true. I'll go to bed. First I want to check on Stark real quick, though."

"*Very* quickly," Sister Mary Angela said.

I nodded. Without looking at Heath, I said, "Okay, well, um. I'll see you guys in about eight hours or so."

"Good night, child." Sister Mary Angela hugged me and whispered, "And may our Lady bless and watch over you."

"Thanks, Sister," I whispered back, hugging her tightly.

When I let her go, Heath surprised me by taking my hand. I gave him a question-mark look.

"I'll walk you to Stark's room," he said.

Feeling defeated, I shrugged, and he and I started down the hall, hand in hand. We didn't say anything; we just walked. Heath's hand was warm and familiar in mine and I fell into step easily beside him. I was just starting to let myself relax when Heath cleared his throat.

"Hey, uh, I want to say sorry about that crap outside earlier with Erik and me. It was stupid. I shouldn't let him get to me," Heath said.

"You're right—you shouldn't, but he can be annoying," I said.

Heath grinned. "Tell me about it. You're gonna dump him pretty soon, aren't you?"

"Heath, I am so not going to talk about Erik with you."

His grin just got bigger. I rolled my eyes.

"You can't fool me. I know you too well. You don't go for bossy guys."

"Just shut up and walk," I said, but I squeezed his hand, and he squeezed mine back. He was right—I didn't like bossy guys, and he did know me very, very well.

We'd come to a turn in the hallway. There was a nice picture window with an alcove in front of it, complete with a cushy bench that looked perfect for reading. On the windowsill there was a beautiful porcelain statue of Mary with several votives burning on either side of her. Heath and I slowed down, pausing by the window.

"That's really pretty," I said softly.

"Yeah, I've never paid Mary much attention. But all these statues of her lit up by candles are cool looking. Do you think the nun's right? Could Mary be Nyx and Nyx be Mary?"

"I have no idea."

"Doesn't Nyx talk to you?"

"Yeah, sometimes, but the subject of Jesus' mom hasn't come up," I said.

"Well, I think you should ask her next time."

"Maybe I will," I said.

We just stood there, holding hands and watching the way the warm yellow flames danced off the gleaming statue. I was thinking about how nice it would be if my Goddess would visit me during a time that wasn't filled with life-and-death stress when Heath blurted, "So I hear that Stark swore himself into your service as a Warrior."

I studied him carefully, looking for signs that he was pissed or jealous, but all I saw in his blue eyes was curiosity.

"Yeah, he did."

"Word is that's a majorly special bond."

"Yeah, it is," I said.

"He's the guy who can't miss with an arrow, right?"

"Right."

"So having him on your side is kinda like being protected by the Terminator?"

That made me smile. "Well, he's not as big as Arnold, but I guess it's a pretty good comparison."

"Does he love you, too?"

His question caught me off guard, and I didn't know what to say. As he'd been doing since we were in grade school, Heath seemed to know the exact right thing to say. "Just tell me the truth, that's all."

"Yeah, I think he loves me."

"And you him?"

"Maybe," I said reluctantly. "But it doesn't change how I feel about you."

"But what does that mean for you and me today?"

It was weird that his words echoed Aphrodite's question about where the A-ya memory left Kalona and me. I felt overwhelmed because I didn't have an answer for either of them; I rubbed at the headache that was starting to pound through my right temple. "I guess it leaves us Imprinted and annoyed."

Heath didn't say anything. He just watched me with that sweet, sad, familiar look that said more about how badly I was hurting him than a dozen screaming matches between us would have.

He was breaking my heart.

"Heath, I'm so sorry. I just . . . I just . . ." My voice broke and I tried again. "I just don't know what to do about a lot of things right now."

"I do." Heath sat down on the bench and held out his arms to me. "Zo, come here."

I shook my head. "Heath, I can't—"

"I'm not asking anything from you," he interrupted firmly. "I'm giving you something. Come here."

When I just looked at him in confusion he sighed, reached up, took my hands, and gently drew my stiff but unresisting body to his lap and into his arms. He held me, resting his cheek on top of my head, like he'd been doing since he'd gotten bigger than me somewhere around the eighth grade. My face was pressed against the crook of his neck and I inhaled his scent. It was the fragrance of my childhood—of long summer nights sitting in the backyard by the mosquito zapper while we listened to music and talked—of after-game parties where I stayed snug within his arm as lots of girls (and guys for that matter) gushed about the great passes he'd thrown—of long good-night kisses and the passion that came with discovering love.

And I realized suddenly that while I'd been breathing in familiarity and security, I'd also been relaxing. With a sigh, I curled into him.

"Better?" Heath murmured.

"Better," I said. "Heath, I really don't know—"

"Don't!" His arms tightened around me and then gentled again. "Right now don't worry about me or Erik or that new guy. Right now just remember *us*. Remember what it's been like between us for years. I'm here for you, Zo. Through all the crap that I can't really understand, I'm here. And we belong to each other. My blood says so."

"Why?" I asked, still cradled in his arms. "Why are you still here, still willing to be with me even when you know about Erik and Stark?"

"Because I love you," he said simply. "I've loved you for as long as I can remember, and I'm going to love you for the rest of my life."

Tears stung my eyes and I blinked hard, trying not to cry. "But Heath, Stark's not going to go away. And I don't really know what I'm going to do about Erik."

"I know."

I drew a deep breath and on the exhale said, "And inside of me there's a connection with Kalona that I can't help."

"But you said no to him and chased him away."

"I did, but I—I have memories that are stuck in my soul, and they have to do with who I was in a different lifetime, and during that lifetime I was with Kalona."

Instead of asking me a zillion questions, or pulling away from me, his arms tightened around me. "It's going to be okay," he said, sounding like he really meant it. "You're going to figure all of this out."

"I don't see how. I don't even know what to do about you."

"There isn't anything *to do* about me. I'm with you. That's it." He paused and then added quickly, like he wanted to get the words out of his mouth, "If I have to share you with the vampyres, I will."

Still in his arms, I leaned back so I could meet his gaze. "Heath, you are entirely too jealous for me to believe it's okay with you if I'm with another guy."

"I didn't say it's okay with me. I definitely won't like it, but I don't want to be without you, Zoey."

"That's just too weird," I said.

He took my chin in his hand when I tried to look away from him. "Yeah, it's weird. But the truth is, as long as we're Imprinted I know I have something with you no one else has. I can give you something none of those big, bad Dracula-wannabes can ever touch. I can give you something that even an immortal can't touch."

I stared at him. Heath's eyes were bright with tears. He looked so much older than eighteen that it almost scared me. "I don't want to make you sad," I said. "I don't want to mess up your life."

"Then stop trying to send me away from you. We belong together."

Okay, I realize it was wrong of me, but instead of answering him and arguing that us being together just couldn't work, I curled up in his arms and let him hold me. Yeah, it was selfish of me, but I lost myself in Heath and the touch of my past. The way he held me was perfect. He didn't try to make out with me. He didn't grope me, or grind against me. He didn't try to feel me up. He didn't even offer to cut himself and let me drink his blood, which would have automatically let loose a passion between us that would burn both of us out of control. Heath held me gently and murmured how much he loved me. He told me everything really would be okay. I could feel his heartbeat against me. I could sense the rich, enticing blood that was there, so warm and so close, but just then what I needed even more than his Imprinted blood was familiarity, our joined past, and the strength of his understanding.

And that's the moment Heath Luck, my high school sweetheart, truly became my consort.

CHAPTER SEVEN

Stevie Rae

Feeling like a total butthead, Stevie Rae slammed the abbey door and retreated into the icy night. She wasn't really pissed at Zoey, or at the super-nice, if slightly delusional, nun. Actually, she wasn't pissed at anyone but herself.

"Dang it! I hate that I'm messin' this up!" she yelled at herself. She hadn't meant to screw things up royally, but it seemed like she was diggin' through a pile of shit that just kept getting deeper and deeper no matter how fast she shoveled.

Zoey wasn't a moron. She knew something was wrong. That was obvious, but how could Stevie Rae even start to tell her? There was just so much to explain. *He* was just so much to explain. And she'd never meant for any of it to happen. Especially not the Raven Mocker part. Dang it! Before she'd discovered him almost dead, she wouldn't have even thought it was possible. Had someone told her about him before, she would have laughed and said, "Nope, that ain't gonna happen!"

But it was possible because it had happened. *He* had happened.

As Stevie Rae prowled around the silent abbey grounds looking for pain-in-the-butt Erik, who might very well discover this last, most terrible secret and really throw a wrench in the dang tractor motor, she tried to figure out just how the hell she'd gotten herself into such a gawd-awful mess. Why had she saved him? Why hadn't she just hollered for Dallas and the rest of 'em, and had them finish it?

That had even been what he'd said he wanted before he passed out.

But he'd spoken. He'd sounded so human. And she hadn't been able to kill him.

"Erik!" Where the heck was he? "Erik, come here!" She paused her internal battle and called into the night. Night? Stevie Rae squinted to the east and swore she could see the darkness there beginning to turn the ripe plum color of predawn. "Erik! Time to report in!" Stevie Rae yelled for the third time. She stopped and peered around the silent abbey grounds.

Stevie Rae's gaze slid over to the greenhouse that had been turned into a temporary stable for the horses Z and the rest of the gang had ridden in their escape from the House of Night. But it wasn't so much the greenhouse that drew her gaze. It was the innocent-looking equipment shed next to it that she couldn't quit staring at. The shed appeared totally normal—just an add-on building with no windows. The door hadn't even been locked. She should know. She'd been inside it not too long ago.

"Hey, what's wrong? Did you see something over there?"

"Oh, shit!" Stevie Rae jumped and spun around, heart hammering so hard in her chest she almost couldn't breathe. "Erik! You scared the bejesus right outta me! Would you make some dang noise or somethin' before you bust up on someone like that?"

"Sorry, Stevie Rae, but *you* were calling *me*."

Stevie Rae brushed a blond curl back behind her ear and tried to ignore the fact that her hand was shaking. She was just seriously no good at this sneaking-around-and-hiding-things-from-your-friends stuff. But she lifted her chin and forced her nerves to settle down, and the easiest way to do that was to take a chomp out of pain-in-the-butt Erik.

Stevie Rae narrowed her eyes at him. "Yeah, I was callin' you because you're supposed to be inside with everyone else. What the heck are ya still doin' out here, anyway? You're worrying Zoey—like she needs any more stress from you right now?"

"Zoey was looking for me?"

With an effort, Stevie Rae didn't roll her eyes at Erik. He was sooooo annoying. He acted like Mr. Perfect Boyfriend part of the time, and then would suddenly change up and be an arrogant jerk. She was gonna have to tell Z about him—that was if Z would still listen to her. The two of them hadn't exactly been very close lately. Too many secrets . . . too many issues sitting squarely between them . . .

"Stevie Rae! Pay attention. Did you say Zoey was looking for me?"

Stevie Rae did roll her eyes then. "You're supposed to be inside. Heath and Dallas and the rest of the kids are. Zoey knows that. She wanted to know where the heck you were and why you're not where you're supposed to be."

"If she was that worried she could have come out here herself."

"I didn't say she was worried!" Stevie Rae snapped, exasperated with Erik's self-absorption. "And Z has way too much on her plate to be out here babysittin' you."

"I don't need a damn babysitter."

"Really? Then why did I have to come get you?"

"I don't know, why did you? I was on my way inside. I just wanted to do one more sweep of the perimeter. I thought it'd be smart to go over what Heath was supposed to check. You know humans can't see shit at night."

"Johnny B isn't a human and he was with Heath." Stevie Rae sighed. "Just go on inside. Get something to eat and some dry clothes. One of the nuns will tell you where you're sleepin'. I'll take one more check around the grounds before the sun comes up," Stevie Rae said.

"*If* the sun comes up," Erik said, squinting up at the sky.

Stevie Rae followed his gaze, and with a sense of gawd-how-clueless-could-I-be, realized it was raining again, only the temperature was still on that line between freeze and non-freeze, so the sky was, once again, spitting ice.

"This crappy weather is not what we need," Stevie Rae muttered.

"Well, at least it'll help cover the blood from those Raven Mockers," Erik said.

Stevie Rae's gaze went quickly to Erik's face. Shit! She hadn't even thought about the blood! Had they tracked blood into the shed? Talk about leaving a glaring path that screamed *Here I am!* She realized Erik was expecting her to say something. "Yeah, um, you're right.

Maybe I'll try to kick around some ice and broken branches and stuff to cover up the blood from those three birds," she said with forced nonchalance.

"Probably a good idea in case some humans actually go outside during the day. Want some help?"

"No," she answered too quickly, and then made herself shrug. "What with my super red vamp skills and all it'll just take me a second. Not a big deal."

"Well, okay then." Erik started to walk away, but hesitated. "Hey, you might want to give some extra attention to the blood marks at the edge of the tree line by the condos next door and the road. It was pretty nasty down there."

"Okay, yeah, I know the place." She sure did.

"Oh, and, where did you say Zoey was?"

"Uh, Erik, I don't believe I said."

Erik frowned, waited, and when Stevie Rae just continued to look at him, finally asked, "Well? Where is she?"

"Last time I saw her she was talkin' to Heath and Sister Mary Angela in the hall outside the basement. But my guess is by now she's checked on Stark and is in bed. She looked tired as hell."

"Stark . . ." Erik muttered something unintelligible after the kid's name, and turned back toward the abbey.

"Erik!" Stevie Rae called while she silently cussed herself out 'cause it was stupid for her to have mentioned Heath or Stark. She waited until he looked over his shoulder at her and then said, "As Z's BFF, let me give ya a little piece of advice: she's been through too much today to want to deal with boyfriend issues. If she's with Heath it's because she's making sure he's okay—not because she's all lovey-dovey with him. Same goes for Stark."

"And?" Erik said, his face expressionless.

"*And* that means you should get something to eat, change your clothes, and take your butt to bed *without* trackin' her down and buggin' her."

"She and I are *together*, Stevie Rae. We're going out. So how could her boyfriend caring enough about her to want to be with her be considered 'buggin'' her'?"

Stevie Rae suppressed a smile. Zoey was going to eat him for breakfast, spit him out, and go on about her day. She shrugged. "Whatever. I'm just givin' ya a little advice, that's all."

"Yeah, well, later." Erik turned and stomped off to the abbey.

"For a smart guy, he sure makes some stupid choices," Stevie Rae said softly as she watched his broad back disappear. "'Course me sayin' that about him is what my mama would say was a hog callin' a skunk stinky."

Sighing, Stevie Rae's gaze moved reluctantly down to the row of big trash bins half camouflaged by their placement next to the nuns' carport. She averted her eyes, not wanting to think about the terrible crumpled bodies that had been dumped there. "With the trash." She said the words slowly, as if they each held their own weight. Stevie Rae admitted to herself that Zoey and Sister Mary Angela might have been partially right in their mini counseling session with her, but that didn't make what they'd said any less annoying.

Okay, sure, she'd overreacted, but the guys putting the bodies of the Raven Mockers in the trash had really jolted her, and not just because of *him*. Her eyes slid over to the shed that sat silently beside the greenhouse.

What they had done with the bodies of the Raven Mockers had bothered her because she didn't believe in life being devalued—any kind of life. It was a dangerous thing to think you were godlike and could decide who was worthy of life and who wasn't. Stevie Rae knew that better than the nun or Zoey ever could. Not only had her life, well, actually, her *death* been messed with by a High Priestess who had begun believing she was actually a goddess, but Stevie Rae had once thought *she* had the right to snuff out lives according to her own needs or whims. Just remembering how it had been when she'd been caught up in that anger and violence made her feel sick. She'd left those dark times behind her—she'd made a choice for good and light and the Goddess, and that was the path she was staying on. So when anyone decided a life meant nothing, *any* life, it upset her.

Or at least that was what Stevie Rae told herself as she started walking across the abbey grounds, heading totally *away* from the garden shed.

Keep it together, girl . . . keep it together . . . she kept repeating over and over as she detoured quickly down the ditch and into the tree line, heading directly for the bloodstains she remembered all too well. She found a thick, broken branch that still had a bunch of twigs attached to it, and lifted it easily, glad for the extra strength that came with her new status as fully Changed red vampyre. Using the branch like a broom, she brushed over the blood, pausing every so often to toss another broken branch, or once, a whole side of a collapsed holly bush, onto the telltale crimson pools.

Following her earlier path, she turned to her left, away from the street and back onto the nuns' lawn, staying inside the fence. She hadn't gone far when, just like before, Stevie Rae found a big splotch of blood.

Only this time there wasn't a body lying on top of it.

Distracting herself by humming Kenny Chesney's "(Baby) You Save Me," she hurriedly brushed over the bloodstains and then followed the trail of drops she knew she'd find, kicking ice and branches over the evidence, as the blood path led her directly to the little garden shed.

She stared hard at the door, sighed, and then turned away, walking around the shed to the greenhouse. The door was unlocked and the handle turned easily. She entered the building and paused, breathing deeply and allowing the scents of earth and growing things, mixed with the new spice of the three horses that were temporarily housed there, to soothe her senses, as the warmth of the place thawed the icy dampness that seemed to have penetrated into her soul. But she didn't allow herself to rest there long. She couldn't. She had business to take care of and not much time before dawn. Even if the sun was going to be shrouded by clouds and ice, it was still never a comfortable thing for a red vampyre to be caught outside, exposed and vulnerable, during the day.

It didn't take Stevie Rae long to find what she needed. The nuns obviously liked the old-school way of doing things. Instead of a system of modern hoses, electric switches, and metallic thingies, the sisters had buckets and dippers, watering pails with long, perforated nozzles made for gently showering baby plants, and lots of tools that were obviously as well used as they were well cared for. Stevie Rae filled a bucket with fresh water from one of the many faucets, grabbed a dipper, a few towels from a clean pile she found on a shelf used to store garden gloves and spare pots, and then, on her way out, she paused near a tray of moss that reminded her of a thick, green carpet. She stood there chewing her lip indecisively as instinct warred with her conscious mind, until she finally gave in and pulled up a long row of the moss. Then, mumbling to herself about not knowing how she knew what she knew, Stevie Rae left the greenhouse and returned to the shed.

At the door she stopped and focused her attention—keyed all of her keen, predator-like ability to sense, smell, see anyone, any*thing* lurking around. Nothing. No one was outside. The sleet and the late hour were keeping everyone tucked safe and warm inside.

"Everyone with any dang sense," she mumbled to herself.

She took one more look around, shifted her load so she had a free hand, and then touched the door latch. *Okay—okay. Just get it over with. Maybe he's dead and you won't have to deal with this great big-assed new mistake you made.*

Stevie Rae clicked the latch down and pushed open the door. Automatically, she wrinkled her nose. It was jolting after the earthy simplicity of the greenhouse, this little building that smelled like gas and oil and musty crap, all mixed with the wrong scent of his blood.

She'd left him at the other end of the shed, behind the riding mower and the shelves that held lawn care stuff like garden shears, fertilizer, and spare sprinkler parts. She peered back there and could vaguely make out a dark shape, but it wasn't moving. She listened hard and didn't hear anything except the ice spitting against the roof.

Dreading the inevitable moment when she was going to have to face him, Stevie Rae forced herself to step into the shed and close the door firmly behind her. She made her way around the mower and shelves to the creature that lay at the far end of the shed. It didn't look like he'd moved since she'd half dragged, half carried him there a couple of hours ago and literally tossed him into that back corner. He lay crumpled in on himself, curled into an awkward fetal position on his left side. The bullet that had torn through the upper right side of his chest, had ripped through his wing as it exited his body, utterly decimating it. The huge black wing lay bloody, shattered, and useless along his side. Stevie Rae also thought one of his ankles might be broken, as it was horribly swollen and, even in the darkness of the shed, she could see it looked bruised. Actually, his whole body looked pretty badly battered, which was no big surprise. He had been shot out of the sky and the big old oaks at the edge of the abbey's property had broken his fall enough for him not to have been killed immediately, but she really had no way of knowing how badly he was wounded. For all she knew his insides were as broken as his outsides looked. For all she knew, he was dead. He sure looked dead. She watched his chest and couldn't be 100 percent certain, but she didn't think she saw it rising or falling with his breath. He was probably dead. She kept staring at him, unwilling to move closer, and unable to turn and walk away.

Was she batshit crazy? Why hadn't she stopped to think before she'd dragged him in here? She stared at him. He wasn't human. He wasn't even animal. It wasn't playing God to let him die; he should never have been born.

Stevie Rae shuddered. She continued to stand there as if she was frozen by the horror of what she'd done. What would her friends say if they found out she'd hidden a Raven Mocker? Would Zoey turn away from her? And what repercussions would this creature's presence cause with the red fledglings, *all* of the red fledglings? As if they didn't have enough dark, evil things to deal with?

The nun had been right. He shouldn't evoke pity in her. She was going to take the towels and stuff back to the greenhouse, go inside the abbey, find Darius and tell him that there was a Raven Mocker in the shed. Then she'd let the warrior do his job. If he wasn't dead already, Darius would take care of business. It would actually be putting the bird guy out of his misery. She let out a long breath she hadn't realized she'd been holding in relief at her decision, and his red eyes opened and met hers.

"Finish it . . ." the Raven Mocker's voice was weak and filled with pain, but it was clearly, absolutely, undeniably human.

And that was it. Stevie Rae realized the reason she hadn't called

Dallas and the rest of them when she'd discovered him. When he'd spoken before and told her to kill him, he'd sounded like a real guy— one who had been hurt and abandoned and scared. She hadn't been able to kill him then, and she wasn't able to turn away from him now. His voice made all the difference, because even though he looked like a being that shouldn't be possible, he sounded like a regular guy who was so desperate and in such pain that he expected the very worst to happen to him.

No, that was wrong. He didn't just expect the very worst to happen to him, he wanted it to. What he had gone through was so horrible he couldn't see any way out of it except through his own death. To Stevie Rae, even though what he'd been through was largely of his own making, that made him very, very human. She'd been there. She understood such complete hopelessness.

CHAPTER EIGHT

Stevie Rae

Stevie Rae controlled her automatic impulse to step back because guy voice or no guy voice, and the question of his humanity put temporarily aside, the honest truth was he was one big, bird guy whose blood smelled seriously wrong. And Stevie Rae was very much alone with him.

"Look, I know you're hurt and all, so you're not thinkin' right, but if I was gonna kill you I definitely wouldn't have dragged you in here." She made her voice sound normal and instead of backing away from him like she wanted to, she stood her ground and she met those cold red eyes that looked so bizarrely human.

"Why won't you kill me?" The words were little more than an agonized whisper, but the night was so silent that Stevie Rae had no trouble hearing him.

She could have pretended she didn't hear what he'd said, or at least didn't understand him, but she was sick of evasions and lies, so she continued to hold his gaze and told him the truth, "Well, actually, that has a lot more to do with me than you, and that makes it a kinda long, confusing story. I guess mostly I'm not real sure why I won't kill you, 'cept for the fact that I tend to do things my own way, and I can definitely say I'm not a big fan of killing."

He stared at her until she wanted to squirm under that strange red gaze. Finally he said, "You should."

Stevie Rae's eyebrows went up. "I should know, I should kill ya, or I should do things my own way? You're gonna have to be more specific.

Oh, and you should also consider being less bossy. You're not exactly in a position to tell me what I *should* do."

Obviously at the very end of his strength, his eyes had begun to close, but her words had him reopening them. She could see some kind of emotion changing his expression, but his face was so foreign, so unlike anything or anyone she was used to, that she couldn't read him. His black beak opened as if he was going to say something. At that moment a shudder rippled through his body. Instead of speaking, he closed his eyes tightly and moaned. The sound was filled with an agony that was completely human.

Automatically she took a step toward him. His eyes reopened and, even though they were glazed with pain, she could see his scarlet gaze was focused on her. Stevie Rae stopped and spoke slowly and distinctly. "Okay, here's the deal. I brought water and stuff to bandage you up with, but I'm not really cool with coming over there by you unless you give me your word you won't try anything I'm not gonna like."

This time Stevie Rae was sure the emotion she saw within the red of those human eyes was surprise.

"I cannot move." His words were halting, and it was an obvious effort for him to speak at all.

"Does that mean I have your word you won't bite me or do anything else that's not very nice?"

"Yesssss."

His voice had gone all guttural and the word ended in a hiss, which Stevie Rae didn't find at all reassuring. Still, she straightened her spine and nodded like he hadn't just sounded like a snake. "Well. Good. Okay, let's see what I can do to make ya feel better."

Then, before she could talk some sense into her own dang head, she walked right up to the Raven Mocker. She plopped the towels and the moss on the ground beside him, and set the water bucket down more carefully. He really was big. She'd forgotten that. Well, maybe it was more like she'd blocked it from her memory, because "forgetting" his size was pretty hard. It hadn't been exactly easy to drag/carry him into this shed before Erik or Dallas or Heath or *anyone* had seen her, even though he'd been weirdly light for how heavy he looked.

"Water." The word was almost a croak.

"Oh, yeah, sure!" Stevie Rae jumped and then fumbled with the handle of the dipper. It fell on the floor, and as embarrassed as she was frazzled, she dropped it again—had to pick it up, wipe it on a towel, and then finally dip it into the water. She moved closer to him. He stirred weakly, obviously trying to raise an arm, but the attempt caused him to moan again and his arm seemed to only be able to hang at his side, as useless as his broken wing. Not pausing to think about what she was doing, Stevie Rae bent, lifted his shoulders gently, tilted his head back, and held the dipper to his beak. He drank thirstily.

When he'd had his fill, she helped him lie back, but not until she'd put one of the towels under his head.

"Okay, I don't have anything to clean you up with except water, but I'll do my best. Oh, and I brought some strips of moss. If I pack your wounds with them, they'll help." She didn't bother to explain that she really didn't know how she knew the moss was good for his wounds—it was just one of the snatches of information she'd get from time to time—out of nowhere. One second she wouldn't have a clue about something. The next she'd be sure of how to, well, plug up a wound, for instance. She wanted to believe it was Nyx whispering to her, like the Goddess whispered to Zoey, but the truth was, Stevie Rae didn't know for sure. "Just keep choosing good over evil . . ." she muttered to herself as she started to tear one of the towels into strips.

The Raven Mocker's eyes opened and he looked questioningly at her.

"Oh, don't mind me. I talk to myself. Even when I'm not alone. It's kinda like my own version of therapy." She paused and met his gaze. "This is gonna hurt. I mean, I'll try to be careful and all, but you're pretty messed up."

"Go ahead," he said in that pain-filled whispery voice that sounded too human to be coming from such an inhuman-looking creature.

"Alright, well, here goes." Stevie Rae worked as quickly and as gently as possible. The hole in his chest was terrible. She flushed it with water and picked off as much of the twigs and crap from around it as possible. His feathers made what she was doing super weird. There was chest and skin under them, but it was just so dang odd! He had *feathers*, and under them she found downy little black puffs that felt soft as cotton candy from the state fair.

She glanced at his face. He'd laid his head back down on the towel pillow. His eyes were squeezed shut, and he was breathing in short little pants.

"Sorry, I know this hurts," she said. His only response was a grunt which, ironically, made him seem more guy-like. Seriously—the grunt was well known to be a major guy communication method. "Okay, I think it's ready for the moss." She spoke more to soothe her own nerves than his. Tearing off a section of the moss, she carefully packed it into the wound. "It doesn't seem as bad now that it's not bleeding so much." She kept chattering, even though he barely responded to her. "Here, gotta move you a little." Stevie Rae rolled him further on his stomach so she could get to the rest of the wound. He pressed his face into the towel and stifled another moan. Stevie Rae spoke quickly, hating that agonized sound. "The hole where it came out of your back is bigger, but it's not as dirty, so I won't have as much cleaning to do back here." It took a larger chunk of moss to cover the exit wound, but she got it done quickly.

Then she shifted her attention to his wings. The wing on his left side was tucked tightly against his back. It didn't look like it had been injured at all. But his right wing was another story. It was totally messed up—shattered and bloody and hanging lifelessly down his side.

"Well, I guess it's time to admit I'm totally out of my comfort zone back here. I mean, the bullet wound was nasty, but at least I knew what to do about it—kind of. Your wing is something else. I have no clue what to do to help it."

"Bind it to me. Use the cloth strips." His voice was gravelly. He didn't look at her and his eyes were still tightly closed.

"Are you sure? Maybe I should just leave it alone."

"Less pain—if it's bound," he said haltingly.

"Well, shit. Okay." Stevie Rae got to work tearing another towel into long strips, and then knotting them together. "All right. I'm gonna arrange your wing on your back kinda in the same position your other wing's in. Is that right?"

He nodded once.

She held her breath and picked up his wing. He jerked and gasped. She dropped it and jumped back.

"Shit! I'm sorry! Crap!"

His eyes slitted and he looked up at her. Between panting gasps he said, "Just. Do. It."

She gritted her teeth, leaned forward and, blocking out his muffled moans of pain, rearranged the shattered wing into a position that vaguely resembled the unwounded wing. Then, with barely a pause for breath, she said, "You're gonna have to hold yourself up a little so I can get this tied around you."

Stevie Rae felt his body tense and then he heaved himself up, leaning mostly on his left arm, so that he was in a tilted-over, half-sitting-up position—and his torso was far enough off the floor of the shed for her to quickly wrap the towel strips around him and secure the wing.

"Okay, got it."

He collapsed. His entire body was trembling.

"I'm wrappin' your ankle now. I think it's broken, too."

He nodded once.

She tore more towel strips and then securely wrapped up his surprisingly human-looking ankle, just like she remembered her volleyball coach wrapping up one of her teammates' weak ankles back when she was in high school at Henrietta High, home of the Fighting Hens.

Fighting Hens? Okay, her hometown's mascot had always been silly, but at that moment it struck Stevie Rae as super-funny, and she had to bite her lip to keep a hysterical giggle from bubbling out of it. Thankfully she got herself under control in just a couple breaths, and managed to ask him, "Are you hurt bad anywhere else?"

He shook his head in a short, jerky motion.

"Okay, then I'm gonna stop messin' with you, 'cause I think I got the worst of it tended." When he nodded once in agreement, she sat

on the floor beside him, wiping her shaking hands on one of the left-
over towels. Then she just sat there, looking at him and wondering
what the heck she was going to do next. "I'll tell you one thing," she
said aloud, "I hope I never have to tie up another broken wing in my
whole dang life."

His eyes opened, but he didn't speak.

"Well, it was totally horrible. That wing hurts worse than a regular broken arm or leg, doesn't it?"

She was talking because she was nervous, and Stevie Rae didn't
expect him to answer, so she was surprised when he said, "It does."

"Yeah, that's what I thought," she continued, as if they were two
normal people having an ordinary conversation. His voice was still
weak, but it seemed easier for him to speak and she guessed immobi-
lizing his wing had really helped his pain level.

"I need more water," he said.

"Oh, sure." She grabbed the dipper, glad her hands had stopped
shaking. This time he was able to hold himself up and tip back his
own head. She only had to pour the water into his mouth, or beak, or
whatever the correct word for it was.

Since she was already up, Stevie Rae decided she might as well
gather up the bloody pieces of towel, thinking that she should get
them away from the shed. The red fledglings' sense of smell wasn't as
good as hers, but it also wasn't as undeveloped as regular fledglings.
She didn't want to chance any of them having a reason to sniff
around there. A quick search of the shed and she discovered extra-
big lawn and garden trash bags, into which she stuffed the rags. There
were three towels she hadn't used, and without really giving it much
thought, she unfolded them and spread them out, covering as much
of the Raven Mocker as was possible.

"Are you the Red One?"

His voice made her jump. His eyes had been closed and he'd been
so quiet while she was cleaning up that she had assumed he was asleep,
or maybe passed out. Now those human eyes were open again and
trained on her.

"I don't know how to answer that. I am a red vampyre, if that's
what you mean. The first red vampyre." She thought briefly about

Stark and his completed red tattoos, which made him the second red vampyre, and wondered where he was going to fit in their world, but no way was she going to mention him to the Raven Mocker.

"You are the Red One."

"Well, okay, I guess I am."

"My father said the Red One was powerful."

"I am powerful," Stevie Rae said with no hesitation. Then she held his gaze and continued, "Your father? You mean Kalona?"

"Yes."

"He's gone, ya know."

"I know." He looked away from her then. "I should be with him."

"No offense, but from what I know of your daddy, I think it's best that you're here and he's not. He isn't exactly a nice guy. Not to mention Neferet has gone completely batshit crazy, and the two of them are like peas in a nasty pod."

"You talk a lot," he said and then grimaced painfully.

"Yeah, it's a habit." *A nervous habit*, but she didn't add that. "Look, you need to rest. I'm gonna go. Plus, the sun started to come up five minutes ago, and that means I need to be inside. The only reason I can walk around at all out there is because the sky's so full of clouds." She tied the trash bag closed and scooted the water bucket and dipper within his reach—*if* he was able to do any reaching. "So, bye. I'll, um, see ya later." She started to hurry away, but his voice stopped her.

"What will you do with me?"

"I haven't figured that part out yet." She sighed and fidgeted, picking nervously at her fingernails. "Look, I think you're safe here for at least one day. The storm isn't letting up and the nuns aren't going to be messin' around out here. All of the fledglings will probably stay inside until sunset. By that time I should know what to do with you."

"I still do not understand why you don't tell the others about me."

"Yeah. Well, that makes two of us. Try to rest. I'll be back."

Her hand was on the door latch when he spoke again. "My name is Rephaim."

Stevie Rae smiled over her shoulder at him. "Hi. I'm Stevie Rae. Nice to meet ya, Rephaim."

* * *

Rephaim watched the Red One leave the building. He counted one hundred breaths after the door clicked closed, and then he began shifting his body until he'd forced himself into a sitting position. Now that he was fully conscious he wanted to take inventory of his injuries.

His ankle was not broken. It pained him, but he could move it. His ribs were bruised but, again, he didn't think any of them were broken. The bullet wound in his chest was serious, but the Red One had cleaned it and packed it with moss. If it didn't fester and putrefy, he would heal. He could move his right arm, though it was difficult, and it felt unnaturally stiff as well as weak.

Finally, he shifted his attention to his wing. Rephaim closed his eyes and probed with his mind, following sinew and ligaments, muscle and bone, through his back and down the length of his shattered pinion. He gasped, almost unable to breathe, as he truly comprehended the full extent of the damage the bullet, and then the terrible, ripping fall had done.

He would never fly again.

The reality of the thought was so horrible that his mind skittered away from it. He would think of the Red One instead and try to remember everything Father had told him about her powers. Maybe he would find some clue in his memory that would explain her unusual behavior. Why had she not killed him? Perhaps she still would—or at least perhaps she would betray his presence to her friends.

If she did, so be it. Life as he had known it was over for him. He would welcome the chance to die battling anyone who tried to keep him prisoner.

But it hadn't seemed she'd been imprisoning him. He thought hard, forcing his mind to work through pain and exhaustion and despair. *Stevie Rae.* That had been the name she'd given him. What was her motive in saving him if not to imprison and use him? Torture. It made sense that she had kept him alive so that she and her allies could force him to tell her all he knew about Father. What other reason could she have for not killing him? He would have done the same had he been lucky enough to have been in her place.

They will discover that the son of an immortal will not be easily broken, he thought.

Stressed beyond the reserves of even his great strength, Rephaim collapsed. He tried to position himself so that he could attain some relief from the agony that wracked his body with every beat of his heart, but it was impossible. Only time could relieve his physical pain. Nothing would relieve the soul-deep pain of never being able to fly again—of never being whole.

She should have killed me, he thought. *Perhaps I can goad her into it if she returns alone. And if she comes back with her allies and attempts to torture my father's secrets from me, I will not be the only one to shriek in pain.*

Father? Where are you? Why did you desert me?

That was the thought foremost in his mind when unconsciousness finally claimed Rephaim again and, at last, he slept.

CHAPTER NINE

Zoey

"Hey, remember you promised the nun you'd go to bed. And I'm pretty sure that didn't mean going to *his* bed." Heath jerked his chin at the door to Stark's room.

I raised my brows at Heath.

He sighed. "I said I'd share you with the stupid vamps if I had to, but I didn't say I'd like it."

I shook my head. "You're not *sharing me* with anyone tonight. I'm just going to make sure Stark's okay, then go to my own bed. Alone. By myself. Got it?"

"Got it." He grinned and then kissed me softly. "See you soon, Zo."

"See you soon, Heath."

I watched him walk away down the hall. He was tall and muscular and looked every inch the star quarterback. He was all set to go to OU on a full-ride scholarship next year, and then, after college, he was going to be either a cop or a fireman. Whichever he chose there was one thing for certain—Heath would be one of the good guys.

But could he do all that, *would* he do all that, and also be a vampyre High Priestess's consort?

Yes. Hell, yes. I am going to make sure Heath gets the future he's dreamed of and planned since we were kids. Sure, some parts of it will be different. Neither of us planned on the vamp stuff. Some parts of it will be hard—like, well, the vamp stuff. But the truth is, I care about Heath too much to force him out of my life *and* I care about him too much to mess up his life. So we are just going to have to make it work. Period. The end.

"You going to go in, or are you just going to stand out here and stress?"

"Holy crap, Aphrodite! Could you not sneak up and scare me?"

"No one was sneaking, and 'holy crap,' is that a curse? 'Cause if it is, I'm afraid I'm going to have to wake up the Potty Mouth Police and have them make an arrest." Darius followed Aphrodite into the hall and gave her a *be nice* look, which made her sigh and say, "So. Stark's not dead yet."

"Gosh, thanks for that update. You just made me feel ever so much better," I said sarcastically.

"Don't be a pain in my ass while I'm trying to be nice."

I turned my attention to the only responsible adult in the area and asked Darius, "Does he need anything?"

The warrior hesitated for only an instant, but it was an instant that I caught. Then he said, "No. He is doing well. I believe he will recover completely."

"*Well* . . ." I dragged out the word, wondering what the hell was really going on. Was Stark hurt worse than Darius was admitting? "I'll check on him real quick, then I'm going to bed." I raised a brow at Aphrodite. "You and I are roomies. Darius is rooming with Damien and Jack. Uh, that means you're not sleeping with him 'cause that would freak the nuns. You got that, right?"

"Oh. No. You so didn't need to give me that *Anne of Green Gables* lecture! Like I can't behave with some propriety? Are you remembering my parents purchased propriety for Tulsa? My. Dad. Is. The. Mayor. I can't believe I have to deal with this shit."

Darius and I stared, speechless, as Aphrodite worked herself up into a seriously extraordinary hissy fit.

"I heard the damn nun. Plus, it's not like this abbey is exactly romantic. Like I want to have hot monkey sex while the penguins cross themselves and pray? Ugh. Not hardly. Goddess! I may melt if I stay here too long."

When she paused to take a breath, I inserted, "I didn't mean I didn't think you knew how to act. I was just kinda reminding you, that's all."

"Yeah? Bullshit. You're a really bad liar, Z." She walked over to

Darius and kissed him hard on the mouth. "Later, lover. I'll miss you in my bed." She gave me a disgusted glance. "Just say night-night to boyfriend number three and get your butt to our room. I do not like to be awakened after I've retired to my boudoir." Aphrodite tossed her long, gorgeous blond hair and twitched away.

"She's really amazing," Darius said as he gazed lovingly after her.

"If by amazing you mean a total pain in the butt, then I'll agree with you." I held up my hand, stopping his she's-really-not-that-bad comment before he could make it. "I don't want to talk about your girlfriend right now. I just want to know how Stark's really doing."

"Stark is healing."

I could almost see the big gap in the rest of his sentence. I raised both brows at the warrior. "But . . ."

"But nothing. Stark is healing."

"Why do I think there's more to it than that?"

Darius waited a beat and then he smiled a little sheepishly. "Perhaps because you are intuitive enough to feel that there is more to it than that."

"All right, what is it?"

"It's about energy and spirit and blood. Or rather Stark's need of and lack of them."

I blinked a couple times, trying to understand exactly what Darius was saying, and then I sucked in air as the lightbulb went on over my head and I felt like a total idiot for not understanding sooner. "He's been hurt—like I was—and he has to have blood to heal, just like I did. Well, why didn't you say something before? Crap!" I kept babbling on as my mind raced, "I don't especially want him to bite Aphrodite, but—"

"No!" Darius interrupted, looking more than a little upset at the thought of Stark drinking from his girlfriend. "Aphrodite's Imprint with Stevie Rae makes her blood repellent to other vampyres."

"Well, hell! Let's get him a blood baggie or whatever, and I guess I could try to find a human he could bite . . ." My voice trailed off. I hated, hated, hated thinking about Stark drinking from anyone else. I mean, I had already had to deal with his extracurricular biting before he'd pledged himself as my Warrior and gone through the

Change. I had hoped that the days of his biting other girls were behind him. I still hoped it! But I wouldn't be so selfish that my feelings kept him from getting what he needed to heal.

"I've already given him some blood the sisters had on ice in the infirmary. He's not in danger of dying. He will recover."

"*But?*" I was exasperated that Darius's sentences all seemed to have these big unfilled-in blanks at the end of them.

"But when a Warrior is pledged to the service of a High Priestess, there is a special bond between them."

"Yeah, I already know that."

"That bond is more than just an oath. Since ancient times Nyx has blessed her High Priestesses and the Warriors who serve them. The two of you are linked through the Goddess's blessing. It gives him intuitive knowledge about you that makes it easier for him to protect you."

"Intuitive knowledge? You mean like an Imprint?" *Goddess! Was this like I was Imprinted with two guys?*

"An Imprint and a Warrior Bond have similarities. Both bind two people together. But an Imprint is a cruder form of a connection."

"Cruder? What do you mean?"

"I mean that even though an Imprint often happens between a vampyre and a human for whom she cares deeply, it is a connection that originates in the blood and is ruled by the basest of our emotions: passion, lust, need, hunger, pain." He hesitated, obviously trying to choose his words carefully. "You have experienced some of that with your consort, have you not?"

My nod was stiff and my cheeks felt hot.

"Contrast that bond with the Oath Bond you have with Stark."

"Well, I haven't had it very long. I really don't know much about it." But as I said the words, I realized that I did already know that the connection I had with Stark went beyond wanting to drink from him. Actually, I hadn't even really thought about drinking from him—or him drinking from me.

"As your Warrior serves you longer, you will understand more of your bond with him. Your link with your Warrior means he could develop the ability to sense many of your emotions. For instance, if a

High Priestess is suddenly threatened, the Warrior pledged to her may feel her fear, and follow that emotional trail to his Priestess so that he may protect her from whatever is threatening."

"I-I didn't know that," I stuttered nervously.

Darius's smile was wry. "I hate to sound like Damien, but you really should find time to read your *Fledgling Handbook*."

"Yeah, that's on the top of my to-do list as soon as my world stops exploding. Okay, so, Stark might be able to tell if I'm afraid. What does that have to do with him being hurt?"

"Your connection isn't as simple as just the possibility of him sensing your fear. It's also about energy and spirit. Your Warrior may eventually be able to feel many of your strong emotions, especially as he spends more and more time in your service."

The memory of the very emotional experience I'd shared with A-ya while she'd trapped Kalona had my stomach tightening at Darius's explanation. "Go on," I said.

"A Warrior can absorb his Priestess's emotions. He can also absorb spirit from her, especially if his Priestess has a strong affinity. Often he can tap into that affinity."

"What in the hell does that mean, Darius?"

"It means he can literally absorb energy through your blood."

"Are you saying it's me Stark needs to bite?" Okay, I'll admit that my heart started to speed up at the thought. Seriously—I was already mega-attracted to Stark and I knew sharing blood with him would be a very hot experience.

It would also break Heath's heart, and what if drinking from me let Stark into my mind and he saw what was going on with my memories of A-ya? Hell! Hell! Hell! Hell! Hell! Hell! Then a new thought hit me. "Hey, wait. You said Stark couldn't bite Aphrodite because she's Imprinted with someone else and other vamps don't want her blood. I'm Imprinted with Heath. Does that mess up my blood for Stark?"

Darius shook his head. "No, the Imprint only changes a human's blood."

"So mine will work for Stark?"

"Yes, your blood would definitely help him to heal, and he knows

it, which is why I'm taking the time to explain all of this to you."
Darius continued as if I wasn't having a mini emotional breakdown
right in front of him. "And you should also know he is refusing to
drink from you."

"*What?* He's *refusing* to drink from me?" Okay, sure, a second before I'd been worried about what would happen if Stark bit me, but
that didn't mean I wanted to be rejected by him!

"He knows you've recently healed from the Raven Mocker's attack. The creature almost killed you, Zoey. Stark doesn't want to take
anything from you that might weaken you. If he drank from you he
wouldn't just be absorbing your blood; he would be taking energy
and spirit from you. Factor in that none of us knows where Kalona
and Neferet have gone, and that means we don't know when you
might have to face them again. I agree with his decision to refuse to
drink. You need to be at full strength."

"So does my Warrior," I countered.

Darius sighed and nodded his head slowly. "Agreed, but he can be
replaced. You cannot."

"He can't be replaced!" I blurted.

"I do not mean to sound unfeeling, but you must be wise—in *all*
of your decisions."

"Stark can't be replaced," I repeated stubbornly.

"As you will, Priestess." He bowed his head slightly, and then suddenly changed the subject. "Now that you understand the ramifications of a Warrior's Oath, I would like to ask your permission for me
to pledge myself formally."

I swallowed hard. "Well, Darius, I really like you and you've taken
seriously good care of me, but I think I'd feel kinda awkward having
two guys pledged to me." As if I didn't have enough guy issues?

Darius's smile was quick. He shook his head and I got the distinct
impression he was trying not to laugh at me. "You misunderstand.
I will stay with you and lead those who guard you, but I would like to
pledge my Warrior's Oath to Aphrodite—that is what I'm asking
your permission to do."

"You want to be bound to Aphrodite?"

"I do. I know it is irregular for a vampyre Warrior to pledge to a human, but Aphrodite is not a normal human."

"You're telling me," I mumbled. He went on as if I hadn't spoken.

"She is truly a prophetess, which puts her in the same category as a High Priestess of Nyx."

"It won't mess up your Warrior's bond to have her Imprinted with Stevie Rae?"

Darius shrugged. "We shall see. I am willing to take the chance."

"You love her, don't you?"

He met my gaze steadily and his smile warmed. "I do."

"She's seriously a pain in the butt."

"She's unique," he countered. "And she needs my protection, especially in the days to come."

"Well, you have a point there." I shrugged. "Okay, you have my permission. Don't say I didn't warn you about the pain-in-the-butt part, though."

"I wouldn't think of it. Thank you, Priestess. Please, do not say anything to Aphrodite. I would like to make my offer privately to her."

"My lips are totally sealed." I made a little pantomime of zipping up my lips and throwing away the key.

"Then I bid you good night." He fisted his hand over his heart, bowed, and he was gone.

CHAPTER TEN

Zoey

I stayed out in the hall, trying to sift through the mess of thoughts in my head.

Wow! Darius was going to ask Aphrodite to accept his Warrior's Oath. Jeesh. A vampyre warrior and a human prophet of the Goddess. Huh. Who knew?

On an equally freaky note: Stark could feel my emotions if they were strong enough. Well, I had a *strong* feeling that was going to be inconvenient. And then I realized I was feeling strong about feeling strongly, and I tried to clamp down on everything, which just stressed me out, which he could probably sense. Undoubtedly, I was going to drive my own self crazy.

Stifling a sigh, I opened the door quietly. The only light was coming from one of those tall prayer candles—the kind you can find in the grocery store that have really weird religious pictures on them. This one wasn't so weird. It was pink, had a pretty picture of Mary on it, and it smelled like roses.

I tiptoed over to Stark's bedside.

He didn't look good, but he also wasn't as pale and awful as he had been not long before. He seemed to be asleep—or at least his eyes were closed—his breathing was regular, and he looked relaxed. He didn't have a shirt on, and the hospital sheet was pulled up under his arms so that I could just see the white top of what must have been a huge bandage covering his chest. I remembered how terrible the burn had been and wondered if, even considering the possible ramifications, I should make a cut in my arm like Heath had done for me, and then shove it against his mouth. He'd probably latch on to it automatically and, without thinking, drink what he needed to heal. But would he be pissed when he'd realized what I'd done? Probably. I knew Heath and Erik certainly would be.

Crap. Erik. I hadn't even begun to deal with him yet.

"Stop stressing."

I jumped and my gaze instantly went to Stark's face. His eyes weren't closed any longer. He was watching me with an expression that was somewhere between amused and sarcastic.

"Stop psychically eavesdropping."

"I wasn't. I could tell by watching you gnaw your lip that you were stressing yourself out. So, I guess Darius talked to you."

"Yeah, he has. Did you know about all that went along with giving me your Warrior's Oath before you did it?"

"Yeah, mostly. I mean I'd read about it at school, and we talked about it in Vamp Soc Class this past year. It's different to actually experience it, though."

"Can you really feel what I feel?" I asked hesitantly, almost as afraid to know the truth as to not know it.

"I'm starting to, only it's not like I can hear your thoughts or anything crazy like that. I just feel things sometimes, and I know they're not coming from me. I mostly ignored it when it first happened, but then I realized what was going on and paid more attention to it." He started to smile.

"Stark, I have to tell you that kinda makes me feel spied on."

His expression went totally serious. "I'm not spying on you. This isn't about me following you around with my mind. I'm not going to invade your privacy; I'm going to keep you safe. I thought you—" He broke off, looking away from me. "Never mind. It's not important. You should just know I'm not going to use this thing between us to be like a creeper and mentally stalk you."

"You thought I what? Finish what you started to say."

He let out a long, exasperated breath and met my eyes again. "What I started to say is that I thought you trusted me more than that. That's one of the reasons I decided to give you my oath, because you trusted me when no one else did."

"I do trust you," I said quickly.

"But you think I'd spy on you? Trust and spying don't go together."

When he put it that way, I could see his point, and some of my initial freak-out started to fade. "I don't think you'd do it on purpose, but if my emotions are blabbing at you, or whatever they do, then it would be easy for you to, well . . ." I trailed off and fidgeted, not comfortable with the whole conversation.

"*Spy*?" he finished for me. "No. I won't. How's this: I'll pay attention to the psychic stuff I get from you if you're scared. Other than that I'll ignore how you're feeling." He met my eyes and I could see his hurt there. Crap! I hadn't meant to hurt him.

"You'll ignore *everything* I'm feeling?" I asked softly.

He nodded and the movement made him grimace in pain, but his voice was steady when he answered. "Everything except what I need to know to protect you."

Without speaking, I reached out slowly and took his hand.

He didn't pull away from me, but he also didn't say anything.

"Look, I started this whole conversation wrong. I do trust you. I was just surprised when Darius told me about the psychic thing."

"Surprised?" Stark's lips tilted up.

"Okay, maybe completely freaked is a better word. It's just that I have a bunch of stuff going on and I guess I'm stressing."

"You're stressing for sure," he said. "And by *bunch of stuff* do you mean those two guys, Heath and Erik?"

I sighed. "Sadly, I do."

He laced his fingers through mine. "Those other guys don't change anything. My Oath binds us."

For a second he sounded too darn much like Heath, and I had to force myself not to fidget again.

"I really don't want to talk about them with you right now." *Or ever* I thought, but didn't say.

"I got ya," he said. "I don't feel like talking about those punks right now either." He tugged on my hand. "Why don't you sit by me for a little while?"

I sat gingerly on the edge of the bed, not wanting to jostle him too much or hurt him.

"I'm not gonna break," he said, giving me his cocky grin.

"You almost broke," I said.

"Nah, you saved me. And I'm going to be okay."

"So, does it hurt really bad?"

"I've felt better," he said. "But the creamy stuff the nuns gave Darius to spread on the burn helps. Except for my chest being all tight, it's mostly numb right now." But even as he spoke he shifted restlessly, as if he couldn't get comfortable. "How's it going out there?" He abruptly changed the subject before I could ask him any more about how he was feeling. "Did all the Raven Mockers take off with Kalona?"

"I think so. Stevie Rae and the guys found three of them dead." I paused, remembering Stevie Rae's weird reaction to Dallas telling her that they'd put the bodies in the trash.

"What is it?" Stark asked.

"I don't know exactly," I answered him honestly. "There're things going on with Stevie Rae that are worrying me."

"Like?" he prompted.

I looked down at our joined hands. How much could I tell him? Could I really talk to him?

"I'm your Warrior. You can trust me with your life. That means you can also trust me with your secrets." I met his eyes, and he continued, smiling sweetly at me. "We're Oath-bound. That's a stronger tie than what happens between an Imprint or even between mates. I'll never betray you, Zoey. Ever. You can count on me."

For an instant I wanted to tell him about my memory of A-ya, but instead I blurted, "I think Stevie Rae's hiding red fledglings. Bad ones."

His easy smile vanished and he started to sit up, then sucked in a sharp breath and went totally white.

"No! You can't get up!" I pressed his shoulders gently back.

"You have to tell Darius," Stark said through clenched teeth.

"I have to talk to Stevie Rae first."

"I don't think that's—"

"Seriously! I have to talk to Stevie Rae first." I took his hand again, trying to will him through my touch to understand. "She's my best friend."

"You trust her?"

"I want to trust her. I have trusted her." My shoulders slumped in defeat. "But if she doesn't come clean with the truth when I talk to her, I will go to Darius."

"I need to get out of this damn bed so I can make sure you're not surrounded by enemies!"

"I'm *not* surrounded by enemies! Stevie Rae isn't my enemy." I sent up a silent prayer to Nyx that I was right about that. "Look, I've kept things from my friends before—bad things." I raised a brow and shot him a Look. "I kept *you* from my friends."

He grinned. "Well, that's different."

I didn't let him tease me out of being serious. "No, it's really not."

"Okay, I hear what you're saying, but I'm still not okay with it. I don't suppose I can get you to bring Stevie Rae here when you talk to her?"

I squidged my forehead at him. "No, not likely."

"Then promise me that you'll be careful and you won't go off alone with her somewhere to talk."

"She wouldn't do anything to hurt me!"

"Actually, I'm assuming she can't hurt you, being as you have control of five elements to her one. But you don't know what kind of powers these rogue fledglings she's hiding have, or how many of them there are. And I know a little something about being a badass red fledgling. So promise you'll be careful."

"Yeah, okay. I promise."

"Good." He relaxed a little bit back on the bed.

"Hey, I don't want you to worry about me right now. You just need to concentrate on getting better." I drew a deep, fortifying breath and continued, "I think it's a good idea for you to drink from me."

"No."

"Look, you want to be able to protect me, right?"

"Right," he said, nodding tightly.

"Then that means you have to get well fast so you can. Right?"

"Yeah."

"And you'll get well quicker if you drink from me, so it's only logical that you do."

"Have you looked in a mirror lately?" he asked abruptly.

"Huh?"

"Do you have any idea how tired you look?"

I could feel my cheeks getting warm. "I really haven't had time lately to worry about stuff like makeup and doing my hair," I said defensively.

"I'm not talking about makeup or hair. I'm talking about how pale you look. You have dark circles under your eyes." His gaze slid down to where my shirt covered the long scar that stretched from one of my shoulders to another. "How's your cut?"

"Fine." With my free hand I tugged up my shirt, even though I knew none of the scar was exposed.

"Hey," he said gently. "I've already seen it, remember?"

I met his eyes. Yes, I remembered. Actually, he'd not just seen my scar—he'd seen all of me. Naked. Okay, now my entire face felt hot.

"I'm not mentioning it to embarrass you. I'm just trying to remind you that you've almost died lately, too. We need you to be strong and well, Zoey. *I* need you to be strong and well. And that's why I'm *not* going to take anything from you right now."

"But I need you to be strong and well, too."

"I will be. Hey, don't worry about me. Apparently, I'm practically impossible to kill." He grinned his cute, cocky smile.

"Keep my stress level in mind. *Practically* impossible is not the same as impossible."

"I'll try to remember that." He pulled on my hand. "Lay down next to me for a little while. I like it when you're close."

"Are you sure I'm not going to hurt you?"

"I'm almost positive you will hurt me." He smiled, making his words teasing, "but I still want you close. Come here to me."

I let him tug me down so that I was lying next to him. Curled on my side I faced him, resting my head carefully against his shoulder. He reached across his body and draped an arm over me, pulling me more firmly against him. "I said I'm not going to break. Now relax."

I sighed, and willed myself to relax. I wrapped my arm around his waist, being careful not to jostle him too much or touch his chest. Stark closed his eyes and I watched his face go from tight and pale to relaxed and pale as his breathing deepened. I swear within a minute he was sound asleep.

That was exactly what I wanted him to be for what I'd decided to do. I drew three deep, cleansing breaths, centered myself, and then whispered, "Spirit, come to me."

Instantly I felt the familiar stirring within me, like I'd just understood something unbelievably magickal, as my soul responded to the infilling of the fifth element, spirit.

"Now, quietly, carefully, gently, go to Stark. Help him. Fill him. Strengthen him, *but don't wake him up.*" I spoke softly, mentally crossing my fingers that he'd stay asleep. As spirit left me I felt Stark's body stiffen for an instant, then he trembled, and then he let out a long, sleepy sigh while spirit soothed and, hopefully, strengthened him. I watched for a little while more; then slowly, I untangled myself from Stark and, with a last whisper asking spirit to stay with him while he slept, tiptoed from the room, closing the door gently behind me.

I'd only taken a couple steps when I realized I didn't have a clue where I was going. I stopped and felt my shoulders slump. A nun, who had been walking with her eyes cast down, hurried past me and gave a little jolt as she looked up and our gazes met.

"Sister Bianca?" I thought I recognized her.

"Oh, Zoey, yes it's me. It's so dark in the hall I almost didn't see you."

"Sister, I guess I'm lost. Can you point me in the right direction to my room?"

She smiled kindly, reminding me of Sister Mary Angela, even though she wasn't nearly as old. "Keep going down this hall until you come to the stairwell. Take it up to the top floor, and I do believe the room you're sharing with Aphrodite is number thirteen."

"*Lucky* thirteen," I sighed. "That figures."

"Don't you believe we make our own luck?"

I shrugged. "Actually, Sister, I'm too tired to know what I believe right now."

She patted my arm. "Well, go on to bed then. I'll say a prayer to Our Lady for you. Her intervention is better than luck any day."

"Thanks."

I headed in the direction of the stairwell. By the time I got to the top floor I was sucking air like an old woman, and the scar that stretched across my chest was burning and throbbing in time with the fast beating of my heart. I opened the door, went out into the hallway, and leaned heavily against the wall, trying to catch my breath. Absently, I rubbed at my chest, wincing because it was still really sore. I pulled down the neck of my shirt, hoping the stupid wound hadn't broken open again. My breath caught as I saw the new tattooing that decorated either side of the raised red line.

"I'd forgotten about that," I whispered to myself.

"That's amazing!"

With a little squeal I let go of the front of my shirt and jumped back so suddenly that I bonked my head against the wall.

"Erik!"

CHAPTER ELEVEN

Zoey

"I thought you knew I was here. It wasn't like I was trying to hide." Erik was slouching just a few feet away, next to a door that had a brass number thirteen emblazoned on it. He stood up and, with his signature handsome-movie-star smile, sauntered over to me. "Damn, Z, I've been waiting here for you for ages." He bent and, before I could say a word, planted a major kiss smack on my mouth.

I pushed against his chest and stepped sideways out of the embrace he'd started to pull me into.

"Erik, I'm not much in the mood for kissing."

One of his dark brows went up. "Really? Is that what you told Heath, too?"

"I am *so* not going into this right now."

"Then when are you? The next time I have to watch you drink from your human boyfriend?"

"You know what? You're right. Let's talk about it now." I could feel myself getting more and more pissed, and it wasn't just the fact that I was tired and stressed and Erik was being utterly insensitive that was making me so mad. I'd had it with Erik's possessiveness. Period. "Heath and I are Imprinted. Either deal with it or don't. And this is the only discussion we're ever going to have about it."

I watched his expression flare to totally pissed, but then, surprisingly, he clamped down on his temper. His shoulders slumped and he let out a long sigh that ended in a kind of half laugh. "You sound just like a High Priestess."

"Well, I don't feel much like one."

"Hey, I'm sorry." He reached out and brushed a strand of my dark hair back. "Nyx gave you new tattoos, huh?"

"Yeah." It was almost automatic for me to clutch the neck of my shirt and lean against the wall so that I was just out of his reach. "It happened when Kalona was banished."

"Do you mind if I see them?"

His voice was deep and seductive—he'd hit the perfect boyfriend tone. But before he could move closer and think that he could help himself to looking down my shirt, I held up my hand like a stop sign.

"Not now. I just want to get some sleep, Erik."

He'd stopped moving toward me and his eyes narrowed. "So how's Stark?"

"He's hurt. Bad. But Darius says he'll be okay." I kept my voice guarded. His attitude was making me feel seriously defensive.

"And you just came from his room, didn't you?"

"Yes."

Clearly frustrated, he ran his hand through his thick dark hair. "It's just too much."

"Huh?"

He threw his arms out to the side in what looked to me like a well-practiced dramatic gesture. "All of these other guys! I have to put up with Heath because he's your consort and just when I'm trying to get used to that, this *other* guy shows up—Stark." Erik said the name with a sneer.

"Erik, I—"

Acting like I hadn't tried to say anything, he spoke over me. "Yeah, sworn to be your Warrior. I know what that means! He's always going to be with you."

"Erik—" Again I tried to get a word in, but he kept blaring over me.

"So I'm going to have to put up with *him*. And as if that's not bad enough, it's obvious there's something going on between you and Kalona! Come on! Everyone's seen the way the guy looks at you," He scoffed. "Like that doesn't remind me of Blake?"

"Stop." I spoke the word softly, but the anger and irritation that had been building inside me exploded at his sarcastic mention of Kalona, and spirit, that I'd so recently conjured, filled the word with a power that had Erik, eyes wide, taking a step back. "Let's get this over with," I continued. "You do *not* have to put up with any other guy because as of this moment you and I are *not* together."

"Hey, I didn't—"

"No! It's my turn to talk. We're done, Erik. You're too possessive, and even if I wasn't exhausted and stressed out of my brain—two things that apparently don't matter at all to you—I still wouldn't be up for tolerating your crap."

"After everything you've put me through, you think you can just walk out on me like this?"

"No." Feeling the spirit swirl around me I channeled it into my next words as I stepped forward, backing him down the hall. "I don't *think* anything. I *know* this is how it's going to be. We're done. Now you need to go away before I do something I might, in like fifty years, be sorry for." I purposely pushed hard with the power of the element that was flowing through me, causing him to stumble.

His face had gone utterly white. "What the hell's happened to you? You used to be so sweet. Now you're a freak! And I'm sick of you cheating on me with everyone who has a dick. You should be with Stark and Heath and Kalona. They're what you deserve!" He stomped angrily past me, slamming the door to the stairwell.

Just as angry, I marched over to room number thirteen and flung open the door.

And Aphrodite almost fell right out, face-first.

"Oopsie," she said, running her fingers through her always perfect hair. "Guess I was, uh—"

"Listening to my big breakup scene with Erik?" I finished for her.

"Yeah, that would be what I was doing. And may I just say I don't blame you. Talk about an asshat. Plus, you so don't cheat on him with everyone who has a dick. You and Darius are just friends. Plus there's Damien and Jack . . . well, not that they really count, being as they like dick themselves. Still, it was a ridiculous exaggeration."

"You're not really making me feel better." I plopped down on the twin bed that wasn't all ruffled and obviously just laid on.

"Sorry. I'm not very good at the 'making someone feel better' part."

"So you heard all of that?"

"Yep."

"Even the part about Kalona?"

"Yes, and again I call him an asshat."

"Aphrodite, what the hell is an asshat?"

She gave me an exaggerated eye roll. "Erik is an asshat, you dork. Anyway, as I was trying to say before you interrupted, it was seriously not cool that he brought up Kalona. Plus, he had enough evidence for his stupid jealous insecurity already with Heath and Stark. It was totally not necessary to mention the winged guy."

"I do *not* love him."

"Of course you don't. You've outgrown Erik. Now, I suggest you get some sleep. Goddess knows I hate to mention it, but you look like crap."

"Thanks, Aphrodite. It really helps me right now to hear that I look as terrible as I feel," I said sarcastically, completely avoiding the fact that when I said I didn't love him I'd meant Kalona and not Erik.

"Hey, anytime. I'm just here to help."

I was searching for a sarcastic comeback when I noticed what she had on and a little bubble of unexpected laughter escaped from me. Aphrodite, Queen of Fashion, was wearing a floor-length, cover-her-from-ankles-to-neck, white cotton nightgown. Like she'd gone Amish. "Uh, what is that lovely little thing you're wearing?"

"Don't start with me. This is the penguins' idea of nightwear. Well, I can almost understand it. I mean, they take those stupid chastity vows, and if this is what they wear to bed, the vow would be practically unnecessary. Seriously. The thing almost makes me look unattractive."

"Almost?" I giggled.

"Yes, smart-ass, *almost*. And before you're too gleeful, cast your eyes over there. That thing folded up on the end of your bed isn't an extra sheet. It's your very own designer nun sleepwear."

"Oh, well, at least it looks comfortable."

"Comfort is for sissies and unattractive people."

As Aphrodite snootily retucked herself into bed, I made my way over to the little sink in the corner of the room and washed my face and used one of the new, still-in-its-wrapper guest toothbrushes to brush my teeth. As nonchalantly as I could I said, "Hey, uh, can I ask you something?"

"Ask away," she said, plumping her pillows.

"It's a serious question."

"So?"

"So, I need a serious answer."

"Yeah, fine, whatever. Ask," she said flippantly.

"You said before that you knew Erik got too possessive."

"That's not really a question," she said.

I raised my brows at her in the mirror. She sighed.

"Okay, yes, Erik was a stage-five clinger."

"Huh?"

She sighed. "Clinger. Stage five. Totally not fucking cool."

"Aphrodite, what language are you speaking?"

"Teenage American. Way upper-class. You could speak it too with a little imagination and a few real cuss words."

"Goddess help me," I muttered to my reflection before I continued. "Okay, so. Erik was too possessive with you, too."

"That's what I just said."

"And it made you mad?"

"Yeah, definitely. Basically, it broke us up."

I squished Crest on my toothbrush. "So it made you mad. You and Erik broke up, but you were, still, uh, all, well . . ." I chewed my lip for a second and then tried again. "I saw you with him and you were all, um—"

"Oh, for crap's sake! You can just say it without melting. You saw me go down on him."

"Uh, yeah," I said awkwardly.

"That's not a question either."

"Fine! Here's the question: You were broken up with him because he was a possessive jerk, but you were still trying to be with him, so much so that you were even doing *that*. I don't get why," I blurted, and stuck my toothbrush in my mouth.

Watching her reflection in the mirror, I saw her cheeks turn bright pink. Aphrodite flipped back her hair. She cleared her throat. Then she met my gaze in the mirror. "It wasn't about wanting Erik. It was about wanting control."

"Huh?" I said through the bubbles of Crest.

"Things had started to change with me at school even before you showed up."

I spit and rinsed. "What things?"

"I knew something was up with Neferet. It bothered me, and that was weird."

I wiped my mouth and went over to my bed, using kicking off my shoes, pulling off my clothes, putting on the soft, warm cotton nightgown, and climbing in bed as an excuse to stay quiet while I tried to figure out how to put into words the stuff babbling through my mind. But without me saying anything, Aphrodite continued, "You know I used to keep my visions from Neferet, don't you?"

I nodded. "And humans died because of it."

"Yeah, you're right. They did. And Neferet didn't care. I could tell. That was when I started to feel weird. That's also when my life started to fall apart. I didn't want it to. I wanted to stay the bitch in charge, who would someday be High Priestess and, preferably, rule the world. Then I could tell my mother to go straight to hell—and maybe even be so powerful that I could scare her like she deserves to be scared." Aphrodite blew out a long breath. "It didn't work out that way."

"Instead you listened to Nyx," I said softly.

"Well, first I tried like hell to stay queen of my bitchy kingdom, and being with the hottest guy at school, even if he was a possessive asshat, was part of that."

"It makes sense, I guess," I said.

Aphrodite hesitated then added, "It makes me sick to remember it."

"You mean doing *it* with Erik?"

Her lips curled up and she shook her head, laughing a little. "Goddess, you're such a prude! No, doing *it* with Erik was actually not bad at all. It makes me sick to remember how I kept quiet about my visions and basically shit on Nyx's path."

"Well, recently you've pretty much cleaned up any poo you put on Nyx's path. And I am *not* a prude."

Aphrodite snorted.

"You're really unattractive when you do that," I said.

"I'm never *really* unattractive," she said. "Are you done with your serious nonquestion question?"

"Yeah, I suppose."

"Good. My turn. Have you been able to talk to Stevie Rae? Alone?"

"Uh-uh, not yet."

"But you're going to?"

"Uh-huh."

"Soon?"

"What do you know?"

Aphrodite said, "She's definitely hiding things from you."

"Things like red fledglings? Like you told me before?" Aphrodite didn't answer, which completely made my stomach clench. "Well?" I prompted. "What?"

"It feels like there's more going on with Stevie Rae than just hiding some random red fledglings from you."

I didn't want to believe Aphrodite, but my gut said she was telling the truth, as did my common sense. Aphrodite's Imprint with Stevie Rae gave her a connection to my BFF no one else had. So Aphrodite knew things about her. Plus, no matter how much I wished otherwise, I realized things weren't right with Stevie Rae. "You can't tell me anything more specific?"

Aphrodite shook her head. "No. She's really shut down."

"Shut down? What does that mean?"

"Well, you know how your bumpkin BFF usually is, like our own transparently perky version of a countrified goodwill ambassador for 'Hey there, y'all! Check out how nice and sweet and white bread I am! Yuck! Yuck!'"

Aphrodite's exaggerated Okie accent mimicked Stevie Rae's voice a little too well, and I frowned severely at her when I said, "Yes, I know she's usually honest and open, if that's what you meant to say."

"Yeah, well, she's not being honest and open anymore. Take it from me—and Goddess knows I wish you could take this damn Imprint from me—she's hiding a very big something that feels way more important than a few fledglings."

"Crap," I said.

"Yep," she said. "But, hey, there's not shit you can do about it right now, so get some sleep. Our world will still need saving tomorrow."

"Great," I said.

"Oh, speaking of— How's your boyfriend?"

"Which one?" I asked glumly.

"Mr. Pain in the Ass Arrows."

I shrugged. "Better, I think."

"You didn't let him chomp on you, did you?"

I sighed. "No."

"Darius was right about that, you know? As annoying as it might be for some of us, and as unqualified as you appear, you are *the* High Priestess right now."

"Which makes me feel ever so much better."

"Hey, no problem. Look, what I'm saying is you need to be one hundred percent, and not drained like an extra-dry martini during brunch at my mom's country club."

"Your mom really drinks martinis at brunch?"

"Of course she does." Aphrodite shook her head and looked utterly disgusted. "Try not to be so naïve. Anyway, just don't do something stupid because you're feeling all *Lifetime Movie of the Week* and in love with Stark."

"Give it a rest, would ya? I won't do anything stupid!" I leaned over and blew out the fat pillar candle that was on the end table between our beds.

The darkness of the room was comforting, and when neither of us had said anything for a little while I felt myself beginning to drift off, until Aphrodite's voice snapped me back to über-aware.

"Are we going back to the House of Night tomorrow?"

"I think we have to," I said slowly. "No matter what, the House of Night is our home, and the fledglings and vampyres there are our people. We have to go back to them."

"Well, you better get some sleep. Tomorrow you're going to land right in the middle of what one of my mom's ex-military assistants would call a huge cluster fuck," Aphrodite said in her best happily sarcastic tone.

As usual, Aphrodite was as right as she was annoying.

CHAPTER TWELVE

Zoey

After Aphrodite's gloomy, but probably accurate, prediction I didn't think I'd be able to sleep, but exhaustion caught up with me. I closed my eyes and then, for a little while there was blissful nothingness. Sadly, bliss didn't ever seem to last very long in my life.

In my dream the island was so blue and beautiful it dazzled me. I was standing on . . . I looked around . . . the roof of a castle! One of those real old-looking castles, made of big blocks of rough stone. The roof was massively cool. Framing it were those stone-sticking-up-things that looked like a giant's teeth. There were plants everywhere on the roof. I even noticed lemon and orange trees, branches all heavy and full of sweet-smelling fruit. In the center of everything was a fountain in the shape of a beautiful naked woman whose hands were lifted over her head, and from those cupped hands flowed crystal water. Something about the stone woman looked familiar, but my gaze kept getting pulled from the gorgeous rooftop garden to the even more awesome view that stretched around the castle.

Holding my breath, I moved to the edge of the roof and looked down and down and down and out at the brilliant blue of the sea. The water was beyond beautiful. It was the color of dreams and laughter and perfect summer skies. The island itself was made of jagged mountains, covered in unusual-looking pine trees that reminded me of giant umbrellas. The castle was at the very top of the highest of the island's mountains, and as I peered down in the distance I could see graceful villas and a pretty little town.

Everything was bathed in the blue of the sea, which gave the place a sense of magick. I inhaled the breeze, smelling salt and oranges. The day was sunny—the sky utterly clear of clouds, but in my dream the brightness of it didn't bother my eyes at all. I loved it! It was a little cool, and more than a little windy, but I didn't care. I liked the crispness of the breeze against my skin. At that moment the island was the color of aquamarines, but I could imagine how it would look as dusk approached and the sun no longer ruled the sky. The blue would deepen, darken, and change to sapphire.

My dreaming self smiled. Sapphire . . . The island would turn the exact color of my tattoos. I tilted back my head and threw my arms wide, embracing the loveliness of this place I'd created out of my sleeping imagination.

"So it seems I cannot escape you, even when I flee your presence," Kalona said.

He was behind me. His voice crawled across the skin of my back, up over my shoulders, and wrapped around my body. Slowly, I let my arms drop to my sides. I did not turn around.

"You're the one who sneaks around in people's dreams, not me." I was glad my voice sounded calm and über-under-control.

"So you are still unwilling to admit you are drawn to me?" His voice was deep and seductive.

"Look, I didn't try to find you. All I meant when I closed my eyes was to sleep." I spoke almost automatically, avoiding his question and willing myself not to remember the last memory I'd had of his voice and his arms around me.

"You are obviously sleeping alone. Were you with someone else, it would be much more difficult for you to be touched by me."

I suppressed the confused longing his voice made me feel and filed away that little bit of info—sleeping with someone *did* make it more difficult for him to reach me, just as Stark had told me the night before. "That's none of your business," I said.

"You are correct. All of those sons of man who swarm around you, eager to bask in your presence, are completely beneath my concern."

I didn't bother to call him on his twisting of what I'd said. I was too busy trying to stay calm and will myself to wake up.

"You chase me away from you, yet you find me in your dreams. What does that say about you, A-ya?"

"That is not my name! Not in this lifetime!"

" 'Not in this lifetime' you say. That means you have accepted the truth. You know your soul is the reincarnation of the maiden fashioned by the Ani Yunwiya to love me. Perhaps that is why you keep coming to me in your dreams, because even though your waking mind resists, your soul, your spirit, your very essence yearns to be with me."

He used the ancient word for the Cherokee people—my grandma's people and mine. I knew the legend. A beautiful, winged immortal had come to live with the Cherokee, but instead of being a benevolent earthbound god, he was cruel. He abused the women and used the men. Finally, the Wise Women of the tribes, known as Ghigua Women, came together and created a maiden from the earth. They gave A-ya life, as well as special gifts. Her purpose was to use Kalona's lust to lure him underground so that he could be trapped within the earth. Their plan worked. Kalona couldn't resist A-ya and he was trapped within the earth—or at least he had been until Neferet had freed him.

And now that I'd shared a memory with A-ya, I knew only too well the truth of that legend.

Truth, my mind reminded me. *Use the strength of the truth to fight him.*

"Yes," I admitted. "I know I am the reincarnation of A-ya." I drew a deep, centering breath, turned around, and faced Kalona. "But I am *today's* reincarnation of her, which means I make my own choices, and I will not choose to be with you."

"And yet you continue to come to me in your dreams."

I wanted to deny that I'd come to him—to say something smart and High Priestess–like, but all I could do was stare at him. He was so beautiful! As usual, he was underdressed. I guess the better description would be *un*dressed. He had on jeans, and that was it. His skin was bronze and perfect. It covered his muscles with a smoothness that made me want to touch him. Kalona's amber eyes were luminous. They met my gaze with a warmth and kindness that made my breath catch. He appeared about eighteen, but when he smiled he seemed even younger, more boyish, more accessible. Everything about him screamed *super hot guy I should be going crazy over!*

But that was a lie. Kalona was actually super-scary and super-dangerous, and I could never forget that—no matter what he *appeared* to be—no matter what the memories planted deep within my soul yearned for him to be.

"Ah, so you finally deign to look at me."

"Well, you wouldn't go away and leave me alone, so I figured I'd be polite," I said with forced nonchalance.

Kalona threw back his head and laughed. The sound was infectious and warm and very seductive. It made me ache to move closer to him and join him in the freedom of his laughter. I wanted it so much that I'd almost taken a step toward him when his wings chose that moment to stir. They quivered and then spread partially open so that the sunlight glistened against their black depths, illuminating the indigo and purple that usually hid within their darkness.

The sight of them was like running into an invisible wall. I remembered again what he was—a dangerous fallen immortal who would like to steal my free will and, eventually, my soul.

"I don't see why you're laughing," I said quickly. "I'm telling you the truth. I'm looking at you because I'm polite, even though I really wish you'd fly away and let me dream in peace."

"Oh, my A-ya." His expression sobered. "I can never leave you in peace. You and I are bound. We will be each other's salvation, or each other's doom." He took a step closer to me and I mirrored his movement by taking a step backward. "Which shall it be? Salvation or doom?"

"I can only speak for myself." I made my voice stay calm, and was even able to add a touch of sarcasm to it, though I could feel the cool stone of the balcony balustrade pressing like the walls of a prison cell against my back. "But both sound pretty bad. Salvation? Jeesh, you're reminding me of the People of Faith, and since they'd consider you a *fallen* angel, that doesn't make you much of an expert on salvation. Doom? Well, seriously, you're *still* reminding me of the People of Faith. Since when did you become so boringly religious?"

In two steps he closed the space between us. His arms became bars, caging me between the stone balustrade and him. His wings shivered, opening around him so that he eclipsed the sun with his own dark brilliance. I could feel the terrible, wonderful chill that always emanated from him. It should have repelled me, but it didn't. That awful coldness drew me at a soul-deep level. I wanted to press myself against him and be carried away by the sweet pain he could bring.

"Boring? Little A-ya, my lost love, for centuries mortals have been calling me many things, but *boring* is not one of them."

Kalona towered over me. There was just so much of him! And there was all that naked skin . . . I wrenched my gaze from his chest and looked up into his eyes. He was smiling down at me, perfectly relaxed and completely in control. He was so darn hot I could hardly breathe. Sure, Stark and Heath and, yes, Erik, were cute guys—exceptionally cute guys, actually. But they were nothing compared to Kalona's immortal beauty. He was a masterpiece, the statue of a god that personified physical perfection, only he was even more attractive because he was alive—he was here—he was here for me.

"I-I want you to step back." I tried unsuccessfully to keep my voice from shaking.

"Is that truly what you want, Zoey?"

His use of my name jolted through me, affecting me much more than when he called me A-ya. My fingers pressed hard into the stone of the castle as I tried to ground myself and not fall under his spell. I drew a deep breath and got ready to lie and tell him yes, I sure as hell did want him to step away from me.

Use the power of truth. The words whispered through my mind.

What was the truth? That I had to fight myself not to leap into his arms? That I couldn't stop thinking about A-ya's surrender to him? Or that other truth—that I wished I was just a normal kid whose most stressful problems were homework and mean girls?

Tell the truth.

I blinked. I *could* tell the truth.

"Right now what I really want is sleep. I want to be normal. I want to worry about school and paying my car insurance and how stupidly expensive gas is right now. And I'd seriously appreciate it if you could do anything about those things." I held his gaze with my own, letting that one sliver of truth lend me strength.

His smile was young and mischievous. "Why don't you come to me, Zoey?"

"Well, see, that wouldn't actually give me any of those things I just mentioned."

"I could give you so much more than those mundane things."

"Yeah, I'm sure you could, but none of it would be normal, and right now what I'd truly like more than anything is a very big dose of *normal*."

He met my gaze, and I could tell that he was waiting for me to falter, for me to get all nervous and stuttery, or worse, to panic. But I had told him the truth, and that was a small, shining victory for me, one that lent me power. It was Kalona who finally looked away, Kalona whose voice was suddenly halting and unsure. "I don't have to be like this. For you, I could be more." His eyes met mine again. "I could choose a different path were you by my side."

I tried not to show the flood of emotions his words had caused within me as he touched the part of me that A-ya had awakened.

Find the truth, my mind insisted; and, again, I found it and spoke it. "I wish I could believe you, but I don't. You're gorgeous and magical, but you're also a liar. I don't trust you."

"But you could," he said.

"No," I said honestly. "I don't think I could."

"Try. Give me a chance. Come to me and let me prove myself to you. Truly, my love, say one small word, *yes.*" He bent and, in a movement that was graceful and strong and seductive, the fallen immortal whispered into my ear, allowing his lips to only brush my skin enough to send chills skittering through my body. "Give yourself to me and I promise that I will fulfill your deepest dreams."

My breath was coming fast and I pressed my palms harder against the stone at my back. At that instant, I only wanted to say one word, *yes.* I knew what would happen if I did. I'd already experienced that kind of surrender through A-ya.

He chuckled, a sound that was deep and confident. "Go on, my lost love. One word, *yes*, and your life will forever be changed."

His lips weren't by my ear anymore. Instead his gaze had captured mine again. He was smiling into my eyes. He was young and perfect, powerful and kind.

And I wanted to say yes so badly I was afraid to speak.

"Love me," he murmured. "Love only me."

Through my desire for him my mind processed what he was saying, and I finally found a word other than yes. "Neferet," I said.

He frowned. "What of her?"

"You say I'm supposed to love only you, but you're not even free. You're with Neferet."

Some of his easy confidence disappeared. "Neferet is not your concern."

His words made my heart squeeze and I realized that a big part of me had wanted him to deny that he was with her—to tell me that was over. Disappointment lent me strength, and I said, "I think she is my concern. Last time I saw her she tried to kill me, and that was when I was rejecting you. I say yes to you and she's going to lose her mind— what's left of it. On me. Again."

"Why are we discussing Neferet? She is not here. Look at the beauty that surrounds us. Consider what it would be to rule this place at my side—to help me bring back the ancient ways to this world that has become far too modern." One of his hands slipped down to caress my arm. I ignored the sensations that were shivering across my skin and the alarm bells that were blaring in my head at his comment about bringing back the ancient ways, and put on my best whiny teenage tone.

"Seriously, Kalona, I really don't want any more drama with Neferet. I don't think I could handle it."

He threw his hands up in frustration. "Why are you still speaking of the Tsi Sgili? I command you to forget her! She is nothing to us."

The instant his arms no longer imprisoned me against the stone, I scrambled sideways, determined to put some space between us. I needed to think, and I couldn't do that with his arms around me.

Kalona followed, this time backing me against one of the low parts of the rooftop wall—a gap in the stone teeth. There was only support as high as the back of my knees. From there up I could feel the cool wind brushing against my back and moving my hair. I didn't need to look behind me. I knew the drop-off was dizzying and that the blue of the sea waited far, far below.

"You cannot escape me." Kalona's amber eyes narrowed. I saw anger beginning to simmer beneath his seductive exterior. "And you must realize that I am going to rule this world very soon. I will bring the ancient ways back, and in doing so I will divide these modern people, separating the wheat from the chaff. The wheat shall stay by my side, growing and thriving as they feed me. The chaff shall be burnt into nothingness."

I felt a terrible sinking inside me. He was using old, poetic words, but I had absolutely no doubt he was describing the end of the world as I knew it, and the destruction of countless people—vampyres, fledglings, and humans. Feeling sick, I tilted back my head and gave him a totally clueless look. "Wheat? Chaff? Sorry, you lost me. You'll have to translate that into something I get."

He didn't say anything for a long moment. He only studied me silently. Then, with a slight smile curling his full lips, he reached out and caressed the side of my face with his hand. "You play a dangerous game, my little lost love."

My body froze.

His hand slid slowly from my cheek down the side of my neck, searing a path of cold heat across my skin.

"You toy with me. You think you can act the schoolgirl who understands nothing more than the next dress she will wear or the next boy she will kiss. You have underestimated me. I know you, A-ya. I know you too well."

Kalona's hand continued down and I sucked in a shocked gasp when he cupped my breast. He rubbed his thumb across the most sensitive spot there and a frigid stab of desire shook me. No matter how hard I tried I couldn't keep myself from trembling at his caress. There on the rooftop of my dream, with the sea behind me and Kalona before me, I was trapped by his hypnotizing touch and I knew then with a terrible certainty that it wasn't just A-ya's memories that drew me to him. It was *me*—*my* heart—*my* soul—*my* desires.

"No, please stop." I meant for the words to come out loud and strong, a command he couldn't ignore, but instead I sounded breathy and weak.

"Stop?" He chuckled again. "It seems you have lost your truth. You do not wish I would stop. Your body yearns for my touch. You cannot deny it. So shake off this foolish resistance. Accept me and your place by my side. Join me and together we will create a new world."

I swayed toward him, but managed to whisper, "I can't."

"If you do not join me you will be my enemy, and I will burn you with the rest of the chaff." As he'd been speaking his gaze had moved from my face down to my breasts. Now he cupped both of them in his hands. His amber eyes had gone all soft and looked unfocused as he caressed me, sending icy waves of unwanted desire through my body, and sickness through my heart, my mind, and my soul.

I was trembling so hard my words sounded shaky. "This is a dream . . . only a dream. This is not real." I spoke as if to convince myself.

His lust for me made him even more seductive. He smiled intimately at me while he continued to stroke my breasts. "Yes, you dream. Though there is truth and reality here, as well as your deepest, most secret desires. Zoey, in this dream you are free to do anything you wish—*we* can do anything you wish."

It's just a dream. I repeated the words to myself. *Please, Nyx, let the power of this next truth wake me up.*

"I do want to be with you," I said. Kalona's smile was fierce with victory, but before he could lock me within his immortal and all-too-familiar embrace, I added, "But the truth is no matter how bad I want you, I'm still Zoey Redbird and not A-ya, and that means in this lifetime I have chosen to follow Nyx. Kalona, I will not betray my Goddess by giving in to you!" As I shouted the last words I threw myself backward, so that I fell from the roof of the castle and plummeted toward the rocky seashore far, far below.

Through my screams I could hear Kalona crying my name.

CHAPTER THIRTEEN

Zoey

I sat straight up in bed, screaming like someone had just tossed me into a pit of spiders. My ears were ringing and my body was shaking so hard that I thought I would be sick, but somewhere through my panic I realized mine wasn't the only voice screaming. I peered around in the darkness, made myself shut up, sucked air, and tried to get my bearings. Where the hell was I? At the bottom of the sea? Smashed dead on the rocks of the island?

No . . . no . . . I was at the Benedictine Abbey . . . in the dorm room they'd assigned me with Aphrodite . . . who was currently in the bed across from me screaming like a crazy woman.

"Aphrodite!" I yelled over her shrieks. "Stop! It's me. Everything's okay."

Her scream broke off, but she was breathing in short little panicky gasps. "Light! Light!" she said, sounding like she'd taken up residence in the Land of Panic Attacks. "I need light! I need to see!"

"Okay—okay! Hang on." Remembering the pillar candle on the end table between our beds, I fumbled awkwardly around until I felt a lighter. I had to steady my right hand by grasping my wrist with my left so that I could get the candle lit, and still it took five tries before the wick caught and the warmth of candlelight illuminated Aphrodite's ghostly white face and completely blood-filled eyes.

"Ohmygod! Your eyes!"

"I know! I know! Shit! Shit! Shit! I still can't see," she sobbed.

"Don't worry—don't worry—this happened last time. I'll get you a wet cloth and a drink of water, just like I did before and—" my words shut off as I realized the exact meaning of Aphrodite's scarlet eyes, and I froze halfway between the bed and the sink. "You had another vision, didn't you?"

She didn't say anything. She just put her face in her hands and nodded while she sobbed.

"It's okay. It's gonna be okay," I kept repeating over and over as I hurried to the sink, grabbed a hand towel, soaked it in cold water, and filled up one of two nearby glasses. Then I rushed back to Aphrodite. She was still sitting on the edge of the bed with her face in her hands. Her sobs had gone from hysterical snot-crying to pitiful little gasps. I reached around behind her and plumped her pillows. "Here, drink this. Then I want you to lie back so I can put this wet towel across your eyes."

She took her hands from her face and reached blindly for the glass. I guided her to it and then watched as she guzzled down the whole thing. "I'll get you more in a second. Lie back first and put this over your eyes."

Aphrodite leaned back against the propped-up pillow. She blinked blindly up at me. She looked scarily horrible. Her eyes were completely bloody and looked bizarre and ghostly framed by her too-white face.

"I can see the outline of you, just a little," she said faintly. "But you're all red, like you're bleeding." Aphrodite finished on a hiccupy sob.

"I'm not bleeding; I'm fine. This happened before, remember? And you were okay after you closed your eyes and rested for a while."

"I remember. I just don't remember it being this bad."

She closed her eyes. I folded the towel and placed it gently across them. Then I lied, "It was this bad last time, too."

Her hands fluttered by the towel for a second before they dropped to her sides. I went back to the sink and filled up the glass again. Watching her reflection in the mirror I said, "Was the vision terrible?"

I saw her lips quiver. She drew a long, shaky breath. "Yes."

I came back to the bed. "Do you want more water?"

She nodded. "I feel like I've just run a marathon through a blazing desert—not that I ever would. All that sweating is so unattractive."

Glad she was sounding more like herself, I smiled and guided her hand to the glass of water again. Then I sat on my bed facing her and waited.

"I can feel you looking at me," she said.

"Sorry. I thought I was being patient by not saying anything." I paused. "Do you want me to go get Darius? Or maybe Damien? Or both of them?"

"No!" Aphrodite said quickly. I saw her swallow a couple of times, and then, in a calmer voice, she continued. "Don't go anywhere for a little while, okay? I don't want to be alone right now—not when I can't see."

"Okay. I won't go anywhere. You want to tell me about the vision?"

"Not particularly, but I suppose I have to. I saw seven vampyres. They looked important—powerful, all obviously High Priestesses. They were in a seriously gorgeous place. Definitely old money and none of that nouveau riche crap that tends to decorate with questionable taste." I rolled my eyes at her, which she, sadly, couldn't see. "At first I didn't even know it was a vision. I thought it was a dream. I was watching these vamps sitting in chairs that looked like thrones and waiting for something freakily dreamish to happen, like they all turn into Justin Timberlake, jump up, and start stripping for me and singing about bringing sexy back."

"Huh," I said. "Interesting dream. He is totally dorkishly hot, even though he's getting old."

"Oh, give it a rest. You already have way too many boys to even dream about another one. Leave Justin to me. So, anyway, they didn't turn into Justin, nor did they strip. I was just wondering what was going on when it became mega-obvious I was having a vision because Neferet walked in."

"Neferet!"

"Yeah. Kalona was with her. She did all the talking, but the vamps weren't watching her. They couldn't stop gawking at Kalona."

I didn't say so, but I knew how they felt.

"Neferet was saying something about accepting the changes she and Erebus brought, moving everything, bringing old ways back . . . blah . . . blah . . ."

"Erebus!" I interrupted her blah-blahing. "She's still claiming Kalona is Erebus?"

"Yeah, and she was also calling herself Nyx Incarnate, which she shortened to just Nyx, but I didn't catch everything she was saying because it was about then that I started to burn up."

"Burn up? Like you caught on fire?"

"Well, it wasn't *me* exactly. It was some of the vamps. It was weird—one of the weirdest visions I've ever had, actually. One part of me was watching Neferet talking to the seven vamps, and at the same time another part of me was leaving the room, one by one, with them. I could feel that not all of them believed what Neferet was saying, and it was those vamps I stayed with. Until they burned."

"Do you mean they just caught on fire?"

"Yeah, but it was real strange. One second I could tell that they were thinking negative things about Neferet, and the next they were on fire, but when they burned they were in the middle of a field. And it wasn't just them burning." Aphrodite paused and drained the rest of the glass of water. "Lots of other people burned with them—humans, vamps, and fledglings. All of them were burning in this same field, which seemed to expand to include the whole damn world."

"What?"

"Yeah, it was seriously bad. I've never had a vision about vamps dying. Well, except those two I had about you, and you're just a fledgling so I don't count them."

I wasted energy frowning at her, which she couldn't see. "Did you recognize anyone except the burning vamps? Were Neferet and Kalona there, too?"

Aphrodite didn't say anything for a moment. Then she reached up and took the damp towel from her eyes. She blinked. I could tell the red was already starting to fade. She squinted at me. "That's better. I can mostly see you now. So, here's the end of the vision: Kalona was there. Neferet wasn't there. Instead, you were there. With him. And I do mean you were *with* him. He was all over you and you liked it. Uh, may I just say eew about having to watch that make-out scene, especially since I was watching it from the perspective of the people who were roasting while you did the nasty. Basically it was more than clear that you being with Kalona caused the world as we know it to end."

I rubbed a shaky hand across my face, like I could wipe away the memory of me as A-ya in Kalona's arms. "I'm never going to be with Kalona."

"Okay, what I'm getting ready to say is not because I'm being a bitch—at least not this time."

"Go ahead, just say it."

"You're A-ya reincarnated."

"We've already established that," I said, my voice sounding sharper than I intended.

Aphrodite put up her hand. "Hang on. I'm not accusing you of anything. It's just that this ancient Cherokee girl whose soul you're kinda sharing was created to love Kalona. Right?"

"Yes, but you need to understand that I. Am. Not. Her." I enunciated each word slowly and distinctly.

"Look, Zoey, I know that. But I also know you're a lot more attracted to Kalona than you want to admit to anyone, and that probably includes yourself. You've already had one memory of being A-ya that was so strong it made you pass out. What if you're not completely able to control what you feel for him because the attraction's been hardwired into your soul?"

"You think I haven't already thought about that? Hell, Aphrodite, I'll stay away from Kalona!" I yelled my frustration. "*Completely* away from him. Then there will be no chance I'll ever be with him again, and your vision will not happen."

"It's not that simple. The vision where you're with him wasn't the only one I had. Actually, now that I think about it, it was a little like those stupid visions I had of your death where first I saw you get your throat slit and your head basically cut off, then in the same damn vision I got to drown with you. Talk about stress."

"Yes, I remember. It was *my* death you were seeing."

"Yeah, but so far *I'm* the only one who's experienced your deaths. Again, I say *not pleasant*."

"Would you please finish telling me about your visions?"

She gave me a long-suffering look, but continued. "So, the vision split, like what happened with the two different deaths I saw for you. One minute you're sucking face and doing nasty stuff with Kalona. Oh, and I felt agony, too."

"Well, yeah, that makes sense. You were burning," I said, frustrated that she couldn't just tell the darn vision.

"No, I mean I felt *other* agony. I'm pretty sure it wasn't coming from the burning people. Someone else was there, and they were definitely under duress."

"Duress? That sounds really bad." My stomach was hurting again.

"Yep. Seriously uncomfortable. One minute people were burning, I felt lots of agony, blah, blah, and you were doing it with the evil angel. Then everything changed. It was obviously a different day—in a different place. People were still burning and I still felt the weird agony stuff, but instead of doing the dirty with Kalona you stepped out of his arms. Not very far, though. And you said something to him. Whatever you said changed everything."

"How?"

"You killed him and all the fire and such stopped."

"I killed Kalona!"

"Yep. At least that's what it looked like to me."

"Well, what did I say to him that had the power to do that?"

She shrugged. "Don't know. I couldn't hear you. I was experiencing the vision from the burning peoples' perspective and feeling stupid agony from wherever; I was just a tad bit busy being in unbearable pain to pay attention to every little syllable you uttered."

"Are you sure he died? He's not supposed to be able to die; he's immortal."

"It looked like it to me. Whatever you said made him disintegrate."

"He disappeared?"

"Actually, it was more like he exploded. Kinda. It's hard to describe because, well, I was *burning* and also he got really, really bright, and it was hard to see exactly what happened to him. But I can tell you he more or less faded away, and when he did, all the fire stopped and I knew everything was going to be okay."

"Is that all that happened?"

"No. You cried."

"Huh?"

"Yeah, after you killed Kalona, you cried. Major snot and everything. Then the vision ended and I woke up with a horrendous headache and my eyes hurting like crazy. Oh, and you were screaming like you'd lost your damn mind." She gave me a long, considering look. "Speaking of, why were you screaming?"

"I had a bad dream."

"Kalona?"

"I really don't want to talk about it."

"Too damn bad. You have to talk about it. Zoey, I saw the world burning while you and Kalona partied. That's not a good thing."

"That's *not* going to happen," I said. "Remember, you also saw me killing him."

"What happened in your dream?" she asked insistently.

"He offered me the world. He said he's going to change things back to the ancient ways and he wants me to rule by his side, or some such bullpoopie. I said not no, but hell no. He said he'd burn—" *Oh my Goddess!* "Wait, you said the people were burning in a field? Could it have been a wheat field?"

Aphrodite shrugged. "I suppose. Fields pretty much all look the same to me."

My chest felt tight and my stomach hurt. "He said he was going to separate the chaff from the wheat, and burn the chaff up."

"What the hell is chaff?"

"I don't know exactly, but I'm pretty sure it has something to do with wheat. Okay, try to remember. The field they were burning in— did it have tall golden grassy stuff in it, or was it green, like hay or corn or something, well, not wheatlike?"

"It was yellow. And tall. And grassy. I suppose it could have been wheat."

"So what Kalona threatened in my dream basically came true in your vision."

"Except in your dream you didn't give in and start a big make-out session with him. Or did you?"

"No, I did not! I hurled myself off the top of a cliff, which is why I was screaming my brains out."

Her red-tinged eyes widened. "Seriously? You really jumped off a cliff?"

"Well, I jumped off the top of a castle, and the castle was on the top of a cliff."

"That sounds really bad."

"It was the scariest thing I've ever done, but it wasn't as bad as staying there with him." I shivered, remembering his touch and the terrible, soul-deep longing he made me feel. "I had to get away from him."

"Yeah, well, you're going to need to rethink that in the future."

"Huh?"

"Would you try to pay attention? I saw Kalona taking over the world. He was using fire to kill people, and by people I mean vamps *and* humans. And you stopped him. Honestly, I think my vision is telling us you're the only person alive who *can* stop him. So you can't run away from him. Zoey, you're going to have to figure out what you said that killed him and then *you're* going to have to go to *him*."

"No! I'm not going to him."

Aphrodite gave me a look that was full of pity. "You have to fight against this reincarnation thing and destroy Kalona once and for all."

Ah, hell, was what I was thinking when someone's fist banged on the door.

CHAPTER FOURTEEN

Zoey

"Zoey! Are you in there? Let me in!"

In less than a breath I was off the bed and at the door. I wrenched it open to find Stark leaning heavily against the doorframe. "Stark? What are you doing out of bed?" He was wearing hospital scrub pants and no shirt. His chest was covered by a huge white gauze Band-Aid that wrapped all the way around his torso. His face was the color of bone, and a veil of sweat beaded his forehead. He was drawing short, ragged breaths and looked like he was going to fall over any second.

But in his right hand he clutched his bow, and it was notched with an arrow.

"Shit! Get him in here before he passes out. If he falls down, we'll never get him up again, and he's too damn big to drag around."

I tried to grab Stark, but surprising me with his strength, he shook me off. "No, I'm fine," he said, stalking into the room and looking around us like he expected someone to jump out of the closet. "I'm not going to pass out," he spat out as he got his breathing under control.

I stepped in front of him, calling his attention back to me. "Stark, there's no one here. What are *you* doing here? You shouldn't even be out of bed, let alone climbing stairs."

"I felt you. You were terrified. So I came to you."

"I had a bad dream, that's all. I wasn't in any danger."

"Kalona? Was he in your dream again?"

"Again? How long have you been dreaming about him?" Aphrodite asked.

"Unless you're sleeping with someone, and I don't mean just a roommate, Kalona can get into your dreams if he wants to," Stark said.

"That doesn't sound good."

"They're just dreams," I said.

"Do we know that for sure?" Aphrodite asked.

She directed the question to Stark, but I answered her. "Well, I'm not dead. So it was just a dream."

"Not dead? You need to explain that," Stark said. His breathing had leveled off, and even though he still looked pale, he sounded every bit like a dangerous Warrior who was ready to fulfill his oath and protect his High Priestess.

"In her dream Zoey hurled herself off the top of a cliff to get away from Kalona," Aphrodite said.

"What did he do to you?" Stark's voice was low and filled with anger.

"Nothing!" I said way too quickly.

"That's because you jumped off a cliff before he could do anything," Aphrodite said.

"What was he trying to do?" Stark asked again.

I sighed. "The same old stuff. He wants to control me. That's not how he puts it, but it's what he wants, and I'm never going to give him what he wants."

Stark's jaw tightened. "I should have known he'd try to get to you through your dreams. I know his tricks! I should have made sure you slept with Heath or Erik."

Aphrodite snorted. "That's a new one. Boyfriend number three *wants* you to sleep with boyfriend one or two."

"I'm *not* her boyfriend!" Stark practically roared. "I am her Warrior. I've given my oath to protect her. That means more than some bullshit crush or stupid jealousy."

Aphrodite just stared at him; for once she didn't seem to know what to say.

"Stark, it was just a dream," I said with a lot more conviction than I felt. "It doesn't matter how many times Kalona butts into my dreams, the result is going to be the same. I'm not going to give in to him."

"You better make sure of that because if you do, the rest of us are in for some serious shit," Aphrodite said.

"What does she mean?"

"She had another vision, that's all."

"That's *all*? Talk about being underappreciated." She gave Stark a long look. "So, Arrow Boy, if you sleep with Zoey, will that keep Kalona out of her dreams?"

"It should," Stark said.

"Then I think you should sleep with Zoey, and since three is definitely a crowd in situations like this, I'm out of here."

"Where are you going?" I asked.

"Wherever Darius is, and, no, I do not give a shit if it annoys the penguins. Seriously, I *do* have a massive headache. So I'll *just* be sleeping, but I'm going to be with my vamp. And that's all there is to it."

She grabbed her clothes and her purse. I figured she was going to duck into a bathroom and change out of her granny nightgown before finding Darius, which made me remember I was standing there in my very own granny nightgown. I sat down on my bed and sighed. Oh, yeah, he'd already seen me blazingly naked, which was way more embarrassing than a white cotton granny nightgown. My shoulders slumped. Goddess, for a girl who had multiple boyfriends, I was seriously impaired in the ooh-look-how-cool-I-am department.

Before Aphrodite made it out the door, I called, "Don't say anything about your vision until I have a chance to think more. I mean," I hurried on, "you can tell Darius, but that's it, okay?"

"I get it. You want to avoid hysteria. Whatever. I'm not much up for listening to the nerd herd and the rest of the masses shriek, either. Get some sleep, Z. I'll see you at sunset." She gave Stark a little wave and then shut the door firmly behind her.

Stark came over to the bed, sitting heavily beside me. He flinched a little as the pain in his chest must have finally registered. He set his bow and arrow on the bedside table and gave me a rueful grin. "So, I won't be needing these?"

"Ya think?"

"Which means my hands are now conveniently free." He opened his arms to me and shot me a cocky look. "Why don't you come here, Z?"

"Hang on." I hurried over to the window, buying time while I wondered how I could move from one man's arms to another. "I definitely can't rest until I make sure you're not going to incinerate," I babbled. While I was pulling the blinds I couldn't resist peeking out, and was rewarded with the sight of a day that included very little light. It was a silent gray world filled with ice and gloom. Nothing was moving. It was like life outside the abbey, along with the trees and grass and fallen power lines, had been frozen. "Well, I guess this explains how you made it up here without being fried to a crisp. There is no sun out there." I kept staring out the window, mesmerized by the world turned to ice.

"I knew I wasn't in any danger," Stark said from the bed. "I could feel that the sun was up, but it's not shining through all that icy stuff and the clouds. It was safe for me to come to you." Then he added, "Z, would you come over here! My mind is telling me you're okay, but my gut's still a little shaky."

I turned around, surprised that the cocky tone in his voice was gone. I left the window and put my hand in his, sitting on the edge of the bed.

"I *am* okay—a lot more okay than you'd be right now if you'd come rushing up here in the middle of a sunny morning."

"When I felt your fear I had to come. Even at the risk of my own life. That's part of the oath I swore to you."

"Really?"

He nodded, smiled, and lifted my hand to his lips. "Really. You're my lady and my High Priestess. I'll always protect you."

I cupped his face in my hand and couldn't stop staring at him, for some reason that suddenly made me cry.

"Hey, don't do that—don't cry." He brushed the tears from my cheek. "Come here to me."

Wordlessly, I slid in beside him, being careful not to bump his chest. He put his arm around me and I leaned against him, hoping that the warmth of his touch could wipe away the memory of Kalona's cold passion.

"He does it on purpose, you know?"

I didn't have to ask. I knew he was talking about Kalona.

Stark kept talking. "It's not real—the stuff he makes you feel. That's what he does. He finds a person's weakness and he uses it." Stark paused, and I could tell there was more he wanted to say. I didn't want to hear it. I wanted to curl up, and in the safety of my Warrior's arms, I wanted to sleep and forget.

But I couldn't. Not after A-ya's memory. Not after Aphrodite's visions.

"Go on," I said. "What else?"

His arm tightened around me. "Kalona knows your weakness is the connection you have with that Cherokee girl who trapped him."

"A-ya," I said.

"Yeah, A-ya. He'll use her against you."

"I know."

I could feel his hesitation, but finally Stark said, "You want him— Kalona, I mean. He makes you want him. You fight against it, but he gets to you."

My stomach squeezed and I wanted to be sick, but I answered Stark honestly. "I know and it scares me."

"Zoey, I believe you'll keep saying no to him, but if you ever give in, you can count on me to be there. I'll stand between you and Kalona, even if it's the last thing I do."

I laid my head on his shoulder, remembering all too well that Aphrodite hadn't said anything about Stark being in either of her visions.

He turned his head and kissed me softly on the forehead. "Oh, by the way, nice nightgown."

A little bubble of unexpected laughter escaped me. "If you weren't hurt I'd smack you."

He gave me his cocky grin. "Hey, I like it. Makes me think I'm in bed with a bad little Catholic schoolgirl from one of those twisted all-girl prep schools. Want to tell me about the naked pillow fights you and your roommates used to have?"

I rolled my eyes at him. "Uh, maybe later when you haven't just almost died."

"Okay, cool. I'm too tired to do any impressive proving anyway."

"Stark, why don't you drink from me? Just a little," I hurried on when he started to protest. "Look, Kalona isn't here. Actually, from my dream it's pretty clear that he's far away, since there aren't any islands anywhere close to Oklahoma."

"You don't know where he is. He could have been making you see him as being anywhere in your dream."

"No, he's on an island." As I spoke I felt the truth of my guess. "He needed to go to an island to recharge. Do you have a clue where that might be? Did you ever hear him talking about an island with Neferet?"

Stark shook his head. "Nope. He never said anything about it around me, but the fact that it's an island tells us you hurt him. Bad."

"Which means I'm safe right now, which *also* means it's okay for you to drink from me."

"No," he said firmly.

"You don't want to?"

"Don't be insane! I want to, but I can't. We can't. Not right now."

"Look, you need my blood and my energy, or spirit, or whatever, to get better." I lifted my chin so he had a clear view of my jugular. "So, go ahead. Bite me." I closed my eyes and held my breath.

Stark laughed, which had my eyes popping open to see him chuckling while he clutched painfully at his chest, wheezed, and then laughed some more.

I frowned at him. "What is so funny?"

Stark managed to control himself enough to say, "It's just that you look like something out of an old Dracula movie. You should be asking if I *vant to suck yur blood*." He made a creepy face and bared his teeth.

I felt my cheeks burning and pulled away from him. "Never mind. Forget I even mentioned it. Let's just go to sleep, 'kay?" I started to roll over, but he caught my shoulder and turned me back to him.

"Hang on, hang on—I'm messing this up." He was suddenly

serious. "Zoey." Stark touched my cheek. "I'm not drinking from you, because I *can't*. Not because I don't want to."

"Yeah, I heard you before." I was still embarrassed and tried to turn my head, but he forced me to meet his gaze.

"Hey, I'm sorry." His voice had gone deep and sexy. "I shouldn't have laughed at you. I should have just told you the truth, but I'm new to being a warrior. It's gonna take me a little while to get it right." His thumb caressed my cheekbone, following the line of my tattoos. "I should have told you that the only thing I want more than a taste of your blood is to know that you're safe and strong." He kissed me. "Plus, I don't need to drink from you, because I know that I'm going to be okay." He brushed his lips against mine. "Want to know how I know that?"

"Uh-huh," I murmured.

"I know because your safety is my strength, Zoey. Go to sleep now. I'm here." He lay back, settling me against his side.

Just before my eyes fluttered shut I whispered, "If someone tries to wake me up, would you please kill them?"

Stark chuckled. "Anything for you, my lady."

"Good." I closed my eyes and fell asleep with my Warrior holding me tightly and keeping me safe from dreams and ghosts of the past.

CHAPTER FIFTEEN

Aphrodite

"Seriously, gay boys. Just go back to bed—together—eesh. I need my vamp for the rest of the night." Aphrodite was standing, arms crossed, just inside the door to the room Darius, Damien, Jack, and Duchess were sharing. She noted, with a vague sense of irritation, that Damien and Jack and Duchess were all curled up in one bed together. Sure, they reminded her of puppies, but it wasn't exactly fair that the penguins were cool with them sleeping together while at the same time they'd banished her to rooming with Zoey. Or at least they'd tried.

"What is it, Aphrodite? What's wrong?" Darius hurried toward her, pulling a T-shirt over his completely gorgeous chest with one hand and slipping on his shoes with the other.

As usual, Darius had caught on before anyone else was fully functional—yet another reason why she'd fallen for him.

"Everything's fine. It's just that Zoey is sleeping with Stark. *In our room.* And I'm not cool with tagging along for that. So we're going to do a little roommate trading of our own."

"All is well with Zoey?" Damien asked.

"My guess is that about now all is more than well with her," Aphrodite said.

"I didn't think Stark was up to, well, *stuff*," Jack said delicately. He looked sleepy, with tousled hair and puffy eyes; Aphrodite thought he was even more puppyish than usual, and really cute. Of course she'd gouge out her eyes before she admitted that out loud.

"He managed the steps up to our top-floor room, so I'm thinking he's on the mend."

"Oooh, Erik's not gonna like that," Jack said happily. "There's gonna be some serious boyfriend drama tomorrow."

"The drama's over in that department. Z dumped Erik earlier tonight."

"She did!" Damien said.

"Yeah, and it's about time, too. His possessive crap had to go," Aphrodite said.

"And she's really okay?" Damien asked.

Aphrodite didn't like Damien's typically too-keen gaze. She absolutely was not going into the fact that Kalona had entered Zoey's dream, and that was why Stark was sleeping with her. She was also not going to talk about her vision—something she was happy to blame on Zoey, and definitely would in the future when Damien got pissed that she'd kept her mouth shut about it. So, to throw off Miss Nosy, she lifted one perfect brow and gave him her standard keep-them-guessing sneer. "Who are you, her gay mom?"

As Aphrodite knew it would, Damien's fur instantly ruffled. "No, I'm her friend!"

"Please. Yawn. Like we all don't know that. Zoey. Is. Fine. Goddess, try giving her some breathing room."

Damien frowned. "I let her breathe. I was just worried about her, that's all."

"Where's Heath? Does he know about her breakup with Erik and that she's, well, *sleeping with Stark*?" Jack finished the sentence in a stage whisper.

Aphrodite rolled her eyes. "I could care less where Heath is, and unless Z needs a snack I'm thinking she's probably not too interested in where he is, either. *She's busy*," she enunciated clearly. Aphrodite really didn't like hurting Damien and his girl/boyfriend Jack's feelings, but cutting them short was the only way to keep Damien out of her business, and that didn't even work 100 percent of the time. She turned to Darius, who was standing near her watching her closely with an expression that was a mixture of amusement and concern. "Ready to go, handsome?"

"Of course." He looked back at Damien and Jack before he closed the door. "I'll see you two at sunset."

"'Kay!" Jack trilled while Damien just looked long and hard at her.

Out in the hall Aphrodite had only taken a couple of steps when Darius took her wrist and pulled her to a stop. Before she could say anything, he put his hands on her shoulders and looked into her eyes.

"You've had a vision," he said simply.

Aphrodite felt her eyes fill with tears. She was totally, absolutely crazy about this big hulk of a guy who knew her so well, and who seemed to care so much about her.

"Yeah."

"Are you all right? You look pale and your eyes are still bloodshot."

"I'm okay," she said, although even to her own ears she didn't sound convincing.

He folded her into his arms and she let him hold her, comforted beyond words by his strength. "Was it as bad as last time?" he asked.

"It was worse." Face tucked down against his chest she spoke in a voice so soft and sweet that it would have shocked almost everyone who knew her.

"Another death vision of Zoey?"

"No. This time it was an end-of-the-world thing, but Zoey did figure in it."

"Are we going back to her?"

"No, she really is sleeping with Stark. Seems Kalona's been getting in her dreams and sleeping with a guy keeps him out."

"Good," Darius said. There was a sound at the end of the hall, and Darius pulled her around the corner and deeper into the shadows while a nun passed by, oblivious to their presence.

"Hey, speaking of sleep—I know Z's the big High Priestess, but she's not the only one who needs her beauty rest," Aphrodite whispered when they were alone in the hallway again.

Darius gave her a considering look. "You are right. You must be exhausted, especially after having a vision."

"I wasn't just talking about me, Mr. Macho. I was thinking about where we could go on the way down here and I came up with an idea—a brilliant idea, if I do say so myself."

Darius smiled. "And I'm sure you do."

"Of course. Anyway, I remembered you telling the penguin nurses that Stark shouldn't be interrupted for at least a solid eight hours. So, he's not in his very private, very dark, very cozy room. Instead it is tragically empty." Aphrodite nuzzled the side of his neck, lifted herself on her tiptoes and nipped at his earlobe.

He laughed and tucked his arm around her. "You are brilliant."

On the walk to Stark's vacated room, Aphrodite filled him in on her vision, and on Zoey's dream. He listened to her with the quiet attentiveness that had been the second thing about him that had drawn her to him.

The first being his utter hotness, of course.

Stark's room was cozy and dark, lit only by a single candle. Darius pulled a chair over to the door and propped it against the handle, effectively barring anyone from busting in on them. Then he rummaged through the dresser in the corner of the room and pulled out fresh sheets and blankets, which he remade the bed with, saying something about not wanting her to sleep on a wounded vampyre's sheets.

Aphrodite watched him as she pulled off her boots and jeans, and then slid her bra off under her shirt. She thought about what a weird feeling it was to have someone take care of her—someone who actually seemed to like her for herself, which was a total surprise. Guys liked her because she was hot, or because she was rich, popular, and a challenge, or, more often than not, simply because she was a bitch. It always amazed her how many guys just flat-out liked bitches. Guys didn't like her because she was Aphrodite. Actually, guys usually didn't take time to find out who she was underneath all the good hair, long legs, and attitude.

But the biggest shock of all about her relationship with Darius, and it was definitely becoming a relationship, was the fact that they hadn't had sex. Yet. Sure, everyone believed they were doing it like bunnies, and she'd let them believe they were—she'd even encouraged them to believe it. They weren't, though. And somehow, that didn't feel weird. They slept together, and had even had some seriously hot make-out sessions, but that's as far as they'd gone.

With a jolt of shocked realization, Aphrodite understood what it was that was happening between her and Darius—they were going slow and getting to know each other. Really, truly getting to know each other, and she was discovering that she liked going slow almost as much as she liked getting to know Darius.

They were falling in love!

That terrifying thought had Aphrodite's knees going weak so suddenly that she backed up to the chair that was in the corner of the room and, feeling light-headed, sat down.

Darius finished making the bed and looked bemusedly across the room at her. "What are you doing all the way over there?"

"Just sitting," she said quickly.

He cocked his head to the side. "Are you really okay? You did say you burned along with the vampyres in your vision. Are you still feeling the effects of that? You look pale."

"I'm a little thirsty, and my eyes still sting, but I'm fine."

When she continued to sit across the room without making any move to come to bed, he gave her a confused smile and said, "Aren't you tired?"

"Yeah, yeah, I am."

"Shall I get you some water?"

"Oh, no! I'll get it myself. No problem." Aphrodite boinged up like one of those freaky puppets with strings and walked over to the sink in the opposite corner of the room. She was filling up a paper cone with water when Darius was suddenly behind her. His strong hands were on her shoulders again. This time his thumbs gently began to knead the ultratight muscles in her neck.

"You carry all your tension here," he said, working from her neck to her shoulders.

Aphrodite downed the cup of water and then couldn't make herself move. Darius massaged her shoulders silently, letting his touch tell her how much he cared for her. Finally, she allowed the cup to slide from her fingers. Her head lolled forward and Aphrodite breathed a deep, contented sigh. "Your hands are totally magic."

"Anything for you, my lady."

Aphrodite smiled and leaned into his hands, allowing herself to relax more and more. She loved it that Darius treated her like she was his High Priestess, even though she had no Mark and would never be a vampyre. She loved that he had no doubt that she was special to Nyx—that she was Chosen by the Goddess. He so obviously didn't care whether a Mark went along with that or not. She loved that he—

Ohmygoddess! She actually loved him! Holy shit!

Aphrodite's head snapped up and she turned around so quickly that Darius took a short, startled step back, automatically giving her room.

"What is it?" he asked.

"I love you!" she blurted, and then pressed her hand against her mouth like she was trying, *too late*, to keep the words from exploding from it.

The warrior's smile was long and slow. "I am glad to hear you say it. I'm in love with you, too."

Aphrodite's eyes began to fill with tears and she blinked hard to stop them as she shoved past him. "Goddess! This sucks!"

Instead of responding to her outburst, Darius simply watched her stalk over to the bed. Aphrodite could feel his steady gaze on her as she considered whether she should sit on the bed, or get in it. Finally, she did neither, deciding she didn't like the picture she'd be creating in bed. She already felt vulnerable and exposed enough standing there in her T-shirt, panties, and nothing else. She turned to face Darius.

"What?" she snapped.

He tilted his head. A sad smile lifted just the corners of his lips. She thought his eyes looked decades older than the rest of his face. "Your parents are not in love, Aphrodite. From what you've shared with me about them, they may not be capable of feeling that emotion for anyone, and that includes you."

She lifted her chin and met his gaze. "So tell me something I don't know."

"You aren't your mother."

He'd said the words gently, but she felt them as if he'd flung knives at her that had buried themselves in her heart.

"I know that!" She spoke through lips that were suddenly cold.

Darius moved slowly toward her. Aphrodite thought how graceful he was—how powerful he always looked. *He* loved *her*? How? Why? Didn't he realize what an awful bitch she was?

"Do you really know that? You *are* capable of love, even if your mother is not," he told her.

But am I capable of being loved? She wanted to scream the question, but she couldn't. Pride, who spoke louder to her than the understanding in Darius's eyes, stopped the words. Instead she did what made her feel safe—she went on the offensive.

"Of course I know that. But this whole thing between us still sucks. The truth is you're a vampyre. I'm a human. The most I can ever be to you would be your consort, and I can't even be that because I'm already fucking Imprinted with stupid-ass Stevie Bumpkin Rae—an Imprint I can't seem to get rid of even though you've bitten me, too." Aphrodite paused, trying not to remember the tenderness Darius had shown her when he drank from her, even though to him her Imprinted blood was tainted. She tried, unsuccessfully, not to think about the pleasure and peace she'd found in his arms, all *without* having sex with him.

"I don't think you're right about all of that. You're not just a human, and your Imprint with Stevie Rae doesn't affect us. I see it as further evidence of your importance to Nyx. She knows Stevie Rae has need of you."

"But you don't need me," Aphrodite said bitterly.

"I do need you," he corrected her firmly.

"For what? We're not even fucking!"

"Aphrodite, why are you doing this? You know I desire you, but you and I are more than just bodies and lust. We're connected beyond that."

"I don't see how!" Aphrodite was perilously close to tears again, which made her even more pissed off.

"I do." He closed the rest of the space between them and, taking one of her hands in his, Darius dropped to one knee before her. "I need to ask you something."

"Oh, Goddess! What?" Was he going to do something ridiculous like ask her to marry him?

He fisted his right hand over his heart and stared into her eyes. "Aphrodite, Beloved Prophetess of Nyx, I ask you to accept my Warrior's Oath. Sworn to you this day I pledge to protect you with my heart, my mind, my body, and my soul. I pledge to belong to you before all others, and to be your Warrior until I draw my last breath on this world, and beyond, if our Goddess so wills it. Do you accept my oath?"

Aphrodite was filled with an overwhelming tide of joy. Darius wanted to be her Warrior! But that joy was short-lived as she thought about the repercussions of his oath.

"You can't be my Warrior. Zoey is your High Priestess. If you're going to pledge yourself to someone, it has to be her." Aphrodite hated saying the words—and hated even more thinking about Darius being on his knee in front of Zoey.

"Zoey is my High Priestess, just as she is yours, but she already has a Warrior. I have witnessed young Stark's enthusiasm for his oath-sworn position. She will need no other Warrior shadowing her. Also, Zoey already gave me her blessing to pledge to you."

"She did what?"

The warrior nodded solemnly. "It was only right that I explained to Zoey what I intended."

"So this isn't just an impulse? You've actually thought this out?"

"Of course." He smiled up at her. "I want to protect you forever."

Aphrodite was shaking her head from side to side. "You can't."

Darius's smile faded. "My pledge is mine to give, so that is no hindrance. I am young, but my skills are vast. I assure you that I *can* protect you."

"I don't mean that! I know you're good—you're too damn good! That's the problem." Silently, Aphrodite began to cry.

"Aphrodite, I don't understand."

"Why would you want to be sworn to me? I'm a total bitch!"

His smile returned. "You are unique."

Aphrodite shook her head. "I'll hurt you. I always hurt anyone who gets close to me."

"Then it is a good thing I am a strong warrior. Nyx was wise in giving me to you, and I am more than content with our Goddess's choice for me."

"Why?" Tears were running freely down Aphrodite's cheeks now, dripping from her chin and soaking into the T-shirt.

"Because you deserve someone who values you beyond wealth and beauty and status. You deserve someone who values you for yourself. Now, I ask you again, do you accept my oath?"

Aphrodite stared down into his strong, gorgeous face, and something within her broke free as she saw her future in his honest, unflinching gaze.

"Yes, I do accept your oath," she said.

With a joyous shout, Darius stood and took his Prophetess into his arms. Then he held her gently until sunset as she cried out the knot of sadness and loneliness and anger that had for so long bound her heart.

CHAPTER SIXTEEN

Stevie Rae

Steve Rae usually didn't have problems sleeping. Okay, it was a terrible cliché, but during the daytime she slept like she was, well, dead. But not that day. That day she hadn't been able to shut off her mind—or, maybe it was more truthful to say she hadn't been able to shut off her *guilty* mind.

What was she going to do about Rephaim?

She should tell Zoey—that's what she should do. Absolutely no doubt about it.

"Sure, and then Z would freak out like a long-tailed cat in a room filled with rockin' chairs," she muttered to herself, and continued to pace back and forth in front of the entrance to the root cellar's tunnel. Stevie Rae was alone, but she kept throwing furtive glances around her like she expected to be snuck up on.

And so what if someone came down here looking for her? She wasn't doing anything wrong! She just couldn't sleep, that's all.

At least she wished that was all.

Stevie Rae stopped pacing and stared into the calming darkness of the tunnel she'd cut through the raw earth not long before. *What the hell was she going to do about Rephaim?*

She couldn't tell Zoey about him. Zoey wouldn't understand. No one would. Heck, Stevie Rae didn't even really understand herself! She just knew that she couldn't turn him in—couldn't betray him to everyone else. But when she wasn't around him, when Stevie Rae couldn't hear his voice and see the too-human pain in his eyes, she was mostly on the verge of panic and worried that hiding the

Raven Mocker only proved that she was losing every bit of her good sense.

He's your enemy! The thought kept circling around in her mind, flapping and spiraling out of control like an injured bird.

"No, right now he's not my enemy. Right now he's just hurt." Stevie Rae spoke into the tunnel, to the earth that grounded her and strengthened her.

Stevie Rae's eyes widened as a thought struck her. It was the fact that he was hurt that had caused this mess! If he'd been whole and attacking her, or any of the others, she wouldn't have hesitated to protect herself or anyone else.

So, what if I just get him someplace he can heal? Yes! That was the answer! She didn't have to protect him. She just didn't want to hand him over to be slaughtered. If she got him to safety, someplace where he wouldn't be bothered, Rephaim could get well and then he could choose his own future. She had! Maybe he would choose to join the good guys against Kalona and Neferet. Maybe he wouldn't. Whichever, it wouldn't be her concern.

But where could he go?

And then, staring into the tunnel, she realized the perfect answer. It would mean that she'd have to admit some of her secrets, and in doing so she wondered if Zoey could possibly understand why Stevie Rae had kept things from her. *She has to understand. She's had to make some pretty unpopular choices, too.* And anyway, Stevie Rae had the sneaking suspicion Zoey wouldn't be all that surprised by what she had to tell her; she'd probably been on to her for a while now.

So she'd tell Z about the stuff, which would, at the very least, ensure that where she sent Rephaim wouldn't turn into fledgling Grand Central anytime soon. He wouldn't exactly be all alone and totally safe, but he would be out of her hair and no longer her responsibility—or her liability.

Feeling excited and more than a little giddy that she'd figured out a solution to her massively terrible problem, Stevie Rae centered herself and checked her ever-accurate internal clock. She had just over an hour until sunset. On a normal day she could never get away with what she was planning, but today she could feel the weakness of the sun as it tried, but failed, to shine through the thick layer of gray clouds, heavy with the ice that seemed to have settled permanently over Tulsa. She was pretty sure she wouldn't burn up if she stepped outside. She was also pretty sure that there wouldn't be any nosy nuns poking around with ice still pelting down and everything outside the abbey being frozen and slick. Same went for the regular fledglings. The red fledglings were the least of her problems, at least from dawn till dusk. They were all still tucked in their cots in the basement. Of course everyone would be getting up in the next hour and, if she knew Z, and she did, they'd be having a big powwow about their next move, which meant Zoey would expect her to be present.

Stevie Rae picked at her fingernails nervously. It was during the big "what are we going to do now?" meeting that she'd have to clue Zoey, and everyone else, in to her secrets. Man, she was so not looking forward to that meeting.

To add to the not-looking-forward-to-it part, there was also the fact that Aphrodite had had another vision. Stevie Rae didn't know what she'd seen, but through their Imprint she'd sensed the turmoil that the vision had caused Aphrodite, turmoil that had risen and then faded, which probably meant Aphrodite was currently sound asleep. That was a good thing 'cause she didn't want her psychically being aware enough to get any clue as to what Stevie Rae was up to. She could only hope Aphrodite didn't already know too much.

"So it's now or never. Time to cowboy up," Stevie Rae whispered to herself.

Not giving herself a chance to chicken out, she went quickly and quietly up the stairs from the root cellar and into the basement proper of the abbey. Sure enough, all the red fledglings were still crashed and totally out. Dallas's distinct snoring drifted through the dark room, almost making her smile.

She went to her empty cot and pulled the blanket off it. Then retraced her steps down to the cellar and moved with preternatural confidence in the unrelieved darkness to the mouth of the tunnel. With no hesitation she stepped into it, loving the scent and the feel of being surrounded by the earth. Even though she knew what she was about to do might become the biggest mistake in her life, the earth was still able to touch her and calm her, soothing her frazzled nerves like the familiar embrace of a parent.

Stevie Rae followed the tunnel a short way to the first gentle curve. There she stopped and put the blanket down. She took three deep breaths, centering herself. When she spoke, her voice was little above a whisper, but it carried such power with it that the air around her literally shivered like heat waves off a blacktop road in the summer.

"Earth, you are mine, just like I am yours. I call you to me." The tunnel around Stevie Rae was instantly filled with the scents of a hayfield, and the sound of wind soughing through trees. She could feel grass that wasn't there beneath her feet. And that wasn't all Stevie Rae could feel. She felt the earth all around her, and it was that sense of her element—an acknowledgment of earth as an ensouled, sentient entity, that Stevie Rae tapped into.

She raised her arms and pointed her fingers at the low, dirt ceiling of the tunnel. "I need you to open for me. Please." The ceiling trembled and dirt showered down, slowly at first, and then, with a sound like an old woman sighing, the earth split open above Stevie Rae.

Instinct had her jumping back into the protective shadows of the tunnel, but she'd been right about the sun; it was definitely nowhere to be seen or felt. Was it raining? No, she decided as she peered up at the dismal sky and a few drops found her face, it wasn't raining; it was sleeting, and pretty hard at that, which was all the better for what she had to do.

Stevie Rae wrapped the blanket around her shoulders and began the short climb up the collapsed side of the tunnel to the world above. She emerged not far from Mary's Grotto, between it and the trees that lined the western edge of the abbey grounds. It was dark enough that it seemed that the sun had already set, but still Stevie Rae squinted uncomfortably, not liking how vulnerable daylight made her feel, even if that light was so well filtered it was practically nonexistent.

She shook off the unease and got her bearings quickly, sighting the shed where she'd left Rephaim a little way off to her left. Putting her head down against the stinging pellets of frozen rain, she jogged to the shed. Just like the night before, as she touched the latch she couldn't help but think *Please let him be dead . . . It'd be easier if he was dead . . .*

The shed was warmer than she'd imagined, and it smelled strange. Along with the scents of the lawn mower and other oiled and gassed yard equipment, as well as the various pesticides and fertilizers stored on the shed's shelves, there was something else. Something that made her skin crawl. She'd just made her way around the lawn-implement obstacle course and was moving slowly to the back of the shed when Stevie Rae realized what the scent reminded her of, and that realization made her steps falter and then stop completely.

The shed, perfumed by Rephaim and his blood, smelled like the darkness that had surrounded her after she had un-died and her humanity had been almost totally destroyed. It reminded her of that black time and those days and nights that had been filled with nothing but anger and need, violence and fear.

She stifled a little gasp of realization as she made the rest of the scent connection. The red fledglings, those *other* red fledglings—the ones she was so reluctant to reveal to Zoey—had this same scent about them. It wasn't a perfect match, and she doubted whether a nose less keen than hers could even draw the connection, but she could. She did. And the connection made her own blood cold with foreboding.

"Again you come to me alone," Rephaim said.

CHAPTER SEVENTEEN

Stevie Rae

Rephaim's words drifted to her out of the darkness. Without seeing the monster he was, his voice had a quality that made him sound hauntingly, heartbreakingly human. That was, after all, what had saved him the day before. His humanity had reached Stevie Rae, and she hadn't been able to kill him.

But today he sounded different, stronger than he had before. That relieved and worried her at the same time.

Then she shook off the worry. She wasn't some helpless kid who went running for the hills at the first sign of danger. She could definitely kick some bird butt. Stevie Rae straightened her spine. She'd made the decision to help him get away, and that's dang well what she was gonna do.

"And who'd ya expect? John Wayne and the cavalry?" Pretending to be her mom when one of her brothers was being sick and annoying, Stevie Rae marched forward. The shape that had been a dark blob hunkered in the back of the shed came into focus and she gave him her best no-nonsense look. "Well, you're not dead and you're sittin' up. So you must be feelin' better."

He cocked his head slightly to the side. "Who is John Wayne and cavalry?"

"*The* cavalry. It just means the good guys comin' to the rescue. Don't get excited, though. There isn't an army comin'. All you got is me."

"Don't you consider yourself one of the good guys?"

He surprised her with his ability to have an actual conversation with her, and she thought if she could close her eyes or look away from him, she might almost fool herself into thinking he was just a normal guy. Of course she knew better. She could never close her eyes around him *or* look away, and he definitely wasn't a normal anything.

"Well, yeah, I'm good, but I'm not exactly an army." Stevie Rae made an obvious show of looking him over. And he did still look like crap—definitely battered and bloodied and broken—but he wasn't lying on his side in a crumpled heap anymore. He was sitting up, leaning, mostly on his uninjured left side, against the back of the shed. He'd arranged the towels she'd left with him over his body like pieces of a blanket. His eyes were bright and alert and never wavered from her face. "So, you *are* feelin' better?"

"As you said, I am not dead. Where are the others?"

"I told ya before, the rest of the Raven Mockers left with Kalona and Neferet."

"No, I mean the other sons and daughters of man."

"Oh, my friends. They're sleepin' mostly. So we don't have much time. This isn't gonna be easy, but I think I figured out how to get you outta here in one piece." She paused, and stopped herself from picking at her fingernails. "You can walk, can't you?"

"I will do what I need to do."

"Now what the heck does that mean? Just give me a simple yes or no. It's kinda important."

"Yessss."

Stevie Rae swallowed hard at the sound of his hissed word and decided she'd been wrong about the whole if-she-didn't-look-at-him-he'd-seem-normal thing. "All right, well, let's get goin' then."

"Where are you taking me?"

"All I could think of was that I need to get you someplace where you can be safe and heal. You can't stay here. They'll find you for sure. Hey, you don't have your daddy's problem with bein' underground, do ya?"

"I prefer the ssssky to the earth." He sounded bitter, practically biting off the words and adding a special hissing emphasis to "sky."

Stevie Rae put her hands on her hips. "So does that mean you can't go underground?"

"I prefer not to."

"Well, do you *prefer* to stay alive and hidden underground, or up here and about a minute away from bein' found and dead?" *Or worse,* she thought but didn't say aloud.

He didn't speak for quite a while and Stevie Rae began to wonder if maybe Rephaim didn't really want to live, which was a thought she hadn't considered. She guessed it might make sense, though. His own folks had left him for dead and the modern world was like a zillion times different than it had been when he'd been alive and in the flesh before—and terrorizing Cherokee villages. How badly had she messed up by not just letting him die?

"I prefer to live."

By the look on his face, Stevie Rae thought that maybe his announcement was as much a surprise to him as it had been to her.

"Okay. Fine. Then I need to get you outta here." She took a step toward him, but stopped. "Do I need to make you promise to be good again?"

"I am too weak to be a danger to you," he said simply.

"All right, then I'll just consider your word that you gave me earlier still holding. Just don't try anything stupid and we might get through this." Stevie Rae walked over to him and squatted down. "I better take a look at your bandages. They might need to be changed or tightened before we leave." She checked him over methodically, all the while keeping up a running verbal commentary of what she was doing. "Well, the moss looks like it's workin'. I don't see much blood. Your ankle's pretty swollen, but I don't think it's broken. Can't feel any breaks, anyway." She rewrapped the ankle and tightened his other bandages, leaving the shattered wing for last. Stevie Rae reached behind him and started to straighten the bandages that had come loose and Rephaim, who had been silent and perfectly still during her examination, flinched and groaned in pain.

"Ah, shoot! Sorry. I know the wing's bad."

"Wrap more of the cloth around me. Tie it more tightly against my body. I will not be able to walk if you do not completely immobilize it."

Stevie Rae nodded. "I'll do what I can." She ripped more lengths from one of the towels and then he leaned forward so that she had access to his back. She gritted her teeth and worked as quickly and gently as she could, hating the way he trembled and kept stifling moans of pain.

When she'd finished with the wing, she ladled out some water and helped him drink it. After he stopped trembling, she stood and held out her hands to him. "Okay, let's cowboy up."

He gazed at her and even in his strange face she could read confusion. She smiled. "It just means stepping up and doin' what you need to do, even when it's hard as hell."

He nodded, and then slowly reached up and clasped her hands. Bracing herself, she pulled, allowing him time to shift his weight and gather himself. With a painful gasp, he managed to stand, though he put little weight on his hurt ankle and he didn't seem very steady.

Stevie Rae kept hold of his hands, giving him a chance to get used to being upright, and while she worried that he might pass out, she thought how weird it was that his hands felt so warm and so human. She'd always thought of birds as cold and flitty. Actually, she didn't like birds much—never had. Her mom's chickens tended to scare the bejesus outta her, what with their hysterical flapping and stupid squawking. She had a brief flashback of gathering eggs and having one fat, grumpy hen peck at her and just miss her eyes.

Stevie Rae shivered, and Rephaim dropped her hands.

"Are you okay?" she asked to cover up the awkward silence that gathered between them.

With a grunt, he nodded.

She nodded, too. "Hang on. Before you try much walkin', let's see what I can find to help you." Stevie Rae looked through the garden stuff, finally settling on a good, sturdy wooden-handled shovel. She came back to Rephaim, measured it against him, and in one swift motion, snapped the handle from the spade end and handed it to him. "Use this like a cane. You know, to take some of the weight off your bad ankle. You can lean on me for a little while, but once we get in the tunnel you're gonna have to go on by yourself, so you'll need this."

Rephaim took the wooden handle from her. "Your strength is impressive."

Stevie Rae shrugged. "It comes in handy."

Rephaim took a tentative step forward, using the handle to help carry his weight, and he was actually able to walk, though Stevie Rae could see that it caused him a lot of pain. Still, he hobbled by himself to the door of the shed. There he paused and looked expectantly at her.

"First, I'm gonna wrap this around you. I'm countin' on no one seeing us, but on the outside chance that some nosy nun is gawkin' out a window, she'll just see me helpin' someone wrapped in a blanket. Or at least that's what I hope."

Rephaim nodded, and Stevie Rae wrapped the blanket around him, positioning it over his head and tucking it into the side of the bandage across his chest to hold it closed.

"So here's my plan: You know about the tunnels we've been stayin' in under the depot downtown, right?"

"Yes."

"Well, I kinda added to them."

"I don't understand."

"My affinity is for the element earth. I can control it, more or less. At least some aspects of it I can control. One of the things I recently found out I can do is to make it move—as in creating a tunnel through it. And I did that to link up the depot to the abbey."

"It is this type of power that my father spoke of when he talked of you."

Stevie Rae definitely didn't want to discuss Rephaim's horrible daddy with him, and she didn't even want to think about why he might have been talking about her and her powers. "Yeah, well, anyway—I opened up part of the tunnel I made so I could climb out of it and come here. It's not far from this shed. I'm gonna help you get there. Once you're in the tunnel I want you to follow it back to the depot. There's shelter there, and food. Actually, it's pretty dang nice. You can get well there."

"And why are the rest of your allies not going to find me in those tunnels?"

"First, I'm gonna seal up the one that connects the depot to the abbey. Then I'm gonna tell my friends somethin' that's gonna make sure they stay outta the depot tunnels for a while. And I'm hopin' that 'a while' translates into enough time for you to get well and get yourself away from here before they start pokin' around."

"What will you tell them that will keep them from going into the tunnels?"

Stevie Rae sighed and wiped her hand across her face. "I'm gonna tell them the truth. That there're more red fledglings—that they're hiding in the depot tunnels—and that they are dangerous because they haven't made the choice for good over evil."

Rephaim was silent for several heartbeats. Finally he said, "Neferet was right."

"Neferet! What do you mean?"

"She kept telling my father that she had allies among the red fledglings—that they could be soldiers in her cause. These red fledglings are the ones she was speaking of."

"They must be," Stevie Rae murmured miserably. "I didn't want to believe it. I wanted to believe they'd eventually do the right thing—choose humanity over the darkness. They just needed some time to get things straight in their heads, that's all. I think I was wrong."

"It is these fledglings that will keep your friends from the tunnels?"

"Kinda. Really, it's more me that'll keep them out. I'm gonna buy time—for you and for them." She met his eyes. "Even if I'm wrong." Without saying anything else, she opened the door, went to his side, lifted his arm, wrapped it around her shoulders, and the two of them stepped out into the icy dusk.

Stevie Rae knew Rephaim had to be in terrible pain as they walked haltingly from the shed toward the opening in the ground she'd created to the tunnel. But the only sound he made was his panting breath. He leaned heavily on her, and Stevie Rae was again surprised by his warmth and by the familiar feel of a guy's arm around her shoulder, mixed with the feathered body she was helping to support. She kept

glancing around them, almost holding her breath in fear that someone, like annoying gotta-prove-how-macho-I-am Erik, had slipped
outside. The veiled sun was setting. Stevie Rae could feel it leaving the
ice-shrouded sky. It was just a matter of time before the fledglings,
vamps, and nuns started to stir.

"Come on, you're doing good. You can make it. We gotta hurry."
She kept murmuring to him, encouraging Rephaim and trying to
calm her own guilty fears.

But no one yelled after them. No one ran up to them, and in much
less time than Stevie Rae had anticipated, the opening to the tunnel
gaped at their feet.

"Climb down backward, with your hands and feet. It's not far. I'll
hold on to you for most of the way to help steady you."

Rephaim didn't waste time or energy on words. He nodded,
turned, flung the blanket off of him, and then, as Stevie Rea held on
to his good arm—glad that though he was big and appeared strong
and solid, he actually weighed less than she did—with her help he
slowly and painfully disappeared down into the earth. Stevie Rae
followed him.

In the tunnel, Rephaim leaned against the dirt wall, trying to
catch his breath. Stevie Rae wished she could let him rest there, but
the crawling sensation in the back of her neck was screaming that
the others would be waking up and coming to look for her, *and finding her and her Raven Mocker!*

"You gotta keep going. Now. Get out of here. Go that way." She
pointed into the darkness in front of them. "It's gonna be really dark.
Sorry 'bout that, but I don't have time to get a lamp for you. Are you
okay in the dark?"

He nodded. "I have long preferred the night."

"Good. Follow this tunnel until you come to the place where it
changes from dirt to cement walls. Then turn to your right. It's gonna
be confusing 'cause the closer you get to the depot, the more tunnels
there are. But stay in the main one. It'll be lit—or at least I hope it's
still lit. Either way, if you keep goin', you'll find lanterns and food and
rooms with beds and everything."

"And there are dark fledglings."

He didn't phrase it as a question, but Stevie Rae answered him. "Yeah, there are. While the other red fledglings and I were livin' there, they stayed away from the main tunnels and our rooms and such. I don't know what they're doin' now that we're not there and I honestly don't know what they'll do with you. I don't think they'll want to eat you—you don't smell right. But I can't tell for sure. They're—" she paused, searching for the right words. "They're different than I am— than the rest of us."

"They are of the darkness. As I said, I am well acquainted with that."

"All right. Well, I'm just gonna believe you'll be okay." Stevie Rae paused again, not knowing what to say and finally blurting out, "So, I guess I'll see ya around sometime."

He stared at her and said nothing.

Stevie Rae fidgeted. "Rephaim. You gotta go. Now. It's not safe here. As soon as you're down the tunnel a ways, I'm gonna collapse this part so that no one can follow you from here, but you still gotta hurry."

"I do not understand why you would betray your people to save me," he said.

"I'm not betraying anyone; I'm just not killing you!" she yelled, and then lowered her voice and continued. "Why does letting you go have to mean I betrayed my friends? Can't it just mean that I choose life over death? Look, I chose good over evil. How is me lettin' you live any different than that?"

"Did you not consider that choosing to save me was making a choice for what you would call evil?"

Stevie Rae looked at him for a long time before she answered. "Then let that be on your conscience. Your life is what *you* want it to be. Your daddy's gone. The rest of the Raven Mockers are gone, too. My mamma used to sing a kinda silly song to me when I was a kid and I'd messed up and gotten myself hurt. She'd sing that I needed to pick myself up, dust myself off, and start all over again. And that's what you need to do. I'm just givin' you a chance to do it." Stevie Rae stuck out her hand. "So, here's hoping that next time we meet, we're not enemies."

Rephaim looked from her outstretched hand to her face, and back to her hand. Then slowly, almost reluctantly, he grasped it. Not in a modern handshake, but in the traditional vampyre greeting of clasping forearms.

"I owe you a life, Priestess."

Stevie Rae's cheeks felt hot. "Just call me Stevie Rae. I don't feel much like a Priestess right now."

He bowed his head. "Then it is to Stevie Rae that I owe a life."

"Do the right thing with yours and I'll consider myself paid up," she said. "Merry meet, marry part, and merry meet again, Rephaim."

She tried to pull her arm from his grasp, but he didn't let her go. "Are they all like you? All of your allies?" he asked.

She smiled. "Nah, I'm weirder than most of the others. I'm the first red vamp, and sometimes I think that makes me kinda an experiment."

Still gripping her arm he said, "I was the first of my father's children."

Though he held her gaze steadily, she couldn't read his expression. All she saw in the dim light of the tunnel was the human shape of his eyes and their unearthly red glow—the same red glow that haunted her dreams and sometimes overwhelmed her own vision, tainting everything with scarlet and anger and darkness. She shook her head, and more to herself than to him said, "Being the first can be hard."

He nodded and finally released her arm. Without another word, he turned and hobbled away into the darkness.

Stevie Rae counted slowly to one hundred, then she raised her arms. "Earth, I need you again." Instantly her element responded, filling the tunnel with the scents of a springtime meadow. She breathed in deeply before continuing. "Collapse the ceiling. Fill up this part of the tunnel. Close the hole you made for me; plug it up; make it solid again, so that nobody can pass here."

She stepped back as the dirt in front and above her started to move, and then it rained down, shifting and solidifying until there was nothing but a solid wall of earth in front of her.

"Stevie Rae, what the hell are ya doing?"

Stevie Rae whirled around, pressing her hand over her heart.

"Dallas! You scared the livin' daylights right outta me! Dang, I think you 'bout gave me a heart attack for real."

"Sorry. You're so hard to sneak up on I thought you knew I was standing here."

Heart pounding even harder, Stevie Rae searched Dallas's face, trying to find a sign that he had even a hint that she hadn't been alone, but he didn't look suspicious or mad or betrayed—he just looked curious and kinda sad. His next words reinforced that he hadn't been there long enough to have caught even a glimpse of Rephaim.

"You sealed it off to keep the rest of them from getting to the abbey, didn't you?"

Stevie Rae nodded and tried not to let the wave of relief she felt show in her voice. "Yeah. I didn't think it was smart to give 'em such easy access to the nuns."

"It would be kinda like an old-lady smorgasbord for them." Dallas's eyes glinted mischievously.

"Don't be gross." But she couldn't help grinning at him. Dallas really was adorable. Not only was he her unofficial boyfriend, but he was also a genius with anything to do with electricity or plumbing or basically whatever you'd find at Home Depot.

Grinning back at her, he moved closer and tugged on one of her blond curls. "I'm not being gross. I'm being real. And you can't tell me you haven't at least thought about how easy it would be to chomp on these nuns."

"Dallas!" She narrowed her eyes at him, truly shocked by what he'd said. "Heck no I haven't thought about eatin' a nun! It doesn't even *sound* right. And like I told ya before, it's not smart to think a lot about eatin' people. It's not good for you."

"Hey, relax, cutie. I'm just messing with you." He glanced behind her at the wall of earth. "So, how are you going to explain this to Zoey and the rest of them?"

"I'm gonna do what I probably shoulda done a while ago. I'm gonna tell them the truth."

"I thought you wanted to stay quiet about the rest of the fledglings because you thought they might come around and be more like us."

"Yeah, well, I'm startin' to think I've messed up with some of my choices."

"All right, it's up to you. You're our High Priestess. Tell Zoey and them whatever you want. Actually, you can do that right now. Zoey just called a meeting in the cafeteria. I came looking for you to tell you about it."

"How'd you know where to find me?"

He smiled at her again and slipped his arm around her shoulders. "I know you, cutie. It wasn't very hard to figure out where you'd be."

They started walking out of the tunnel together. Stevie Rae wrapped her arm around Dallas's waist. She let herself lean against him, glad that he felt normal and totally guy-like beside her. It was a relief to have her world shift back to what she knew was right. She'd put Rephaim out of her mind. She'd helped someone who'd been hurt, that's all. And now she was done with him. Seriously, he was just one badly injured Raven Mocker. How much trouble could he cause?

"You know me, huh?" She butted him with her hip.

He pressed right back against her. "Not as well as I wish I knew you, cutie."

Stevie Rae giggled, ignoring the fact that she sounded kinda manic in her effort to be normal.

She also ignored the fact that she could still smell Rephaim's dark scent on her skin.

CHAPTER EIGHTEEN

Zoey

I was in that magical, misty place between awake and asleep when he pulled me against his body. He was so big and strong and hard that the contrast between his physical presence and the soft, sweet breath that tickled the side of my neck along with the gentle kisses he placed there had me shivering.

I was mostly asleep and didn't want to wake up all the way yet, but I sighed happily and stretched so that he could reach more of my neck. His arms felt so right around me. I loved being close to him and was thinking about how glad I was Stark was my Warrior when I murmured sleepily, "You must really be feeling better."

His touch became sexier and less gentle.

I shivered again.

Then my groggy mind registered two things simultaneously. First: I wasn't shivering just because I liked what he was doing, even though I definitely liked what he was doing. I was shivering because his touch was *cold*. Second: The body that pressed against me was too big to be Stark's.

At that instant he whispered, "Do you see how your soul longs for me? You will come to me. You are fated to do so, and I am fated to wait for you."

I sucked in a gasp, came wide awake, and sat up.

I was completely alone.

Calm down . . . calm down . . . calm down . . . Kalona is not here . . . everything's fine . . . it was just a dream . . .

Without thinking about it, I automatically started to control my breathing and steady my emotions, which were definitely in overdrive. Stark wasn't in the room, and the last thing I wanted him to do was to come running back to me because he could feel how panicked I was, when I was not in any real danger. I might be uncertain about a bunch of things, but I was dead sure about one thing: I didn't want Stark to start thinking he couldn't leave my side.

Yeah, I was crazy about him, and glad we shared a bond, but that didn't mean I wanted him to believe I couldn't function without him. He was my Warrior, not my babysitter or my stalker, and if he started to think he had to watch me constantly . . . gawking at me while I slept . . .

I suppressed a groan of horror.

The door that led to the little bathroom my room shared with the guest room next door opened and Stark strode in, his gaze going straight to me. He had on jeans and a black Street Cats Catholic Charities T-shirt, and he was towel-drying his still-wet hair. I guess I must have calmed myself down and fixed the panicked expression on my face enough that as soon as he saw me sitting up in bed, alone and in no danger, his worried look changed to a smile.

"Hey, you are awake. I thought so. You okay?"

"Yep. Fine and dandy," I said quickly. "I just woke myself up by almost rolling off the bed. It kinda freaked me out."

His smile turned cocky. "You were probably flailing around missing me and my hot body, and that's what had you rolling off the bed."

I raised a brow at him. "I'm so sure that wasn't it." His mention of his body (yes, it is hot, but I'm not gonna let him think I'm drooling over him) had me studying him, and I realized he did look good—as in more than just cute and hot. He was a lot less pale than he had been when we'd gone to sleep, and he was a lot steadier on his feet. "You seem better."

"I am better. Darius was right—I heal quickly. A solid eight hours of sleep, plus the three baggies of blood I snagged while you were still snoring, have me feeling pretty good." He walked over to the bed, bent, and kissed me softly. "Add to that me knowing I can keep you safe from Kalona's nightmares, and I'd say I'm ready to face just about anything."

"I don't snore," I told him firmly, then I sighed and wrapped my arms around his waist, leaning into him, letting the strength of his physical presence chase away what remained of Kalona's nightmare presence. "I'm glad you're feeling better."

Should I have told Stark that Kalona had still snuck into my dreams, even with him so close and so focused on protecting me? Probably. Maybe telling him would have made a difference in what happened later. Then I was only thinking about not messing up the positive energy he had going, so I rested in his arms until I remembered I hadn't even brushed my hair or anything. Running my fingers through my wicked-ugly bed head, and averting my face from him to keep from blasting Stark with morning mouth, I pulled away from his embrace and hurried toward the bathroom. Over my shoulder I said, "Hey, would you do me a favor while I'm taking a shower?"

"Sure." He shot me a cocky grin, which telegraphed how good he really was feeling. "Want me to wash your back?"

"Uh, no. But thanks. I think." Jeesh, guys had such one-track minds! "I want you to round up the fledglings, red and blue, and find Aphrodite, Darius, Sister Mary Angela, my grandma, and anyone else you can think of who needs to be in on the discussion of when and how we're getting back to the school."

"I'd rather wash your back, but no problem. Your wish, my lady, is my command." He bowed his head and saluted me, his hand over his heart.

"Thank you." The words came out soft. His expression of respect and trust suddenly making me feel close to tears.

"Hey." His smile faded. "You look kinda sad. Is everything okay?"

"I'm just glad you're my Warrior." What I said was the truth, if not all of it.

His smile was back. "You are one lucky High Priestess."

I shook my head at his unending cockiness and blinked the ridiculous tears from my eyes. "Just get everyone together for me, 'kay?"

"'Kay. Want to meet in the basement?"

I grimaced. "Definitely not. How about you ask Sister Mary Angela if we can meet in their dining room? Then we can eat and talk."

"Will do."

"Thanks."

"I'll see you soon, my lady." Eyes shining, he saluted me formally again before hurrying from the room.

More slowly, I entered the bathroom. Mechanically, I brushed my teeth and got in the shower. I stood for a long time just letting the hot water pour down over me. And then, when I knew I could keep my emotions calm, I thought about Kalona.

I'd relaxed in his arms. I hadn't been reliving one of A-ya's memories, or even under her influence, but I'd let myself go when he touched me, and the result had been as terrifying as it was revealing. It had felt right to be with him—so right that I'd mistaken him for my oath-bound Warrior! And it hadn't seemed like a dream. I'd been too awake; too close to full consciousness. Kalona's last visit had shaken me to my core.

"No matter how hard I try to fight against it, my soul recognizes him," I whispered to myself. And then, as if my eyes were jealous of the water already running down my face, I began to cry.

To find the dining room I followed my nose and my ears. All down the hallway leading to it, I could hear familiar voices laughing amid the clanking of plates and silverware and I wondered briefly if the nuns were really cool with what amounted to an invasion of teenage vampyres-to-be. I paused outside the wide, open-arched entry to the big room, checking out how the nuns were getting along with the kids. There were three rows of long tables. I'd expected the nuns to be clustered together, naturally segregating themselves from us, but they weren't. Sure, they tended to be sitting in twos and threes, but they were surrounded by fledglings—red and blue—and everyone was chattering, which totally killed the stereotypical image I had in my head of the nuns' dining room being a place of prayer and quiet (boring) reflection.

"So are you going to loiter or are you going to actually go in there?"

I turned to see Aphrodite and Darius standing behind me. They were holding hands and looking very glowy and, as the Twins would say, happy-smappy.

"Merry meet, Zoey." Darius saluted me formally, but his smile gave his respectful gesture a warm, casual feel.

I threw Aphrodite a see-someone-has-manners look before smiling at the warrior. "Merry meet, Darius. You two look pleased with yourselves. You must have found someplace to get some sleep last night." I paused, glanced at Aphrodite again, and added, "Sleep or whatnot."

"They assured me they *slept*." Sister Mary Angela emphasized the word as she joined us in the doorway.

Aphrodite rolled her eyes at the nun, but didn't say anything.

"Darius explained to me that the fallen angel has been visiting your dreams, and that Stark seemed to be able to stop him," said the nun in her usual manner of getting right to the point.

"What'd Stark do?" Heath skidded to a stop and gave me a giant hug, planting a kiss squarely on my lips. "Do I need to kick his butt?"

"Not likely you could," Stark said, joining us from inside the dining room.

Unlike Heath, he didn't grab me, but his look was so warm and intimate that it seemed to touch me as thoroughly as Heath's hug.

And suddenly I was feeling very guy-claustrophobic. I mean, a buffet of boys sounds like a good idea in theory, but I was quickly finding out that, much like straight-leg designer jeans, it's only in theory that the idea is good. As if to reinforce my thoughts, Erik chose that instant to join us. Venus, the red fledgling who was Aphrodite's old roommate, was practically Velcroed to his side. Ugh. Just ugh.

"Hi everyone. Man, I'm starving!" Erik said. He blazed the big, warm, movie star smile that I used to heart so much.

Through my peripheral vision I could see Heath and Stark gawking at Erik and his Venus leech, who was definitely suckerfished to his side, which was when I remembered that neither of my other guys knew I'd dumped Erik. I stifled a sigh of pure irritation and instead of ignoring him with the icy attitude I'd have liked to throw his way, I planted my own fake smile on my face and beamed.

"Hi, Erik, Venus. Well, you guys have definitely come to the right place if you're hungry. Everything smells super-good."

Erik's smile faltered for just an instant, but his acting skills were way up to the task of making it look as though he'd moved on, like, fifteen seconds after we'd broken up. "Hi, Zoey. Didn't see you over there. As usual, you're surrounded by guys. Damn, it always was crowded around you." With a sarcastic chuckle he pushed past me, bumping Stark with his shoulder.

"If I shot an arrow and thought about an ass, would it surprise you that I hit Erik?" Stark asked me in a pleasant, nonchalant voice.

"Wouldn't surprise me," Heath said.

"I can tell you *boys,* from personal experience, that Erik does have one nice ass," Venus said as she moved to follow Erik into the dining room.

"Hey, Venus, I have two words for you," Aphrodite said.

Venus hesitated and glanced over her shoulder at her ex-roommate. Aphrodite smiled her best mean-bitch sneer and said, "Re. Bound." She paused and gave a bitchy smirk and then said, "Good luck with that."

It was about then that I noticed every eye in the dining room was turned to us and all the conversations had skidded to a halt.

Erik made a possessive little motion with his hand and Venus practically trotted up to him. Slipping her arm through his, she mashed her boob against his elbow. And then the whispers started like someone had lit them with a match.

"Erik and Zoey broke up!"

"Erik's with Venus!"

"Zoey and Erik aren't together!"

Well, hell.

CHAPTER NINETEEN

Zoey

"I never did like him." Heath kissed me on the top of my head and then ruffled my hair like I was two years old.

"You know I hate it when you do that!" I said, trying to smooth back my hair that was already too poofy because apparently nuns didn't believe in flatirons.

"I never liked him, either." Stark took my hand and kissed it. Then he looked Heath in the eye. "I don't like it much that you and Zoey are Imprinted, but I don't have a problem with you."

"I'm cool with you, too, dude," Heath said. "But I don't like it much that you slept with Zo."

"Hey, just part of the job description of being her Warrior, keeping her safe and all."

"Okay, vomit," Aphrodite said. "By the way, testosterone dorks, you should know Z dumped Erik—no matter what kind of spin he tries to put on it. Keep in mind she could do that to either of you if you get too damn annoying." She unwrapped herself from around Darius, marched over to me, and looked me in the eye. "Ready to go in there and face the pain-in-the-ass masses?"

"In a sec." I turned to Sister Mary Angela. "How's Grandma this morning?"

"Worn out. I'm afraid she did entirely too much yesterday."

"Is she okay?"

"She will be."

"Maybe I should go to her and—"

I started to walk away from the dining room, but Aphrodite

caught my wrist. "Grandma's going to be fine. Right now I can promise you she'd rather have you figure out what we're doing next than stress about her."

"Stress? Did someone say they were stressin'?" Stevie Rae jogged around the corner of the hallway with Dallas at her side. "Hey there, Z!" She enveloped me in a big hug. "Sorry that I snapped your head off before. I guess we both have been stressin' too much lately. Forgive me?" she whispered.

"Of course," I whispered back and tried not to wrinkle my nose as I hugged her. She smelled like basement and earth and something else stinky I couldn't identify.

"Hey," I said quickly under my breath to her. "I dumped Erik and he's hooked up with Venus—in front of everybody."

"Well, that sucks like your mama forgettin' your birthday," she said out loud, not paying any attention to our audience.

"Yeah," I said. "It definitely sucks."

"You gonna go in and face him, or turn tail and run?" she asked with a wickedly cute smile.

"What do you think, Ado Annie?" Aphrodite said. "Z doesn't run from a fight."

"Who's Ado Annie?" Heath asked.

"Dunno," Stark said.

"That's a character from the musical *Oklahoma*!" Sister Mary Angela said as she tried to stifle a giggle by clearing her throat. "Shall we have breakfast?" Smiling, the nun headed into the cafeteria.

I sighed and had the urge to run shrieking down the hall in the opposite direction.

"Come on, Z. Let's go in there and get somethin' to eat. Plus, I got stuff to tell y'all that's gonna make your boyfriend issues seem like nothin'." Stevie Rae grabbed my hand, and swinging it, pulled me into the dining room. Trailed by Stark, Heath, Darius, Aphrodite, and Dallas, we found seats beside Sister Mary Angela at the same table where Damien, Jack, and the Twins were already sitting.

"Hey, Z! You're finally up! Check out the seriously yummy pancakes the nun cooks made us," Jack bubbled at me.

"Pancakes?" My world instantly brightened.

"Yeah! There're plates and plates of this stuff *and* bacon and hash browns. It's better than IHOP!" He glanced down the table and yelled, "Hey! Pass the pancakes!"

Platters started to clatter our way, and my mouth began to water. I seriously heart me some pancakes.

"We like French toast better," Shaunee said.

"Yeah, it's not as mushy," Erin said.

"Pancakes aren't mushy," Jack said.

"Merry meet, Z," Damien spoke up, obviously defusing a pancake debate.

"Merry meet," I smiled at him.

"Hey, except for your poofy hair you look lots better than you did before," Jack said.

"Thanks. I think." I said it through a big bite of pancake.

"I think she looks amazing," Stark said from where he was sitting a little way down the table.

"Me, too. I like Zoey's bed head," Heath grinned at me.

I was rolling my eyes at both of them when Erik's voice drifted across the room to me.

"Really, *really* crowded over there." His back was turned to us, but that didn't stop his voice from projecting obnoxiously.

Why couldn't breakups be easy? Why couldn't Erik just not be a butt? *Because you really hurt his feelings* flitted through my mind, but I was sick of being worried about Erik's feelings. He'd been a possessive jerk! And what a damn hypocrite. He'd called me a ho, but it'd taken him less than a day to hook up with someone else. Jeesh.

"Wait, Erik's with Venus?" Jack's voice caught my attention.

"We broke up last night," I said, nonchalantly forking pancakes onto my plate and waving at Erin to pass me the platter of bacon.

"Yeah, that's what Aphrodite told us. But now he's with *Venus*? Just like that?" Jack repeated, staring at Erik and the aforementioned Venus, who was spider monkeying all over him so much that I was shocked that he could eat. "I thought he was a nice guy." Jack sounded totally young and disillusioned, like Erik had just burst his perfect-guy bubble.

I shrugged. "It's okay, Jack. Erik's not really a bad guy. We're just bad *together*," I said, hating how upset Jack looked. Wanting to change the subject, I announced, "Aphrodite had another vision."

"What did you see?" Damien asked her.

Aphrodite glanced at me, and I nodded almost imperceptibly. "Kalona burning up vamps and people."

"*Burning* them?" Shaunee spoke right up. "Sounds like something I should be able to discourage. I am Miss Fire."

"Right you are, Twin," Erin said.

"Brain sharers—*you* weren't in the vision." Aphrodite jabbed her syrupy fork at the Twins. "Fire and blood and horror and whatnot were. You two were probably shopping."

Shaunee and Erin narrowed their eyes at Aphrodite.

"Where was Zoey?" Damien asked.

Aphrodite's gaze found mine as she answered. "Zoey was there. In one of my visions that was a good thing. In the other, not so good."

"What's that supposed to mean?" Jack asked.

"The vision was confusing. Seemed like what I saw was a double-edged sword."

To me it was obvious that she was stalling, and I was just opening my mouth to tell her to go ahead and tell them everything when Kramisha, who was sitting down the table to my right, raised her arm and waved around the piece of paper she was holding.

"I know what it means," she said. "Or I know part a what it means. I wrote this before I went to bed last night." She smiled at Sister Mary Angela. "After we finished watching that nun movie."

"I'm glad you liked it, dear," Sister Mary Angela said.

"I did, but I still think them kids was bad."

"What are you flailing around?" Aphrodite asked.

"You could be a little patient," Kramisha said. "And show some manners. It's for Zoey anyway. Here, pass it down to her."

The piece of paper was passed from person to person till it got to me. As everyone had probably suspected, it was one of Kramisha's poems. I stifled a sigh.

As if reading my mind, Aphrodite said, "Please tell me it's not another one of those prophetic poems. Goddess, they give me a headache."

"Better stock up on Tylenol," I said. I read the first line to myself, blinked, and then looked up at Aphrodite. "What did you say just a second ago? Something about a sword?"

"She said you bein' there with Kalona was a double-edged sword. That's what made me give you the poem now, 'stead of waitin' for a more private time." Kramisha's sharp gaze found Erik, then she added, "I have more sense than some people 'bout puttin' my business all out in public."

"That's the first line of this poem, 'A double-edged sword,'" I said.

"That's spooky," said Stevie Rae.

"Yep," I said, staring at the poem. "Spooky is a good word for it."

"What do you want to do about it?" Damien asked me.

"I want to take the poem and, with the help of my friends, figure it out. But I want to do it at home," I said simply.

Damien smiled and nodded. "Home. That sounds good."

I looked at Aphrodite. "What do you think?"

"I think I miss the Vichy shower in my room," she said.

"Darius?" I asked.

"We have to go back before we can focus on going forward."

"Shaunee and Erin?"

They glanced at each other, and then Erin said, "Home. Definitely."

"Stevie Rae?"

"Well, I have somethin' to tell y'all before you make any big decisions."

"Okay, go ahead," I said.

I watched Stevie Rae suck in a big, long breath and then blow it out through her pursed lips, like she was taking an asthma test. Her words followed her breath and she spoke quickly and clearly, letting what she said carry throughout the room.

"There're more red fledglings than just the kids here. They didn't change when I did like these guys. They're still bad. I think—I think they might still be connected to Neferet." She turned to me and her eyes begged me to understand. "I didn't say anything to you 'cause I wanted to give them a chance. I thought that they'd find their humanity again if they were just left alone and could think through

148

things on their own, or if maybe I could help them. I'm sorry, Z. I didn't mean to cause any problems and I never wanted to lie to you."

I couldn't be pissed at Stevie Rae. All I could do was feel relieved that she'd finally told me the truth.

"Sometimes you can't tell your friends everything you'd like to tell them," I said.

Stevie Rae let out her breath on a sob. "Oh, Z! You don't hate me?"

"Of course not," I said. "I've had to keep some pretty crappy secrets, so I get it."

"Where are they?" Damien's question would have seemed harsh, but his voice was gentle, his warm brown eyes filled with understanding.

"They're in the depot tunnels. That's why I just sealed off the dirt tunnel that I made to get everyone here. I didn't want any of the others following us and causing the nuns problems."

"You should have warned us last night," Darius said. "We would have posted guards while everyone was sleeping."

"There were rogue red fledglings at the other end of your tunnel?" Sister Mary Angela's hand found the rosary that hung around her neck.

"Oh, Sister, you weren't in any danger. Darius, we didn't need to post guards, promise!" she quickly explained. "Those other kids are affected by daylight big-time. They never move around while the sun's up, not even in the tunnels."

Darius's frown said he still would have posted a guard. Sister Mary Angela didn't say anything, but I saw her fingers worrying her rosary beads. It was then that I noticed none of the red fledglings were speaking. I glanced at the only other red vampyre in existence. "Did you know about these other fledglings?"

"Me? Hell no. I would've told you right away," Stark said.

"I should have told you right away. I'm real sorry I didn't," Stevie Rae said.

"Sometimes the truth can get buried and it's hard to figure out how to uncover it," I told her, and then I looked around the room at the other red fledglings. "You guys all knew, didn't you?"

Kramisha spoke up. "We knew. We don't like them other kids. They's bad news."

"They smell bad, too," little Shannoncompton said from a ways down the table.

"They suck," Dallas said. "And they remind us of how it used to be."

"That's something we don't like to remember," said muscle-y Johnny B.

I turned my attention back to Stevie Rae. "Is there anything else you want to tell me?"

"Well, I don't think it's smart for us to go back to the depot tunnels right now, so going home to the House of Night sounds good to me, too."

"Then it's settled. We go home," I said.

CHAPTER TWENTY

Zoey

"I'm all for getting back where we belong, but your grandma should stay here," Aphrodite said suddenly. "We don't know what all we're going to have to deal with at the House of Night."

"Did your visions show you something else?" I asked, noticing that she was looking at Stevie Rae instead of me.

Aphrodite shook her head slowly. "No, I told you everything I saw in my visions. I just have a feeling, that's all."

Stevie Rae laughed nervously. "Well, heck, Aphrodite, we're all *feelin'* jumpy and on edge, which makes total sense. We just chased away some major booger monsters, but that's no reason to freak Zoey out."

"I'm not freaking her out, bumpkin," Aphrodite said. "I'm just being careful."

"It is wise to anticipate dangers," Darius said thoughtfully.

Since there was nothing wrong with being careful, I opened my mouth to agree with both of them when Stevie Rae turned to Darius and in a cold, flat voice said, "Just because you've sworn your Warrior's Oath to her doesn't mean you have to agree with everything she says."

"What?" Stark said. "You gave Aphrodite your Oath?"

"Really?" Damien said.

"Wow, too cool," Jack said.

Erik snorted from the table behind us. "I'm shocked Zoey let you and didn't just add you to her private collection."

By that time I'd had enough. I yelled over at him, "Oh, go to hell, Erik!"

"Zoey!" Sister Mary Angela gasped.

"Sorry," I muttered.

"Don't be sorry," Aphrodite said, glaring at Stevie Rae. "Hell isn't a bad word. It's a place. And some people do need to be sent there."

"What?" Stevie Rae said innocently. "You didn't want everyone to know about you and Darius?"

"My business is *my* business," Aphrodite said.

"Just like I was sayin' before," Kramisha nodded sagely. "It just ain't right to put your personal business all out in public." She turned her dark eyes on Stevie Rae. "I know you our High Priestess and all, so I don't mean no disrespect, but I think you was raised better than that."

Stevie Rae looked instantly contrite. "You're right, Kramisha. I guess I didn't think it was that big a deal. I mean, everyone would know sooner or later." She smiled at me and shrugged her shoulders. "A Warrior's Oath isn't exactly somethin' you can hide." She turned to Aphrodite. "Sorry, I wasn't tryin' to be mean."

"I'm not interested in your apology. I'm not Zoey. I'm not going to automatically believe everything you say."

"Okay, *enough!*" I shouted. Anger and frustration added power to my words, and I saw several kids flinch. "All of you need to listen up and get something straight. We can't fight big, world-ending evil if we're bickering with each other! Stevie Rae and Aphrodite—get over the fact that you're Imprinted and learn not to embarrass each other." I saw hurt in Aphrodite's eyes and shock in Stevie Rae's, but I kept going. "Stevie Rae, don't keep important stuff from me, even if you think you have a good reason to." I looked squarely at Erik, who had turned around in his chair so he could stare at me. "And Erik, we have lots bigger problems than you being pissed I dumped you." I heard Stark chuckle and I rounded on him. "You don't get a free pass, either."

Stark raised his hands like he was surrendering. "I'm just laughing because Erik the Great got put in his place."

"Which is real crappy of you since you can feel how much this whole thing with you and Erik and Heath has hurt my feelings."

Stark's cocky smile faded.

"Darius, it's an icy mess out there, but do you think you can drive the Hummer back to the House of Night?" I asked.

"I do," said the warrior.

"Who's good on a horse?" Instantly several hands went up like I was a mean teacher and they were all scared of being in trouble. "Shaunee, you and Erin can ride the horse you got here on." I looked around at the kids still holding up their hands. "Johnny B, can you and Kramisha double on the other mare?"

"Yep, we can," he said. Kramisha nodded briskly, and they both put down their hands.

"Stark, you can ride behind me on Persephone," I said without looking at him. "Damien, Jack, Aphrodite, Shannoncompton, Venus, and . . ." I stared at a brunette red fledgling whose name I absolutely could not remember.

"Sophie," Stevie Rae said hesitantly, like she was scared I might snap her head off.

"And Sophie. You guys go with Darius in the Hummer." I looked at Stevie Rae. "Can you be sure the rest of the red fledglings and Erik get to the House of Night safely?"

"If that's what you want me to do, then that's what I'll do," she said.

"Good. Finish breakfast and then let's go home." I stood up and took in all the nuns with one long look. "I appreciate you helping us more than I'll ever be able to tell you. As long as I'm alive, the Benedictine Sisters will have a High Priestess as a friend." Then I turned to leave. As I passed Stark, I saw him start to get up, but I caught his eyes and shook my head. "I'm going to say bye to Grandma—by myself." I could see that I'd hurt him, but he only saluted me respectfully and said, "As you wish, my lady."

Ignoring the silence I left in my wake, I walked out of the room, alone.

"So, *u-we-tsi-a-ge-ya,* you made everyone angry?" Grandma said after listening to me rant while I paced back and forth beside her bed.

"Well, not everyone. I hurt some people's feelings instead of making them mad."

Grandma studied me for a long time. When she finally spoke her words were typically simple but straight to the point. "That is unlike you, so you must have had a good reason for acting so out of character."

"Well, I'm scared and confused. Yesterday I felt like a High Priestess. Today I'm just a kid again. I have boyfriend issues and a best friend who's been keeping stuff from me."

"All that means is neither you nor Stevie Rae is perfect," Grandma said.

"But how do I know that's all it means? What if I'm a shallow ho and Stevie Rae's gone evil?"

"Only time will show whether your trust in Stevie Rae has been misplaced. And I think you should stop being so hard on yourself for being attracted to more than one boy. You're making good judgments about the relationships in your life. From what you've said, Erik's behavior was controlling and boorish. There are many young women who would have ignored all of that because he's, how do you put it, *so hot!*" Grandma did a bad teenage imitation. "You'll learn to balance Heath and Stark, many High Priestesses do. Or you won't, and you'll decide committing yourself to one man is the right path for you. But, darling, that is something you have many, many years to decide."

"I suppose you're right," I said.

"Of course I'm right. I'm old. Which means I can also tell there's more bothering you than boys or Stevie Rae. What is it, Zoeybird?"

"I had a memory of A-ya, Grandma."

Grandma's sharp intake of breath was the only outward sign of her inward shock. "Did the memory involve Kalona?"

"Yes."

"Was it pleasant or unpleasant?"

"Both! It started out as terrifying, but as I got closer and closer to A-ya, it changed. She loved him, Grandma. And I could feel that."

Grandma nodded and spoke slowly. "Yes, *u-we-tsi-a-ge-ya*, that makes sense. A-ya was created to love him."

"It scares me and makes me feel out of control!" I cried.

"Sssh, daughter," Grandma soothed. "We are all affected by our pasts, but it is within our power not to let what we have done dictate what we will do."

"Even at a soul-deep level?"

"Especially at a soul-deep level. Ask yourself where is it your great gifts originate."

"Well, from Nyx," I said.

"And did the goddess gift your body or your soul?"

"My soul, of course. My body's just a shell for my soul." I was surprised at the firmness of my voice. I blinked in surprise. "I have to remember it's *my* soul now, and treat A-ya like I would any memory from my past."

Grandma smiled. "Ah, there, I knew you'd find your center again. When you make mistakes, whether they are from this life or another, learn from them—then they become opportunities."

Not if my mistakes let Kalona burn up the world, I thought, and almost said aloud, but just then Grandma closed her eyes. She looked so tired and hurt and *old* that it made my stomach clench and feel more than a little sick.

"I'm sorry I dumped all this on you, Grandma," I said.

She opened her eyes and patted my hand. "Don't ever be sorry for speaking your mind to me, *u-we-tsi-a-ge-ya.*"

I kissed Grandma lightly on her forehead, being careful not to hurt any of her cuts and bruises. "I love you, Grandma."

"And I love you, *u-we-tsi-a-ge-ya.* Go with the Goddess, and the blessings of our ancestors."

My hand had just touched the doorknob when her voice rang between us, sounding strong and sure and wise as ever.

"Hold to the truth, *u-we-tsi-a-ge-ya.* Do not ever forget, as our people have always known, there is a deep power in words that speak the truth."

"I'll try my best, Grandma."

"And that is all I will ever ask of you, my Zoeybird."

CHAPTER TWENTY-ONE

Zoey

The ride back to the House of Night was slow and weird and awkward.

It was slow because even with Shaunee and me directing fire to warm the hooves of the horses so that we could trot down Twenty-first Street and take a left at the Utica Street light (which was totally dark), it was still a slick, frigid, difficult trek.

It was weird because everything was so darn dark. Here's what happens when your city loses light: it doesn't look right. It sounds simplistic, especially coming from a kid who is supposed to be one of the children of the night or whatnot, but the world doesn't look the same when the lights go out.

And it was awkward because Shaunee and Erin kept throwing looks at me like they thought I was a bomb that might explode. Johnny B and Kramisha hardly talked to me at all, and Stark, who was sitting behind me on my amazing mare, Persephone, wouldn't so much as rest his hands on my waist.

Me? I just wanted to go home.

Darius drove the Hummer behind us at I'm sure what must have felt like a crawl to him, even though the three horses were managing a steady trot. The red fledglings, led by Stevie Rae and Erik, followed the Hummer. Except for the car and the hooves of the horses, the night was as silent as it was dark, though once in a while, creepily, a branch would give up under its icy weight and, with a terrible *crack!* a tree would break.

We'd turned left on Utica before I said anything.

"So are you just not going to ever talk to me again?" I asked Stark.

"I'll talk to you," he said.

"Why does it seem like there should be a 'but' at the end of that sentence?"

He hesitated and I could practically feel the tension that radiated off him. Finally he let out a long breath and said, "I don't know whether to be pissed at you, or to say I'm sorry for the messed-up shit that happened in the cafeteria."

"Well, the cafeteria wasn't your fault. Or at least most of it wasn't."

"Yeah, see, I know that, but I also know your feelings were hurt by the whole Erik thing."

I didn't know what to say to that, so we rode on in silence for a while until Stark cleared his throat and said, "You were pretty hard on everyone back there."

"I had to shut up the bickering, and that seemed like the quickest way."

"Next time you could try saying something like, 'Guys, shut up your bickering!' I dunno, maybe it's just me, but that makes more sense than freaking on your friends."

I stifled the urge to snap back and say I'd like to see him do any better. Instead I thought about what he'd said. He might be right. I didn't feel comfortable with the fact that I'd snapped at everyone—especially since a bunch of the "everyones" were my friends.

"I'll try to do better next time," I finally said.

Stark didn't gloat. He didn't turn all tough-guy–like and patronize me, either. He just rested his hands on my shoulders, squeezed, and said, "The fact that you actually listen to other people is one of the things I like best about you."

I could feel my cheeks get warm at his unexpected compliment. "Thanks," I said softly. I ran my fingers through Persephone's cold, wet mane, liking how her ears twitched back in response. "You're a really good girl," I crooned to her.

"Thought you mighta noticed by now that I'm not a girl," Stark said with a cocky smile in his voice.

"I noticed." I laughed and the tension between us evaporated. The Twins, Johnny B, and Kramisha looked our way with tentative smiles.

"So, uh, you and I are okay?" I asked him.

"You and I will *always* be okay. I'm your Warrior, your protector. No matter what else is going on, I'll have your back."

When my throat cleared enough for me to speak, I said, "Being my Warrior might not always be an easy job."

He laughed, full and loud and long. He also slid his arms around my waist and said, "Zoey, sometimes being your Warrior will suck royally."

I was going to mention that, just perhaps, his *mom* sucked royally, but his arms were warm around me and his touch was soothing. So I grumbled something about him being full of bullpoopie, and let myself relax back against him.

"You know," he said. "If you could forget all the craziness the storm is causing, and the whole Kalona-Neferet mess, the ice really does look cool. It's almost like it's taken us out of the real world and transported us to a weird winter land. Like someplace the White Witch would really like."

"Oooh, *The Lion, the Witch and the Wardrobe!* That was a great movie."

He cleared his throat. "I didn't see it."

"You didn't see it?" My eyes widened and I glanced over my shoulder at him. "You read the book?"

"Book*s*," he said, putting special emphasis on the plural. "C. S. Lewis wrote way more than one Narnia book."

"You read?"

"I read," he said.

"Huh," I said, feeling befuddled (as Grandma would have said).

"What's wrong with that? Reading's good," he said defensively.

"I know! It's cool you read. Actually it's hot that you read." And it was. I loved it when cute guys showed they had brains.

"Really? Well, you'd definitely be interested in the fact that I just read *To Kill a Mockingbird*."

I smiled and elbowed him. "Everyone's read that."

"I've read it five times."

"Nu-uh."

"Yep. I can quote parts of it."

"That's bullpoopie."

And then Stark, my big, bad, macho Warrior, raised his voice, put on a little girl's Southern drawl, and said, "'Uncle Jack? What's a whore-lady?'"

"I do not think that's the most important quote from that book," I said, but laughed anyway.

"Okay, how about: 'Ain't no snot-nosed slut of a schoolteacher ever born c'n make me do nothin'!' That one's really my favorite."

"You got a twisted mind, James Stark." I was smiling and feeling warm and happy when we turned into the long driveway that led to the House of Night. I was just thinking how magical it looked, all lit up and welcoming, when I noticed there was more light than usual coming from the school's backup generators and old-fashioned oil lanterns. Then I realized the light wasn't coming from any of the school buildings. Instead it was flickering from an area between Nyx's Temple and the school proper.

I felt Stark tense instantly.

"What is that?" I asked.

"Stop the horses," he said.

"Whoa." I pulled Persephone to a halt, calling for Shaunee and Johnny B to stop their horses, too. "What's going on?"

"Keep your eyes open. Be ready to ride back to the abbey. Go and go quickly if I tell you to. And don't wait for me!" was all Stark said before he slid off Persephone and sprinted behind us to the Hummer.

I twisted around and could see that Darius was already getting out of the Hummer as Heath took his place behind the driver's wheel. The two warriors talked briefly, and then Darius called Erik and all the male red fledglings to him, plus Stevie Rae. I was just getting ready to head Persephone over to the Hummer when Stark jogged back to me.

"What is it?" I asked.

"Something's on fire inside the school grounds."

"Can you tell what it's from?" I asked Shaunee.

"Don't know," Shaunee said, wrinkling her forehead in concentration. "But it feels sacred."

Sacred? What the hell?

Stark took Persephone's bridle to get my attention. "Look under the trees."

I looked to my right, to the row of Bradford pear trees that lined the lane leading to the House of Night. There were things under them—shadows within shadows of crumpled forms. My stomach felt sick when I realized what I was seeing.

"Raven Mockers," I said.

"They's dead," Kramisha said.

"We have to check. We have to know for sure," Stevie Rae said. She had stepped up with the red fledgling males and Erik.

"That we will," Darius said. Then, pulling a knife for each of his hands from inside his leather jacket, he told Stark, "Stay with Zoey." Nodding to Stevie Rae and Erik to follow him, he started toward the trees.

It didn't take long.

"Dead," he called, after pausing by each one.

When the group rejoined us, I couldn't help but notice how white Stevie Rae's face looked.

"You okay?" I asked her.

She looked up at me, her eyes more than a little startled. "Yeah," she said quickly. "Fine. It's just . . ." Her voice trailed off and her gaze went back to the grisly lumps under the trees.

"It's 'cause they smell bad." Kramisha said. We all looked at her. "Well, it's true. Them Raven Mockers have something nasty in they blood."

"Their blood does smell wrong. I know because I had to clean it up from where Darius had shot some of them down from the sky back at the abbey," Stevie Rae spoke quickly, like the subject made her uncomfortable.

"That's what I smelled on you!" I was relieved I'd finally identified the odd scent.

"Everyone needs to focus on the here and now," Darius said. "We don't know what's happening in there." He motioned toward the school grounds and the flickering flames that were illuminating its heart.

"What is that? Is the school really on fire?" Stevie Rae spoke our thoughts aloud.

"I can tell you what it is." The voice startled all of us except the three horses we rode, which should have clued me in instantly to who was standing in the shadows on the field house side of the lane. "It is a funeral pyre," said Lenobia, Professor of Equestrian Studies, and one of the few adult vamps who had stood by us after Kalona and Neferet had taken over the school.

She went straight to the horses, greeting them, checking them, and generally ignoring us until she was sure they were okay. Finally, looking up from caressing Persephone's muzzle she said, "Merry meet, Zoey."

"Merry meet," I responded automatically.

"Did you kill him?"

I shook my head. "We chased him away. Kramisha's poem was right. When the five of us joined, we were able to banish him with love. But whose—"

"Is Neferet dead or just fled with him?" she interrupted my question.

"Fled. Whose funeral is the pyre for?" I couldn't wait any longer to ask.

Lenobia's beautiful blue-gray eyes met mine. "Anastasia Lankford lost her life. The last act Kalona's favorite son, Rephaim, did before he called his brothers with him to follow you to the abbey was to slit her throat."

CHAPTER TWENTY-TWO

Zoey

I heard Stevie Rae's horrified gasp echoed by everyone surrounding us, but Darius didn't hesitate. "Are there any Raven Mockers left alive here?"

"None. May their souls rot eternally in the deepest depths of the Otherworld," Lenobia said bitterly.

"Did anyone else die?" I asked.

"No, though there are several wounded. They've filled the infirmary. Neferet was our only real healer, and now that she . . ." Lenobia's voice trailed off.

"Then Zoey needs to get to the wounded," Stark said.

Lenobia and I wrinkled our foreheads questioningly at him.

"Me? But I'm—"

"You're the closest thing we have to a High Priestess. If there are hurt fledglings and vampyres at the House of Night, they need their High Priestess," Stark said simply.

"Especially if she has an affinity for spirit. You could definitely help soothe the wounded," Darius added.

"You are correct, of course," Lenobia said, brushing her long white-blond hair back from her face. "I'm sorry. Stasia's death has taken a toll on me. I'm not thinking clearly." She smiled at me, but it was really more of a grimace of upturned lips than a true smile. "Your help is welcome and needed, Zoey."

"I'll do whatever I can." I put pretend confidence in my voice, but the truth was, just the thought of hurt people was making my stomach sick.

"We'll all help out." Stevie Rae spoke up. "If one affinity can help, maybe five can help times five."

"Perhaps," Lenobia said, still looking defeated and sad.

"It'll bring hope back in."

I glanced down in surprise to see Aphrodite move to Darius's side and wrap her arm through his. Lenobia gave her a skeptical look. "I think you'll see things have changed at the House of Night, Aphrodite."

"That's okay. We're getting good with change," Aphrodite said.

"Yeah, change is almost our same," Kramisha said. Several of the other kids made sounds of agreement.

I was so proud of them I almost burst into tears.

"I think we're all ready to be home," I said.

"Home." Lenobia repeated the word in a sad, soft voice. "Then follow me into what home has become." She turned, made a clucking sound, and, as one, the three horses followed her without any direction from us.

From the main entrance of the school we moved through the parking lot, which was where Darius motioned for Heath to park the Hummer, and we all paused to dismount and regroup. The edge of the professor's building and the infirmary blocked our view of the center of the school grounds so, eerily, all we could see were the dancing shadows made by the flames.

Except for the crackling of fire consuming wood, the school was absolutely silent.

"It's bad," Shaunee said softly.

"What do you mean?" I asked.

"I can feel sadness through the flames. It's bad," she repeated.

"Shaunee is correct," Lenobia said. "I'll take the horses to the stable. Do you want to come with me, or would you rather . . ." Her voice faded as her gaze was drawn to the flickering shadows the firelight cast against the boughs of the ancient oaks that grew throughout the center of the school grounds.

"We'll go in there," I said, motioning toward the heart of the school. "Might as well face it."

"I'll follow as soon as the horses are cared for," Lenobia said. She disappeared into the darkness with the horses at her heels.

Stark's hand was warm and steady on my shoulder. "Remember, Kalona is gone, and so is Neferet. That leaves fledglings and vamps for you to handle, which should be simple after what you've gone through," he said.

Heath stepped up to flank my other side. "He's right. Even dealing with hurt fledglings and vamps isn't as bad as Neferet and Kalona."

"It is our home, no matter what has happened," said Darius.

"Yeah, home. It's about time we took it back," Aphrodite said.

"Let's see what kind of mess Neferet left for us," I said abruptly. I stepped away from Stark and Heath, leading everyone to the sidewalk that went around the pretty fountain and garden area outside the professors' entrance and the castle-like round wooden doors, beside the turret that was really a media center. Finally, the central grounds of the school came into view.

"Oh, Goddess!" Aphrodite gasped.

My feet stopped without me consciously telling them to. The scene was just so awful that I couldn't make myself move forward. The funeral pyre was an enormous mound of firewood that had been placed under and around a wooden picnic bench. I knew it was a picnic bench because even though it was burning, the structure was still completely recognizable, as was the body that lay on top of the table. Professor Anastasia, the beautiful wife of our Fencing Master, Dragon Lankford, had been dressed in something long and flowing and covered by a white linen shroud. Horribly, her body could still be seen through it. Her arms were crossed over her chest and her long hair fell toward the ground, lifting and crackling in the fire.

A terrible noise, like a heartbroken child's cry, pierced the night, and my gaze, which had been fixed on the grisly pyre, shifted to a place near the head of the bench. Dragon Lankford was there on his knees. His head was bowed and his long hair swept forward, though it didn't hide the fact that he was weeping. Beside him a huge cat I recognized as Shadowfax, his Maine Coon, leaned into him, staring up into his face. In his arms was a delicate white cat who was yowling and struggling to get free, apparently willing to hurl herself onto the pyre with her vampyre.

"Guinevere," I whispered. "That's Anastasia's cat." I pressed my hand to my mouth, trying to hold in the sob that was building there.

Shaunee stepped quickly away from us and walked over to the pyre, standing way closer than any of us could have. At the same time, Erin moved to Dragon's side. As Shaunee raised her arms and called loudly, "Fire! Come to me!" I heard Erin's softer voice asking water to join her. While the pyre and the body were suddenly engulfed in camouflaging flames, Dragon was surrounded by a cool mist that reminded me of tears.

Damien moved close to Erin. "Wind, come to me," he said. I watched him direct a soft breeze to blow away the terrible smell of burning flesh.

Stevie Rae joined Damien. "Earth, come to me," she said. Instantly the breeze that had blown away the scent of death was filled with the delicate sweetness of a meadow, bringing to mind images of springtime, growing things, and the verdant meadows of our Goddess.

I knew my part was next. Filled with sadness I walked to Dragon and gently put one hand on his shoulder, which shook with his sobs. I raised my other hand and said, "Spirit, come to me." When I felt the beautiful rush that was the element answering my call, I continued, "Touch Dragon, spirit. Soothe him and Guinevere and Shadowfax. Help their grief to be bearable." Then I concentrated on directing spirit through me, into Dragon and the two devastated cats. Guinevere stopped yowling. I felt Dragon's body jerk and slowly his head raised and his eyes met mine. His face was terribly scratched, and there was a deep gash over his left eye. I remembered that last time I'd seen him he had been battling three Raven Mockers. "Blessed be, Dragon," I said softly.

"How will it ever be bearable, Priestess?" His voice was rough. He sounded completely broken.

I felt an instant of panic—an instant of *I'm seventeen! I can't possibly help him!* Then, like a perfect circle, spirit spiraled from Dragon, through me, and into the Fencing Master again, and I pulled strength from my element. "You'll see her again. She's with Nyx now. She'll either wait for you in the Goddess's meadows, or she'll be reborn and her soul will find you again during this lifetime. You can bear it because you know that spirit never really ends—we never really end."

His eyes searched mine, and I held his gaze steadily. "Did you defeat them? Are the creatures gone?"

"Kalona and Neferet are gone. So are the Raven Mockers," I assured him.

"Good . . . good . . ." Dragon bowed his head and I heard him praying softly to Nyx, asking the Goddess to look after his beloved until they met again.

I squeezed his shoulder once and then, feeling like an intruder, stepped away to allow him some privacy for his grief.

"Blessed be, Priestess," he said without lifting his head.

I probably should have said something mature and wise in response, but just then I was so filled with emotion I couldn't talk. Stevie Rae was suddenly there beside me, Damien next to her. Erin moved away from Dragon to stand at my other side, and Shaunee stepped into the space beside her. We stood there silently, respectfully, a circle uncast but present as Shaunee's magickally enhanced fire took the last of Anastasia's physical shell.

The silence that surrounded us was broken only by the sounds of flames and Dragon's murmured prayers. Which was when a new thought struck me. I glanced around the pyre. Dragon had placed it in the middle of the paved drive that circled between Nyx's Temple and the main school buildings. It was a good choice—there was plenty of room for the fire. There was also plenty of room for the other professors and fledglings who should have been there, standing beside Dragon and sending prayers to Nyx for Anastasia, as well as her mate, not intruding on his grief, but bearing silent witness that they loved and supported him.

"No one's out here with him," I said quietly, not wanting Dragon to hear the disgust in my voice. "Where the hell is everyone?"

"He shouldn't be out here alone," Stevie Rae said, wiping tears from her face. "It's just not right."

"I was with him until I felt the horses approaching," Lenobia said, jogging up to join us.

"What about everyone else?" I asked.

She shook her head, the disgust I felt was mirrored in her expression. "The fledglings are in the dorms. The professors are in their rooms. Anyone else is in the infirmary—anyone else who would have cared to stand with him, that is."

"That doesn't make any sense." I couldn't wrap my mind around it. "How could his students and the professors not care to stand with him?"

"Kalona and Neferet might be gone, but their poison remains," Lenobia said cryptically.

"You need to be in the infirmary," Aphrodite said, coming up behind us. I noticed she kept her gaze from moving to the pyre or Dragon.

"Go," Lenobia said. "I'll remain here with him."

"So will we," Johnny B said. "He was my favorite professor before, you know."

I did know. Johnny B meant before he'd died and then un-died.

"We'll all stay with him," Kramisha said. "It ain't right that he's alone, and you and your circle's got business to take care of in there." She turned her eyes to the infirmary part of the school building. "Come on," she called, and the rest of the red fledglings stepped out of the shadows to take places beside Dragon, creating a circle around the pyre.

"I'll stay, too," Jack said. He was crying steadily, but he didn't hesitate to take his place in the circle the red fledglings were making. Duchess stayed close beside him, her tail and ears down as if she truly understood. Without saying anything, Erik stepped beside Jack. Then Heath surprised me by filling the space next to Erik. He nodded at me solemnly before bowing his head.

I wasn't sure of my voice, so I simply turned and, with my circle following me, along with Aphrodite, Stark, and Darius, we reentered the House of Night.

CHAPTER TWENTY-THREE

Zoey

The school's infirmary wasn't very big. Actually, it was only three little hospital-like rooms on one of the floors of the professors' building. So it was no surprise that there were hurt kids spilling out of the rooms. Not that it wasn't shocking to see an additional three pallets, each filled with a hurt fledgling, scattered in the hallway. The wounded kids blinked in surprise as my group and I paused in the entrance.

"Zoey?" I looked up from trying not to stare at the hurt kids—and not to smell the blood that seemed to hang in the air around us—to see two vampyres hurrying toward me. I recognized them as Neferet's assistants, kinda like the equivalent of nurses, and had to think hard to remember that the tall blonde called herself Sapphire, and the short, Asian one was Margareta. "Were you injured, too?" Sapphire asked, looking me over quickly.

"No, I'm fine. We're all fine," I assured her. "Actually, we're here to help."

"Without a healer we've done all that can be done for them," said Margareta bluntly. "None of the fledglings are in immediate danger of dying, though one never knows how an injury will affect the Change, so it is always possible that several of them might—"

"Okay, yeah, we get it." I cut her off before she could say "die" all loud and obvious in front of the group of kids who might very well die. Jeesh, talk about bad bedside manner.

"We aren't here because of our medical skills," Damien explained.

"We're here because our circle is powerful, and within it we might be able to soothe those who have been injured."

"None of the other uninjured fledglings are here," said Sapphire, as if that was a reason for us to not be here, too.

"None of the other fledglings have affinities for the elements," I said.

"Really, we have done all that can be done," Margareta repeated coolly. "Without a High Priestess—"

This time Stark cut her off. "We have a High Priestess, so it's time for you to step aside and let her, and her circle, help these kids."

"Yeah, back off," Aphrodite said, literally getting in the vamp's face.

The two vampyres backed off, though I could feel their icy, disapproving stares.

"What the hell is their problem?" Aphrodite asked in a low voice as we walked into the hallway.

"I don't have a clue," I said. "I don't really even know them."

"I do," Damien said softly. "I volunteered in the infirmary my third-former year. They've always been dour. I thought it was because they had to deal with fledglings dying."

"'Dour'?" Shaunee said.

"Translate him, will ya, Stevie Rae?" Erin said.

"Dour means 'stern and kinda gloomy.' You know, y'all really should read more."

"I was just gonna say that," Stark said.

Damien sighed.

Unbelievably, I had to stifle a smile. The circumstances were bad, but my friends being their normal selves made everything seem just a teensy bit better.

"Nerd herd, focus. You're here to help the fledglings. Dour One and Dour Two aren't important," said Aphrodite.

"Dr. Seuss reference. I like it," Stark said, giving me a check-me-out-I've-*always*-read-books hottie grin.

Aphrodite frowned at him. "I said 'focus,' not 'flirt.' "

"Stevie Rae?" A guy called from a pallet halfway down the hall, interrupting all of us.

"Drew?" Stevie Rae said, and then she hurried to his side. "Drew, are you okay? What happened? Is your arm broke?"

The kid's arm was in a sling. One of his eyes was all bruised and puffy, and his lip was split, but he managed to smile at Stevie Rae. "I'm really glad you're not dead anymore."

She grinned. "Hey, me, too. And I can tell you I don't so much recommend the dying and un-dying stuff, so you gotta rest and get well." Then she sobered as her eyes went back to his wounds, and she added quickly, "But you're gonna be okay. You don't have to worry about that."

"It's no biggie. I didn't break my arm. It just got dislocated when I was wrestling with a Raven Mocker."

"He tried to save Anastasia." My gaze followed the girl's voice into a hospital room beside where Drew was lying. The door was open and I could see a fledgling half reclined in bed with one arm propped on one of those aluminum side tray things that fit on hospital beds. Her entire forearm was wrapped in thick gauze. There was also a nasty cut that ran down the side of her neck and disappeared into her hospital gown. "He almost did it, too. Drew almost saved her."

"Almost isn't good enough," Drew said tightly.

"Almost is better than what lots of kids did," said the girl. "At least you tried."

"What the hell happened, Denio?" Aphrodite asked, moving past me and into the girl's room. I suddenly realized who the girl was. She and her two buddies, Enyo and Pemphredo (named after the three sisters of the Gorgon and Scylla), had been part of Aphrodite's bitchy inner circle before I came to the House of Night and, as Aphrodite herself has said, her life imploded. I braced myself for Denio to make some haggish comment to Aphrodite, since none of her "friends" had actually stayed her friends once she'd fallen from Neferet's good graces and I'd replaced her as Leader of the Dark Daughters. Thankfully, the girl's response wasn't hateful at all, though she sounded frustrated and more than a little pissed.

"Nothing happened. Well, that is, unless you stood up to the damn bird things. Then they attacked you. We"—she gestured with her good arm out at the infirmary— "stood up to them. So did Dragon and Anastasia."

"They attacked Professor Anastasia while Dragon was fighting a bunch of them down the lane. He wasn't close enough to help her. He didn't even see it happening," Drew said. "I grabbed one of them and pulled it off her, but another one came up behind me."

"I grabbed that one," Denio said. She pointed across the hall. "Ian tried to help when the thing turned on me. The Raven Mocker snapped his leg like a twig."

"Ian Bowser?" I asked, sticking my head through the open doorway of the room Denio had pointed to.

"Yeah, it's me," said the scrawny, but kinda cute kid who had one leg propped up and wrapped all the way to his thigh in a cast. He looked way too white against the bleached sheets.

"That looks like it hurts," I said. I knew him from drama class. He'd had a massive crush on our teacher, Professor Nolan—before she was murdered a month or so ago.

"I've felt better," he said, trying to smile.

"Yeah, we've all felt better," said a girl on a pallet farther down the hallway.

"Hanna Honeyyeager! I didn't see you over there," Damien said, moving around me to go to the girl's side. I could understand why he hadn't noticed her before she said something. She was covered by a big white comforter, which she disappeared against because she was seriously the whitest kid I think I've ever seen. You know, one of those blondes who had skin so fair it never tanned and she always looked pink-cheeked and either embarrassed or surprised. I only knew her through Damien. I'd heard him talking to her about flowers—apparently the girl was a genius with anything that bloomed. I remembered that about her, and the fact that everyone always called her by her first and last names, kinda like Shannoncompton, only they didn't run the two together.

"What happened to you, sweetie?" Damien crouched down beside her and took her hand. Her little blond head was wrapped in a gauze bandage that had a bloody spot near the forehead.

"When Professor Anastasia was attacked, I screamed at the Raven Mockers. A lot," she said.

"She has a seriously shrill voice," said a kid from the last hospital room, who I couldn't even see.

"Well, apparently Raven Mockers don't like shrill voices," said Hanna Honeyyeager. "One of them knocked me out."

"Hang on." Erin marched down the hall toward the room of the kid I couldn't see. "Is that you, T.J.?"

"Erin!"

"Oh. My. Goddess!" Erin squealed and rushed into his room.

Right behind her, Shaunee yelled, "Cole? What about Cole?"

"He didn't stand up to them," T.J. answered in a strained voice, which made Shaunee stop at the open door to his room like she'd been smacked in the face.

"Didn't stand up? But . . ." Shaunee's voice faded, like she was utterly confused.

"Oh, shit, boy! Look at your hands!" Erin's exclamation drifted from T.J.'s room.

"Hands?" I repeated.

"T.J.'s a boxer. He even placed in the last Summer Games, against vampyres," Drew explained. "He tried to knock out Rephaim. It didn't quite work out like he expected, and the bird guy tore up his hands."

"*Oh, Goddess, no.*" I heard Stevie Rae say softly, her words filled with horror.

I was watching Shaunee as she stood outside T.J.'s room, looking like she didn't know what to do with herself, which gave me a really bad feeling. Cole and T.J. had been best friends, and they'd been dating the Twins. T.J. was seeing Erin; Cole was seeing Shaunee. The two couples had done a lot of hanging out together. All I could think was, "How could one stand up to the Raven Mockers and not the other?"

"Exactly what I'd like explained to me." I hadn't realized I'd spoken aloud until Darius commented.

The last kid in the hall answered him. "It just happened. The stables caught on fire, then Neferet and Kalona freaked. The Raven

Mockers went crazy. If you stayed out of their way they didn't mess with you, which is what we were doing until one of them grabbed Professor Anastasia. Then some of us tried to help her, but most of the fledglings just ran for the dorms."

I looked at the kid. She had really pretty red hair and eyes that were bright, gorgeous blue. Both of her biceps were wrapped in gauze, and one side of her face was all bruised and swollen. I swear I'd never seen her before in my life.

"Who the heck are you?" I asked.

"I'm Red." She smiled shyly and shrugged. "Yeah, my name's obvious, but that's me. Um, you guys don't know me because I just got Marked. Right before the ice storm hit. Professor Anastasia was my mentor." She swallowed hard and blinked back tears.

"I'm really sorry," I said, thinking how awful it must be for her to be newly Marked, newly uprooted from her family and everything she'd ever known, and plopped down in the middle of this mess.

"I tried to help her, too," Red said. A tear escaped and slid down her face. She brushed it away, wincing as the movement caused pain in her arm. "But that huge Raven Mocker slashed my arms and then threw me against a tree. I couldn't do anything but watch when he—" Her voice broke on a sob.

"Did none of the professors stand with you?" Darius asked, his voice sounding harsh, though it was obvious his anger wasn't directed at Red.

"The professors knew the Raven Mockers had simply become overexcited because Neferet and her consort were highly upset. We knew better than to further agitate them," said Sapphire in a clipped voice from where she and Margareta still stood in the entrance to the infirmary hallway.

Incredulous, I turned to face her. "*They simply became overexcited*? Are you kidding me? Those creatures were attacking House of Night fledglings and none of you did anything about it because you didn't want to agitate them?"

"Unforgivable!" Darius almost spat the word out.

"And what about Dragon and Professor Anastasia? They obviously didn't buy into your whole don't-agitate-them theory," Stark said.

"Wouldn't you know more about what happened than anyone, James Stark? I recall that you were very close to Neferet and Kalona. I even remember seeing you leave the school with them," said Margareta smoothly.

Stark took a step toward her, his eyes beginning to glow a dangerous red. I grabbed his wrist. "No! Fighting our own isn't how we win this," I said to him before I rounded on the two vampyres. "Stark went with Neferet and Kalona because he knew they were attacking me *and* Aphrodite *and* Damien *and* Shaunee *and* Erin *and* a whole abbey full of nuns." With every *and* I'd taken a step toward Sapphire and Margareta. I could feel the elemental force of spirit, which I'd so recently called on to soothe Dragon, swirling dangerously around me. The vampyres felt it too, because they'd both stumbled several steps away from me. I stopped and got a handle on my temper, lowering my voice and my blood pressure. "He stood with us *against* them. Neferet and Kalona are not who you think they were. They're a danger to everyone. But right now I don't have time to try to convince you of something that should have been obvious to you when the winged guy exploded from the ground in a shower of blood. Right now I'm here to help these kids, and since you seem to have a problem with that, I think it would be a good idea if you scuttled to your rooms like the rest of the House of Night."

Looking shocked and offended, the two vampyres backed from the entryway and hurried up the stairwell that led to the professors' rooms. I sighed. I'd told Stark we couldn't win this by fighting our own, and then I'd threatened them. But when I turned to our little infirmary group, I was met with grins, cheers, and clapping.

"I've wanted to tell those cows off since we got here," called Denio from her room as she beamed a smile at me.

"And they call *her* Terrible," Aphrodite said, obviously referring to the fact that Denio, in Greek, means terrible.

"I'm just good at sensing what people are feeling. I can't smack them around with an element or five," Denio said. She rubbed her wounded arm absently then turned her attention from me to Aphrodite. "Hey, I shouldn't have been such a bitch to you the last couple months. Sorry about that."

I expected Aphrodite to puff up and tell her about herself. I mean, Denio had been awful to her—as had all of Aphrodite's supposed friends.

"Yeah, well, all of us screw up now and then. Forget about it," Aphrodite said, totally surprising me.

"You sound all grown," I said to her.

"Don't you have a circle to cast?" she said.

I grinned at her because I swear her cheeks looked pink. "Actually, I do." I looked from Stevie Rae to Damien and Shaunee, then called, "Erin, can you quit playing nurse long enough to get in on this circle?"

She popped out of T.J.'s room like one of those old jack-in-the-boxes. "Yep, easy-peasy."

I noticed she and Shaunee didn't look at each other, but no way did I have the time or the energy to get into Twin problems just then.

"Okay, so, which way's north, earth girl?" I asked Stevie Rae.

She marched over to stand opposite the entrance to the hallway. "This is definitely north."

"All right. The rest of you guys know what to do," I said.

Like pros they moved into place: Damien taking the position in the east for air, Shaunee south for fire, Erin west for water, and Stevie Rae firmly stationed in the north for earth. When they were ready I took my place in the center of the circle. Beginning with Damien in the east, I called each element into our circle, moving deasil, or clockwise, until I finished by calling spirit to me.

I'd closed my eyes during the casting, and when the circle was complete, I opened them to see a glowing silver thread binding the five of us. I threw back my head, raised my arms, and shouted with the joy of being touched by all five elements. "It's good to be home!"

My friends laughed, happy and whole, fulfilled by their elements and, even if just for a moment, able to forget the chaos and hardship that surrounded us.

But not the pain. I wouldn't forget the reason I'd cast the circle, even though it was easy to get caught up in the thrill of the elements.

I centered and calmed myself. In a strong, confident voice, I began to speak. "Air, fire, water, earth, and spirit—I have called you here to our circle for one specific reason. Our fledgling friends at the House of Night have been hurt. I'm not a healer. I'm really not even technically a High Priestess." I paused and glanced out of the circle, meeting Stark's gaze. He winked at me. I smiled and continued. "But my purpose is clear. I would like you to please touch these hurt kids. I can't heal them, but I can ask that you soothe and strengthen them, so that they can heal themselves. Actually, I think that's what all of us want—a chance to fix ourselves. In the name of Nyx, and through the power of your elements, fill these fledglings!" Concentrating with my mind, body, and soul, I tossed out my hands, imagining I was hurling the elements through me and out at the wounded kids.

I heard the exclamations of surprise and pleasure, and even some gasps of pain as the five elements swirled around the infirmary, infilling the fledglings. I stayed there, being a living conduit for the elements until my arms ached and sweat poured down my body.

"Zoey! I said, 'Enough!' You've helped them. Close the circle."

I heard Stark, and realized that he had been talking to me for a while, but I'd been concentrating so hard and for so long that he literally had to shout to finally break through to me.

Wearily, I dropped my hands and whispered sincere thanks and goodbyes to the five elements, and then I somehow lost my legs and fell to the floor smack on my butt.

CHAPTER TWENTY-FOUR

Zoey

"No, I do *not* need a bed in the infirmary," I repeated for the third time to Stark, who kept hovering around me looking way too worried. "And there are no extra beds here anyway."

"Hey, I'm feeling lots better," Denio called. "You can have my bed, Z."

"Thanks, but no thanks," I told her. And then I stuck my hand out to Stark. "Just help me stand up, would ya?"

He frowned dubiously at me, but helped me up. I stood very still so that no one was aware that the room was spinning like a crazy mini-tornado around me.

"I think she looks worse than I feel," said Drew from his pallet on the floor.

"*She* can hear you," I said. "And I'm fine." I let my slightly blurry vision wander from wounded kid to wounded kid. They were all looking better, which gave me a great sense of relief. I checked "be sure the hurt kids aren't writhing in pain and dying horribly" off my mental to-do list. Time for the next list item. I stifled a sigh because I didn't want to waste the oxygen. "Okay, things are better here. So, Stevie Rae, we need to figure out where the red fledglings will be staying when the sun comes up *before* the sun comes up."

"Good idea, Z," said Stevie Rae, who was sitting on the floor next to Drew. I remembered then that she'd had kind of a thing for the kid before she'd died and un-died, and I acknowledged to myself that seeing her flirting with him, when I thought she probably had a thing for that red fledgling kid named Dallas, gave me a little moment of selfish glee. It might be borderline mean of me, but it would sure be nice if my BFF and I could talk about how to juggle multiple-guy problems.

"Z? Do ya think that's a good idea?"

"Oh, sorry, what?" I realized Stevie Rae had been talking away at me while I'd been hoping she'd accumulate a zillion (or at least two) boyfriends.

"I said the red fledglings could stay in empty dorm rooms. There should be enough, even if they have to sleep three to a room. We could be sure their windows are covered. It's not as good as being underground, but it'll do, at least until this stupid ice storm stops and we can figure something else out."

"Okay, then let's get that going. And while the room situation is being fixed, *we*"— I enunciated the word carefully, taking in my circle plus Aphrodite, Darius, and Stark—"need to have a talk with Lenobia."

My gang nodded, everyone apparently clued in to the fact that we needed to quickly be brought up to speed on what had happened at the House of Night while we were gone.

"You guys are all going to be okay," I told the hurt kids as my gang said their goodbyes and we started straggling toward the exit.

"Hey, thanks, Zoey," Drew called.

"You really are a good High Priestess—even if you're not really one yet," Ian yelled from his room.

I wasn't sure his lopsided compliment required a thanks or not, and as I was standing in the entrance to the infirmary, looking back at the kids and thinking that, except for the fact that they'd just battled Raven Mockers and witnessed the murder of a professor, they all seemed so normal.

Then it hit me. *They seemed normal.* Just the day before, almost everybody at the school, with the exception of my group, Lenobia, Dragon, and Anastasia, had fallen under the charismatic spell of Kalona and Neferet, and hadn't acted normal at all.

I walked back into the infirmary hallway. "I have a question for all of you guys. It may sound weird, but I really need honest answers, even if that might be embarrassing."

Drew grinned over my shoulder, where I was sure my BFF was standing, "Ask me anything you want, Z. Any friend of Stevie Rae's is cool by me."

"Uh, thanks, Drew." I managed not to roll my eyes at him. "This question is for all of you, though. Here's the thing: Did you guys think there was anything wrong with the Raven Mockers, or even Kalona and Neferet, before Professor Anastasia was attacked?"

Not surprisingly, Drew answered first. "I didn't trust the winged guy, but I didn't know why." He shrugged. "I dunno, maybe because he had wings. It's just too weird."

"I thought he was hot, but those man-bird sons of his were super-disgusting," said Hanna Honeyyeager.

"Yeah, the Raven Mockers were gross, but also Kalona was *old*, and I couldn't figure out how come so many fledgling girls had a thing for him," said Red. "I mean, George Clooney's hot and all, but he's too old, and I wouldn't want to, like, do him. So I didn't get why practically everyone else wanted to do Kalona."

"How about the rest of you?" I asked the rest of them.

"Like you said before, Kalona exploded from the ground. That's just bizarre." Denio paused, looked at Aphrodite, and then continued. "Plus, some of us have known for a while that Neferet wasn't everything she seemed to be."

"Yeah, you knew it, but you didn't do anything about it." Aphrodite's voice wasn't hateful or pissed. She was just making a statement, an awful but true statement.

Denio lifted her chin. "I did do something about it." She gestured at her bandaged arm. "It was just too late."

"Nothing's felt right to me since Professor Nolan was killed," Ian said from his room. "The stuff with Kalona and the Raven Mockers was more of that same feeling."

"I saw what he was doing to my friends," T.J. called from the last room down the hall. "They were like zombies and believed anything he said. When I tried to talk to them about anything, like asking how we could be sure he was really Erebus come to earth, they'd get pissed or laugh at me. I didn't like him from the very beginning. And those damn bird things were evil. I don't know why everyone couldn't see it."

"Neither do I, but that's something we're going to figure out," I said. "Right now y'all don't worry about any of this. Kalona is gone, and so's Neferet and the Raven Mockers. Just get well. Okay?"

"Okay!" they yelled back at me, sounding way healthier than they had when we first saw them.

On the other hand, channeling all five elements had me feeling like poo, and I was glad Stark grabbed my elbow and lent me his strength as we left the building. Unbelievably, the ice and rain had stopped. The clouds that had blanketed the sky for days actually had breaks in them through which I glimpsed sections of a starry night. My gaze moved to the center of the school grounds. The fire that had completely consumed Anastasia's pyre was beginning to die, though Dragon was still on his knees in front of it; Lenobia stood beside him, one hand resting on his shoulder. The circle made of red fledglings, plus Erik, Heath, and Jack, stretched all the way around the smoldering funeral pyre. They stood quietly, bearing witness to their respect for Dragon and his beloved.

I motioned for my group to follow me a little way into the shadows and huddle up. "We gotta talk, but we don't need to do that with an audience. Stevie Rae, can you delegate getting rooms ready for your kids to someone?"

"Sure, Kramisha is so organized she's almost OCD. Plus, she was a sixth-former when she died and un-died. She knows all sorts of stuff about this place."

"Good. Put her on it." I turned to Darius. "The bodies of the Raven Mockers have to be gotten rid of—now. If we're lucky, this storm is finally clearing, which means humans are going to start to stir as soon as it's light. They can't find those creatures."

"I'll take care of it," Darius said. "I'll get the red fledgling males to help me."

"What are you going to do with the bodies?" Stevie Rae asked.

"Burn them," Shaunee answered, then she looked at me. "If that's okay with you."

"It's perfect," I said. "Just don't burn them anywhere around Anastasia's pyre. That would be too much for Dragon to handle."

"Burn them at the east wall. Right where their disgusting father exploded from the earth." Aphrodite's gaze went to Shaunee. "The old oak that broke apart when Kalona escaped, can you make it burn?"

"I can make *anything* burn," Shaunee said.

"Go with Darius and the guys then, and make sure every feather of those creatures is burned beyond anyone's recognition. Then the two of you meet the rest of us in my room. Agreed?"

"Agreed," Darius and Shaunee said together.

I thought it was weird that Erin hadn't said anything to her Twin, but as Shaunee started to follow Darius over to the circling red fledglings, she called, "I'll fill you in on anything you miss, Twin."

"Of course you will, Twin," Shaunee said, smiling over her shoulder at Erin.

"Okay, we really need Lenobia with us." I looked over to where the Horse Mistress stood beside Dragon. "But I don't know how to pull her away from that."

"Just tell him," Damien said.

I gave him my *question mark* look.

"Dragon understands how dangerous Kalona and Neferet are. He'll understand that we need Lenobia." Damien's gaze went over to the vampyre, who was still on his knees. "He's going to stay there and grieve until he feels right leaving. We can't change that or hurry him up. So just tell him we need Lenobia."

"You're a smart kid, you know it?" I said.

"Affirmative," he said with a smile.

"All right." I drew a long, weary breath. "Stevie Rae—explain to Kramisha what she needs to do. The rest of you guys can meet in my room. I'll be there as soon as I get Lenobia."

"Z, I'm going to tell Jack to help Kramisha," Damien said.

I raised my brows at him.

"Your room's only so big. Plus, I can fill him in on stuff later. Right now *we* need to get our heads on straight."

I nodded and started trudging toward Lenobia and Dragon. Around me I could see Darius and Stevie Rae pulling kids aside and speaking quietly to them. Damien petted Duchess's head while he talked to his boyfriend.

Through it all Stark stayed by my side. I didn't have to look for him. I could feel him. I knew if I stumbled, he would make sure I didn't fall. I also knew he understood better than anyone else exactly how much channeling the elements in the infirmary had taken from me.

As if reading my mind, he whispered, "You'll be able to sit down soon. And I'll find something for you to eat and drink."

"Thank you," I whispered back. He took my hand and together we went to Lenobia and Dragon. The cats were quiet, though both were pressed against Dragon's body. His bruised and battered face was wet with tears, but he'd stopped crying.

"Dragon, I need Lenobia to come with me for a little while. I don't want to leave you here alone, but I really do need to talk to her."

He looked up at me. I thought I'd never seen anyone so sad.

"I won't be alone. Shadowfax and Guinevere will be with me, and our Goddess will be with me," he said. His gaze returned to the pyre. "I'm not ready to leave Anastasia yet."

Lenobia squeezed his shoulder. "I will return soon, my friend," she said.

"I will be here," Dragon said.

"I'll wait with Dragon. Kramisha doesn't really need me. She already has enough fledglings to boss around," Jack said to me. He and Damien had joined us. Duchess stopped several feet away and was lying on the grass with her nose on her paws. The cats paid no attention to her. "I'd like to stay with you, that is, if you don't mind," he finished, speaking to Dragon nervously.

"Thank you, Jack," Dragon said, his voice catching on a sob.

Jack nodded, wiped his eyes and, without saying anything else, sat next to Dragon and began gently petting Shadowfax.

"Well done you," I said softly to Jack.

"I'm proud of you," Damien whispered to Jack and kissed him gently on the cheek, which made Jack smile through his tears.

"Okay," I said. "Let's meet in my room."

"Lenobia, Zoey has to take a detour through the kitchen," Stark said abruptly. "She and I will meet you in the dorm as soon as possible."

Lenobia nodded absently, already walking toward the dorms with Damien, Erin, and Aphrodite.

"Why are—," I started, but Stark cut me off.

"Just trust me. This is what you need."

He took my elbow and guided me toward the center of the school building where the entry hall led to the cafeteria. We were almost to the doors when he said, "Go on in to the cafeteria. I gotta grab something and then I'll be right with you."

Too tired to question him, I went in. It was weird how deserted everything was. The lobby was lit by half the gaslights that usually blazed at this time of night. I glanced up at a clock. It was a little past midnight. School should be going on. There should be fledglings and vamp professors all over. I wished the place was packed. I wished I could turn back time and make the past two months disappear so I could go back to worrying about Aphrodite being a mean girl and Erik being an untouchable hottie.

I wanted to go back to a time when I didn't know anything about Kalona or A-ya or death and destruction. I wanted normal. I wanted it so bad I felt sick.

I walked slowly into the cafeteria, which was also completely empty, and darker than the hallway had been. There were no yummy food smells, no clusters of kids gossiping about other kids, no professors giving dirty looks to kids sneaking Doritos.

I stumbled over to the picnic bench–like booth I usually shared with my friends and let my knees give out, sitting heavily on the well-polished wood. Why had Stark told me to come in here? Was he going to attempt to cook for me? For a second the vision of him with an apron tied around his waist was almost funny. Then I realized why he'd pushed me to come in here. One of the fridges in the massive school kitchen was kept filled with baggies of human blood. At that moment he was probably grabbing several bags o' blood and would bring them for me to drink like thick red juice boxes.

Okay, I know it's gross, but the thought made my mouth water.

Stark was right. I had to recharge, and a bag o' blood (or two) would be a good way to do that.

"Zo! There you are! Stark said you'd be in here."

I blinked in surprise and turned to see Heath walking into the cafeteria—alone.

And I suddenly understood that I'd only been partially right. Stark had gone to get me blood, but instead of it coming from the side-by-side, stainless steel kitchen refrigerators, my blood was coming from the cutie football player Heath.

Ah, hell.

CHAPTER TWENTY-FIVE

Rephaim

Awakening was difficult. Even in the wispy realm that was the boundary between the conscious and unconscious mind, even before he fully felt the pain that wracked his abused body, Rephaim was aware of her scent.

At first he thought he was back in the shed and the nightmare had just begun—just after the accident when she'd come, not to kill him, but to bring him water and bind his wounds. Then he realized it was too warm for him to still be in the shed. He shifted slightly and the pain that coursed through his body brought full consciousness with it, and with consciousness came memory.

He was belowground, in the tunnels she'd sent him to, and he hated it.

It wasn't a hatred that bordered on paranoia, as did his father's. Rephaim simply despised the confined feeling of being beneath the earth. There was no sky above him—no green and growing world beneath him. He couldn't soar belowground. He couldn't—

The Raven Mocker's thoughts ended abruptly.

No. He wouldn't think of his permanently damaged wing and what that meant for the rest of his life. He couldn't think of that. Not yet. Not while his body was still so weak.

Rephaim thought of her instead.

It was an easy thing to do, surrounded by her scent as he was.

He shifted again, this time being more careful of his shattered wing. With his good arm he pulled the blanket over himself and burrowed, nestlike, into the warmth of the bed. Her bed.

Even underground there was an odd and illogical sense of security that came to him from being somewhere she'd called her own. He didn't understand why she had this singular effect on him. Rephaim just knew that he'd followed Stevie Rae's directions, stumbling through agony and exhaustion until he realized what he was really following was the scent of the Red One. It had led him through the winding, apparently deserted tunnels. He'd stopped at the kitchen and forced himself to eat and drink. The fledglings had left behind refrigerators filled with food. Refrigerators! That was one of the many miracles of the modern age he'd been observing for the long years he was only spirit. He'd spent what felt like an eternity watching and waiting . . . dreaming of the day he could touch and taste and truly live again.

Rephaim had decided he liked refrigerators. He wasn't at all sure whether he liked the modern world, though. In just the short time his body had been returned to him, he'd realized that most modern humans had no real respect for the power of the ancients. The Raven Mocker didn't count vampyres among the ranks of the ancients. They were nothing more than attractive playthings. Amusements and distractions. No matter what his father said, they were unworthy to rule beside him.

Was that why the Red One had allowed him to live? Because she was too weak and ineffective—too *modern* to take the steps she should have and killed him.

Then he thought about the strength she had exhibited, and not just her physical strength, which was impressive. She also commanded the element earth, so fully that it ripped itself apart to obey her. That was not weakness.

Even his father had spoken of the Red One's powers. Neferet, too, warned that the leader of the Red Ones was not to be underestimated.

And there he was, drawn by her scent to her bed, where he was practically nesting.

With a cry of disgust, he lurched from the comfortable warmth of blankets and pillows and thick mattress and staggered to his feet. He stood there, leaning against the table that was near the end of the bed, struggling to remain upright and not let the unrelenting darkness of this place pull him under.

He would trace his path back to the kitchen. He would eat and drink again. He would light every lantern he could find. Rephaim would will himself to heal, and then he would leave this tomblike place and return aboveground to find his father—to find his place in the world.

Rephaim pushed aside the blanket that served as a door to Stevie Rae's room and limped into the tunnel. *I'm already better . . . stronger . . . I don't have to use the cane to walk,* he told himself.

The darkness was almost complete. There were intermittent lanterns, though many of them were guttering. Rephaim picked up his pace. He'd refill and light the lanterns after he stuffed himself. He'd even drink the bags of blood he'd found one of the refrigerators filled with, though it held no special appeal to him. His body needed fuel to mend, just as the lanterns needed fuel to burn.

Fighting against the agony each movement caused, Rephaim followed the curve in the tunnel and finally entered the kitchen. He opened the first refrigerator and was pulling a bag of sliced ham from it when he felt the cold blade of a knife against his lower back.

"One move I don't like, birdboy, and I cut your spinal cord in half. That *will* kill you dead, won't it?"

Rephaim went absolutely still. "Yes, that would kill me."

"He looks part dead to me anyway," said another female voice.

"Yeah, that wing is totally fucked up. He don't look like he can do shit to us," said a male.

The knife didn't move from his spine. "Others underestimating us is what got us here. So we don't *ever* underestimate *anyone*. Got it?" said the voice that belonged to the knife.

"Yeah, sorry, Nicole."

"I got it."

"So, birdboy, here's how we're gonna play this: I'm gonna step back and you're gonna turn around—real slow. Don't get any smart ideas. My knife won't be on you, but Kurtis and Starr both have guns. Make a wrong move and you'll be just as dead as if I'd cut through your spine."

The point of the knife pressed hard enough against Rephaim to draw a bead of blood.

"He smells wrong!" said the male voice that belonged to Kurtis. "He ain't even good eatin'."

Nicole ignored him. "You understand me, birdboy?"

"I do."

The knife pressure left his spine and Rephaim heard the shuffling noise of moving feet.

"Turn around."

Rephaim did as he was told and found himself facing three fledglings. The red crescent moons on their foreheads identified them as part of the Red One's flock. But he knew instantly that though they, too, were red, they were as different from Stevie Rae as was the moon from the sun. He gave Kurtis, a huge male fledgling, and Starr, an ordinary-looking, light-haired girl, cursory glances, though they were holding handguns up and pointed at him. It was Nicole on whom he focused his attention. She was obviously the leader. She was also the one who'd drawn his blood, something Rephaim would never forget.

She was a small fledgling with long dark hair and large eyes so brown they appeared black. Rephaim looked into those eyes and felt a moment of complete shock—Neferet was there! In this fledgling child's eyes lurked the distinctive darkness and intelligence that Rephaim had seen so many times in the Tsi Sgili's gaze. That recognition shocked the Raven Mocker so deeply that for a moment he could only stare, his single thought was *Does Father know she has attained the ability to project herself?*

"Damn! He looks like he seen a ghost," Kurtis said, the gun bobbing up and down with his chuckles.

"I thought you said you didn't know any of the Raven Mockers," said Starr, her tone clearly suspicious.

Nicole blinked, and the familiar shade of Neferet was gone, leaving Rephaim to wonder if he'd imagined the presence.

No. Rephaim didn't imagine things. Neferet had been present, even if only for an instant, within the fledgling.

"I've never seen one of these things before in my life." Nicole turned to Starr, though she still kept her gaze trained on Rephaim. "Are you saying you think I'm a liar?"

Nicole hadn't raised her voice, but Rephaim, who was accustomed to being in the presence of power and danger, recognized that this particular fledgling seethed with an aggression that was barely controlled. Starr obviously recognized it, too, as she instantly backed down.

"No, no, no. I didn't mean anything like that. It's just weird that he freaked when he saw you."

"That was weird," Nicole said smoothly. "And maybe we should ask him why. So, birdboy, what's with you being down here in our territory?"

Rephaim noted that Nicole hadn't actually asked him the question she'd implied she was going to ask.

"Rephaim," he said, willing strength into his voice. "My name is Rephaim."

All three fledglings' eyes widened, as if surprised he would actually have a name.

"He sounds almost normal," Starr said.

"He's anything but normal, and you better remember that," Nicole snapped. "Answer my question, *Rephaim*."

"I escaped into the tunnels after being wounded by a warrior from the House of Night," he said truthfully. Rephaim's instincts, which had served him well for centuries, told him to remain silent about Stevie Rae, that even though these must be the rogue red fledglings she had been protecting, they were not truly of her flock, nor did they follow her.

"The tunnel between here and the abbey collapsed," said Nicole.

"It was open when I entered it."

Nicole took a step toward him and sniffed the air. "You smell of Stevie Rae."

Rephaim made a dismissive gesture with his good hand. "I reek of the bed I slept in." He cocked his head to the side, as if confused by what she'd said. "You say I carry Stevie Rae's scent. Is she not the Red One, your High Priestess?"

"Stevie Rae's a red vampyre, but she isn't our High Priestess!" Nicole snarled, and her eyes took on a red glow.

"Not your High Priestess?" Rephaim pushed. "But there was a red vampyre priestess called Stevie Rae who stood with a group of fledglings against my father and his queen. She had your markings. Is she not your High Priestess?"

"That was the battle where you were hurt?" Nicole ignored his question to ask her own.

"It was."

"What happened? Where's Neferet?"

"Gone." Rephaim didn't hide the bitterness in his voice. "She fled with my father and those of my brothers who still live."

"Where'd they go?" Kurtis asked.

"If I knew that, I would not be hiding in the earth like a coward. I would be at my father's side where I belong."

"Rephaim." Nicole gave him a long, considering look. "I've heard that name before."

The Raven Mocker stayed silent, knowing it was better for her to come to the understanding of who he was without him having to brag about his position like a braying ass.

When her eyes widened, he knew she'd remembered where it was she'd heard his name.

"She said you were Kalona's favorite—his most powerful son."

"Yes, that is who I am. Who is this *she* who's been talking about me?"

Again, Nicole ignored his question. "What covered the door to the room you slept in?"

"A checked blanket."

"Stevie Rae's room," Starr said. "That's why he smells like her."

Nicole acted as if Starr hadn't spoken. "Kalona took off without you, even though you're his favorite."

"Yesssss," Rephaim drew out the hiss of anger that came with the acknowledgment.

Nicole spoke to Kurtis and Starr. "You know this has to mean that they're coming back. This birdboy is Kalona's favorite. No way is he going to leave him here forever. Just like we're her favorites. He'll come back for him; she'll come back for us."

"Do you speak of the Red One, Stevie Rae?"

In a motion so fast her body blurred, Nicole moved to Rephaim's side, clamped her hands around his battered shoulders, and in one smooth motion lifted the huge Raven Mocker off the ground and slammed him against the side of the tunnel. Eyes blazing red, she breathed rancid breath into his face as she said, "Get this, birdboy. Stevie Rae, or the Red One as you keep calling her, isn't our High Priestess. She isn't our boss. She isn't one of us. She's tight with Zoey and that bunch, and that's not cool. See, we don't have a High Priestess, we have a queen, and her name is Neferet. Now, what's with this obsession with Stevie Rae?"

Agony seared through Rephaim. His broken wing was on fire, lighting his body with white-hot agony. With everything inside him he wished he was whole again so that he could destroy this arrogant red fledgling with one slice of his beak.

But he wasn't whole. He was weak and wounded and abandoned.

"My father wanted her captured. He said she was dangerous. Neferet didn't trust her. I am not obsessed. I am only following my father's will," he choked out through the pain.

"How about we see if you're really telling us the truth," Nicole said. Then she tightened her already viselike grip on his arm, closed her eyes, and bowed her head.

Incredibly, Rephaim felt her palms begin to heat. The heat radiated through him, tracing his bloodstream, pounding in time with the frantic beating of his heart, and slamming into his body.

A shudder went through Nicole, then she opened her eyes and lifted her head. Her smile was sly. She continued to hold him against the wall for one very long minute more before she dropped him. Looking down at where he'd crumpled on the floor, she said, "She saved you."

"What the fuck?" Kurtis shouted.

"Stevie Rae saved him?" Starr said.

Nicole and Rephaim acted as if neither had spoken.

"She did," Rephaim gasped, fighting to get his breathing under control so he wouldn't pass out. Then he said nothing more, only tried to figure out what had just happened while he breathed through the radiating pain in his wing. The red fledgling had done something to him when she'd touched him—something that had given her a glimpse into his mind, maybe even his soul. But he also knew that he was unlike any being she'd ever before touched; his thoughts would be difficult, if not nearly impossible for her to read, no matter her talents.

"Why would Stevie Rae do that?" Nicole asked him.

"You saw into my mind. You know that I have no idea why she did what she did."

"That much is true," she said slowly. "It's also true that I didn't pick up that you have any bad feelings toward her. What's with that?"

"I'm not sure what you mean. Bad feelings? That makes no sense to me."

She scoffed. "No sense—like you have any sense? Your mind was the weirdest thing I've ever looked into. So it's like this, birdboy, you say you're still doing what your dad told you to do. At the very least that should mean you want to capture her—maybe kill her."

"My father did not want her killed. He wanted her brought to him unharmed so he could study her, and maybe use her powers," Rephaim said.

"Whatever. But, see, the problem is, when I looked into that bird-brain of yours, I didn't find anything that said you're after her."

"Why would I be after her right now? She isn't here."

Nicole shook her head. "No, see, that's just weird. If you want to get Stevie Rae, you *want to get her*, whether she's here or not."

"That isn't logical."

Nicole stared at him. "Look, this is what I have to know. Are you with us or not?"

"With you?"

"Yeah, *with us*. We're going to kill Stevie Rae." She spoke matter-of-factly while she moved with her preternatural speed to his side and grasped his arm in her iron grip. Rephaim's bicep heated instantly as she probed his thoughts. "So, what's your choice? Are you with us, or not?"

Rephaim knew he had to answer. Nicole might not be able to read all of his thoughts, but obviously she had enough power that she could discover things he'd rather keep hidden. Making the decision quickly, he met the red fledgling's scarlet gaze with his own and said truthfully, "I am my father's son."

She stared at him, her hand burning the flesh of his arm and her eyes glowing red. Then she smiled her sly smile again. "Good answer, birdboy, 'cause that's the major thing I found inside your bird head. You definitely are your dad's kid." She let loose of him. "Welcome to my team, and don't worry. Since your dad's not here right now, I don't think he'll care whether Stevie Rae's dead or alive when you catch her."

"And dead's easier," Kurtis said.

"Most definitely," Starr said.

Nicole laughed, sounding so much like Neferet that the feathers at the nape of Rephaim's neck lifted in response. *Father! Beware!* His mind shrieked, *The Tsi Sgili is more than what she seems!*

CHAPTER TWENTY-SIX

Zoey

"Heath, what are you doing in here?"

Heath clutched his chest like she'd shot him and staggered around, making mock gasping sounds. "Your coldness is killing me, baby!"

"You are a dork," she said. "If anything's killing you, it's your absolute lack of good sense. So, what *are* you doing in here? I thought you'd be out there doing bird burning with Darius and Shaunee."

"Well, I was gonna, 'cause they can definitely use my superhuman strength to help them out." He waggled his brows at her and flexed. Then he plopped onto the bench beside her. "But Stark found me and said you needed me—so here I am."

"Stark was wrong. You should go back and help Darius."

"You look bad, Zo," he said, all kidding gone from his tone.

I sighed. "I've been through a bunch of stuff lately, that's all—just like all of us have."

"Helping the hurt kids kicked your butt," he said.

"Well, yeah, it did. But I'll be okay. I just need to get today over with so I can get some sleep. That's all."

Heath watched me for a little while without speaking, then he held his hand out to me. It was an automatic reflex for me to thread my fingers through his.

"Zo, I'm trying hard not to let it drive me crazy that you have some kind of special thing with Stark—something you don't have with me."

"It's a Warrior Bond. I can only have it with a vampyre." I said the words apologetically, and I was sorry—sorry that I kept hurting this guy whom I'd loved since grade school.

"Yeah, I heard about that. Anyway, what I was sayin' is that I'm trying to deal with the Stark thing, but it makes it doubly hard for me when you push me away."

I couldn't say anything because I knew exactly what he was really talking about. It was why Stark had sent him in here. Heath wanted me to drink from him. Just thinking about it made my mouth water and my breath come faster.

"I know you want to," he whispered.

Unable to meet his eyes, I stared down at our joined hands. In the dim light of the deserted cafeteria the tattoos on my palms were almost invisible and our hands looked so ordinary—so much like they'd looked for so many years that it made my stomach hurt.

"You know I want you to."

I met his gaze then. "I know you do. I just can't, Heath."

I expected him to explode and get all pissed, but instead he deflated. His shoulders sagged and he shook his head. "Why won't you let me help you in the one real way I can?"

I drew a deep breath and told him the complete truth. "Because I can't deal with the sex part of it right now."

He blinked in surprise at me. "Is that the only reason?"

"Sex is a kinda big reason," I said.

"Well, yeah, not that I'd know from experience, but still I get what you're saying."

I felt my cheeks get warm. Heath was still a virgin? I'd thought for sure that after I was Marked and left my human life for the House of Night, my ex-BFF had totally gone after him. Actually, I *knew* skanky Kayla had gone after him.

"What about Kayla? I thought you two hooked up after I left."

He gave a humorless little laugh. "She wishes. Not no, but hell, no. I wasn't with Kayla. There's only one girl for me." The humorlessness left his expression and he grinned at me. "And even though you're a big-time High Priestess and so not technically just a 'girl' anymore, to me you're still my girl."

Again, I didn't know what to say. I'd always thought when I had sex for the first time it would be with Heath, but then I'd messed up majorly and lost my virginity to Loren Blake, which was literally the biggest mistake of my life. It still made me feel sick and more than a little guilty.

"Hey, stop thinking about Blake. You can't change what happened with him, so let's forget it."

"Are you a mind reader now?"

"I've always been able to get inside your head, Zo." His grin faded. "Well, I guess I haven't been able to do that so good recently."

"I'm sorry about all of this, Heath. I hate that it hurts you."

"I'm not a kid anymore. I knew what I was getting into when I got in my truck and drove to Tulsa to see you. It doesn't have to be easy between us, but it does have to be honest."

"Okay. I want to be honest, too. So I'm telling you the truth when I tell you that I can't let myself drink from you. I can't deal with what will happen between us because of it. I'm not ready to have sex, even if the whole world wasn't going to hell in a handbasket all around us."

"Hell in a handbasket—you sound like your grandma when you say that."

"Heath, changing the subject won't change my mind. I'm not having sex, so I'm not drinking from you."

"Jeesh, Zo, I'm not a moron; I get that," he said. "So we don't have sex. We've spent a whole lot of years not having sex. We're experienced at it."

"There's more to it than just wanting each other. You know what the Imprint does to both of us. It was intense enough before when I was hurt so bad I was almost dead. It would be that times ten if I drank from you now."

Heath swallowed hard and ran his hand through his hair. "Yeah, okay, I know that. But here's what I'm saying about it—the Imprint goes both ways, right? While you're drinking my blood you feel stuff I feel, and I feel stuff you feel."

"Yeah, and the 'stuff' is all about pleasure and sex," I said.

"Okay, so, instead of us focusing on the sex part, we'll focus on the pleasure part."

I raised my brows at him. "You're a guy, Heath. Since when do you *not* focus on the sex part?"

Instead of the kidding response I expected, his expression was absolutely serious. "When have I ever pressured you about sex?"

"There was that time in the tree house."

"You were in fourth grade. That doesn't count. Plus you knocked the crap out of me." He didn't exactly smile, but his brown eyes twinkled.

"How about the back of your truck last summer at the lake?"

"You really can't count that, either. You had that new bikini on. And I didn't actually pressure you."

"You had your hands all over me."

"Well, there was a lot of you showing!" He paused, lowering his voice to a normal level again. "My point is, we've been together for a long time. We can definitely be together without having sex. Do I want to have sex with you? Hell, yes. Do I want to have sex with you when your head is all messed up from that Blake guy and you're worried as hell about everything that's going on, and *you don't actually want to have sex with me*? Hell, no! Hell, hell, no." He put his finger under my chin and made me meet his gaze. "I promise that this won't be about sex because you and me, what we have, means more than sex. Let me do this for you, Zoey."

My mouth opened and before I could stop it I heard myself whisper, "Okay."

His smile was like he'd just won the Super Bowl. "Excellent!"

"But no sex," I said.

"Absolutely none at all. Just call me Heath No Sex. Hell, my middle name is No Sex."

"Heath." I put a finger on his lips to shut him up. "You're dorking this up."

"Oh, yeah. Okay," he mumbled around my finger. Then he let loose my hand and reached into the pocket of his jeans, pulling out a small pocketknife. He slid off his coat and opened the knife. The blade looked weirdly like a kid's toy in the dark cafeteria.

"Hang on!" I kinda shrieked when he started to lift the knife to the side of his neck.

"What?"

"Um. Right here? We're doing this right here?"

He raised his brows at me. "Why not? We're not having sex, re-member?"

"Of course I remember," I said. "It's just, well, someone might come in."

"Stark's guarding the door. No one will get past him."

That shocked me into silence. I mean, obviously this had been Stark's idea, but guarding the door to make sure Heath and I had private time? That was just—

The scent of Heath's blood hit me and all thoughts of Stark flew from my mind. My eyes found the small ribbon of red that lay along the soft spot where his neck met his shoulder. He shifted, putting the knife on the table and holding his arms open to me.

"Come here, Zo. It's just you and me right now. No one else for you to think about. No one else for you to worry about. Come here," he repeated.

I went into his arms inhaling his scent: Heath, blood, desire, home, and my past all wrapped up together in a strong, familiar embrace. When my tongue touched the line of scarlet I felt him shiver and knew he was suppressing a moan of pure desire. I hesitated, but it was too late. His blood exploded in my mouth. Unable to stop myself, I pressed my lips against his skin and drank. At that moment I didn't care that I wasn't ready for sex, or that the world around me was one big ball of chaos, or even that we were in the middle of the cafeteria while Stark guarded the door (and probably was experiencing everything I was feeling). At that moment all I cared about was Heath and his blood and his body and his touch.

"Sssh." Heath's voice had gone all deep and kinda raspy, but it was weirdly soothing. "It's okay, Zo. It can just feel good and that's it. Think about how strong it makes you. You need to be strong, remem-ber? You have, like, a zillion people counting on you. I'm counting on you; Stevie Rae is counting on you; Aphrodite is counting on you, even though I kinda think she's a bitch. Erik's even counting on you—not that anyone cares about him . . ."

Heath's words went on and on. And as he spoke a weird thing

happened. His voice stopped being all deep and raspy. He started sounding just like Heath—like he and I were sitting here talking about normal stuff and I wasn't sucking blood from his neck. Then, without me hardly knowing it, the surge of feeling that filled me as I drank from him changed from raw sex to something else. Something I could think through. Something I could handle. Don't get me wrong, it still felt good. Really, really, seriously good. But good was tempered with what I can only describe as normal, and normal made it manageable. So when I felt strong and rejuvenated I was actually able to pull back. *Close now*, I thought, and licked the bleeding line on Heath's neck, automatically changing the endorphins in my saliva from coagulants to anticoagulants. I watched the bleeding stop and the small wound begin to knit together, leaving only a slim, pink line to betray to the world what had happened between us.

My eyes lifted to meet Heath's gaze.

"Thank you," I said.

"Anytime," he said. "I'll always be here for you, Zo."

"Good, because I'll always need you to remind me of who I really am."

Heath kissed me. It was a gentle kiss, but it was deep and intimate and filled with a desire I knew he was holding back, waiting for me to be ready to finally say yes to him. Instead, I broke the kiss and snuggled into his arms. I felt him sigh, but his embrace didn't falter and he held me tightly.

The sound of the door to the cafeteria swinging open made us both jump.

"Zoey, you really should get to the dorm. They're waiting for you," Stark said.

"Okay, yeah, I'm coming," I said, pulling out of Heath's arms and helping him put on his coat.

"I'd better find Darius and those guys and give them some awesome human help with stuff," Heath said.

Like guilty kids, we walked together over to where Stark stood, expressionlessly holding the door open.

"Stark." Heath nodded at him. "Thanks for getting me to her."

"It's part of my job," Stark said sharply.

"Well, I think you deserve a raise," Heath told him with a grin, then he bent and gave me a quick kiss before telling me bye and hurrying toward the door that led to the central school grounds.

"It's not a part of my job I like," I heard Stark mutter as both of us watched Heath disappear outside.

"Like you said, guess we better get to the dorms," I said, starting to walk briskly down the hall that led to the exit nearest the dorms. Stark followed me—along with a very uncomfortable silence.

"So," he finally said, his voice sounding strained. "That sucked."

I spoke before thinking, and the ridiculous words seemed to babble out of my mouth of their own accord. "Yep. Yep it did. Literally." Then, unbelievably, I giggled.

Okay, in my defense, I was feeling amazingly good. Heath's blood had made me feel better than I had since Kalona burst through the ground and messed up my life.

"It's not funny," Stark said.

"Sorry. It was a bad pun," I said, giggled again, and then clamped my lips shut.

"I'm going to pretend really hard that you're not all giggly and I didn't just feel everything you felt in there," Stark said in a strained voice.

Even through my blood rush I understood that it must have been really hard on Stark to experience the intense pleasure another guy had just brought me, and to realize how close Heath and I actually are. I slid my arm through Stark's. At first he was cold and stiff, and barely responded, like I was trying to hold on to a statue, but as we continued walking he thawed and I felt him relax. Just before he opened the door to the girls' dorm for me, I looked up at him and said, "Thank you for being my Warrior. Thank you for making sure I'm strong, even though it hurt you."

"You're welcome, my lady." He smiled at me, but he looked old and really, really sad.

CHAPTER TWENTY-SEVEN

Zoey

"Do you want a brown pop, too?" I called over my shoulder to Stark, who was waiting impatiently for me out in the very silent, very weird main room of the dorm. I say weird because it was silent, even though there were a bunch of fledglings, girls and guys, sitting in the clusters of chairs staring at the flat-screen TVs. Seriously. They just sat and stared. No talking. No laughing. Nothing. They did look up when Stark and I walked into the room. Actually, I was semi-sure some of the kids sent us hateful glares, but they still didn't say anything.

"No, I'm fine. Just grab your pop and let's get upstairs," he said, already walking toward the stairway.

"Okay, okay. I'm coming. I just—" And I ran smack into a kid named Becca. "Jeesh, sorry!" I said, stepping back. "I didn't see you 'cause I was—"

"Yeah, I know what you were doing. What you're always doing. You were checking out a guy."

I frowned. I didn't know Becca very well. Except that she'd had a big crush on Erik. Oh, and I'd caught Stark biting and practically raping her—*before* he'd chosen good and sworn himself as my Warrior. Of course, Becca hadn't remembered the raping part. She'd only remembered the biting pleasure part, again thanks to the jerk Stark used to be.

Still, that didn't give her permission to pop this ridiculous attitude on me. But I didn't have time to get things right with her and, honestly, I didn't really care that she was a big, festering pile of

I'm-jealous-of-Zoey. So I just made one of Aphrodite's unattractive snorting noises and walked around her and over to a fridge, opened it, and started my quest for brown pop.

"You did this, didn't you? You messed up everything."

I sighed. I found my can of brown pop and turned around. "If you mean, did I get rid of Kalona, who is not Erebus come to earth but really an evil fallen immortal, and chase away Neferet, who is not Nyx's High Priestess anymore but really an evil Tsi Sgili who wants to take over the world, then yes. Yes, with the help of some friends I did that."

"Why do you think you know everything?"

"I definitely don't know everything. If I did, I'd know why you still can't see that Kalona and Neferet and the Raven Mockers are evil, even after they killed Professor Anastasia."

"The Raven Mocker only killed her because you pissed them off by running away and then fighting Kalona, who a bunch of us think really is Erebus."

"Get a clue, Becca. Kalona isn't Erebus. He's the Raven Mockers' dad. He created them by raping Cherokee women. Erebus wouldn't do that. Has *that* occurred to the whole bunch of you?"

She acted like she hadn't heard a word I'd said. "Everything was fine when you were gone. Now you're back and everything's screwed up again. I wish you would just leave for good and let the rest of us do what we want to do."

"The rest of you? You mean like the kids in the infirmary who were almost killed by your winged friends. Or do you mean Dragon, who is out there mourning the death of his wife by himself?"

"That only happened because of you. No one was attacked before you took off."

"Seriously, are you not hearing a word I'm saying?"

"Hey, Becca." Stark was standing in the doorway to the kitchen, just behind Becca.

She turned her head, tossed her hair, and gave him a flirty smile. "Hey there, Stark."

"Erik's free meat," he said bluntly.

She blinked and looked a little confused.

"He and Zoey broke up," he added.

"Oh, really?" She tried to sound nonchalant, but her body language gave away her pleasure. She glanced back at me. "It's about time he dumped you."

"Other way around, you . . . you . . . *bitch!*" I blurted.

Becca actually took a step toward me, raising her hand like she was going to try to hit me, which shocked me so badly that I didn't even think about calling one of the elements to smack her down. Thankfully, Stark wasn't so shocked, and he stepped quickly between us.

"Becca, I've done enough bad to you. Don't make me toss you out of here. Just walk away," he said, looking very warriorlike and dangerous.

Becca backed down instantly. "Oh, whatever. Like I care enough about her to mess up my nails?" She spun around and huffed out.

I opened my pop and took a long drink before saying, "Well, that was really disturbing."

"Yeah, I must be losing it. The real me would never stop a good girl fight."

I rolled my eyes at him. "You're such a guy. Come on, let's get upstairs where there's less crazy."

We walked out of the kitchen and had to go through the main dorm room to get to the stairs, which meant jumping back into a whole bunch of crazy. Becca was all whispery with the biggest cluster of kids, though she stopped talking to give me the stank eye, which was the same stank-eye-kill-you-dead that all the other kids were giving me, too.

I picked up the pace and practically vaulted up the stairs.

"Okay, that's freaky," Stark said as we hurried to my dorm room.

I just nodded. It was hard for me to find the words to describe how it felt to me that almost everyone at my school, my *home*, obviously hated my guts. Opening the door to my room, I was instantly assaulted by an orange ball of fur that hurled herself into my arms as she *"mee-uf-owed"* like a disgruntled old woman.

"Nala!" I ignored her annoyance and kissed her on the nose, which made her sneeze in my face. I laughed and juggled my brown pop to my other hand so I didn't spill it or my cat. "I've missed you, little girl." I pressed my face into her soft fur, which stopped her complaining and started her purr machine.

"When you're done making out with your cat, we have stuff to discuss—important stuff," Aphrodite said.

"Oh, don't be so odious," Damien told her.

"Ode this, Damien." Aphrodite made a rude gesture at him.

"Stop it!" Lenobia spoke before I could tell them to be quiet. "The body of my good friend is still smoldering out there and I don't feel like listening to teenage bickering."

Aphrodite and Damien actually muttered apologies and looked uncomfortable, which I decided was an excellent cue for me to start talking. "Okay, so, every single one of those kids down there is hating my guts."

"Really? They were just being Stepfords when we came in," Damien said.

"Really," Stark said. "I almost had to pull that Becca girl off Zoey."

I could see by the looks on Aphrodite and Damien's faces that they were remembering Stark's not-so-nice past. Neither of them said anything.

"That doesn't surprise me," Lenobia said.

I looked at the Horse Mistress. "What is going on? Kalona's gone. Way gone. Like I don't even think he's in the country anymore. How can he still be affecting fledglings?"

"And vampyres," Damien added. "No other professor except for you came out to be with Dragon. That means the rest of them are still under Kalona's influence, too."

"Or they're simply allowing fear to defeat them." Lenobia said. "It's hard to tell whether they're afraid, or whether the demon began something within them that is still at work, even though he's no longer present."

"He isn't a demon," I heard myself say.

Lenobia gave me a sharp look. "Why would you say that, Zoey?"

I shifted uncomfortably under her scrutiny and sat on my bed, curling Nala into my lap. "It's just that I know things about him, and one of the things I know is that he isn't a demon."

"What difference does it make what we call him?" Erin asked.

"Well, true names are powerful," Damien said. "Traditionally using someone's true name in a spell or ritual can be more binding than sending out energy generally, or even just using their first name."

"You make a good point, Damien. So we won't call Kalona a demon," Lenobia said.

"And we also won't forget he's evil, like those other kids have," Erin said.

"But not all of them have," I said. "Those kids in the infirmary weren't under Kalona's spell, and neither are Lenobia and Dragon—neither was Anastasia. But why? What do you guys have that everyone else doesn't?"

"We already decided that Lenobia and Dragon and Anastasia all had heightened gifts from Nyx," Damien said.

"Okay, so what's special about the kids that stood up to the Raven Mockers?" Aphrodite said.

"Hanna Honeyyeager can make flowers bloom," Damien said.

I stared at him. "Flowers? Seriously?"

"Yeah." Damien shrugged. "She has a green thumb."

I sighed. "What else do we know about the kids in the infirmary?"

"T.J. is a wicked good boxer," Erin spoke up.

"And Drew's an awesome wrestler," I said.

"But are any of these abilities true gifts?" Lenobia said. "Vampyres are talented. That's the norm and not unusual at all."

"Does anyone know anything about that Ian Bowser kid?" I asked. "I just know him a little from drama class. He used to have a big crush on Professor Nolan."

"I know him," Erin said. "He's really sweet."

"Okay, he's sweet," I said, feeling overwhelmed by the hopelessness of our task. The kids were nice and good at things, but being good at something didn't equal being gifted by Nyx. "What about that new girl, Red?"

"None of us know her at all." Damien glanced at Lenobia. "Do you?"

Lenobia shook her head. "No, only that she was being mentored by Anastasia, and she had become close enough to her in just a few days so that she was willing to risk her life to save her professor."

"Which doesn't mean there's anything special about her except that she made the right choice and—" My words broke off as I realized what I was saying. Suddenly I was laughing. "That's it!"

Everyone gawked at me.

"She's lost it," Aphrodite said. "It was bound to happen sooner or later."

"No! I haven't lost it. I found it. Found the answer. Goddess, it's so obvious! Those kids aren't über-gifted. They're just kids *who made the right choice.*"

No one said anything for several seconds, and then Damien picked up the thread of my thought. "Just like in life. Nyx gives us all choices."

I grinned at him. "And some of us choose wisely."

"Some of us mess up," Stark said.

"Goddess! It really is obvious," Lenobia said. "There's no mystery to Kalona's spell."

"It's all about choice," Aphrodite said.

"And truth," I added.

"It does make sense." Damien broke in. "I couldn't understand why only three of our professors were able to see through Kalona. I've always thought that *all* of the vampyres here were special and had Goddess-given gifts."

"And most are," Lenobia said.

"But gift or no gift, finding the truth and following the right path is always a choice." Stark spoke softly as his gaze trapped mine. "That's something none of us should forget."

"Which could be why Nyx has brought us here. To remind us that all of her children have free choice," Lenobia said.

That's my whole point with A-ya. I have the choice not to follow her path. But wouldn't that mean Kalona also has free choice, and can choose good over evil? The thoughts whirled through my mind. I pushed them away and said, "Okay, so, any ideas on where we go from here?"

"Absolutely. You follow Kalona. We come with you," Aphrodite said. When we all stared at her, she continued, "Look, Kalona has proven he's evil, so let's make the *choice* to destroy him." Before I could say anything, Aphrodite added, "It's not impossible. One of my visions showed Zoey taking him out."

"Visions?" Lenobia said.

Aphrodite briefly recapped the two visions she'd had, leaving out the specific mention that in the "not so good" one I'd joined with Kalona. So when she was done, I cleared my throat, put on my big-girl panties (figuratively), and said, "In the bad vision I was with Kalona. As in *with* him. We were lovers."

"But in the other vision you did something to vanquish him," Lenobia said.

"That was clear, even if everything else was a jumbled mess," Aphrodite said. "So, like I was saying before, she has to go to him."

"I don't like it," Stark said.

"Neither do I," Lenobia said. "I wish we knew more—had more details about what caused each vision to happen."

"Goddess! I'm a moron," I said, fishing in my pocket for the piece of paper I'd put there. "I forgot all about Kramisha's poem."

"Ugh, so did I," Aphrodite said. "I hate poetry."

"A fact that baffles me, my beauty," Darius said as he came into the room with Stevie Rae and Shaunee close behind. "Someone with your intelligence should enjoy it."

Aphrodite gave him a sweet smile. "I'd like it if you read some to me, but then again, I'd like anything you read to me."

"Disgusting," Shaunee said, going over to sit by Erin.

"Totally," Erin agreed, grinning at her twin.

"Good, we didn't miss the poem part," Stevie Rae said, plopping down next to me and petting Nala. "I was wonderin' what Kramisha had come up with."

"Okay, well, I'll just read it out loud," I said, and began,

> *A double-edged sword*
> *One side destroys*
> *One releases*
> *I am your Gordian knot*
> *Will you release or destroy me?*
> *Follow truth and you shall:*

Find me on water
Purify me through fire
Trapped by earth nevermore
Air will whisper to you
What spirit already knows:
That even shattered
anything is possible
If you believe
Then we shall both be free.

"I hate to say it, but even I can tell that's from Kalona to you," Aphrodite spoke into the thick silence that followed my reading.

"Yep, sounds like it to me, too," said Stevie Rae.

"Ah, hell," I muttered.

CHAPTER TWENTY-EIGHT

Zoey

"I don't like it," Stark said.

"You already said that," Aphrodite said. "And none of us like it, but that doesn't make the stupid poem go away."

"Prophecy," Damien corrected her. "Kramisha's poems are prophetic in nature."

"Which is not necessarily a bad thing," Darius said. "If we have a prophecy that also means we have forewarning."

"So these poems plus Aphrodite's visions combine to create a powerful tool for us," Lenobia said.

"If we can figure them out," I said.

"We figured out the last one," Lenobia reminded me. "We'll decipher this one, too."

"No matter what, I think all of us agree that Zoey has to follow Kalona," Darius said.

"It's what I was created for," I said, which definitely got everyone's attention. "I hate it. I don't know what to do about it. Most of the time I feel like I'm a giant snowball rolling down a mountain in the middle of winter, but I can't ignore the truth." I remembered Nyx's whispers and added, "There's power in the truth, just like there's power in making the right choice. The truth is that I'm connected to Kalona. I remember the connection, and remembering it makes Kalona hard for me to deal with, but something inside me defeated him once. I think I have to find that something and make the choice to defeat him all over again."

"This time maybe for good?" Stevie Rae said.

"I seriously hope so," I said.

"Well, this time you won't be alone," Stark said.

"That's right," said Damien.

"Absolutely," Shaunee said.

"Yep," Erin added.

"All for one and one for Zoey!" Stevie Rae said.

I looked at Aphrodite. She sighed dramatically. "Fine. Where the nerd of herd goes, I'll go, too."

Darius put his arm around her. "You won't be alone, either, my beauty."

It was only later that I realized Stevie Rae hadn't said anything about joining us.

"All of this solidarity is good, but we can't act because we don't know where Kalona is," said Lenobia.

"Well, in my dream I found him on an island. Actually, on top of a castle on an island," I specified.

"Did anything look familiar about it?" Damien asked.

"No. It was really pretty, though. The water was incredibly blue, and there were orange trees everywhere."

"That doesn't exactly narrow it down," Aphrodite said. "Oranges are all over—Florida, California, the Mediterranean. All those places have islands."

"He's not in America." My response was automatic. "I don't know how I know that, but I do."

"Then we'll take it as truth," Lenobia said.

Her confidence in me made me feel good, but nervous, and kinda sick all at the same time.

"Okay, well," Stevie Rae said. "Maybe you know more stuff about where he is, but you just need to not think about it for a while so you can think about it."

"Bumpkin, you make no damn sense," Aphrodite said. "Here, I'll translate from countrified Okie to English." Aphrodite turned to me. "Without thinking about it you knew he wasn't in America. Maybe you're trying too hard to figure this out. Maybe you just need to relax and it'll come to you."

"That's exactly what I said," Stevie Rae muttered.

"They're Twin-like," Shaunee said.

"Hilarious," Erin agreed.

"Shut up!" Aphrodite and Stevie Rae said together, which made the Twins convulse into laughter.

"Hey, what's so funny?" asked Jack as he came into the room. I noticed that he still had tear tracks on his cheeks and his eyes looked haunted.

He went to Damien and sat close beside him. "Nothing's funny. The Twins are just being the Twins," he told Jack.

"All right, enough of this. It's nonproductive and absolutely not helping us figure out where Kalona might be," Lenobia said.

"I know where Kalona is," Jack said, matter-of-factly.

"What do you mean, you know where Kalona is?" Damien said while we all gawked at Jack.

"Well, him and Neferet, that is. Easy." He held up his iPhone. "Internet's back up, and my Vamp Twitter has been going crazy. It's all over the Net about Shekinah dying all sudden and mysterious, and Neferet showing up in Venice at the High Council saying that she's Nyx Incarnate and Kalona's Erebus come to earth, so she should be the next Vampyre High Priestess." We stared at him. I know my mouth was definitely flopped open. Jack frowned at us. "I'm not making it up. Promise. You can see it all right here." He offered up his iPhone again, which Darius took. While he poked at the screen, Damien put his arms around Jack and kissed him smack on the mouth. "You are brilliant!" he told his boyfriend.

Jack smiled and everyone started talking at once.

Everyone except Stark and me.

In the middle of the chaos Heath came into the room. He hesitated for only a second, and then he walked around the bed and flopped down next to me on the side Stevie Rae wasn't taking up. "So, what's happening, Zo?"

"Jack found Kalona and Neferet," Stevie Rae told him.

"That's good," Heath said. His gaze met mine and he added, "Hang on, maybe it's not good."

"Why wouldn't it be good?" Stevie Rae asked.

"Ask Zoey," Heath said.

"What's wrong, Zoey?" Damien asked, shutting everyone up.

"It wasn't Venice," I said. "I'm sure about that. In my dream Kalona wasn't in Venice. I mean, I've never been there, but I've seen pictures and, correct me if I'm wrong, but there are definitely no mountains in Venice, right?"

"None at all," Lenobia said. "I've been there several times."

"Maybe it's not bad that you didn't actually go where he is in your dream. Maybe that means that the dreams aren't as real as you think they are," Aphrodite said.

"Maybe."

"It doesn't feel right," Stark said.

I suppressed a sigh of irritation because it was obvious he'd been psychically eavesdropping on me.

Aphrodite ignored Stark and kept talking. "Remember in my visions how I saw Neferet and Kalona in front of a group of seven powerful vampyres?"

I nodded.

"The Vampyre High Council!" Lenobia interjected. "I don't know why I didn't think of it right away." She shook her head, clearly annoyed at herself. "And I agree with Aphrodite. Zoey, perhaps you've given these dreams too much importance. Kalona is manipulating you," she said gently, as if she expected me to freak out.

"No, I'm telling you, Kalona wasn't in Venice, he was—" I broke off as a memory surfaced and felt like smacking myself in the forehead. "Holy crap! Kalona wasn't in Venice in my last dream, but I think I did dream he was in Venice in one of my dreams. He said he liked it there, that he felt the place's power and . . ." I rubbed my forehead as if trying to massage my brain into working better. "I remember—he said he felt some kind of ancient power there and he understood why *they* chose it."

"He must have been referring to us—to vampyres," Lenobia said.

I thought about the dream and frowned in confusion. "But I don't think where we were in the dream was actually in Venice. I mean, I saw that famous place with the gondolas and the big clock thing in the distance, but it was in the distance. We weren't actually there."

"Z, not to be mean or anything, but don't you ever do any home-work?" Stevie Rae said.

"Huh?" I said.

"San Clemente Island," Lenobia said.

"Huh?" I repeated brilliantly.

Damien sighed. "Do you have your *Fledgling Handbook 101* around here anywhere?"

I jerked my chin at my desk. "It's over there. I think."

He got up, dug around in the mess that was my desk, and then pulled out my *Fledgling Handbook*. He paged through it for, like, two seconds (Did he have the entire thing memorized?), and then handed me the open book. I blinked in shock as I recognized the beautiful, salmon-colored palace that had been a backdrop for one of my Kalona dreams.

"This is definitely where Kalona was in one of my other dreams. Actually, we were on this bench, right there." I pointed to the picture.

Aphrodite suddenly detached herself from Darius and came to peer over my shoulder. "Damn it! I should have recognized this place. I swear making me human has moroned me."

"Aphrodite, what is it?" Stark asked, stepping close to me.

"It's the palace she saw in the second vision she had of my death," I answered for her. I sighed. "I know this is going to sound stupid, but until now I forgot. I mean, I remember realizing in my dream that it could be the place you'd described where I'd drowned, but when I woke up . . . well . . ." I paused and met Stark's eyes. "I woke up and I got distracted." I saw the realization pass through his eyes as he understood he'd been the one to wake me up from the dream—the first time he'd slept with me—when he was just beginning to choose good over evil. "Plus," I added hastily, "you saw me drowning because I was all alone. That was when everyone was mad at me. I'm not alone anymore, so that vision won't come true." I looked from Stark to Aphrodite when she didn't say anything, and saw that she was staring at Stark.

"You weren't completely alone in the second death vision I had of you," Aphrodite said slowly. "I got a glimpse of Stark's face right before you were killed. He was there."

"What! That's bullshit! I'd never let her get hurt," Stark practically exploded.

"I didn't say you were responsible. I just said you were there," Aphrodite said coldly.

"What else did you see?" Heath asked, sitting straight up and looking as warriorlike as Stark ever had.

"Aphrodite had two visions of Zoey being killed," Damien spoke up. "In one she was decapitated by a Raven Mocker."

"That almost happened!" Heath blurted. "I was there. She still has the scar."

"The point is my head *wasn't* cut off. And now that my brain is working, we'll be sure I don't drown. And Aphrodite didn't see much in either vision."

"But you're sure the second death vision happened on San Clemente Island at the site of the High Council?" Lenobia asked.

Aphrodite pointed at the book that was still open on my lap. "There. That's the palace I saw when she was dying."

"Okay, so, I'll just be extra careful," I said.

"We'll all have to make sure you are," Lenobia said.

I sat there trying not to show how claustrophobic I was already feeling. Did that mean no one was ever going to leave me alone?

Stark didn't say anything. He didn't have to. His body language telegraphed frustration.

"Hang on. I just realized something." Damien took the *Fledgling Handbook* from me and flipped the page. When he looked at me, his smile was victorious. "I know where Kalona's island is, and you're right. It's not Venice." He turned the book to face me and said, "Is this where you were in your dream?"

Damien had opened the book to a page that had a bunch of text (that I clearly hadn't read), and an illustration of part of a pretty island, all hilly and blue-tinged by the color of the sea surrounding it. On the drawing I could see the outline of a castle that was all too familiar.

"That's it," I said solemnly. "That's where I was in my last dream. Where the hell is it?"

"Italy, the island of Capri," Lenobia answered for him. "It's the ancient site of the first Vampyre High Council. It only moved to Venice after 79 A.D."

I was glad to see several faces with question marks on them. Damien obviously didn't have one of them. In his schoolteacher's voice he said, "Vampyres were the patrons of Pompeii. Vesuvius erupted in August of 79 A.D." Everyone was still blinking like big, dumb goldfish at him, so he sighed and continued. "Capri is an island not far from Pompeii."

"Oh, yeah, I remember reading somethin' 'bout that in the history chapter," Stevie Rae said.

I didn't remember because I hadn't ever read the chapter, and by the way Shaunee and Erin were fidgeting, they hadn't either. Big surprise.

"Okay, that's interesting, and, yeah, that's the island. But why would he go there if the High Council hasn't been there for a bazillion years?" I asked.

"He wants to bring back the ancient ways," Stark said. "He's said it over and over."

"So is he at the palace in San Clemente or Capri?" I said, still confused.

"Twitter says he went in front of the High Council with Neferet just a couple of hours ago. So he's there now," Jack said.

"But I'll bet his base is on Capri," Stark said.

"So it looks like we'll be making a trip to Italy," Damien said.

"I hope you peasants have your passports in order," Aphrodite said.

CHAPTER TWENTY-NINE

Zoey

"Oh, don't be so hateful, Aphrodite," Stevie Rae said. "You know all fledglings get passports as soon as they're Marked. It's part of the whole 'I'm an emancipated teen' thing."

"Good thing I have a passport," Heath said. "Even though I'm not Marked."

To stop myself from yelling *"You're not going—you'll get killed for sure"* at Heath and embarrassing the bejesus outta him, I made myself focus on logistics. "Anyone know how we're getting to Italy?"

"First class, I hope," Aphrodite muttered.

"That will be the easy part. We'll simply take the House of Night's jet," Lenobia said. "Or rather, you and your group will. I'll authorize it, but I won't be going."

"You won't go with us?" My stomach dropped. Lenobia was wise and so well thought of in the vamp community that even Shekinah had respected her. We needed her to go with us. I needed her to go with us!

"She can't," Jack said. We looked at him in surprise. "She has to stay here with Dragon and be sure the school doesn't go completely over to the Dark Side, 'cause whatever it is Kalona can do, he's still doing it even though he's not here."

Lenobia smiled at Jack. "You're absolutely right. I can't leave the House of Night right now." Her gaze went around the room, touching on each of us and finally coming to rest on me. "You can lead them. You've been leading them. Just keep doing what you've been doing."

But I've messed up! More than once! And I don't even know if I can trust myself around Kalona! I wanted to shriek. Instead, I tried to speak in my grown-up voice. "But someone has to tell the High Council what's really going on with Neferet and Kalona. I can't do that. I'm just a fledgling."

"No, Zoey, you're our High Priestess, the first fledgling High Priestess, and they will listen to you because Nyx is with you. It's obvious to me. It was obvious to Shekinah. It will be obvious to them, as well."

I wasn't so sure, but everyone was giving me big smiles of encouragement, which really just made me want to barf my guts up. Rather than puking or my second choice, bursting into tears, I said, "When do we leave?"

"As soon as possible," Lenobia said. "We have no idea how much damage Kalona is doing right now. Think of the disaster he wrought here in only a matter of days."

"It's almost dawn. We're going to have to wait for the sun to set." Stark's voice was tight with frustration. "Because I would imagine now that the ice storm is over, the sun will actually be visible, and that means Stevie Rae and I will fry getting to the plane."

"You leave here at sunset," Lenobia said. "Until then, pack, eat, and rest. I'll take care of the arrangements."

"I don't think Zoey should stay on San Clemente Island," Stark said. He turned to Darius for support. "Don't you agree it's a bad idea for her to stay exactly where Aphrodite saw her drowning?"

"Stark, she also saw me getting decapitated right here in Tulsa. It didn't happen, though, because my friends didn't turn their backs on me. *Where* I am isn't as important as the fact that I know I'm in danger, and I'm surrounded by people who have my back."

"But she saw me with you! If I can't protect you, who can?"

"I can," Darius said.

"Air can, too," Damien said.

"Fire can kick some butt," Shaunee said.

"I got water, and I'm sure as hell not letting Zoey drown," Erin said indignantly.

"Earth will always protect Zoey," Stevie Rae said, though her expressive eyes seemed sad.

"I'm annoyingly human, but I'm still mean. If someone gets by Darius, you, and the nerd of herd, they'll have to go through me, too," said Aphrodite.

"Add one more annoying to that human, fledgling, and vamp soup," Heath said.

"See," I told Stark as I blinked hard to keep the tears that had filled my eyes from overflowing. "It's not all on you. We're in this together."

Stark's gaze held mine, and I could see how tortured he was. To have an oath-bound High Priestess be killed was every warrior's nightmare. Just the mention that Aphrodite had seen him there, and then seen me being killed anyway, had been enough to completely shake Stark's confidence.

"It really will be okay. I promise," I said.

He nodded and then looked away, like he couldn't bear to meet my gaze any longer.

"All right. Let's get busy. Pack light. You won't have time to carry around a bunch of baggage. Each of you take a book bag with your essentials," Lenobia said. I saw Aphrodite blanch in horror and had to cough to hide a giggle. "I'll meet you in the cafeteria at sunset." She started to leave, then paused at the door. "Zoey, be sure you're not sleeping alone. Let's keep Kalona out of your head as much as possible. We don't want him to have any idea you're coming after him."

I swallowed hard, but nodded. "Yeah, okay."

"Blessed be," she said.

"Blessed be," we all chimed in, even Heath.

Lenobia closed the door, and no one said anything for a few moments. I think we were all a little stunned and hadn't quite grasped the fact that we were actually going to Italy to speak before the Vampyre High Council. Or at least I was going to speak. Ah, hell. *I was going to have to speak in front of the Vampyre High Council.* Or maybe I'd get up there, in front of all those old, powerful vamps and have raging diarrhea and poo myself. Yep. That would certainly make an impression on the Council. "Unique" would be just one of the words they'd call me.

Jack's question stopped my semi-hysterical mind babble. "What are we gonna do with Duchess and the cats?"

I looked down at Nala, purring away beside me, and said, "Uh-oh."

"We can't take them," Stark said. "There's no way." Then sounding more like himself he added, "They're gonna be pissed when we get back, though. Especially those cats. Cats can carry a grudge."

Aphrodite snorted. "You're telling me. Have you met my cat? Speaking of, I'm going to go spend some quality time with her while I grab something to eat and pack." She gave Darius a coy smile. "If you'd like to get in on that quality time, you're invited."

"I don't have to be asked twice," he said. "Blessed be, Priestess," he told me before taking her hand heading to her room to do Goddess-was-the-only-one-who-wanted-to-know what.

"We better get our stuff taken care of, too," Damien said.

"I can't believe we're supposed to take *one* book bag of clothes. Where are all my shoes going to go?" Jack asked.

"I think we're only supposed to take one pair of shoes," Heath said helpfully.

Jack was still gasping in horror as he and Damien left.

That left me with Stark and Heath and Stevie Rae. Before things could get mega-awkward, Stark surprised me by saying, "Heath, would you sleep with Zoey?"

"Hey, man, as far as I'm concerned, I'd like to *always* sleep with Zoey."

I punched his arm, but he still grinned like a dork.

"What are you going to do?" I asked Stark.

He wouldn't meet my eyes. "I want to check the perimeter before dawn, and I'll see if Lenobia needs help settling things. Then I'll get something to eat."

"Where are you going to sleep?"

"In the dark." He turned to me, bowed formally with his right fist over his chest. "Blessed be, my lady." Before I could say anything else to him, he left.

I was stunned silent.

"He's freaked 'cause of Aphrodite's vision," Stevie Rae said, getting off my bed and going to rummage through the drawers that used to be hers before she died and un-died. I was glad I'd made Neferet and the vamps give me some of her stuff back, so she actually had things to rummage through.

"Don't let Stark hurt your feelings, Zo," Heath said. "He's pissed at himself, not at you."

"Heath, I appreciate you wanting to make me feel better, but it's just too weird to have you be on Stark's side."

"Hey, I'm on your side, baby!" He bumped me with his shoulder, and then stretched all long and obvious before reaching an arm around me.

"Uh, Heath, could you do me a big ol' favor?" Stevie Rae asked.

"Sure!"

"Could you go down to the kitchen—that's through the common room and to the right—and try to scare up somethin' for us to eat? They always have a bunch of sandwich stuff in the fridges. You can search for chips, but the closest you'll come is probably pretzels or those good-for-you baked chips."

"Yuck," Heath and I said at the same time.

"So is that okay? Would you do that?"

"Yeah, Stevie Rae, no problem." Heath hugged me and gave me a sloppy kiss on my forehead before bounding out of bed. At the door he grinned back at Stevie Rae and said, "But next time you want to talk to Zo alone, all you have to do is say so. I'm human and I play football, but I'm really not stupid."

"I'll keep that in mind for next time," she said.

He winked at me and took off.

"Goddess, he has a lot of energy," I said.

"Z, I can't go with y'all to Italy," Stevie Rae blurted out with no preamble whatsoever.

"What? You have to! You're earth. I need the whole circle there."

"You've circled without me before. Aphrodite can step in if you help her."

"She can't be earth. It zaps her," I said.

"But I know you've given her spirit before, and it worked fine. Just give her spirit again."

"Stevie Rae, I need you."

My BFF bowed her head and looked completely defeated. "Please, please don't say that. *I have to stay.* I don't have any choice. The red fledglings need me even more than you do."

"Not any more they don't," I said earnestly. "They're here at the school, with a whole bunch of adult vamps. Even if the adult vamps are acting all weird, their presence will be enough to keep your kids from rejecting the Change."

"It's not just that. It's not just them."

"Oh, no! Stevie Rae, you are *not* still thinking about those bad fledglings."

"I'm their High Priestess," she said quietly, pleading with her eyes for me to understand. "They're my responsibility. While you're gone, before you have to go down there and do something awful to them, I can try once more to reach them—to get them to turn back to their humanity."

"Stevie Rae—"

"Zoey! Listen to me! It's a *choice.* I made the right one. Stark made the right one. The kids here are all on the right path, too, and we used to be bad. Like you said, you know how horrible it used to be for us, but that's changed. We're different now because we're choosing to be different. I can't help believing that those other kids can choose good, too. Just let me try."

"I don't know. What if they hurt you?"

Stevie Rae laughed, and her short blond curls bounced around her shoulders. "Ah, heck, Z! They can't hurt me. They're *inside* the earth. If they try anything with me I can call on my element to kick their butts, and they know it."

"Maybe they were meant to die, and that's why they can't get their humanity back," I said softly.

"I can't believe that, at least not yet." Stevie Rae went to her old bed and sat across from me, just like she used to before our world started to explode around us. "I want to go with you. I really do. Heck, Z, you're in more danger than I am! But I have to do the right thing, and that's to try to reach those other kids and give them one more chance. Do you understand?"

"Yeah, I do. It's just that I've really missed you and I wish you were coming with me."

Tears filled Stevie Rae's eyes. "I've missed you, too, Z. It's been horrible keeping stuff from you. I was just so scared you wouldn't understand."

"I know what it's like to keep secrets. It sucks."

"Seriously, that's an understatement," she said. "We're still best friends, right?"

"We'll always be best friends," I said.

Grinning, she launched herself at me and we hugged so hard that Nala woke up, grumbling at us like she was someone's mom.

Heath chose that instant to burst back into the room. Arms filled with food, he stopped and stared. "Yes! I have died and gone to girl-on-girl heaven!"

"Ohmygoddess!" I said.

"Heath, you are nasty as roadkill—stinky, disgusting, middle-of-the-summer-opossum roadkill."

"Eesh, that's disgusting," I said.

"Well, that's your boyfriend."

"But I brought food," he said.

"Fine, you're forgiven," I said.

"Hey, just so you know, I'm sleepin' right here in my old bed. So there won't be any groping and making out going on because I'm not cool with that." Stevie Rae was talking to Heath, but I answered.

"Uh, I have two words for girls who make out with their boyfriends with other girls in the room: Not okay. So you don't need to worry about that stuff going on over here." I patted my bed. "Heath is going to be good because we already talked about how our relationship is based on more than sex. Right, Heath?"

Stevie Rae and I skewered him with our eyes.

"Right. Sad and tragic, but right," he admitted reluctantly.

"Good. Let's eat, then I'll help Z pack, and then we can get some sleep. Finally," Stevie Rae said.

* * *

I was just drifting off to sleep, snugly curled into Heath's strong, familiar arms when it hit me: *Heath really couldn't come with us.*

"Heath," I whispered. "We gotta talk."

"Changing your mind about that no-making-out thing?" he whispered back.

I elbowed him.

"Ow, what?" he said.

"I don't want you to get mad, but you really can't go with me to Italy."

"The hell I can't."

"Your parents will never let you miss that much school."

"We're on winter break."

"No, you *were* on ice storm break. The storm's clearing up. You'll be back at school in a day or so," I said.

"Then I'll make up my homework when I get back."

I tried a different tactic. "You've gotta stay here and focus on your grades. It's your last semester before you go to college. If you mess up your grades now, you mess up your scholarship."

"Look, this is simple. Broken Arrow has that online grade book thing, remember?"

"How could I forget something as totally annoying as my parental units being able to gawk at my grades and assignments every single day?" Then I clamped my mouth shut because I realized what I'd said.

"See! I can get my assignments online. I'll stay caught up. You can even help me. Or, better yet, Damien can help me. No offense, Zo, but I think he's a better student than you are."

"I *know* he is, but that's beside the point. Your parents will never let you go."

"They can't stop me. I'm eighteen."

"Heath, please. I already feel bad enough about all the poo I've brought into your life. Don't make me responsible for screwing up your last semester of school, getting you grounded until you leave for college, *and* putting your life in danger."

"I've told you before I can take care of myself," he said.

"Fine, let's compromise. Call your parents when we get up and ask them if you can come to Italy with me. If they say yes, then you come with me. If they say no, you stay here and get your butt back to class."

"Do I have to tell them about Kalona and that stuff?"

"I don't think it's smart for the general public to know there's a fallen immortal and a crazy ex–High Priestess trying to take over the world. So, no, you don't have to tell them that part."

He hesitated and then said, "Okay, I can live with that."

"Promise?"

"Promise."

"Good, because I'll be listening to the whole conversation so you won't be able to bullpoopie me."

"You know that's not a real word, Zo."

"It's *my* real word. Go to sleep, Heath."

He tightened his arms around me. "I heart you, Zo."

"I heart you, too."

"I'll keep you safe."

I fell asleep with Heath's arms around me and a smile on my face, my last conscious thought was about how strong he felt and that I'd have to tell him I really appreciated how buff he'd been keeping himself.

My next thought was not conscious and it was totally not soothing: *What in the hell am I doing on the roof of this castle again?*

CHAPTER THIRTY

Zoey

It was the same castle rooftop; there was no doubt about it. The orange trees were filled with fat fruit that scented the cool breeze. In the center was the same fountain shaped like a naked woman with water cascading from her raised hands. Seeing her twice, I realized why she looked familiar. She reminded me of Nyx, or at least of one of the faces I'd seen the Goddess wear. And then I remembered what I'd learned about this place—that it was the ancient site of the original Vampyre High Council, so it totally made sense that the fountain would look like our Goddess. I wanted to sit beside it and breathe deep the smell of citrus and the sea air. I didn't want to turn where my gut was telling me to turn—and see who I knew I was going to see. But, like the snowball down the mountain, I couldn't seem to control the avalanche that was happening to me, so I turned in the direction my soul was leading me.

Kalona knelt by the edge of the castle's toothlike roof. His back was to me and he was on his knees. He was dressed, or rather, *un*dressed, like he'd been the last time we'd been here—he had on jeans and that was it. His dark wings spread down around him, leaving only his bronze shoulders visible. His head was bowed, and he didn't seem to know I was there. As if I couldn't stop them, my feet moved toward him, and as I approached, I realized that he was kneeling exactly where I'd been standing when I'd flung myself off the rooftop.

I wasn't far from him when I saw his shoulders tense. His wings rustled and then his head lifted and he glanced over his shoulder.

He was crying. Tears made wet paths down his face. He looked crushed, broken, completely defeated. But the instant he saw me his expression changed. His face was suffused with such incredible joy that my breath literally caught at his incomparable beauty. He stood, and with a shout of happiness strode toward me.

I thought he would pull me into his arms, but at the last second he checked himself so that he only lifted one hand as if he was going to touch my cheek, but his fingers stopped short of my skin, hesitated there for an instant, and then, without touching me, his hand dropped back to his side.

"You came back."

"Dreams aren't real. I didn't die," I said, though it was hard for me to speak.

"The realm of dreams is part of the Otherworld; don't ever underestimate the power of what happens here." He wiped his face with the back of his hand and, surprising me again, gave an embarrassed little chuckle. "I must seem foolish to you. I knew you weren't dead, of course. Yet it still felt so real—so horribly familiar."

I stared at him, not knowing what to say. Not knowing how to react to this version of Kalona—the version who looked and acted more like an angel than a demon. He reminded me of the Kalona who had surrendered to A-ya, willingly giving himself to the trap of her embrace with a vulnerability that still haunted me. It was such a contrast from the last time I'd been here, when he'd been in superseduction mode, all groping me, and . . .

I narrowed my eyes at him. "Just exactly how can I be here again? I'm not sleeping alone, and I don't mean I'm with one of my girlfriends. Or rather, friends who are girls," I corrected hastily. "I'm sleeping in the arms of the human guy I've Imprinted. He and I are definitely more than friends. You shouldn't be able to get in here." I pointed to my head.

"I am not inside your head. You have never called me into your dreams. I draw your essence to me. The invasion was mine, not through any invitation of yours."

"That's not what you said before."

"I lied to you before. I am speaking the truth to you now."

"Why?"

"For the same reason I was able to draw you here through your sleep even though you are in the arms of another. This time—for the first time—my motives are pure. I am not attempting to manipulate you. I am not attempting to seduce you. And I will speak only truth to you."

"How can you expect me to believe that?"

"Whether you believe it or not does not change the nature of truth. You are here, Zoey, when you should not be. Is that not proof enough for you?"

I chewed my lip. "I don't know. I don't know the rules here."

"You do know about the power of truth, though. You showed me that during your last visit. Can you not draw on that power to judge the veracity of what I'm saying?"

Thanks to Damien, I knew veracity meant truth, so I wasn't standing there chewing my lip with a big question mark on my face because I didn't get what he meant. I question marked because I didn't know how to respond to him. Kalona was completely baffling me. Finally I opened my mouth to tell him that, no, I couldn't count on the power of truth when I didn't have a clue what he might be lying about, but he held up one hand and stopped my words.

"You asked me once before if I have always been as I am now, and I only gave you evasions and lies. Today I'd like to give you the truth. Will you let me, Zoey?"

Again, he called me Zoey! He hadn't once called me A-ya, as he liked to do. And he wasn't touching me. At all.

"I-I don't know," I stuttered like a moron and took a half step back, expecting the good-guy act to fade and the seductive immortal to reappear. "What are you going to do to show me?"

His beautiful amber eyes darkened with sadness. He shook his head. "No, Zoey. You need not fear that I'll try to make love to you. Should I attempt to shift from truth to seduction, this dream would shatter and you would find yourself waking in another man's arms. For me to show you what you need to see, you need only take my hand." He held it out to me, strong and normal-looking.

I hesitated.

"I give you my oath that my skin will not burn you with the cold power of the lust I have for you. I know you have no reason to trust me, so I ask only that you trust in truth. Touch me, and you will see that I am not lying to you."

It's just a dream. I reminded myself. *No matter what he says about the Otherworld, a dream is a dream. This isn't real.* But truth was real, whether in dreams or the waking world, and the sad truth was that I wanted to take his hand. I wanted to see what it was he needed to show me.

So I lifted my hand and pressed my palm to his.

He'd been telling the truth. For the first time, his skin didn't freeze me with a passion and power that I couldn't accept, even when I couldn't make myself completely reject it.

"I want to show you my past." The hand not holding mine swept in front of us like he was wiping an invisible window once, twice, three times. Then the air wavered and with an awful ripping sound something opened before us, like he'd torn a piece of the dream realm open. "Now behold the truth!"

At his command the rip in the sky shivered and then, like a big flat-screen TV had suddenly been turned on, I began watching pieces of Kalona's past.

The first scene I saw had me breathless at its beauty. Kalona was there, half naked as always, but this time he held one long, dangerous-looking sword while another one was in a scabbard strapped across his back, *and his wings were pure white!* He was standing outside a magnificent door to a marble temple. He looked dangerous and noble— every bit a true Warrior. As I watched, his stern expression changed to something softer, and as the woman walked up the stairs of the temple, he smiled at her with obvious adoration.

Merry meet, Kalona, my Warrior.

Her voice echoed eerily from the past and I gasped. I didn't need to see the woman's face. I instantly recognized her voice. "Nyx!" I cried.

"Indeed," Kalona said. "I was Nyx's Oath-sworn Warrior."

The Kalona in the vision followed his Goddess into her temple. The scene changed, and suddenly Kalona was using both his swords to battle something I couldn't quite focus on. The thing was black and kept changing shape. One instant it would be a huge serpent, in another it was an open mouth filled with glistening teeth, in yet another it appeared to be a hideous spiderlike creature with claws and fangs.

"What is that?"

"Just an aspect of evil." Kalona spoke slowly, as if the words were hard for him to say.

"But weren't you in Nyx's realm? How could evil get there?"

"Evil is everywhere, just as good is everywhere. It's the way the world and the Otherworld were made. There must be balance, even in Nyx's realm."

"That's why she needed a warrior?" I asked, watching the scene shift again to show Kalona, white wings blazing, walking behind Nyx as she strolled through a lush meadow. His eyes were never still, but constantly scanned the area around and behind the Goddess. One sword was drawn and in his hand. The other was ready in its scabbard.

"Yes, that is why she needs a warrior," he said.

"Needs." I tested the word, and then managed to look from the scenes of Kalona's past to the Kalona of the present. "If she still needs a warrior, then why are you here instead of there?"

His jaw tightened and his eyes filled with pain. His voice was broken when he answered me. "Look there, and you shall see the truth."

I focused my gaze back on the changing scenes to see Nyx standing before Kalona. He was on his knees in front of her, and just as he had been when I stepped into this dream, he was weeping. This incarnation of Nyx looked so much like the statue of Mary at the Benedictine nuns' grotto that I felt a little jolt of shock. But as I kept watching, I saw that something was off about Nyx. Unlike the serene beauty of the nuns' Mary, Nyx's expression was hard and appeared weirdly more stonelike than the statue.

Please do not do this, my Goddess. Kalona's voice lifted to us. It sounded as if he were begging.

I do nothing, Kalona. You have a choice in this. I give even my Warriors free will, though I don't require them to use it wisely. I was shocked by how cold Nyx sounded. For a second she actually reminded me of how Aphrodite used to be.

I cannot help myself. I was created to feel this. It is not free will. It is preordination.

Yet as your Goddess I tell you what you are is not preordained. Your will has fashioned you.

I cannot help how I feel! I cannot help what I am!

You, my Warrior, are mistaken; therefore, you must pay the consequences of your mistake.

Nyx raised one perfect arm and flicked her fingers at Kalona. The Warrior was lifted from his knees and hurled backward, tumbling end over end.

Kalona fell.

I watched it.

I watched him scream and writhe in agony as he fell and fell and fell. When he finally landed, crumpled, broken, and bloody, in a lush field that reminded me of the Tall Grass Prairie, his wings had turned from white to the raven black they are today.

With a cry filled with pain, Kalona lifted his hand and wiped away the vision of the past. As the air before us shimmered and then became the rooftop garden of the castle again, he let loose of my hand and stepped away from me to sit on a bench under an orange tree. He didn't say anything. He just sat there looking out at the sparkling blue of the Mediterranean.

I followed, but didn't sit beside him. Instead, I stood in front of him, studying him as if I could really judge truth with my eyes.

"Why did she kick you out? What was it that you did?"

His eyes met mine. "I loved her too much." His voice was so emotionless he sounded like a ghost.

"How can you love your Goddess too much?" I asked automatically, even as the obvious answer came to me. There were different types of love—I was über-aware of that. Kalona's love for Nyx was obviously the wrong type.

"I was jealous. I even hated Erebus."

I blinked in shock. Erebus was Nyx's consort, her eternal lover.

"My love for her made me break my oath. I was so obsessed with her, I couldn't protect her anymore. I failed as her Warrior."

"That's terrible," I said, thinking of Stark. He'd only been sworn to me for days, and already I knew it would be like ripping away a part of his soul if he failed to protect me. And how long had Kalona been Nyx's Warrior? Centuries? How long was a piece of eternity?

Incredulous, I realized I was feeling sorry for Kalona. I couldn't be feeling sorry for him! Sure, he'd had his heart broken and fell from the Goddess's realm, but then he'd turned into a bad guy. He'd become the evil he used to fight.

He nodded his head and, as if he could hear my thoughts, said, "I did terrible things. I've continued to do them. Falling changed me. Then, for so long I was numb inside. I searched and searched, century after century, trying to find something, some*one* to fill the bloody wound Nyx had left within my soul, within my heart. When I found her, I didn't know she wasn't real, that she was just an illusion created to entrap me. I went willingly into her arms. Did you know that when she began to shift her form back to the clay from which she'd been made, she wept?"

My body jerked. I knew what he was talking about. I'd experienced it with her.

"Yes." My voice was a rough whisper. "I remember."

His eyes widened in shock. "You remember? You have A-ya's memories?"

I didn't want to admit the extent of the A-ya memory, but I knew I couldn't lie. So I fashioned a small piece of the truth and gave it to him in short, tight words. "Only one. I just remember dissolving. And I remember A-ya crying."

"I am glad you don't remember anything else, because her spirit stayed with me, trapped there in the darkness, for a long time. I couldn't touch her, but I could sense her presence. I think it was the only thing that kept me sane." A shiver rippled through his body and I saw his hands begin to lift, as if he would literally try to push away the memory. He was silent for a long time. I thought he might be done with his retelling of the past, and I was trying to sift through the shock and disbelief in my mind to find a question to ask him when he began to speak again. "Then A-ya was gone. That is when I began calling. I whispered my need to be free to the world, and the world finally heard me."

"Don't you mean Neferet heard you?"

"It is true that she heard me, but it wasn't only the Tsi Sgili who answered my call."

I shook my head. "You didn't call me to the House of Night. Nyx Marked me. That's why I'm there."

"Is it? I must speak only the truth or our dream disappears, so I will not try to persuade you by pretending I know more than I do. I will only say what I believe, and I do believe you heard me, too. Or at least the part of you that was once A-ya heard and recognized my voice." He hesitated, and then added, "Perhaps Nyx's hand was guiding your reincarnation. Perhaps the Goddess sent you to—"

"No!" I couldn't listen to any more. My heart was beating so hard I thought it would burst from my chest. "Nyx didn't send me to you, just like I'm not really A-ya. It doesn't matter that I have some random memory that's hers. In this lifetime I'm a *real* girl, with free will and a mind of my own."

His expression changed again. His eyes softened as he smiled at me tenderly. "I know, Zoey, and that is why I have had such a struggle with my feelings for you. I woke from the earth wanting the maiden who had imprisoned me, to find a girl with free will fighting against me."

"Why are you doing this? Why do you sound like this? You're not really this guy!" I shouted at him, trying to yell down the terrible, wonderful way his words were making me feel.

"It happened when you fell. I saw myself falling again, and in that vision I also saw my heart breaking again. I couldn't bear it. I swore to myself that if I could draw you to me one more time I would show you the truth."

"If this is really true, then you have to know that you've become the evil you used to fight."

He looked away from me, but not before I saw shame in his eyes. "Yes. I know."

"I've chosen a different path. I can't love evil. And *that* is the truth," I said.

His eyes came instantly back to me. "And if I choose to reject evil? What then?"

His questions threw me totally off guard, so I blurted the first thing that came to my mind. "You can't reject evil, not while you're with Neferet."

"What if I'm only evil with Neferet? What if the truth is that if I were with you, I could choose good?"

"Impossible." I was shaking my head back and forth, back and forth.

"Why do you call it impossible? It has happened before. You know because you caused the choice for good. The warrior who is bound to you is proof of it."

"No. This version of you isn't real. You're not Stark. You're a fallen immortal, Neferet's lover. You've raped women—made people your slaves—killed people. Your sons almost killed my grandma. One of them did kill Professor Anastasia!" I grabbed on to all the negatives I could and hurled them at him. "The fledglings and professors at the House of Night started to question Nyx because of you. They're still acting wrong. Whether it's their choice or not, they're filled with fear and hate and jealousy, just like you were with Nyx!"

He acted like I wasn't standing there shrieking at him. He simply said, "You saved Stark. Can't you save me, too?"

"No!" I screamed.

And sat straight up in bed.

"Zo, it's okay. I got ya." Heath was there, wiping sleep from his eyes with one hand and rubbing my back with the other.

"Oh, Goddess," I said, blowing out a long, trembling breath.

"What's wrong? Bad dream?"

"Yeah, yeah. Weird, bad dream." I glanced at the bed across the room. Stevie Rae hadn't moved. Nala was curled by her shoulder. My cat sneezed at me. "Traitor," I told her, trying to force myself to sound normal again.

"Well, then, go back to sleep. This switching up days and nights is finally working for me and I want to stay in practice," Heath said, holding his arms open for me to slide back into.

"Okay, yeah, sorry." I lay back, curling into a ball that was frighteningly similar to a fetal position.

"Go back to sleep," Heath repeated around a huge yawn. "Everything's okay."

I lay awake for a long time wishing desperately that it was true.

CHAPTER THIRTY-ONE

Zoey

When we woke up near dusk I couldn't bear to think about Kalona and the dream, so I pounced on Heath. "Okay, time to call your mom and dad so they can tell you to come home."

"Are you okay, Z?" Stevie Rae asked while she towel-dried her hair. She and I had stuffed things in my book bag while Heath showered, then we'd taken turns getting ready. Her question made me realize that in all that time I hadn't done much more than mumble monosyllabic responses to anything she or Heath said.

"Yep. I'm okay. I'm just going to miss Heath, that's all," I lied. Okay, well, it wasn't actually a lie, because I would miss Heath while we were in Italy, but that's not why I hadn't felt like talking.

Kalona was why I hadn't felt like talking. I was afraid that if I said too much last night's dream would start to babble from my mouth and I'd tell Stevie Rae everything, and I didn't want to do that in front of Heath. No, there was more to it than that. I didn't want to tell anyone about the new version of Kalona I'd seen.

I didn't want to hear them tell me it was all smoke and mirrors.

Heath's hug made me jump. "Aw, that's sweet, Zo," he said, oblivious to the terrible deception going on inside my head. "But you're not going to have to miss me. I have a good feeling about this phone call."

I shook my head at him. "No way is your mommy going to let you take off to Italy with me."

"Not with *you*, maybe. But with your school—that's another thing."

Before I could say anything he punched his phone, and his end of the conversation began:

"Hey, Ma, it's me."

"Yep, I'm okay."

"Yep, I'm still with Zoey." Here he paused and then looked at me and said, "Mom says to say hi."

"Tell her 'hi' for me." Then I whispered: "*Get to it!*"

He nodded. "Hey Ma, speaking of Zo, she and some of the House of Night kids are going to Italy. Venice actually, well more like that island that's by Venice. You know, San Cle-something. Where the vamp High Council meets and stuff. I want to know if I can go with them."

I could hear his mom's voice rising and I had to suppress a smile. I'd known his mom would freak.

Of course I hadn't known the card Heath had up his fibbing sleeve.

"Hang on, Mom. It's really no big deal. It's like that trip I wanted to take with the Spanish teacher last summer, but couldn't go 'cause of football practice starting. Remember?" He nodded to whatever his mom was saying. "Yeah, it's a school thing. We'll be gone eight days, just like the Spanish trip. Actually, I bet I can use my Spanish 'cause Italian is, like, a cousin." He paused again and then said, "Okay, yeah, that's cool."

"She says I have to ask Dad," he whispered, covering the phone with his hand.

Then I heard a deeper voice get on the line, and Heath said, "Hey, Dad. Yeah, I'm good." He waited while his dad talked, and then continued, "Yeah, that's basically the deal. It's a school trip. I can do my homework online." Heath smiled in response to what his dad was saying. "Really? They're calling off school for all of next week 'cause of power outages in the neighborhoods?" He waggled his eyebrows at me. "Wow, that makes this trip super-convenient. And, get this Dad, since we're flying on the House of Night's private jet, and staying at the vamp's island, it's not gonna cost me anything."

I ground my teeth together. I could not believe he was working his parents so easily. Of course, it was true that even though Nancy and

Steve Luck were nice people and pretty good parents, they were absolutely clueless about teenage stuff. Seriously. Heath had been drinking for years and they never noticed, not even when he came home smelling like puke and beer. Ugh.

"Great, Dad! Thanks a bunch!" Heath's exuberance had me blinking and refocusing on him and not my mind babble. "Yeah, I'll call you guys every day." He paused while his dad said something else. "Oh, I almost forgot that. Okay, well, while Zo and the rest of the kids are getting ready, I'll run home and grab my passport and some clothes. Tell Mom we're only supposed to take one book bag of stuff each, though, so not to go all crazy on the packing. Okay, I'll see you in a few! Bye!" Grinning like he was back in grade school and had just been given an extra carton of chocolate milk during snacktime, he hung up.

"That was slick," Stevie Rae said.

"I'd forgotten all about that Spanish trip," I said.

"I hadn't. So it looks like I need to get home quick and grab my passport and stuff. I'll meet ya at the airport. Don't leave without me!" He kissed me quickly, grabbed his coat, and rushed out of the room like he wanted to escape before I could tell him once and for all, no matter what his clueless parents said, he was so *not going*.

"You're really lettin' him go with y'all?" Stevie Rae said.

"Yeah," I said apathetically. "I guess I am."

"Well, I'm glad. Not to be mean or anything, but I think it's a good idea because of the whole blood thing."

"Blood thing?"

"Z, he's your Imprinted human. His blood is super-good for you. You're going into a dangerous situation, with confronting Kalona and Neferet and the High Council, so you might need some super-good-for-you blood."

"Yeah, I guess you're right."

"Okay, Z. What the heck's up?"

I blinked at her. "What do you mean?"

"I mean you're acting like a zombie. So tell me about that 'weird' dream that woke you up."

"I thought you were asleep."

"That's what I wanted you to think in case you and Heath wanted to do some makin' out."

"With you in the room? That's just gross," I said.

"True, but still I was tryin' to be polite."

"Jeesh," I said. "Gross. I seriously wouldn't do that."

"And I'm seriously not gonna let you change the subject. The dream—remember? Tell me."

I sighed. Stevie Rae was my best friend, and I really should talk about it. "It was about Kalona," I blurted.

"He got in your dream even though you were sleepin' with Heath?"

"No. He didn't get in my dream," I said truthfully, though evasively. "It was more like a vision than a dream."

"A vision of what?"

"His past. Way back. Before he fell."

"Fell? From where?"

I drew a deep breath and told her the truth. "From Nyx's side. He used to be her Warrior."

"Ohmygood*ness*!" She sat down on her bed. "Are you sure?"

"Yes . . . No . . . I don't know! It seemed real, but I don't know for sure. I don't know how I can ever know for sure." Then my breath caught. "Oh, no."

"What?"

"In the memory I had of A-ya, she said something about Kalona not being meant to walk this world." I gulped and clasped my hands together to stop them from shaking. "And she called him her Warrior."

"Uh-oh. You mean like she knew he'd been Nyx's Warrior before he fell?"

"Oh, Goddess, I don't know." But I did. In my heart I knew A-ya had been trying to comfort Kalona with familiarity. He'd been a warrior once; he would want to be a warrior again.

"Maybe you should talk to Lenobia about—" Stevie Rae began.

"No! Stevie Rae, promise me you won't tell anyone. They already know I've had a memory of A-ya being with Kalona. Add that to Aphrodite's visions, it would just freak them out and make everyone think I'm going to suddenly lose my mind and be with him again—and that's just not going to happen." I said it like I meant it, and I did. I didn't care that it made my stomach feel sick. I couldn't be with Kalona. Like I'd told him, it was impossible.

But I didn't have to worry about Stevie Rae telling on me. She was nodding her head and looking at me with eyes filled with understanding. "You want to figure him out for yourself, don't you?"

"Yeah. Sounds stupid, doesn't it?"

"No," she said firmly. "Sometimes things just aren't anyone else's business. And some things that seem totally impossible end up being different than we'd ever expected."

"You really think so?"

"I hope so," she said earnestly. It seemed Stevie Rae wanted to say something more, but was interrupted by the knock on the door and Aphrodite's "Would you guys hurry the hell up? Everyone's already eating and we have a jet to catch."

"We're ready," Stevie Rae yelled, and then tossed my book bag to me. "I think you should follow what your gut is tellin' you, just like Nyx has always said. Sure, you've messed up in the past. So have I. But both of us have chosen to be squarely on the side of our Goddess, and that's what counts in the end."

I nodded, suddenly finding it hard to speak.

Stevie Rae hugged me. "You'll do the right thing. I know you will," she said.

My laugh sounded more like a sob, and I said, "Yeah, but after how many mess-ups?"

She smiled at me. "Life's about messing up. And I'm startin' to think it wouldn't be as exciting if we were perfect."

"I could do with a little boring right now," I said.

We were laughing when we walked out in the hall and joined an annoyed Aphrodite. I noticed her "book bag" was a Betsey Johnson carry-on, and that it was so full it was bulging at its fashionable seams.

"I think that's cheating," I said, pointing at her bag.

"It's not cheating. It's improvising."

"Cute bag," Stevie Rae said. "I heart me some Betsey Johnson."

"You are way too country for Betsey," Aphrodite said.

"Am not," Stevie Rae said.

"Am too," Aphrodite said, and countered with "Bumpkin exhibit A—those horrid jeans. Ropers? Seriously? I have two words for you: Up. Date."

"Oh, no. You did not just talk about my Ropers . . ."

I let the two of them bicker as I followed them to the cafeteria. Actually, I hardly heard them. My mind was miles away on a rooftop in the middle of a dream.

The cafeteria was busy, but, bizarrely, too quiet as Aphrodite, Stevie Rae, and I joined the Twins, Jack, and Damien, who were already wolfing down bacon and eggs. As I expected, I was drawing a lot of *kill you dead* looks, especially from the booths filled with girls.

"Ignore them. They're haters," Aphrodite said.

"It's so weird that Kalona's still messin' with their heads," Stevie Rae said as we filled our plates and kept throwing glances over our shoulders at the mostly silent and sullen room.

"It's their choice, too." My mouth blurted before I could stop it.

"What do ya mean?" Stevie Rae asked.

I gulped some eggs and said, "I mean the kids,"—I paused and waved my fork at the rest of the room for emphasis—"the ones who are giving us the stank eye and being so insanely horrid, are choosing to be that way. Yeah, Kalona started it, but they're choosing their own paths."

Stevie Rae's voice was soft with understanding, but no less insistent. "That could be true, Z, but you have to remember it's happened because of Kalona—well, him along with Neferet."

"What's *true* is that Kalona is bad shit, and Zoey has to deal with him once and for all," Aphrodite said.

My eggs suddenly looked less tasty.

We were all squished around the booth, eating and trying to pretend like people weren't killing us with their eyes, when Stark joined us. He looked tired, and when his gaze met mine, I recognized the sadness in his eyes. I'd seen it mirrored in Kalona's eyes as he spoke of Nyx. *Stark believes he's failed me.*

I smiled at him, wanting to wipe the worry from his face. "Hi," I said softly.

"Hi," he said.

Then we realized our table, as well as the entire room, was watching and listening to us. Stark cleared his throat, pulled up a chair, lowered his voice, and said, "Darius and Lenobia are already at the airport. I'm driving you guys in the Hummer." He glanced around, and I saw some of the tightness in his face relax. "So, I'm guessing you sent Heath home?"

"To get his passport," Stevie Rae proclaimed.

That, of course, caused a mini-uproar at our table. I sighed and waited for the storm to subside. When everyone finally shut up, I said, "Yes, Heath's coming with us. The end."

Aphrodite raised one blond brow. "Well, I suppose it does make sense to bring the bloodmobile with you. Even Arrow Boy over there with the mean face has to agree with that."

"I said 'the end' because I'm not going to talk about it. And don't call Heath a bloodmobile."

"It's really not polite," Stevie Rae said.

"Bite me," Aphrodite said, clearly without thinking, because the Twins automatically started to giggle.

"Stevie Rae isn't going with us," I broke into the Twins' hilarity. "So that means when we circle, Aphrodite will be representing spirit."

That shut the Twins up. Everyone stared at Stevie Rae.

"They might not be able to be saved," Damien said solemnly.

"I know, but I'm going to give it another try."

"Hey, do me a favor, will ya?" Aphrodite said. "Would you please *not* get killed? Again. I'm sure that would be annoyingly uncomfortable for me."

"I am not gettin' killed," Stevie Rae said.

"Promise you won't go back there alone," Jack said.

"That's a promise you need to make," Stark agreed.

I didn't say anything. I was no longer so cocky about knowing the only right way to do things.

Fortunately, my silence wasn't noticed because just then the red fledglings made their entrance, and the entire cafeteria went from gawking at us, to gawking and whispering at them.

"Better make sure they're fine," Stevie Rae said. She stood up and then smiled at us. "Y'all hurry and get stuff straight over there, so you can come back home over here." She hugged me, whispering, "You'll do the right thing."

"You will, too," I whispered back.

Then she moved away from me and I watched her take charge of the red fledglings (who waved at us as they got into line). Stevie Rae was so normal acting, talking to her kids like they hadn't just stepped into the cafeteria for the first time since each of them had died, that her group instantly started to relax, ignoring the stares and whispers.

"She's a good leader," I said, thinking out loud.

"I hope that doesn't get her into trouble," Aphrodite said. I looked from Stevie Rae to her and she shrugged. "Some people—especially evil, undead-dead people—can't be led."

"She'll do the right thing." I repeated Stevie Rae's words.

"Yeah, but will they?" Aphrodite said.

I didn't have a comeback for that, so I picked at my eggs instead.

"Are you guys about ready?" Stark finally said.

"I am," I said.

Everyone else nodded, and we grabbed our bags and headed to the door. Stark and I brought up the rear.

"Hey, Zoey."

Erik's voice stopped me. Stark stayed with me, his eyes sharp on my ex-boyfriend.

"Hi, Erik," I said guardedly.

"Good luck," he said.

"Thanks." I was pleasantly surprised at his neutral expression and lack of Venus suckerfished to his side. "Are you staying at the school and teaching drama again?"

"Yeah, but just until they get a new professor. So if I'm not here when you get back, I just wanted you to know, that, um"—he looked from Stark to me, and then finished with—"that I said good luck."

"Oh, okay. Well, thanks again."

He nodded and walked quickly out of the cafeteria ahead of us, presumably going up to the professors' dining room.

"Huh. That was kinda weird, but nice of him," I said.

"He acts too much," Stark said, holding the door open for me.

"Yeah, I get that, but I'm still glad he said something nice before we left. I hate the awkward ex-boyfriend stuff."

"Yet another reason to be glad I'm not technically your boyfriend," Stark said.

The rest of the group was several yards ahead of us, so we had an instant of privacy. I was just trying to figure out whether Stark was being borderline hateful in his "not your boyfriend" comment or not when he suddenly asked, "Was everything okay last night? You woke me up once."

"Everything was fine."

He hesitated and then said, "You didn't bite Heath again."

It wasn't a question, but I answered anyway, though my voice sounded sharper than I'd intended. "No. I was feeling fine, so I didn't need to."

"I'll understand if you do, though," he said.

"Can we not talk about this right now?"

"Yeah, fine." We walked on a few feet and were almost to the parking lot, so he slowed down, giving us another moment of privacy. "Are you mad at me?" he asked.

"Why would I be mad at you?"

He lifted his shoulders. "Well, first there's Aphrodite's visions. She sees you in trouble. Serious trouble. But she either sees me and I do nothing, or she doesn't see me at all. And now Heath's coming with us to Italy . . ." His words just trailed off, leaving him looking frustrated.

"Stark, Aphrodite's visions can be changed. We've done it several times. Once for me personally. We'll change the drowning one, too. Actually, *you'll* probably change it. You won't let anything bad happen to me."

"Even though I have an issue with going outside in the sunlight?"

I suddenly understood one of the reasons that this threat to me was bothering him so badly—he felt like he might not be able to be there for me when I needed him. "You'll figure out how to be sure I'm safe, even if you can't be with me physically."

"Do you really believe that?"

"With all my heart," I said honestly. "There is no other vampyre I would ever want as my Warrior. I trust you. Always."

Stark looked like about a zillion pounds had been lifted off his back. "It's good to hear you say that."

I stopped and faced him. "I would have told you that before, but I thought you already knew it."

"I guess I did. In here." Stark touched the spot over his heart. "But my ears needed to hear it."

I stepped into his arms and pressed my face against his neck. "I trust you. Always," I repeated.

"Thank you, my lady," he whispered as his strong arms held me close.

I stepped back and smiled at him. Suddenly Kalona seemed very distant as Stark filled up my here and now. "We'll figure out all this stuff, and through it all we'll be together—a Warrior and his lady."

"That's what I want," he said firmly. "And to hell with everything else."

"Yep. To hell with everyone and everything else." I refused to think about Kalona. He was a maybe—a big, scary, confusing maybe. Stark was a for-sure. I took his hand and, pulling him with me ... always with me ... toward the Hummer, said, "Come on, Warrior, let's go to Italy."

CHAPTER THIRTY-TWO

Zoey

"Venice is seven hours ahead of us," Lenobia explained. She'd met us outside the VIP security checkpoint. "When you land, it'll be late afternoon there. Try to sleep as much as you can on the plane. The High Council will convene just after dusk, and you'll be expected to be there and be alert."

"How's Stark going to handle the sun?" I asked.

"I've apprised the High Council of Stark's needs. They have assured me Stark will be shielded from the sun. You should know they are quite anxious to meet him and extremely curious about this new kind of vampyre."

"Curious as in wanting to study me like a lab rat?" Stark said.

"We will not let that happen," Darius said.

"I think you should keep in mind that the High Council is comprised of seven of the wisest and most ancient High Priestesses alive today. They do not behave inhumanly, nor are they rash," Lenobia said.

"So they're all kinda like Shekinah?" Jack asked.

"Shekinah was the Vampyre High Priestess, so she was unique, but each council member is elected by the body of vampyres for the position. The position is theirs for fifty years, and then a new member is elected. No member can hold the office consecutively. The council members are from all over the world, and they are known for their wisdom."

"Which means they should be smart enough not to fall for Kalona and Neferet," I said.

"It's not smarts we have to worry about," Aphrodite said. "It's choice. There're lots of *smart* vampyres at our House of Night who stood by and let Kalona and Neferet run over them."

"Aphrodite's point is valid," Damien said.

"So we need to be prepared for anything," Darius said.

"My thoughts exactly," Stark agreed.

Lenobia nodded solemnly. "Remember the outcome of this could change the world as we know it."

"Well, shit. No pressure there," Aphrodite said.

Lenobia shot her a sharp look, but didn't say anything to her. Instead she surprised me by looking at Jack. "I believe you should remain here," she told him.

"Oh, no way! I go where Damien goes," Jack said.

"Where Damien is going is dangerous," Lenobia said.

"Then I'm double going with him!"

"I think he should go," I said. "He's part of this. Plus," I continued, following my instincts and knowing by the sense of rightness inside me that I was voicing something Nyx wanted everyone to hear, "Jack has an affinity."

"What? I do?"

I smiled at him. "I think you do. Your affinity is for the magick of the modern world—technology."

Damien grinned. "It's true! Jack understands anything audiovisual or computer. I just thought he was a tech genius, but really he's a tech genius goddess squared."

"Ohmigod! How cool is that?" Jack said.

"Then you're right, Zoey. Jack should go with you. Nyx gifted him for a purpose, and that purpose could very well be of great use to you."

"Yeah, and also—" I was getting around to telling her about our other traveler, when Heath jogged up to us, book bag over his shoulder.

"Your consort goes, too?" Lenobia finished for me, with one brow raised at Heath.

"Damn right!" Heath said, putting his arm around me. "You never know when Zo might need to bite me."

"Okay, Heath, yeah, everyone understands that." I could feel my cheeks getting warm and I purposely kept my gaze from meeting Stark's.

"As a High Priestess's consort, you will be allowed in the Council Chamber," Lenobia told Heath. "But you will not be able to speak."

"There're a lot of rules about how to act in the Council Chamber, aren't there?" Damien said.

My stomach felt even sicker. "Rules?"

"There are," Lenobia said. "It's an ancient system designed to prevent chaos, yet to give speakers a fair hearing. You must follow the rules, or you will be escorted from the Chamber."

"But I don't know the rules!"

"That is why my friend, Erce, Horse Mistress for San Clemente Island, will meet you at the airport. She will take you to your rooms on the island and brief you on Council etiquette."

"I can't say anything?"

"Are you impaired?" Aphrodite asked Heath. "That's what Lenobia just told you."

"I'm not sure you'll be allowed within the Council Chamber at all," Lenobia told Aphrodite.

"What? But I'm . . ." Her words sputtered out. The truth was that, technically, Aphrodite was a human. An abnormal human, but still.

"Erce is requesting that you be present," Lenobia continued. "We shall see if they admit you or not."

"Why don't you guys go get on the plane? I gotta talk to Lenobia for a second."

"You depart out of gate twenty-six," Lenobia said. "Blessed be, and may Nyx stay close to you."

"Blessed be!" everyone said, and they headed for the twisty security line.

"How're the hurt fledglings?" I asked.

"Much improved. Thank you for what you did for them," she said.

I shook off her thanks. "I'm just glad they're better. What about Dragon?"

"Deep in mourning."

"I'm so sorry," I said.

"Defeat Kalona. Stop Neferet. That will help Dragon."

I ignored the skittering of panic inside me and changed the subject. "What are you going to do about the red fledglings?"

"I've considered that, and what I believe we should do is to honor the will of their High Priestess. I'll speak with Stevie Rae when I return to the school and we'll decide what she believes is best for her people."

It felt funny to hear Lenobia call Stevie Rae a High Priestess, but good funny. "You need to know that there are more red fledglings than just the ones with Stevie Rae."

Lenobia nodded. "Darius has informed me."

"What are you going to do about *them*?"

"As with the others, that decision should include Stevie Rae. It's a difficult situation. We don't even know exactly what it is they've become—or haven't become." Lenobia put her hand on my shoulder. "Zoey, you must not allow what might be happening here to distract you. Focus on Kalona and Neferet and the High Council. Trust that I'll take care of our House of Night."

I sighed. "Okay, I will. Or at least I'll try."

She smiled. "I've informed the High Council that we consider you our High Priestess."

I felt a little jolt of shock. "Seriously?"

"Seriously. You are, Zoey. You've earned it. And you're connected to Nyx in a way no other fledgling or vampyre has ever been. Keep following the Goddess and make us proud," she said.

"I'll try my best."

"And that is all we ask of you. Blessed be, Zoey Redbird."

"Blessed be," I said. Then I followed my gang to gate twenty-six, trying not to think too much about the fact that a High Priestess of Nyx had no business dreaming of her Goddess's ex-Warrior.

"Grandma, hi! How are you feeling?"

"Oh, Zoeybird! I am better today. I think the storm ending has strengthened me. Ice is beautiful, but only in small doses," said Grandma.

"Hey, don't think that means you need to rush back out to the lavender farm. Please promise me you'll let Sister Mary Angela take care of you for a while."

"Oh, do not fear, *u-we-tsi-a-ge-ya*. I find I rather like the company of the good sister. Will you come see me tonight? How are things at the school?"

"Well, Grandma, that's what I'm calling about. I'm getting ready to get on the school jet and go to Venice. Kalona and Neferet are there, and it looks like they're messing with the High Council."

"That is bad, *u-we-tsi-a-ge-ya*. You are not going into that battle alone, are you?"

"No way, Grandma. The whole gang's with me, plus Heath."

"Good. Don't feel ashamed to use his connection to you; it is the natural order of things."

Tears burned in the back of my throat. Grandma's constant love, no matter how vampyre-monster–like and weird my life had become, was the foundation of my whole world. "I love you, Grandma," I choked out.

"And I you, *u-we-tsi-a-ge-ya*. Do not fret about an old woman. Focus on your task at hand. I'll be here when you have won your battle."

"You sound so sure I will."

"I am sure of you, *u-we-tsi-a-ge-ya*, and sure you have your Goddess's favor."

"Grandma, I had a really weird dream about Kalona." I lowered my voice, even though I'd walked away from where the rest of the kids were waiting by the gate for our plane to be ready to board. "I saw that Kalona hasn't always been evil. He used to be Nyx's Warrior."

Grandma was silent for several long moments. Finally she said, "This sounds more like a vision than a dream."

I could feel the rightness of what she was saying. "A vision! So does that mean it's true?"

"Not necessarily, though it does give what you saw more importance than a simple dream. Did it seem truthful?"

I chewed my lip, then admitted, "Yes, it felt like what I was seeing was the truth."

"Remember to temper feelings with common sense. Listen to your heart, mind, *and* soul."

"I'm trying."

"Weigh your feelings with logic and reason through them. You are not A-ya. You are Zoey Redbird, and you have free will. If it becomes too overwhelming, look to your friends, especially Heath and Stark. They are connected to *you*, to Zoey, and not the ghost of an ancient Cherokee maiden."

"You're right, Grandma. I'll remember. I'm me, and that's not going to change."

"Zo! Plane's boarding!" Heath called.

"I gotta go, Grandma. I love you!"

"My love goes with you, *u-we-tsi-a-ge-ya*."

I got on the plane feeling renewed by my grandma's love. She was right. I needed to balance what I knew about Kalona and what I *thought* I *might* know about him.

My positive attitude was reinforced by the cool jet we were getting to fly in. It was all like first class with huge leather seats that lay all the way back and super-thick window coverings, which I immediately went around and pulled down.

"The sun's not out there right now, dork," Aphrodite said.

"I'm just taking care of this right now in case any of you *forget*"— I made air quotes around the word—"to close them later."

"I'm not going to burn up your Warrior," Aphrodite said. "Then *my* Warrior would have way too much to do."

"I will never be too busy for you," Darius said, taking the seat beside her and lifting the arm that separated them so they could snuggle.

"Barf," Erin said.

"Moving to the back of the plane so we don't get Aphrodite sick," Shaunee said.

"Is there a beverage service on this plane?" Damien asked.

"I hope so. I could use some brown pop," I said, loving that everyone was sounding as normal as I was suddenly feeling.

"Lenobia said we'd be on our own on this flight, but I would bet you could forage around after we get airborne and find something to drink," Darius said.

"I know where they keep the pop," Stark said. "This is the plane that flew me from Chicago to here. I'll get you some as soon as we take off." Then he gestured to the empty seat next to him. "Sit by me?"

"Hey, Zo!" Heath called from farther back in the plane. "I saved you a seat back here."

I sighed. "You know what, I think I'm going to sit over here by myself and just try to sleep. Jet lag is a killer," I said, choosing a seat midway between Heath and Stark.

"I'm taking a Xanax. I know how to fly," Aphrodite said. "I'll be ready to hit the stores the second we touch down in Venetia."

"Stores?" Shaunee called.

"Shopping?" Erin said.

"Perhaps we should reconnoiter with Aphrodikey," Shaunee said.

"Excellent idea, Twin," Erin agreed.

I smiled to myself as the Twins moved up to seats across from Aphrodite, who sneered at them, but launched quickly into an enthusiastic list of the shopping possibilities in Venice.

"Here." Stark handed me a blanket and a pillow. "It gets cold in planes sometimes, especially when you're trying to sleep."

"Thanks," I said. I wanted to tell him that I would like to curl up with him, but that I wouldn't like how that would make Heath feel (who was now in a big debate with Jack over whether Macs or PCs were better).

"Hey, it's okay. I understand," Stark said, lowering his voice. "You're the best Warrior in the world."

He smiled that cocky little grin I liked so much and kissed the top of my head. "Go to sleep. I'll keep a psychic ear on your feelings. If things get weird, I'll wake you up."

"I'm counting on that," I said.

I curled up with the blanket and pillow my Warrior had given me, and fell asleep almost before we were airborne.

If I dreamed I didn't remember it.

CHAPTER THIRTY-THREE

Stevie Rae

"I still disagree with you," Lenobia said.

"But it's my decision to make, right?" Stevie Rae said.

"It is. I just wish you would reconsider. Let me come with you. Or even Dragon—he could accompany you."

"Dragon is still too messed up from Anastasia's death, and you're pretty much in charge here. The way things are going, I don't think it's smart for you to leave the school right now," Stevie Rae said. "Look, I'll be fine. I know them. They're not gonna hurt me, and even if they've lost every bit of what's left of their minds and they do try to mess with me, they can't. I'll call earth and smack them around or somethin' like that. Don't worry. I've handled them before. This time I'm hopin' I can talk them into comin' back here with me. I think bein' back at the school would really help 'em."

Lenobia nodded. "That is logical. Return them to where they last felt normal and perhaps they can find that feeling again."

"That's kinda what I thought." Stevie Rae paused, and then added in a soft, sad voice, "I still argue back and forth with myself sometimes. Sometimes it feels like the darkness is so close to me that I could touch it. And I see it in my group—the ones who also found their humanity. It's not always easy for them, either."

"Maybe you'll always have a choice. Maybe the line between good and evil is less clear for you and your red fledglings."

"But does that make us bad? Or worthless?"

"No, of course not."

"Then you can see why I have to go back to the depot and talk to the other kids again. I can't turn my back on them. Zoey didn't turn her back on Stark, even though he shot me—which sucked and wasn't very nice of him, by the way—but it turned out okay in the end."

"You will make a fine High Priestess, Stevie Rae."

Stevie Rae's cheeks went all hot. "I'm not really a High Priestess. I'm just all they have."

"No, you are a High Priestess. Trust that. Trust yourself." She smiled at Stevie Rae. "So when will you return to the depot?"

"I think I'll be sure the red fledglings here are set. You know, get the rooms straight and get stuff for them to wear and all. Plus, they have to be put back into all their classes, which is a real pain in the butt since the classes change every semester. But I'd like to get back there tonight still."

"Tonight? Are you sure you shouldn't wait until tomorrow? Shouldn't you get settled here first?"

"Well, the truth is I don't really know if we can settle here."

"Of course you can. The House of Night is your home."

"It *was* our home. Now we feel better resting in the earth during the day." Stevie Rae gave her nervous grin. "It makes me sound like I should be in one of those stupid slasher movies, doesn't it?"

"No, it actually makes sense. You died. When that happens to any of us, all of our bodies return to the earth. Though you were resurrected, you still have a connection with the earth we do not." Lenobia hesitated. "There is a basement under the main House of Night building," she said. "It's used for storage and is not particularly habitable, but with some work . . ."

"Maybe," Stevie Rae said. "Let me see what happens with the kids at the depot. We really did like it there, and we were fixin' it up real nice, too."

"I don't suppose there is any reason why we couldn't bus your fledglings back and forth. Human children do it every day."

Stevie Rae grinned. "The big yellow limo!"

Lenobia laughed. "Either way, we will make it work with your group. You are part of us, and this is your home."

"Home . . . That sounds nice," Stevie Rae said. "Okay, well, I better get busy if I'm gonna make it back to the depot before it gets close to dawn."

"Be sure to give yourself plenty of time. I don't want you stuck there, and the forecast is for lots of Oklahoma sunshine. Travis Meyers even reported it might get above freezing long enough to get rid of some of this ice."

"Trav is my favorite weatherman, and don't worry. I'll be back before dawn."

"Excellent, then you'll have time to tell me how it went."

"I'll come straight here." Stevie Rae started to get up and then changed her mind. She had to ask—Lenobia wouldn't think it was a totally weird question—and she *had to ask*. "Um, so, the Raven Mockers were pretty bad, huh?"

Lenobia's serene expression changed to disgust. "I pray to Nyx they were banished from this realm when their father was forced to flee from Tulsa."

"Have you ever heard of them before? I mean, did you know about them before they all flew out of the ground?"

Lenobia shook her head. "No. I knew nothing of them. I'd never even heard of the Cherokee legend. But I did recognize one thing about them very easily."

"You did? What?"

"Evil. I have battled evil before, and they were simply another of its dark faces."

"Do you think they were totally bad? I mean, they were part human."

"Not part human—part immortal."

"Yeah, that's what I meant."

"And the immortal they are part of is completely evil."

"But what if Kalona wasn't always like he is now? He came from somewhere. Maybe he was good there, and if that's true, then maybe there could be some good found in a Raven Mocker."

Lenobia studied Stevie Rae silently before replying. Then she spoke quietly, but with conviction. "Priestess, do not let the compassion you feel for the red fledglings color your perception of evil. It exists here in our world. It also exists in the Otherworld. It is tangible there, just as it is here. There is a great difference between a broken child and a creature fathered by evil and conceived through rape."

"That's basically what Sister Mary Angela said, too."

"The nun is a wise woman." Lenobia paused and then continued, "Stevie Rae, have you sensed something I should know about?"

"Oh, no!" she said hastily. "I was just thinkin', that's all. You know, about good and evil and the choices we make. So I thought that maybe some of the Raven Mockers might be able to choose, too."

"If they had that ability they made the choice for evil long ago," Lenobia said.

"Yeah, I'm sure you're right. Okay, well, I better get. I'll come back around and see you before dawn."

"I'll look forward to meeting with you. May Nyx be with you, Priestess. And blessed be."

"Blessed be." Stevie Rae hurried from the stables, as if distance from the words she'd spoken could distance her from her guilt. What had she been thinking when she said that stuff about Rephaim to Lenobia? She needed to keep her mouth shut and forget about him.

But how could she forget about him when there was a chance she was going to see him again when she went back to the depot?

She shouldn't have sent him there. She should have figured something else out. Or she should have turned him in!

No. No, it was too late to think about that. Now all Stevie Rae could do was damage control. First, contact the red fledglings. Then, deal with the Rephaim issue. Again.

Of course he might not be an issue. The fledglings might not have found him. He didn't smell like food, and he wasn't in any shape to attack them. He was probably hiding down in the darkest cubbyholed tunnel, licking his wounds. Or he could be dead. Who knows what would happen to a Raven Mocker if a nasty infection set in.

Stevie Rae sighed and pulled her phone from the pocket of her hoodie. Praying the reception was back up in tunnels, she text messaged Nicole:

I need to see u tonite

She didn't have to wait long for a reply.

Busy. Won't be bk til dawn.

She frowned at her phone and responded.

Get bk be4.

She'd started to pace by the time Nicole managed to text her back.

Be there @ 6.

Stevie Rae wanted to grind her teeth together. Six o'clock was only an hour and a half before dawn. Dang it! Nicole pissed her off so bad. She was really the biggest problem down there. The rest of the kids were just followers. Not very nice, but not like her. Stevie Rae remembered Nicole from before she'd died. She'd been a mean girl then, and that hadn't changed. Actually, it'd gotten worse. So what Stevie Rae needed to do was to get to Nicole. If she turned her back on the darkness, then the rest of the kids would probably follow her.

OK.

Stevie Rae texted. Then she added,

Anything weird going on?

She held her breath, waiting for her phone to chime. Nicole would tell her if she'd found a Raven Mocker. She'd probably think Rephaim was cool. Or maybe she'd just kill him right off, without thinking anything. Either way, she'd blab it to Stevie Rae—it would make her feel all powerful and in charge.

Just looking for food. Live food. Wanna join us?

Stevie Rae knew it would do no good whatsoever to remind Nicole they shouldn't be eating people. No, not even homeless people or bad drivers (who they liked to follow and then grab as they got out of their cars). She just texted back:

No. See u @ 6.
Hahahahahaha

Stevie Rae stuck her phone back in her pocket. It was going to be a long night, especially that hour and a half between six and dawn.

Rephaim

"So that's the plan, birdboy. Are you up for this?" Unannounced and uninvited, the red fledgling leader, Nicole, had come into Stevie Rae's room, which Rephaim had claimed as his own, kicked the bed to wake him, and then started talking about her plan to trap Stevie Rae on the roof of a building.

"Even if, close to sunrise, you could lure the Red One to the roof of a building, how do you plan to hold her there?"

"The first part is simple because it's not just any building. It's this building. There're two round towers up there, all nicey-nice with decoration and crap when this place was actually something, back in the day. They're open to the sky 'cause it's *the roof.* We found a big metal grill we can chain over the top of one of them. No way can she get out. She's strong, but she can't break metal. Plus, all the way up there there's no earth for her to reach. She'll be trapped, and when the sun comes up she'll fry like a hamburger."

"Why would she be on the roof, even if it is the roof of this building?"

"That's even simpler. She'll be there 'cause you're gonna get her up there."

Rephaim didn't speak until he could control his shock, and then he chose his words carefully. "You think I can make the Red One come to the roof of a building near dawn? Why would I be able to do that? I'm not strong enough to overpower and carry her," he said, sounding more bored than curious.

"You won't need to. She saved you. And she had to do it without telling anyone. To me that says you mean something to her. Maybe even a bunch of something." Nicole scoffed at the thought. "Stevie Rae's pathetic. Always thinking she can save the world and shit like that. That's why she's stupid enough to come back here close to dawn. She thinks she can save us. Well, we don't want to be saved!" Nicole started laughing and as the laughter overtook her, Rephaim saw the inklike shadow of Neferet slide across her eyes and taint her expression so that she appeared close to hysteria.

"Why would she want to save you?"

Rephaim's question ended Nicole's laughter as if he had slapped her across the face.

"What? You don't think we deserve saving?" Quick as an envious thought, she moved to the bed and grabbed his uninjured arm by the wrist. "How about I see what you do think?"

She stared at him as his arm radiated the heat of her psychic violation, and as that heat spread throughout his body and soul, Rephaim concentrated on one thing: his anger.

Nicole dropped his wrist and took a step back from him. "Wow," she chuckled uncomfortably. "You're really pissed. What's that about?"

"It issss about being wounded and left behind to deal with children and their petty gamesssss!"

Nicole stepped back into his personal space and snarled, "This isn't petty! We're getting rid of Stevie Rae so that we can do the shit we need to do, just like we told Neferet we would. So are you going to make nice and help us trap her, or do we leave you out of this and go with Plan B?"

Rephaim didn't hesitate. "What is it you want me to do?"

Nicole's smile reminded him of a lizard. "We'll show you the stairs that go up to the tower—the one on the opposite side of the roof from that stupid tree. I'm not taking the chance that she can figure out some way to pull it over to her and have it shield her enough so she lives. So you'll go to the other tower and wait. Be all crumpled up like we dragged you there after beating the shit outta you and draining you almost dry of blood. Which is exactly what I'm gonna tell Stevie Rae we did, but I'll make sure she knows you're still alive. Barely."

"She'll go up there to save me," Rephaim said in a perfectly emotionless voice.

"Again. Yeah. We're counting on it. Once she climbs into the tower with you, just stay hunkered down. We'll smack the grate over the top and chain it in place. The sun'll come up. Stevie Rae will burn up. Then we'll let you out. See, simple."

"It will work," Rephaim stated.

"Yeah, and check this out. If you decide at the last minute you're not with us after all, Kurtis or Starr will shoot your feathered ass and we'll throw you into the tower anyway. That'll work for us, too. 'Cause, see, you are Plan A and Plan B. You're just deader in one than the other."

"As I said to you before, my father commanded me to bring the Red One to him."

"Yeah, but I don't see your daddy around here anywhere."

"I do not know why you play this game with me. You have already admitted you know my father has not abandoned me. He will return for his favorite son. When he does I will have the Red One for him."

"And it's cool with you that she'll be charbroiled?"

"The state of her body does not concern me as long as I am in possession of it."

"Well, you can definitely have it. I don't want to eat her, so I don't want her body." She cocked her head to the side and gave him an appraising look. "I saw inside that birdbrain of yours, and I know you're pissed, but I could also tell that you're guilty as hell. What's that about?"

"I should be at my father's side. Anything else is unacceptable."

Her bark of laughter lacked humor. "You are your father's son, aren't you?" She started to duck out of the blanket that was the door to the room. As she left she called back, "Get some sleep. You have a few hours before she'll be here. And if you need anything, Kurtis will be out here with his big gun. He'll get it for you. You just stay in there until I call. Got it?"

"Yesssss."

The red fledging left and Rephaim curled back up in the nest he'd made of Stevie Rae's bed. Before he fell into another healing sleep his single thought was that he wished the Red One had let him die under that tree.

CHAPTER THIRTY-FOUR

Zoey

When we landed at the Venice airport I'd only been awake about a nanosecond. I swear I slept the entire way, and the only dream I'd had had been about me and that giant beaver from the weird sleep medicine commercials playing Scrabble (which I don't play) and me winning like a bazillion pairs of designer shoes from him (and he doesn't really have feet). The dream had been odd, but harmless, and I'd slept like a kid on summer vacation.

Most of the rest of my gang were wiping tears from their eyes and blowing their noses.

"What the heck is wrong with everyone?" I asked Stark as we taxied to our gate. Sometime during the flight he'd moved to the seat right across the aisle from me.

He jerked his chin over his shoulder at everyone behind us, including Heath, who was even looking kinda misty-eyed. "They just got done watching *Milk*. It made them all bawl like babies."

"Hey, that's a good movie. And it's super-sad, too," I said.

"Yeah, I saw it when it came out, but I wanted to keep my manly calm, so I decided to move up here and read." He lifted the book in his lap, which I noticed was called *My Losing Season* by a guy named Pat Conroy.

"You really do read, don't you?"

"Yep. I really do."

"A losing season? How come he wrote about that?"

"You really want to know?"

"Yeah, of course I do," I said.

"He wrote the book to show that suffering can be a source of strength."

"Huh," I said, not so brilliantly and book-smartish.

"He's my favorite author," Stark said, a little shyly.

"I'll have to check him out."

"He doesn't write chick books," Stark said.

"That's a terrible stereotype!" I began, and was getting ready to launch into my lecture about the misogynistic (a word I learned from Damien while we read *The Scarlet Letter* in lit class) idea that manly books are for guys and frilly, pointless, fluffy books are for girls when the plane gave a little lurch and came to a halt.

We all kinda gawked around at each other, not sure what to do, but in just a second or so the door to the cockpit opened and the vampyre copilot stepped out with a smile.

"Welcome to Venetia," she said. "I know at least one of you has special needs, so we've pulled directly into our private hangar." I could hear the Twins snickering about Stark being "special needs/special services," but we ignored them. "Erce is meeting you here. She will be your escort to San Clemente Island. Be sure you take all your carry-ons off with you, and blessed be." Then she moved to the front door and, with a few flips of some levers, opened the plane. There was some noise, and then she said, "You may deplane."

"Let me go first," I told Stark, who was already on his feet, his book zipped into his backpack and slung over his shoulder. "I want to be sure there really isn't any sun out there to fry you."

Stark was going to argue with me, but Darius brushed past both of us with a quick, "Stay here. I'll let you know if all is safe."

"He's being Warrior-like," Aphrodite said, walking down the aisle ahead of everyone else who had to stay back behind her rolling Betsey Johnson luggage. "I like it when he gets all testosteroney, but I wish he'd remember to carry my bag."

"He needs his hands free in case he has to defend you," Stark told her, with the "you moron" part of the sentence left out but implied.

She narrowed her eyes at him, but Darius popped back into the plane. "All is well here." So we turned, sheeplike, and filed down the aisle to the door.

The vampyre standing at the bottom of the stairs leading from the plane was tall and regal-looking, and as dark as Lenobia was fair, but she still definitely reminded me of our Horse Mistress. Erce had that calm way about her that Lenobia had, too. I decided it must have something to do with their affinity for horses. They're calm and wise because horses, who are the coolest animals in the world besides cats, choose people who are soothing and smart.

"I am Erce. Merry meet, Zoey." Her dark eyes found me instantly, even though I was coming down the stairs behind Stark and Darius.

"Merry meet," I said to her.

Then her gaze went to Stark. I saw her eyes widen as she took in his red tattooing of intricately decorated arrows on either side of the crescent in the middle of his forehead.

"This is Stark," I said, needing to break what was becoming an awkward silence.

"Merry meet, Stark," she said.

"Merry meet," he replied automatically, even though he sounded strained.

I understood how he felt, but I was getting used to vamps and fledglings staring at my weird tattoos.

"Stark, I have taken care to be certain our boat has curtains drawn and windows blackened, though sunset is within the hour and it has been snowing on and off all day, so what sun is still shining is rather wan."

Her voice was musical and nice to listen to, so nice that it took me a moment to actually hear what she was saying.

"Boat?" I said. "How does he get to the boat?"

"Well, it's right there, Zo." Heath, who was sliding down the stairs with his feet up and his hands on the cold, slick rail, jerked his chin toward the side of the hangar. Cut out of the floor at one edge of the building was a large rectangular dock with a big door that reminded me of a garage closed at one end. At the other was a slick-looking black wooden boat. The top front was glass, and I could see two tall vampyres standing there by the dash. Behind them shiny wooden stairs led down into what must be the passenger area. I say "must be" because, even though there were windows along the side of the boat, they were, indeed, completely covered.

"If the sun's behind clouds, I can stand it," Stark said.

"So it's true that sunlight isn't simply uncomfortable for you? It will literally burn you?" I could hear the curiosity in her voice, and it didn't sound pushy or "oh-my-god-you're-such-a-freak." She sounded honestly concerned.

"Direct sunlight would kill me," Stark said matter-of-factly. "Setting or indirect sun would be anywhere from very dangerous to uncomfortable."

"Interesting," she mused.

"I guess interesting's one way to look at it. I mostly think of it as annoying and inconvenient," Stark said.

"Are we going to have time to shop before the High Council meeting?" Aphrodite asked.

"Ah, you must be Aphrodite."

"Yes, merry meet, whatever. So can we shop?"

"I'm afraid you won't have time. It will take half an hour to get to the island, then I will get you settled and, most importantly, brief you on the rules of the Council. Actually, we must be going now." She started to shepherd us to the boat.

"Are they letting me speak before them, or am I not good enough now that I'm *just* a human?" Aphrodite said.

"The rule about humans has nothing to do with them not being good enough to speak before the Council," Erce said as we moved from the wharf-like part of the hangar and boarded the boat, stepping down into a dark, luxurious cabin. "Consorts have long been allowed in the Council Chamber because of their importance to their vampyres." She paused here to smile at Heath, who was totally, obviously human. "They are not allowed to speak before the High Council because humans do not have a say in intimate vampyre policies and issues."

Heath sighed dramatically, smooshed himself next to me and, ignoring Stark, who was sitting on the other side of me, draped his arm possessively around my shoulders.

"I'm going to elbow the crap out of you if you don't put your arm down and act right," I whispered.

Heath grinned sheepishly and moved his arm, though he didn't unsmoosh from me.

"So does that mean I can attend the almighty Council Meeting, but I have to shut up like the blood donor over there?" Aphrodite asked.

"You they have made an exception for. You may attend, and you may speak, but you'll have to follow all the other rules of the Council."

"Which means no shopping right now," Aphrodite said.

"That is what it means," Erce said.

I was impressed by her patience. Lenobia would probably have snapped Aphrodite's head off before then for her smart-alecky attitude.

"Can all the rest of us come to the Council Meeting, too? Oh, hi and merry meet, I'm Jack," he said.

"You are all invited to meet before the Council."

"And what about Neferet and Kalona? Are they there also?" I asked.

"Yes, though Neferet now calls herself Nyx Incarnate, and Kalona says his true name is Erebus."

"That's a lie," I said.

Erce's smile was grim. "That, my young and unusual fledgling, is exactly why you are here."

We didn't say much more during the rest of the trip. The motor of the boat had kicked up and it was loud and more than a little disorienting inside the shrouded boat. It lurched a lot, and I was busy concentrating on not puking up my guts.

The speed of the boat slowed, along with the tempo of the watery rolling and lurching, signaling our arrival at the island, when Darius's voice carried above the engine noise. "Zoey!"

He and Aphrodite were sitting in one of the seats two rows behind me and I had to swivel around in my chair to see him. Stark turned around with me, so both of us got to our feet at the same time.

"Aphrodite! What's wrong?" I hurried over to her. She was holding her head in her hands as if she was afraid it was on the verge of exploding. Darius was looking helpless. He kept touching one of her shoulders, murmuring stuff I couldn't hear to her, and trying to get her to look at him.

"Oh, Goddess! My head is killing me. What the fuck?"

"Is she having a vision?" Erce said, coming up behind me.

"I don't know. Probably," I said. I got on my knees in front of Aphrodite and tried to get her to meet my eyes. "Aphrodite, it's Zoey. Tell me what you're seeing."

"I'm too hot. Too damn hot!" Aphrodite was saying. Her face had become flushed and sweaty, even though it was actually cool in the boat. With wide, panicked eyes she stared around, though my guess was that she wasn't seeing the inside of the expensive little boat.

"Aphrodite, talk to me! What is your vision showing?"

She did look at me then, and I realized that her eyes were clear and *not* filled with the painful blood that had started coming with each of her visions.

"I'm not seeing anything." She gulped air, still fanning her sweating face. "It's not a vision: It's Stevie Rae and our damn Imprint. Something's happening to her. Something really, *really* bad."

CHAPTER THIRTY-FIVE

Stevie Rae

Stevie Rae knew she was going to die, and this time it would be for good. She was scared, more scared even than she'd been when she'd bled out her life in Zoey's arms surrounded by her friends. It was different this time. This time it was a betrayal and not a biological act.

The pain in her head was terrible. She reached up and felt gingerly around on the back of her head. Her hand came away soaked in her blood. Her thoughts were woozy. What had happened? Stevie Rae tried to sit up, but a terrible dizziness claimed her, and with a groan, she puked her guts up, crying at the pain the movement caused her. Then she collapsed on her side, rolling away from the vomit. That's when her tear-blurred gaze moved to the metal cage above her, and then the sky beyond it—a sky that was getting increasingly less gray and more blue.

Her memory rushed back, and with it panic made her breath come in short little pants. They'd trapped her here and the sun was rising! Even now, even with the cage above her and the memory of their betrayal fresh in her mind, Stevie Rae didn't want to believe it.

Another wave of nausea washed over her, and she closed her eyes, trying to regain her equilibrium. As long as her eyes were shut, she could control the horrible dizziness and her thoughts began to clear.

The red fledglings had done this. Nicole had been late for their meeting. Not like that had been all that shocking, but Stevie Rae had been pissed and sick of waiting, so she had been in the process of leaving the empty tunnels to return to the House of Night when

Nicole and Starr finally came into the basement. They had been laughing and joking with each other, and had obviously just fed—their cheeks were still flushed and their eyes were glowing red from fresh blood. Stevie Rae had tried to talk to them. Actually, she'd tried to *reason* with them and get them to return to the House of Night with her.

The two red fledglings had spent a long time being sarcastic and giving jerklike excuses not to go with her: "Nah, the vamps don't let us eat junk food and we heart us some junkies!" And "Will Rogers High School is right down the street on Fifth. If I want to go to school I'll go there—after dark—for *lunch*."

Still, she'd tried to be serious and give them good reasons for coming back to school, like not only was it their home, but there was lots of stuff about being vampyres they didn't know—that Stevie Rae didn't even know. They *needed* the House of Night.

They'd laughed at her, called her an old woman, and said they were totally cool staying at the depot, especially now that they had it to themselves.

Then Kurtis had lumbered into the basement, looking breathless and excited. Stevie Rae remembered having a bad feeling from the second she'd seen him. The truth was she'd never liked the kid. He was a big, stupid pig farmer from northeastern Oklahoma who basically thought women were one step below hogs on the redneck What You're Worth Scale.

"Yepper, I found him and bit him!" He practically crowed.

"That thing? You got to be kidding. He smelled nasty," Nicole had said.

"Yeah, and how'd you get him to hold still while you ate him?" Starr asked.

Kurtis wiped his mouth with his sleeve. A splotch of red smeared his shirt and the scent of it hit Stevie Rae, completely shocking her. *Rephaim! That was Rephaim's blood.*

"I knocked him out first. It wasn't hard to do, with his broken wing and all."

"What are you talkin' about?" Stevie Rae snapped the words at Kurtis.

Bovinelike, he blinked at her. She was getting ready to grab him and shake him and maybe even have the earth open up and swallow his big, stupid ass, when he finally answered. "I'm talking about the birdboy. What'd you call 'em, Raven Mockers? One showed up here. We been chasin' it all around the depot. Nikki and Starr got sick of messing with it and went out to chomp on some of the late night Taco Bell fourth meal feeders, but I had me a taste for chicken. So I kept after him. Had to corner him up on the roof in one of those tower things, you know, the far one over there, away from the tree." Kurtis pointed up and to his left. "But I got him."

"Did he taste as bad as he smelled?" Nicole's shock and revulsion were as obvious as her curiosity.

Kurtis shrugged his beefy shoulders. "Hey, I'll eat anything. Or anyone."

They all dissolved into laughter. All except Stevie Rae.

"You have a Raven Mocker on the roof?"

"Yeah. Don't know why the hell he was down here in the first place. Especially all beat up and broken." Nicole lifted a brow at her. "Thought you said it was okay to go back to the House of Night 'cause Neferet and Kalona were gone. Looks like they left some shit behind, huh? Maybe they're not really gone."

"They're gone," Stevie Rae had said, already moving toward the door to the basement. "So none of you want to come back to school with me?"

Three heads shook silently back and forth as red-tinged eyes followed her every move.

"How about the others? Where are they?"

Nicole shrugged. "Wherever they want to be. Next time I see any of them I'll tell 'em you said they should go back to school."

Kurtis cracked up. "Hey, that's great. Let's all just go back to school! Like that's something we really want to do?"

"Look, I gotta go. It's almost sunrise. But I'm not done talkin' about this with you. And you should know that I may want to bring the other red fledglings back here to live, even though we'll officially be part of the House of Night. And if that happens y'all can either be with us and act right, or you need to leave."

"How about this: How about you keep your pussy fledglings at school, and we'll stay here because *this* is where we live now," Kurtis said.

Stevie Rae stopped moving toward the exit. Almost as if it was second nature to her, she imagined she was a tree with roots growing down, down, down into the amazing, incredible ground. *Earth, please come to me.* In the basement, already underground and surrounded by her element, it was a simple thing to pull power up through her body. As she spoke, the ground rumbled and shook with the force of her irritation. "I'm only gonna say this one more time. If I bring the other red fledglings back here, this will be our home. If you act right, you can stay. If you don't, you will leave." She stomped her foot and the entire depot shook, sending plaster cascading from the low basement ceiling. Then Stevie Rae drew a deep breath, forcing herself to calm down, and imagining all the energy she'd called flowing out of her body and back into the earth. When she spoke again her voice sounded normal and the earth didn't shake. "So, y'all decide. I'll be back tomorrow night. See ya."

Without giving them another glance, Stevie Rae hurried out of the basement, through the maze of rubble and metal grates spread haphazardly around the abandoned depot grounds to the stone stairs that led from the parking lot at railroad track level up to the street level of what used to be a thriving railway station. She had to be careful as she rushed up the stairs. It had stopped sleeting, and the sun had actually come out the day before, but night had brought falling temperatures and almost everything that had thawed had refrozen.

She reached the circle drive and the big covered entryway that used to keep Oklahoma weather from train passengers. She looked up and up and up.

The building was just creepy-looking. That's all there was to it. Z liked to describe it as something out of Gotham City. Stevie Rae thought it was more like *Blade Runner* meets *Amityville Horror*. Not that she didn't heart the tunnels under the building, but there was something about the stone exterior with its weird mixture of art deco and machine design that creeped her out.

Of course, some of her freaky feeling could have been because the sky was already starting to shift from black to gray with the coming dawn. In retrospect, that should have stopped her. She should have turned around, gone back down the stairs, climbed into the car she'd borrowed from the school, and driven to the House of Night.

Instead, she'd stepped squarely into her fate and, as Z would have said, then the poopie hit the fan.

She knew there were circular stairs inside the main part of the depot that led up to each tower room—she'd done lots of exploring during the weeks she'd lived there. But no dang way was she going back inside that building and taking a chance that some random red fledgling wouldn't be tucked into bed and would see her—and question her—and find out the truth.

Plan B led her to a tree that at one time had obviously been decorative, but had long since overgrown its concrete circle so that its roots had broken through the ground below in the parking lot, exposing lots of frozen earth and allowing it to grow taller than it should have. Without its leaves, Stevie Rae didn't have a clue what kind of tree it was, other than the kind that was tall enough that its branches brushed the roof of the depot, near the first of the two towers that faced out from the roof on the front side of the building, and that was tall enough for her.

Moving quickly, Stevie Rae went over to the tree and jumped to grab the branch closest to her head. She scrambled up the slick, bare bough, shimmying along it until she got to the main part of the tree. From there she made her way up and up, silently thanking Nyx for her red vampyre enhanced strength 'cause if she'd been a normal fledgling, or maybe even vamp, she'd never have been able to make the treacherous climb.

When she was as high up as she could go, Stevie Rae gathered herself and then jumped onto the roof of the building. She didn't waste time looking in the first of the towers. Pig boy had said Rephaim was in the one farthest from the tree. She jogged across the roof to the other end of the building and then climbed the short distance up so she could look down into the circular space.

He was there. Crumpled in the corner of the tower, Rephaim lay unmoving and bleeding.

Without hesitation, Stevie Rae threw her legs over the stone ridge and then dropped the four feet or so into the room.

He'd been curled up in a ball, his good arm cradling his bad one in its dirty sling. Down the outside of his arm she could see that someone had slashed his skin, which is obviously where Kurtis had fed from him, though he hadn't bothered to close the cut, and the odd, off smell of his inhuman blood filled the little chamber. The bandage that had immobilized his wing had come loose and it was a torn pile of bloody towels half draping his body. His eyes were closed.

"Rephaim, hey, can you hear me?"

At the sound of her voice his eyes instantly opened. "No!" he said, struggling to sit up. "Get out of here. They're going to trap—"

Then there had been a terrible pain in the back of her head, and she remembered falling into blackness.

"Stevie Rae, you have to wake up. You have to move."

She finally felt the hand that was shaking her shoulder and recognized Rephaim's voice. Carefully she opened her eyes, and the world didn't pitch and roll, though she could feel her heartbeat throbbing in her head.

"Rephaim," she rasped. "What happened?"

"They used me to trap you," he said.

"You wanted to trap me?" Her nausea was a little better, but Stevie Rae's mind felt like it was working in slow motion.

"No. What I wanted was to be left alone to heal and make my way back to my father. They gave me no choice." He stood up, moving stiffly, bent at the waist because of the metal grate that made a low, false ceiling. "Move. You have little time. The sun is already rising."

Stevie Rae looked up at the sky and saw the soft pastels of pre-dawn that she used to think were so pretty. Now the lightening sky filled her with absolute terror. "Oh, Goddess! Help me get up."

Rephaim grabbed her hand and pulled her to her feet, where she stood unsteadily beside him, bent like he was. Drawing a deep breath, she raised her hands, gripped the cold metal of the grate, and pushed. It rattled a little, but didn't really move.

"How is it stuck up there?" she asked.

"Chained. They hooked chains through the edges of the metal and then padlocked them to anything on the roof that couldn't be pulled up."

Stevie Rae pushed against the grate again. Again it rattled, but held firm. She was trapped up on a roof and the sun was rising! Gathering all her strength, she pushed and pulled, gripping the metal and trying to slide it to one side so that maybe she could crawl through. With each second the sky got brighter. Stevie Rae's skin shivered like a horse trying to twitch off a fly.

"Break the metal," Rephaim said urgently. "Your strength can do it."

"I might be able to if I was underground, or even standing on the earth," she said between gasping breaths as she continued to struggle impotently against the caging metal. "But up here, a huge building away from my element, I'm just not strong enough." She looked from the sky to his scarlet eyes. "You should probably stand back away from me. I'm gonna burn, and I don't know how big the flames will be, but it could get pretty hot in here."

She watched Rephaim move away and, with a growing sense of hopelessness, went back to struggling with the immovable metal. Her fingers were starting to sizzle and Stevie Rae was biting her lip to keep from screaming and screaming and screaming . . .

"Over here. The metal is rusted and thinner, weaker."

Stevie Rae pulled her hands down, automatically clutching them under her armpits and, bent backed, rushed to him. She saw the rusted metal and grabbed ahold of it with both hands, and then pulled with all her might. It gave a little, but her hands had started to smoke, as had her wrists.

"Oh, Goddess!" she gasped. "I'm not gonna make it. Get back, Rephaim, I'm already startin' to—"

Instead of running from her, he moved as close to her as he could get, spreading his good wing so that it provided some shade. Then he raised his uninjured arm and took hold of the rusted grate. "Think of the earth. Concentrate. Do not think of the sun and the sky. Pull with me. Now!"

In the shadow of his wing, Stevie Rae grabbed the grate on either side of his hand. She closed her eyes and ignored the burning of her fingers and the sensitivity of her skin that was screaming at her to run! Run anywhere, just get out of the sun! Instead she thought about the earth, cool and dark, waiting underneath her like a loving mama. Stevie Rae pulled.

With a metallic snap the grate broke, leaving an opening just big enough for one person at a time to slip out of.

Rephaim stepped back. "Go!" he said. "Quickly."

The instant Stevie Rae was no longer covered by his wing, her body flushed and, literally, began to smoke. Instinctively, she dropped to the floor and curled into a ball, trying to shield her face with her arms. "I can't!" she cried, frozen with pain and panic. "I'll burn up."

"You will burn if you stay here," he said.

Then he pulled himself up through the opening and was gone. He'd left her. Stevie Rae knew he was right. She had to get out of there, but she couldn't push through the paralyzing fear. The pain was too much. It was like her blood was boiling in her body. Just when she thought she couldn't bear it any longer, a small, cool shadow fell on her.

"Take my hand!"

Squinting against the cruel sun, Stevie Rae looked up. Rephaim was there, crouched on the grate, his good wing spread above her, blocking as much of the sun as possible, his uninjured arm reaching for her.

"Now, Stevie Rae. Do it!"

She followed his voice and the coolness of his dark wing and grabbed his hand. He couldn't pull her up by himself. She was too heavy and he only had one arm. So she thrust out her other hand, took hold of the metal, and chinned herself up.

"Come to me. I will shield you." Rephaim opened his wing.

Without any hesitation Stevie Rae stepped into his embrace, burying her head in the feathers of his chest, and wrapping her arms around him. He enfolded her with his wing and lifted her.

"Get me to the tree!"

Then he was running, lurching, and limping, but running across the rooftop. The backs of Stevie Rae's arms were exposed, as was some of her neck and shoulders, and as he ran she burned. With a detached, out-of-body feeling she wondered what that terrible noise was that rang in her ears, and then she realized it was her voice. She was screaming her pain and terror and anger.

At the edge of the roof he yelled, "Hold on. I'm jumping to the tree." The Raven Mocker leaped. His body tumbled, spiraling because of his lack of balance, and they crashed into the tree.

Adrenaline helped Stevie Rae keep her hold on him and, feeling thankful his body was so light, she lifted him, putting herself between Rephaim and the tree. With the bark to her back she told him, "Try to hold on to the tree while I slide us down."

Then they were falling again as the rough bark ripped Stevie Rae's already blistered and bleeding back. She closed her eyes and felt for the earth, finding it serene and waiting below her.

"Earth, come to me! Open and shield me!"

There was a great ripping sound and the ground at the base of the tree broke open just in time for Stevie Rae and Rephaim to slip within a cool, dark pouch in the earth.

CHAPTER THIRTY-SIX

Zoey

When Aphrodite started screaming, Zoey knew only one thing to do. "Spirit, come to me!" she commanded. Spirit instantly filled her with its serene presence. "Help Aphrodite calm down." She felt the element leave her, and almost immediately Aphrodite's shrieks quieted to gasps and sobs.

"Darius, I need Lenobia's cell number. Now!"

Darius was holding Aphrodite in his arms, but he obeyed Zoey, pulling his phone from his jeans pocket and tossing it to her. "It's in the contacts."

Willing her hands not to shake, Zoey pulled up the contact list and punched Lenobia's name. She answered on the first ring.

"Darius?"

"It's Zoey. We have an emergency. Where's Stevie Rae?"

"She went to the depot to try to reason with the other red fledglings. I expected her back by now, though, as it is almost dawn."

"She's in trouble."

"Burning!" Aphrodite sobbed. "She's burning!"

"She's outside somewhere. Aphrodite says she's burning."

"Oh, Goddess! Can she tell anything else?"

I could already hear by the change in Lenobia's voice that she was on the move. "Aphrodite, can you tell where Stevie Rae is?"

"N-no. Just outside."

"She doesn't know where she is, only that she's outside."

"I'll find her," Lenobia said. "Call me if Aphrodite can tell us anything else."

"You call me as soon as Stevie Rae's safe," I said, not able to consider any other outcome. Lenobia disconnected the line.

"Let's get Aphrodite inside where we can deal with this better," Erce said. She led the way out of the boat and into an enclosed building, only this building wasn't airport hangarlike. It was old and made of stone. I only had time to be relieved that Stark was shielded from the sun as Darius carried Aphrodite from the boat and we all hurried with Erce through an arched breezeway.

Stark stayed at my side as we jogged to keep up with Erce. "Aphrodite is Imprinted with Stevie Rae—she's the other red vampyre," I explained.

Erce nodded, holding open a huge wooden door and motioning for Darius to carry Aphrodite within. "Lenobia told me of their Imprint."

"What can you do to help her?"

We entered a huge hallway. I got the impression of amazing opulence, unbelievably high ceilings, and chandeliers, chandeliers, chandeliers; then Erce hurried us through the hall and into a side parlor. "Put her on the chaise over there."

We crowded around the chaise, silently watching Aphrodite. Erce turned to me and in a low voice said, "There is nothing that can be done for a human if their Imprinted vampyre is suffering. She will feel Stevie Rae's pain until the crisis is over, or until she is dead."

"She?" I squeaked. "As in Stevie Rae or Aphrodite?"

"Either or both. Vampyres can survive events that will kill their consorts."

"Well, shit," Heath murmured.

"My hands!" Aphrodite sobbed. "They're burning!"

I couldn't stand it anymore and went to her. She was still mostly in Darius's arms. The warrior was sitting on the chaise, holding her tightly and speaking softly to her. His face was pale and grim. His eyes begged me to help her. I took one of Aphrodite's hands in mine. It felt abnormally warm. "You're not burning. Look at me, Aphrodite. It's not happening to you. It's happening to Stevie Rae."

"Yeah, I know how you feel." Heath was there beside me, crouching down on one knee and holding Aphrodite's other hand. "It sucks to be Imprinted and then have something bad happen to your vampyre. But it's *not* you. It feels like it is, but it's not."

"This isn't about Stevie Rae doing the nasty with someone else," Aphrodite said, her voice all strangely tremble-y and weak.

Heath was unfazed. "What happens doesn't matter. What matters is that it hurts you, and it does. You have to remember that you're not really her, even though it feels like you're so attached that you are a part of her."

He seemed to get through to Aphrodite, and she stared up at him. "But I didn't want this." She hiccupped a little sob. "I didn't want to be connected to Stevie Rae, and you want the thing with Zoey."

Heath gripped her hand, and I saw her hold on to him for all she was worth. Everyone was watching them, but I think I was the only one who felt like an outsider.

"Want it or not, it's too much sometimes. You have to learn to save some stuff inside you for yourself. You have to know you don't really share a soul with her, no matter what the Imprint says."

"That's it!" Aphrodite pulled her hand from mine and covered Heath's with it. "It feels like I'm sharing my soul. And I can't stand it."

"Yes, you can. Just remember it's a feeling. It's not real."

I backed away a few steps.

"Aphrodite, you're safe. We're all here with you." Damien touched her shoulder.

"Yeah, it's okay. And your hair still looks really good," Jack said.

I heard Aphrodite laugh—a little escaped bubble of normalcy in the middle of unbelievable turmoil. Then she said, "Wait, it's better all of a sudden."

"Good, 'cause you can't die on us," Shaunee said.

"Yeah, we need your shopping expertise," Erin said. The Twins tried to sound all nonchalant and unaffected, but it was obvious they were worried about Aphrodite.

"Aphrodite will be fine. She'll make it through this," Stark said. He had moved to my side, as always. He was a steady presence there, a voice of calm in the storm.

"But what's happening to Stevie Rae?" I whispered to him.

He put his arm around me and squeezed.

A beautiful vampyre with bright red hair entered the room, carrying a tray with an icy pitcher, a glass, and several folded, damp towels. She went straight to Erce, who was standing close to the chaise. Erce motioned for her to put the tray on the nearest coffee table. I noticed the new vamp reached into her pocket, brought out a pill bottle, and handed it to Erce before leaving the room as quietly as she'd entered it.

Erce shook a pill out of the bottle and approached Aphrodite. I'd moved before I realized what I was doing, and found myself grabbing her wrist.

"What are you giving her?"

Erce met my gaze. "Something to calm her, to decrease her anxiety."

"But what if she loses contact with Stevie Rae because of it?"

"Would you have two dead friends or one? Choose, High Priestess."

I swallowed down my shriek of primal rage. I didn't want to lose either of my friends! But my mind understood that my best friend was an ocean and half a continent away, and Aphrodite dying with her was absolutely unnecessary. I let loose of Erce's wrist.

"Here, child. Take this." Erce gave Aphrodite the pill and helped Darius hold the glass of ice water to her lips. Aphrodite took the pill and gulped the water like she'd been running a marathon.

"Goddess, I hope it's Xanax," she said tremulously.

I thought things were getting better. Aphrodite had quit crying and my gang had dispersed themselves to well-upholstered chairs in the room. Except for Heath and Stark. Stark was by my side. Heath was still holding Aphrodite's hand. He and Darius were talking quietly to her. Then Aphrodite cried out and pulled away from Heath and out of Darius's arms, curling herself into a fetal position.

"I'm burning!"

Heath looked back at me. "Can't you help her?"

"I'm channeling spirit. That's all I can do. Stevie Rae's back in Oklahoma: I can't help her!" I practically screamed at Heath, my frustration spilling over into anger.

Stark put his arm around me. "It's okay. It's going to be okay."

"I don't know how," I said. "How can both of them make it through this?"

"How can a bad guy become the Warrior of a High Priestess?" he countered, and smiled. "Nyx—she has her hand on both of them. Trust your Goddess."

So I stood there, channeling spirit, watching Aphrodite's agony and trusting in my Goddess.

Suddenly Aphrodite screamed, grabbed at her back, cried, "Open and shield me!" And then she collapsed, sobbing with relief in Darius's arms.

I approached her hesitantly and bent so I could see her face. "Hey, are you okay? Is Stevie Rae alive?"

Aphrodite's tearstained face lifted so she could meet my eyes. "It's over. She's in contact with earth again. She's alive."

"Oh, thank the Goddess!" I said. I touched her shoulder lightly. "Are you okay, too?"

"I think so. No. Wait, I don't know. I feel strange. Like my skin isn't quite right."

"Her vampyre has been damaged," Erce said in a barely audible voice. "Stevie Rae may be safe now, but something is terribly wrong with her."

"Drink this, love," Darius said, taking a fresh glass from Erce and lifting it to Aphrodite's lips. "This will help."

Aphrodite gulped the water. It was a good thing Darius was helping her hold the glass, because she was shaking so hard there's no way she could have kept from spilling the water without his help. Then she lay back, resting in his arms, breathing in shallow gulps, like she couldn't take a deep breath without causing herself too much pain.

"I hurt all over," I heard her whisper to Darius.

I walked to Erce, took her wrist, and pulled her out of Aphrodite's hearing range. "Isn't there a vamp healer you could send for?" I asked.

"She isn't a vampyre, Priestess," Erce said gently. "Our healer could not help her."

"But she's like this because of a vampyre."

"That is the chance every consort takes. Their fate is bound to their vampyre. Most often a consort dies long before the vampyre, and that is difficult enough. This situation occurs less often."

"Stevie Rae isn't dead," I whispered severely.

"Not yet she isn't, but by watching her consort I would say she is in grave danger."

"She's a consort by mistake," I muttered. "Aphrodite didn't mean for this to happen. Neither did Stevie Rae."

"Intentional or not, it is still binding," Erce said.

"Oh my Goddess!" Aphrodite sat straight up, pulling completely away from Darius. Her face was a mask of shock that morphed slowly to reflect first pain and then denial, and then she shivered once, so violently that I could hear her teeth chattering, before covering her face with her hands and dissolving into heart-wrenching tears.

Darius looked beseechingly at me. Steeling myself for hearing that Stevie Rae was dead, I went to Aphrodite and sat beside her on the chaise.

"Aphrodite?" I tried unsuccessfully to keep the tears from my voice. *How could Stevie Rae really be dead? What was I going to do now, a world away from her and completely in over my head?* "Is Stevie Rae dead?"

I could hear the Twins crying, and I saw Damien take Jack in his arms. Aphrodite lifted her face from her hands, and I was shocked to see her old, sarcastic grin shine through her tears.

"Dead? Hell no, she's not dead. She's just Imprinted with someone else!"

CHAPTER THIRTY-SEVEN

Stevie Rae

The earth swallowed her, and for a moment it seemed like everything would be okay. The cool darkness was a relief for her burned skin, and she moaned softly.

"Red One? Stevie Rae?"

It wasn't until he spoke that she realized she was still locked in Rephaim's arms. She unwrapped herself from him and moved away, only to cry out in pain as her back touched the earthen wall of the pocket in the ground her element had opened to shield her, and then closed again.

"Are you well? I-I cannot see you," Rephaim said.

"I'm okay. I think." Her voice surprised her. It sounded so weak, so outside the norm that it was her first hint that even though she'd escaped the sun, she might not have escaped its effects.

"I cannot see anything," he said.

"It's because the earth sealed itself over us to shield me from the sun."

"We're trapped here?" His voice wasn't panicky, but it wasn't exactly calm either.

"No, I can get us out whenever I want," she explained. Then, on second thought, she added, "And, well, the earth over us isn't very deep. If I drop dead you could dig out pretty easily. How are you? That wing must really hurt."

"Do you feel as if you might die?" he asked, ignoring her question about his wing.

"I don't think so. Okay, actually, I don't know. I feel kinda funny."

"Funny? Explain that."

"Like I'm not really attached to my body."

"Does your body hurt?"

Stevie Rae thought about it, and was surprised by what she discovered. "No. Actually, I don't hurt at all." It was weird, though, that her voice kept getting weaker and weaker.

Suddenly his hand was touching her face, sliding down to her neck and arm and—

"Ouch! You're hurting me."

"You're burned badly. I can feel it. You need help."

"Can't leave here or I'll finish burning up," she said, wondering why the earth seemed to be spinning around beneath her.

"What can I do to help you?"

"Well, you can get a big tarp or somethin' and put it over me while you take me to the blood bank downtown. That sounds really good right now." Stevie Rae lay there, thinking she'd never been so thirsty in her life. She wondered, with a detached sense of curiosity, if she was really going to die. It seemed a shame, after all that Rephaim had gone through to help her.

"Blood is what you need?"

"Blood is all I need. It's what makes me tick, which is more than kinda gross, but still. It's the truth. Cross my heart and hope to die." She giggled a little hysterically, and then sobered. "Wait, that's not really very funny."

"If you don't get blood, you'll die?"

"I think I might," she said, finding it hard to care too much.

"Then if blood will heal you, take mine. I owe you a life. That's why I saved you on the roof, but if you die here, you die without my debt being repaid. So if you need blood, take mine," he repeated.

"But you don't smell right," she blurted.

From the darkness he sounded irritated and offended. "That is what the red fledglings said, too. My blood does not smell right to you because I'm not meant to be one of your prey. I am the son of an immortal. I'm not your victim."

"Hey, I don't have victims; not anymore," she protested weakly.

"The truth still holds. I smell different to you because I *am* different. I was not created to be your lunch."

"I never said you were." She meant her words to come out sounding snappy and kinda defensive. Instead her voice was faint, and her head felt strangely huge, like it was going to pop off her neck at any second and float up through the ground and into the clouds like a giant birthday balloon.

"Right-smelling or not, it's blood. I owe you a life. So you will drink, and you will live."

Stevie Rae cried out as Rephaim's hand found her again and he pulled her against his body. She felt the skin of her burned arms and shoulders rip off and mix with the earth. Then she was resting on the softness of his feathers. She sighed deeply. It wouldn't be so bad to die here in the earth, in a nest of feathers. As long as she didn't move, it didn't even hurt much.

She felt Rephaim move, though. And realized he'd sliced his beak across the gash that Kurtis had made in his bicep. It had stopped bleeding, but this new laceration immediately began to weep, filling their little pocket in the earth with the thick scarlet scent of his immortal blood.

Then he shifted again and suddenly his bleeding arm was pressed against her lips.

"Drink," he said harshly. "Help me rid myself of this debt."

She drank, automatically at first. His blood had, after all, been stinky. It'd smelled wrong, wrong, wrong.

Then it touched her tongue. Its taste was like nothing Stevie Rae could have imagined. It wasn't like the scent of him; it wasn't anything remotely like the scent of him. Instead it was an incredible surprise, filling her mouth and her soul with its rich complexity, its absolute difference from anything she'd ever experienced.

She heard him hiss, and the hand that had been on the back of her neck guiding her to his arm, tightened its grip on her. Stevie Rae moaned. Drinking from the Raven Mocker couldn't be a sexual experience, but it wasn't exactly *not* a sexual experience, either. Stevie Rae had the fleeting thought that she wished she'd had some kind of experience with guys—other than making out with Dallas in the dark—'cause she didn't know what to think of all the stuff that was going through her mind and surging through her body. It felt good, all hot and tingly and powerful, but nothing like Dallas had made her feel.

She liked it, though. And there, for that heartbeat of a moment, Stevie Rae forgot that Rephaim was a mixture of immortal and beast, created from violence and lust. For that instant, she only knew the pleasure of his touch and the strength of his blood.

That was when her Imprint with Aphrodite shattered, and Stevie Rae, the first red vampyre High Priestess of Nyx, Imprinted with Rephaim, the favorite son of a fallen immortal.

That was also when she broke his grip on her head and pulled away from him. Neither of them said anything. The silence of their small, earthen room was filled only by the sounds of both of them gasping for breath.

"Earth, I need you again," Stevie Rae spoke into the darkness. Her voice sounded normal again. Her body hurt. She could feel her burns and the rawness of her skin, but Rephaim's blood had allowed her to begin to heal, and she understood all too well that she had been on the verge of dying.

Earth came to her, filling their space with the scents of a springtime meadow. Stevie Rae pointed up, to a spot as far from herself as she could get. "Open just a crack over there—enough to let in light, but not enough to burn me."

Her element complied. The ground above them shivered, dirt raining down as it split, letting in a tiny crack of daylight.

Stevie Rae's eyes adapted almost instantly, so she watched Rephaim blink in surprise as he tried to accustom himself to the sudden light. He was sitting close to her. He looked terrible—bloody and bruised. His broken wing had come completely loose from the towel bandage she'd fashioned for him and it lay helplessly down his back. She knew the instant his vision had cleared. Those human eyes, tinged with scarlet, found hers.

"Your wing's messed up again," she said.

He grunted, and she figured that was his guy word for agreeing with her.

"I better fix it again." She started to get up and his lifted hand stopped her.

"You shouldn't move. You should just rest against your earth and regain your strength."

"No, it's okay. I'm not one hundred percent, but I'm lots better." She hesitated and then added, "Can't you tell that?"

"Why would I—" The Raven Mocker's words ended abruptly. Stevie Rae watched his eyes widen with understanding. "How is it possible?" he said.

"I dunno," she said, getting up and beginning to unwind the messed-up strips of towels from around him. "I wouldn't think it'd be possible. But, well, here we are, and here *it* is."

"An Imprint," he said.

"Between us," she said.

Then neither of them said anything.

When she had the tangled mess of bandages straightened out, she told him, "Okay, I'm gonna set your wing back like I had it and re-wrap it. It's gonna hurt again. Sorry. Of course this time it'll hurt me, too."

"Truly?" he said.

"Yeah, well, I kinda know how these Imprint things work, being as I used to have a human Imprinted to me. She knew all sorts of stuff about me. Now I'm Imprinted to you, so it stands to reason that I'll be knowing stuff about you, which includes when you're in ex-cruciating pain."

"Are you still Imprinted to her?"

Stevie Rae shook her head. "Nope, it's gone, which, I'm sure, will tickle her pink."

"Tickle pink?"

"Just an expression my mama used to use. It means she'll be happy we're not Imprinted anymore."

"And you? What are you?"

Stevie Rae looked into his eyes and answered honestly. "I'm to-tally confused about us, but not sorry at all that I'm not Imprinted with Aphrodite anymore. Now, hold still and let me get this over with." Rephaim stayed perfectly still while Stevie Rae reset his wing.

It was she who did the gasping and made the painful exclamations. She who was white and shaky after it was all over. "Dang, wings hurt. Bad."

Rephaim stared at her, shaking his head. "You did feel it, didn't you?"

"Sadly, yep, I did. It was almost worse than almost dying." She met his eyes. "Is it going to get well?"

"It will heal."

"But?" She felt the word there at the end of his sentence.

"But I do not believe I will ever fly again."

Stevie Rae's gaze stayed steady on his. "That's bad, isn't it?"

"It is."

"Maybe it'll heal better than you think. If you came back to the House of Night with me, I could—"

"I cannot go there." He hadn't raised his voice, but the words had a sense of finality to them.

Stevie Rae tried again. "That's what I used to think, but I'm back there and they accept me. Well, some of them do."

"It wouldn't be like that for me, and you know it."

Stevie Rae looked down. Her shoulders slumped. "You killed Professor Anastasia. She was really nice. Her mate, Dragon, is lost without her."

"I did what I had to do for my father."

"And he deserted you," she said.

"I disappointed him."

"You almost died!"

"He is still my father," he said quietly.

"Rephaim, this Imprint. Does it feel like anything to you? Or is it just me who's had a change?"

"A change?"

"Well, yeah. I couldn't feel your pain before, and now I can. I can't tell what you're thinking, but I can sense things about you, like I think I'd know where you were and what was going on with you even if you were a long way away from me. It's weird. It's different than what I had with Aphrodite, but it's definitely there. Is there anything at all different with you?"

He hesitated a long time before answering her, and when he did speak he sounded confused. "I feel protective of you."

"Well." Stevie Rae smiled. "You did protect me from dyin' up there."

"That was payment of a debt. This is more."

"Like what?"

"Like it makes me sick to think about how close you came to dying," he admitted, his voice defensive and annoyed.

"Is that all?"

"No. Yes. I do not know! I'm not used to this." He thumped his chest with his fist.

"This what?"

"This *feeling* I have for you. I don't know what to call it."

"Maybe we could call it friendship?"

"Impossible."

Stevie Rae grinned. "Well, I was just tellin' Zoey that stuff we once thought was impossible might not be so black-and-white."

"Not black-and-white, but good and evil. You and I are on two opposing sides in the balance of good versus evil."

"I don't think that's set in stone," she said.

"I am still my father's son," he said.

"Well, I wonder where that leaves us?"

Before he could answer her, the sounds of frantic shouting drifted down through the small crack in the earth.

"Stevie Rae! Are you here?"

"That's Lenobia," Stevie Rae said.

"Stevie Rae!" Another voice joined the Horse Mistress's.

"Oh, crap! That's Erik. He knows his way to the tunnels. If they get down there, all hell's gonna break loose."

"Will they shield you from the sunlight?"

"Well, yeah, I'd imagine so. They don't want me to burn up."

"Then call them to you. You should go with them," he said.

Stevie Rae concentrated, waved her hand, and the small crack in the far end of the ceiling of their hiding place trembled and then got bigger. Stevie Rae pressed herself back against the raw ground. Then she cupped her hands around her mouth and called: "Lenobia! Erik! I'm down here!"

Quickly she leaned over, laying her palms against the earth on either side of Rephaim. "Hide him for me, earth. Don't let him be discovered." Then she pushed, and like the swirling of water down a drain, the dirt behind him rippled backward, leaving a Raven Mocker–sized cubbyhole, into which he reluctantly crawled.

"Stevie Rae?" Lenobia's voice came from above them near the crack.

"Yeah, I'm here, but I can't come out unless you can cover this part of the ground with a tent or somethin'."

"We'll take care of that. You just stay down there where you're safe."

"Are you okay? Do we need to get something for you?" Erik's voice asked.

Stevie Rae figured the "something" Erik was asking about was really a bag or ten of blood from the fridge in the tunnels, and no way did she want him going down there.

"No! I'm fine. Just get somethin' to cover me from the sun."

"No problem. We'll be back in a sec," Erik said.

"I'm not goin' anywhere," she called back to them. Then she turned to Rephaim. "What about you?"

"I stay here, hidden in this corner. If you don't tell them I'm here, they will not know."

She shook her head. "I don't mean now. Of course I'm not tellin' 'em you're down here. But where are you gonna go?"

"Not back into those tunnels," he said.

"Yeah, that's definitely not a good idea. Okay, let me think. Once Lenobia and Erik are out of here, you can get away real easy right now. The red fledglings can't come out after you in the daytime, and it's super-early, so most people will still be asleep." She considered his options. She wanted to keep him close, and not just because she figured she'd have to help him get food, and those bandages were nasty dirty, so his wounds would definitely need doctoring. Stevie Rae was also aware that she needed to keep a check on him. He would get better, and become stronger, like he used to be. Then what would he do?

And there was the little fact that she'd Imprinted with him, which meant it was uncomfortable to think about him being very far from her. Strange that she hadn't felt that with Aphrodite . . .

"Stevie Rae, I can hear them returning," Rephaim said. "Where should I go?"

"Ah, crap . . . um . . . well, you need someplace close but hidable for you. And it wouldn't hurt if it had a creepy reputation so people would stay out, or at least wouldn't think it wasn't unusual if you went bump in the night." Then her eyes widened and she grinned at him. "I got it! After Halloween, Z and the gang and I went on a ghost tour of Tulsa. It was in one of those cool old-time trolleys."

"Stevie Rae! You still okay down there?" Erik's voice called from above.

"Yeah, fine," she yelled back.

"We're putting up something like a tent over this crack and around the tree. Will that be good enough to get you out?"

"You just get a space covered for me. I can take care of the getting-out part."

"Okay, I'll let you know when we're ready," he said.

Stevie Rae turned back to Rephaim. "So here's my point. The last trolley stop was at the Gilcrease Museum. It's in north Tulsa. There's a big ol' house smack in the middle of it that's totally unoccupied. They keep talking about renovating it, but they haven't got the money together. You can hide there."

"Won't people see me?"

"Heck no! Not if you stay in the house during the day. It's a mess— all boarded up and locked so tourists don't stumble into it. And here's the best part—it's super-haunted! That's why it was on the ghost tour. Apparently Mr. Gilcrease, his second wife, and even ghost kids hang out there regularly, so if someone sees or hears something weird— meaning you—they'll freak and think it's just more ghost stuff."

"Spirits of the dead."

Stevie Rae raised her brows. "You're not scared of them, are you?"

"No. I understand them too well. I existed as a spirit for centuries."

"Dang, I'm sorry. I forgot about—"

"Okay, Stevie Rae! We're ready for you up here," Lenobia called.

"'Kay, I'll be right up. Stand back, though, so you don't fall down here when I make the crack bigger." She stood up and moved closer to the crack in the ground above them, which was no longer letting in much light. "I'll get them out of here right away. Then you get yourself over the railroad tracks. You'll see highway 244 east—follow it. It turns into OK 51. Go north until you see the Gilcrease Museum exit sign—it's on your right. Then just follow that road and you'll run smack into the museum. The hardest part will be over then, 'cause there're lots of trees and stuff to hide in on that road. It's the highway you're gonna have trouble with. Just move as fast as you can and stay off to the side and in the ditch. If you hunker down anyone who gets a glimpse of you might think you're just a giant bird."

Rephaim made a disgusted sound, which Stevie Rae ignored. "The house is in the middle of the museum grounds. Hide there and I'll bring food and stuff to you tomorrow night."

He hesitated and then said, "It isn't wise for you to see me again."

"None of this has been very smart, if you get right down to it," she said.

"Then I will probably see you tomorrow, as neither of us seems able to be smart where the other is concerned."

"Well, then, bye until tomorrow."

"Stay safe," he said. "If you don't, I— I believe I would, perhaps, feel your loss." He hesitated over the words, like he didn't quite know how to say them.

"Yeah, same right back at ya," she said. Before she raised her arms to open the earth, she added, "Thank you for saving my life. Your debt is totally paid in full."

"Odd how it doesn't feel like I'm free of it," he said softly.

"Yeah," said Stevie Rae. "I know what you mean."

And then, while Rephaim crouched within the earth, Stevie Rae called on her element, opened the ceiling of their chamber, and let Lenobia and Erik pull her free.

No one thought to look behind her. No one suspected. And no one saw a creature, half raven, half man, limping to the Gilcrease Museum to hide himself among the spirits of the past.

CHAPTER THIRTY-EIGHT

Zoey

"Stevie Rae! Are you really okay?" I gripped the cell phone, wishing I could beam myself to Tulsa and actually see with my own eyes that my BFF was alive and well.

"Z! You sound so worried. Don't be! I'm okay. Promise. It was all a big, stupid accident. Goddess, I'm such a dork."

"What happened?"

"Well, I was late leavin' the House of Night. I'm so stupid. I should have just stayed there and waited till tomorrow to come back to the tunnels. But I went anyway. And then, get this—I thought I heard someone up on the roof! So I rushed up there 'cause it was almost dawn and I thought some red fledgling kid might be trapped. Goddess, I need to have my ears checked. It was a *cat*. A great big, fat, calico cat yowling on the roof. I started to leave and, like the totally uncoordinated noncheerleader type I am, I fell and bonked my head so hard I passed out. You would *not* believe all the blood. Totally scary."

"You knocked yourself out on the roof? Right before dawn?" I wanted to reach through the phone and strangle her.

"Yeah, I know. Not the smartest thing I've ever done. Especially since I woke up with the sun shining on me."

"Did you burn?" My stomach felt sick. "I mean, are you still, uh, messed up from it?"

"Well, yeah, I started to burn, and that's probably what woke me up. And I'm still pretty toasty. It could've been a lot worse, though.

Luckily, I had time to run to that tree that's near the roof. Remember it?"

I knew the tree all too well. It had hidden something that had almost killed me. "Yeah, I remember it."

"So I jumped on the tree, slid down it, and had the earth open up to make a little hidey-hole for me. Kinda like a tornado was comin' and I was livin' in a trailer park."

"That's where Lenobia found you?"

"Yeah, Lenobia and Erik. He was real nice, by the way. Not that you should be with him again, but I thought you'd like to know."

"Okay, well, good. I'm glad you're safe." I paused, not sure how to say this next part. "Uh, Stevie Rae, it's been bad for Aphrodite. What with the Imprint between the two of you being broken and all."

"I'm real sorry if it hurt her."

"Hurt her! Are you kidding? We thought she was going to die. She was burning with you, Stevie Rae."

"Oh, my good*ness*! I didn't know."

"Stevie Rae, hang on a sec." I turned my back on everyone who was trying to listen in to my conversation and made my way out into the amazingly beautiful hall. White spun-glass chandeliers, holding real candles, lent a warm flickering light to the creams and golds of the upholstery, making me feel like Alice in Wonderland talking through a rabbit hole to an entirely different world. "Okay, that's better. Less ears out here," I continued. "Aphrodite said you were trapped. She was sure of it."

"Z, I tripped and hit my head. I'm sure Aphrodite picked up on my panic. I mean, when I woke up I was burning. Plus, I'd fallen over some metal trash on the roof, and I was all tangled up in it. I'm tellin' you—it scared the bejesus outta me. She musta felt that."

"So no one grabbed you? You weren't caged in anywhere?"

"No, Z," she laughed. "That's just crazy. But it would make a better story than me trippin' over my own feet."

I shook my head, still not able to take it all in. "It was scary, Stevie Rae. For a while I thought I was gonna lose both of you."

"Everything's okay. You're not losin' me or pain-in-the-butt

Aphrodite. Even though I can tell you I'm not sorry my Imprint with her is broken."

"Okay, that's another weird part. How did that happen? Your Imprint didn't even break when Darius drank from her, and you know they have that *thing* between them."

"Best I can figure is that I was closer to dying than I knew. That must have snapped our Imprint. And it wasn't like we *wanted* to be together. Maybe her thing with Darius had weakened it."

"It sure didn't seem like the Imprint between you was weak," I said.

"Well, it's gone, so when it came down to it, our Imprint was pretty easy to break."

"From where I was watching it didn't seem easy," I said.

"Well, from the perspective of the flaming kid in the sun, I can say it wasn't easy here either," she said.

Instantly I felt bad for the way I'd been firing questions at her. She'd almost died (for good), and here I was, grilling her about details. "Hey, I'm sorry. I was just so darn worried, that's all. And it was awful to watch Aphrodite experiencing your pain."

"Should I talk to her?" Stevie Rae asked.

"Uh, no. At least not right now. Last time I saw her, Darius was carrying her up an amazingly wide staircase to what sounded like a totally expensive suite so she could sleep off the drugs the vamps had given her."

"Oh, good. They medicated her. Aphrodite will like that."

We laughed, and it felt normal between us again.

"Zoey? The High Council is calling the session to order. You must go," Erce's voice called down the hallway.

"I gotta go take care of business," I said.

"Yeah, I heard. Hey, I want to say somethin' to you that you need to remember. Follow your heart, Z. Even if it seems like everyone else is against you, and that you might be messing up royally. Follow what everything inside you tells you to do. What happens because of it might surprise you," Stevie Rae said.

I hesitated and then said what was foremost in my mind. "And it might save your life?"

"Yes," she answered. "It might."

"We need to talk when I get home."

"I'll be here," she said. "Kick ass and take names, Z."

"I'll try," I said. "Bye, Stevie Rae. I'm glad you're not dead. Again."

"Me, too. Again."

We hung up. I drew a deep breath, squared my shoulders, and got ready to face the High Council.

The High Council met in a really old cathedral that sat right next to the super-beautiful San Clemente Palace. It was obvious that it had once been a Catholic church, and I wondered what Sister Mary Angela would think of how the vamps had changed it. They'd gutted the place, except for the enormous light fixtures that hung on thick bronze chains from the ceiling, looking like something that should have been suspended magically over the tables at Hogwarts. They'd built circular seating in tiers in a style I remembered studying about when we read *Medea*. Down on the granite floor, seven carved marble chairs sat side by side. I thought they were pretty, but looked like they'd make your butt fall asleep or freeze.

The stained-glass window scenes of the original cathedral had been changed from bloody Jesus on the cross and a bunch of Catholic saints to a representative of Nyx, arms upraised holding a crescent moon between her hands, a brilliant pentagram close beside her. In the other windows I saw stained-glass versions of the four class emblems that symbolized which year a fledgling ranked at the House of Night. I was looking around the cathedral, thinking how beautiful the windows were, when I noticed the scene depicted directly across from the image of Nyx—and it felt like everything inside me froze.

It was Kalona! Wings fully extended, his naked body muscular and bronzed and powerful. I felt myself begin to tremble.

Stark took my arm and wrapped it through his, like he was being a gentleman and guiding his lady down the stone stairs of the amphitheater-like space to our seats near the floor. But his touch was strong and steady, and he spoke low for my ears alone, "It isn't him. It's just an ancient representation of Erebus, like the symbol of Nyx over there."

"But it looks enough like him that they're going to think Kalona really is Erebus," I whispered frantically back to Stark.

"They might. And that's why you're here," he murmured.

"Zoey and Stark, these seats are for you." Erce pointed down to a tier of seats in the front and off to the side of the seven chairs. "The rest of you may fill in the row back there." She ushered Damien, Jack, and the Twins into seats several tiers behind us saying, "Remember, you may only speak if the Council recognizes you," Erce said.

"Yeah, yeah, I remember," I said. Something about Erce was annoying me. Okay, she was Lenobia's friend, so I wanted to like her, but since Aphrodite's freak-out she'd stepped in and been acting like she was seriously the boss of me and all my friends. I'd insisted Darius stay with Aphrodite, so I'd basically watched without saying much as Erce had droned on and on about the rules of the High Council and What Not to Do.

Okay, a fallen immortal and a rogue ex–High Priestess were trying to manipulate the Vampyre High Council. Wasn't clueing them in to that a little more important than being polite?

Of course, Damien, Jack, and the Twins all chimed in with innocent, intimidated "okays."

"I'm gonna be back here behind you, sitting next to Damien and Jack. I'm not feeling the love in this place for humans, so I'm keeping a low profile," Heath said.

I saw Stark exchange a long look with him. "You watch her back," he said.

Heath nodded. "I'll always have her back."

"Good. I'll focus on everything else," Stark said.

"Got it," Heath said.

And they weren't kidding. They weren't being sarcastic or testosteroney or overly possessive guy-like. They were so worried that they were working together.

That made me really, *really* paranoid.

I know it was ridiculous and immature, but I felt a terrible longing for my grandma. I wished with everything inside me that I was curled up in her cottage back at her Oklahoma lavender farm, eating popcorn that was too buttery, watching a marathon of Rodgers and

Hammerstein musicals, and the worst thing I had to worry about was how much I totally didn't get geometry.

"The Vampyre High Council!"

"Remember to stand up!" Erce whispered over her shoulder to me. I squelched an eye roll. The big room fell absolutely silent. I stood up with everyone else, and then gawked as seven of the most perfect creatures I'd ever seen strode into the room.

All of the High Council were women, but that much I'd known already. Our society is matriarchal, so it figures that its governing council would be female. I knew that they were old, even for vampyres, and they were. Of course you couldn't tell their age from just looking at them. All you could tell was how incredibly beautiful and amazingly powerful they were. On one hand it gave me a little squee of pleasure to see proof that even though vamps did age and, eventually die, they didn't get all grossly Shar-Pei–looking and full of wrinkles. On the other hand, the sense of power they exuded was totally intimidating. Just thinking about speaking in front of them, let alone the rest of those in the cathedral, grim, silent vampyres, made my stomach want to turn itself inside out.

Stark covered my hand with his and squeezed. I held tight to him, wishing I was older and smarter and, quite frankly, a better public speaker.

I heard the sound of someone else entering the room and glanced over to see Neferet and Kalona walking confidently down the stairs to fill two empty places in the same bottom row tier we were on, only the two of them sat directly in front of the High Council. As if they'd waited for them to arrive, the Council sat down, signaling to us it was okay to sit, too.

It was hard not to stare at Neferet and Kalona. She'd always been beautiful, but in just the couple of days since I'd last seen her, she had changed. The air around her seemed to vibrate with power. She was wearing a dress that reminded me of ancient Rome, flowing like a toga. It made her look like a queen. At her side Kalona was spectacular. It sounds stupid to say that he was only half dressed: He had on black slacks—no shirt—no shoes, but he didn't look stupid. He looked like a god who had decided to walk the earth. His wings swept around him like a cape. I knew everyone's eyes were on him, but when he looked at me and our gazes met, the world fell away and there was just Kalona and me.

The memory of our last dream blazed between us. I saw in him Nyx's Warrior, the incredible being who had stood beside her and then fell because he loved her too much. And in his eyes I saw vulnerability and a clear question. He wanted to know if I could believe him. In my mind I heard his words: *What if I'm only evil with Neferet? What if the truth is that if I were with you, I could choose good?*

My mind heard the words and rejected them again. My heart was something else. He'd touched my heart, and even though I was going to have to deny him—to pretend that he hadn't gotten to me—for that moment I wanted him to see the truth in my eyes. So I showed him my heart and let my eyes tell him what I knew I never could.

Kalona's response was to smile with such gentleness that I had to look quickly away.

"Zoey?" Stark whispered.

"I'm okay," I whispered back automatically.

"Stay strong. Don't let him get to you."

I nodded. I could feel people looking at me with even more than their normal curiosity for my added tattoos. I glanced over my shoulder to see Damien, Jack, and the Twins all gawking at Kalona. Then I caught Heath's eye. He wasn't looking at Kalona. He was staring at me, obviously worried. I tried to smile at him, but the expression felt more like a guilty grimace.

Then a Council member spoke, and I was relieved to focus my attention on her.

"The High Council is convened for this special session. I, Duantia, call us to order. May Nyx lend her wisdom and guidance to us."

"May Nyx lend her wisdom and guidance to us," intoned the rest of the room.

During Erce's briefing she'd told us the names of the Council members, and described each of them, and from her I knew that Duantia was the senior member, so it was her job to call it to order and to decide when the session would close. I stared at her. It was unbelievable that she was several hundred years old, and except for the intense confidence and power she commanded, her only outward sign of age was that her thick brown hair was streaked with silver.

"We have further questions for Neferet and the being who calls himself Erebus." I saw Neferet's green eyes narrow just the slightest, though she nodded graciously to Duantia.

Kalona stood and bowed to the Council. "Merry meet again," he greeted Duantia and nodded to each of the other six Council members. Several of them nodded back to him.

"We have questions about your origins," Duantia said.

"It is natural that you would," Kalona said.

His voice was deep and rich. He sounded humble and reasonable and very, very honest. I think I, along with almost everyone present, wanted to listen to him, whether we believed what he said or not.

And then I did something that was silly and totally childish. Like a little girl I closed my eyes and prayed one prayer to Nyx harder than I'd ever prayed before in my life. *Please let him speak only the truth. If he tells the truth, maybe there is hope for him.*

"You say that you are Erebus come to earth," said Duantia.

I opened my eyes to see Kalona smile and respond with, "I am, indeed, an immortal being."

"Are you Nyx's consort, Erebus?"

Tell the truth! I screamed in my head. *Tell the truth!*

"I once stood at Nyx's side. Then I fell to earth. Now I am here at—"

"At the side of the Goddess Incarnate," Neferet interrupted, standing beside Kalona.

"Neferet, we already know your viewpoint of who this immortal is," Duantia said. She didn't raise her voice, but her words were sharp, their warning clear. "What we want is to hear more from the immortal himself."

"As any consort would, I bow to my vampyre mistress," Kalona said, bowing slightly to Neferet who flashed him a triumphant smile that made me clench my teeth.

"Do you expect us to believe that Erebus's incarnation on this earth has no will of his own?"

"Whether on earth or beside Nyx in the Goddess's Realm, Erebus is devoted to his mistress, and his desires reflect hers. I can tell you that I know the truth of these words through personal experience," Kalona said.

And he was speaking the truth. As Nyx's Warrior he had witnessed Erebus's dedication to his Goddess. Of course the way he worded his response made it seem like he was claiming to be Erebus—without actually saying the *un*true words.

But isn't that what I'd prayed he'd do? That he'd only speak the truth?

"Why did you leave Nyx's Realm?" asked another Council member, one who had not nodded her welcome to him.

"I fell." Kalona looked from the Council member to me and spoke the rest of his response as if he and I were alone in the room. "I chose to leave because I no longer believed I served my Goddess well. At first it felt as if I had made a terrible mistake, and then I rose from the earth to find a new realm and a new mistress. Lately I have begun to believe I could, indeed, serve my Goddess again, only this time through her representative on earth."

Duantia's gracefully arched brows rose as she followed his gaze, which rested on me. Her eyes widened only slightly. "Zoey Redbird. The Council recognizes you."

CHAPTER THIRTY-NINE

Zoey

Feeling hot and cold at the same time, I dragged my gaze from Kalona and stood to face the Council. "Thank you. Merry meet," I said.

"Merry meet," Duantia responded and then continued smoothly. "Our sister, Lenobia, notified us that in Neferet's absence from your House of Night, you have been named High Priestess; therefore, you represent their will."

"It is entirely inappropriate for a fledgling to be named High Priestess," Neferet said. I knew she was totally pissed, but instead of showing it, she smiled indulgently at me, as if I were a toddler who'd been caught playing dress up with her mom's clothes. "I am still High Priestess of Tulsa's House of Night."

"Not if your House's Council has deposed you," said Duantia.

"The appearance of Erebus and the death of Shekinah has shaken Tulsa's House of Night greatly, especially following so soon after the terrible and tragic murders of two of our professors by local humans. It saddens me, but the Council members of my House are not thinking clearly."

"That the Tulsa House is in turmoil is undeniable. Nevertheless, we recognize their right to make the appointment of a new High Priestess, though it is highly unusual for a fledgling to be named to the position," Duantia said.

"She is a highly unusual fledgling," Kalona said.

I heard the smile in his voice.

I couldn't look at him.

Another Council member spoke up. Her dark eyes flashed and her voice was sharp, almost sarcastic. I thought she must be Thanatos, the vampyre who'd taken on the Greek name for death. "Interesting you speak in support of her, Erebus, as Lenobia says Zoey believes another version of who it is you are."

"I said she was unusual, not infallible," Kalona said. Several of the other Council members chuckled, as did many vampyres in the audience, though Thanatos appeared unamused. I could feel Stark stiffen where he sat beside me.

"So tell us, unusual and very young Zoey Redbird, who do you believe our winged immortal to be?"

My mouth was so dry I had to swallow twice before I could speak. And then when the words finally came, what I said took me by surprise, as if my heart said them without asking my mind's permission.

"I believe he's been lots of different things. I think he used to be close to Nyx, though he isn't Erebus."

"And if he isn't Erebus, who is he?"

I focused on the wisdom in Duantia's eyes and tried to block out everything else as I spoke only the truth. "My grandmother's people are Cherokee, and they have an old legend about him. They called him Kalona. He lived with the Cherokee after he fell from Nyx's Realm. I don't think he was himself then. He did terrible things to the women of the tribe. He fathered monsters. My grandmother told me how he was trapped. There was even a song the people used to sing that told how he could be freed from his imprisonment—directions Neferet followed, which is why he's here now. I think he's with Neferet because he wanted to be the consort of a goddess, and I think he messed up in his choice. Neferet isn't a goddess. She isn't even a goddess's High Priestess anymore."

My proclamation was met with exclamations of outrage and disbelief, the loudest coming from Neferet herself.

"How dare you! As if you—a fledgling *child*—can know who I am to Nyx?"

"No, Neferet," I faced her across the Council Chamber. "I don't have any idea who you are to Nyx anymore. I don't begin to understand what you've become. But I do know who you *aren't*. You aren't Nyx's High Priestess."

"Because you think you've supplanted me!"

"No, because you turned from the Goddess. It doesn't have anything to do with me," I said.

Neferet ignored me and appealed to the Council. "She's infatuated with Erebus. Why must I be subjected to this jealous child's slander?"

"Neferet, you have made it clear that it is your intention to be the next Vampyre High Priestess. Should you hold that title, you must be wise enough to deal with all types of controversy, even those involving yourself." Duantia looked from Neferet to Kalona. "What say you about Zoey's speech?"

I could feel him looking at me, but I kept my eyes steadily on Duantia.

"I say that she believes she is speaking the truth. And I do admit that my past has been violent. I have never claimed infallibility, either. I have recently found my path, though, and within that path there is Nyx."

There was no way I couldn't hear the truth that rang in his words. Unable to stop myself, my eyes were drawn to him.

"My experiences are why I feel so strongly about bringing back the old ways, where once vampyres and their Warriors strode the earth, proud and strong, instead of hiding in clusters of schools and only letting our young outside our gates if they have their Marks covered, as if the Goddess's crescent is something of which they should be ashamed. Vampyres are Nyx's children, and the Goddess never meant for you to cower in darkness. Let us all step into the light!"

He was magnificent. As he spoke, his wings had begun to unfurl. His voice was filled with passion. Everyone stared at him. Mesmerized by his beauty and passion, we all wanted to believe in his world.

"And when you're ready to be led by Nyx Incarnate and her consort Erebus, then we will bring the ancient ways to life again, so that we may all stand proud and strong—and not bow to human bondage and prejudice," Neferet said, looking glorious beside him as she wrapped her arm possessively through his. "Until then, listen to the whining of children as Erebus and I reclaim Capri from those who have interloped on our ancient home too long."

"Neferet, the Council will not sanction war against humans. You cannot force them from their homes on the island," Duantia said.

"War?" Neferet laughed, sounding shocked and amused. "Duantia, I *purchased* Nyx's Castle from the elderly human who had allowed it to fall into disrepair. Had any one of you on the Council checked, we could have regained our ancient home at any time during the past two decades." Neferet's green eyes swept around the chamber. Intense and appealing in her passion, she captivated the audience as she spoke. "It was there that vampyres founded the beauty of Pompeii. It was there that vampyres ruled the Amalfi Coast, ushering in centuries of prosperity with their wisdom and benevolence. It is there that you will find the heart and soul of Nyx and the richness of the life she wishes for her people. And it is there that you will find Erebus and me. Join us if you dare to live again!"

She turned and, in a swirl of silk, swept out of the chamber. Before following her, Kalona bowed respectfully to the Council, his fist over his heart. Then he looked at me and said, "Merry meet, merry part, and merry meet again."

When they left the chamber utter pandemonium was loosed. Everyone spoke at once, some clearly wanting to call Neferet and Kalona back—some indignant that they'd left. No one—not one vampyre—spoke against them. And whenever his name was spoken, they called him Erebus.

"They believe him," Stark said.

I nodded.

He gave me a sharp look. "Do *you* believe him?"

I opened my mouth, not sure how I was going to explain to my Warrior it wasn't so much that I believed in Kalona, but that I was beginning to believe in what he once had been and might become again.

Duantia's voice echoed through the chamber, silencing everyone. "Enough! This chamber will be cleared immediately. We will not disintegrate into chaotic rabble." Warriors seemed to materialize from the crowd, and the still animated vampyres began leaving.

"Zoey Redbird, we would speak with you tomorrow. Bring your circle here at dusk. We understand the fledgling-turned-human prophetess has experienced the trauma of a broken Imprint today. If she has recovered enough, we would have her join your group tomorrow."

"Yes, ma'am," I said.

Stark and I made a hasty exit. Damien motioned us over to a little side garden that was tucked just off the main path where the rest of the kids were waiting for us.

"What happened in there?" Damien didn't pause before getting right to it. "It sounded like you believed the stuff about Kalona falling from Nyx's side."

"I had to tell them the truth." I drew a deep breath and told my friends the rest of it. "Kalona showed me a vision of the past, and in it I saw that he was Nyx's Warrior."

"What!" Stark exploded. "The Goddess's Warrior? That's insane! I spent time with him. Time where he acted *real* around me. I saw who he is—and he isn't our Goddess's Warrior."

"Not anymore he isn't." I tried to keep my voice calm, but I wanted to yell back at Stark. He hadn't seen the vision. How could he judge whether it was true or not? "He chose to leave Nyx. And, yeah, it was a mistake. And, yeah, he did terrible things. I said all of that."

"But you believe him," Stark said, tight-lipped.

"No! I don't believe he's Erebus. I never said that."

"No, Zo, but what you did say made it sound like you might be on his side—if he dumped Neferet," Heath said.

I had had about enough. As usual, these guys were making my head hurt. "Do you think you two could quit looking at it like you're my boyfriends? Could you cut out the jealous, possessive stuff and try to be objective about him?"

"I'm not jealous or possessive of you, and I think you're mistaken if you're starting to believe Kalona is good," Damien said.

"He got to you, Z," Shaunee said.

"His mojo has definitely zapped you," Erin agreed.

"No, it hasn't! I haven't jumped on Team Kalona! All I'm doing is trying to see the truth here. What if the truth is that he used to be on the right side? Maybe he could find the right side again," I said.

Stark was shaking his head. I rounded on him. "It happened with you, so how the hell can you be so sure it can't happen with him?"

"He's using your connection with A-ya to mess with your head. Think clearly, Zoey." His eyes begged me to listen to him.

"That's what I've been trying to do—to think clearly and to find the truth—*without* everyone else's attitudes, including A-ya's, getting in the way. Just like I did for you."

"It's not the same thing! I wasn't evil for centuries. I didn't turn an entire tribe of people into my slaves and rape their women," Stark said.

"You were going to rape Becca if Darius and I hadn't stopped you!" The words came blurting out of my mouth before my good sense could stop them.

Stark actually took a step away from me like I'd hit him. "He's done it. He's gotten inside your head, and with him there, there's no room for your Warrior." Stark turned and walked away into the shadows.

I didn't realize I was crying until I felt the wetness fall from my chin to my shirt. I wiped my face with a trembling hand. Then I looked at the rest of my friends. "When Stevie Rae first came back, she was so horrible that I almost didn't recognize her. She was scary and mean and bad. Truly bad. But I didn't turn my back on her, either. I believed in her humanity, and because I didn't give up on her, she got it back," I said.

"But, Zoey, Stevie Rae was good before she died and then came back. We all know that. What if the truth is that Kalona never had any goodness and *humanity* to lose? What if his choice has always been for evil?" Damien asked quietly. "For you to be saying all of this, what he showed you seemed real, but you have to at least consider the fact that the vision might have been nothing more than smoke-and-mirrors. He might have been showing you 'truth,' but a dressed-up, partial version of truth."

"I have been considering that," I said.

"Like Stark said, have you really thought about the fact that the soul connection you have with A-ya, and the memories you've had about her, might be clouding your judgment?" Erin asked.

I nodded, crying harder.

Heath took my hand. "Zo, his favorite son killed Anastasia and almost killed those other kids who stood up to him."

"I know," I sobbed. *But what if he only let them do that because Neferet wanted it?* I didn't say the words aloud, but Heath seemed to read my mind.

"Kalona's trying to get to you 'cause you're the one who had the strength to pull everyone together to banish him from Tulsa," Heath said.

"And Aphrodite's vision shows that you're the only one who has the strength to defeat him permanently," Damien said.

"Part of you was made to cause his destruction," Shaunee said.

"And that same part of you was made to love him," Erin said.

"You have to remember that, Zo," Heath said.

"I think you need to talk to Aphrodite," Damien said. "I'm going to wake her up, and get Darius, too. We're going to talk this out. You need to describe exactly what Kalona showed you in that vision."

I nodded, but I knew I couldn't do what they wanted me to do. I couldn't talk to Aphrodite and Darius. Not when I felt so raw.

"Okay, but I need a minute." I wiped my face with my sleeve. Jack, who'd been watching everything with big, worried eyes, opened his man purse and handed me a little travel Kleenex package. "Thank you," I sniffled.

"Just keep it. You'll probably cry more later," he said, patting my shoulder.

"Why don't you guys go on up to Aphrodite's suite? I'll get myself together and be up there in a little while."

"Don't take long, okay?" Damien said.

I nodded and my friends walked slowly away. I looked at Heath. "I gotta be alone."

"Yeah, I figured, but I wanted to tell you something." He took me by both of my shoulders and made me meet his gaze. "You have to fight this thing you feel for Kalona, and I'm not saying that because I'm jealous or whatever. I've loved you since we were kids. I'm not gonna leave you. I'm not gonna turn away from you, no matter what you say or do, but Kalona isn't like Stevie Rae or Stark. He's immortal. He's from another whole kind of world, and Zo, I get 'I want to rule this world' vibes from him. You're the only one who can stop him, so he has to have you on his side. He gets into your dreams. He gets into your mind, and there's part of him that's even connected to your soul. I understand that because I'm connected to your soul, too."

Being alone with Heath was actually calming me down. He was so familiar. He was my human rock—always there—always standing up for what was really best for me.

"I'm sorry I called you jealous and possessive." I sniffled and blew my nose.

He grinned. "I am, kinda. But I always know what me and you have is special." He jerked his chin in the direction Stark had gone. "Your Warrior boyfriend doesn't have my confidence."

"Yeah, well, he doesn't have as much Zoey experience as you do."

His grin widened. "No one does, babe!"

I sighed and stepped into his arms, hugging him hard. "You're like home to me, Heath."

"That's what I'll always be, Zo." He pulled back and kissed me softly. "Okay, I'm gonna let you be alone 'cause you still got some snot and tears going on. And while you clean up, how about I track down Stark, tell him that he's a jealous dork, maybe even punch him."

"Punch him?"

Heath shrugged. "A good punch makes guys feel better."

"Uh, not if they're receiving instead of giving," I said.

"Fine. Then I'll go find someone else for him to punch." He waggled his brows at me. "'Cause you obviously don't want my pretty face messed up."

"If you find him, would you bring him to Aphrodite's room?"

"That's what I planned on," he said. Then he ruffled my hair. "I love ya, Zo."

"I love you, too, but I really hate it when you mess up my hair," I said.

He grinned over his shoulder at me, winked, and then went after Stark.

I was actually feeling a little better. I sat on the bench, blew my nose again, wiped my eyes, and stared off into the distance. Then I realized what I was staring at and where I was sitting.

It was the bench from one of my first Kalona dreams. It was built up on a mound so that from there I could look over the top of the huge wall that circled the island and see, off in the distance, the illuminated St. Mark's Square looking like a magical wonderland in the wintry night. At my back was San Clemente Palace, all lit up and glistening. Around the palace to my right was the ancient cathedral turned High Council Chamber. All this beauty—all this power and majesty around me and I'd been too self-absorbed to *see* any of it.

Maybe I'd become too self-absorbed to *see* Kalona, either.

I knew what Aphrodite would say. She'd say I was making the bad vision come true. Maybe she was right.

I lifted my head and stared up at the night sky, trying to see though the layers of clouds and concealment to the moon. And then I prayed.

"Nyx, I need you. I think I'm lost. Please help me. Please show me something that will make things clearer to me. I don't want to mess up . . . again . . ."

CHAPTER FORTY

Heath

Heath wondered if Zo knew she was breaking his heart. Not that he wanted to be away from her. He didn't. Actually, he wanted more of her. The problem was he also wanted what was best for her—he always had. Ever since grade school. He remembered the day he fell in love with her. Her mom had freaked out on her and had taken her to some girlfriend who worked at one of those girl beauty shops. They'd decided—Zo's mom and her girlfriend—that it would be cute to chop off all of Zo's long, dark hair. So the next day she'd showed up for third grade with hair that was super-short and kinda weirdly sticking out all over and fuzzy looking.

The kids had all been whispering and laughing at her. Her big brown eyes had been huge and scared, and Heath had thought he'd never seen anyone who was so beautiful. He'd told her he liked her hair—in front of the whole cafeteria at lunch. She'd looked like she was going to cry, so he'd carried her tray for her, and sat with her, even though it wasn't cool to sit with a girl. That day she'd done something to his heart. She'd been doing something to it ever since.

So, here he was, going to find a guy who had a piece of her heart because it was what was best for Zoey. Heath ran his hand through his hair. All of this would be over someday. Someday Zo would go back to Tulsa, and even though the House of Night would take up a bunch of her time, she'd be with him when she could. They'd go to the movies again. She'd come watch him play football at OU. It would be normal again, or as normal as it could be.

He could hang in till then. When this crap with Kalona got

straight—and Zo would get it straightened out, Heath was sure of it—when this crap was fixed, things would be better. He'd have his Zo back. Or at least as much of her as she could give him. And that would be enough.

Heath followed the path that led away from the palace, still going in the general direction Stark had taken. He looked around and couldn't see much except the big stone wall on his left, and a parklike area filled with hedges that were almost as high as his head, on his right. He studied the park as he walked, realizing the hedges created some kind of circular, interwoven pattern. He decided it must be one of those old mazes—a labyrinth, he finally remembered from the Greek mythology story about the Minotaur on the island of some rich king, whose name there was no way he could remember.

Damn, he hadn't realized how dark it was until he'd gotten away from the lights of the palace. It was quiet out here, too. So quiet he could hear the lapping of the waves just on the other side of the wall. Heath wondered if he should yell out for Stark, but decided, nah, like Zo, he didn't mind a little time to himself.

All this vamp stuff was a lot to take in, and it was normal that he needed time to process. Not that he couldn't deal with Stark and the other vamps. Hell, he kinda liked some of the vamps—and fledglings, too. If it came right down to it, he actually thought Stark was an okay guy. It was just Kalona who was fucking things up.

Then, as if his thoughts had drawn the immortal to him, Heath heard Kalona's voice drifting through the empty night, and he slowed down, careful not to crunch any loose stones on the path.

"It goes exactly as planned," Kalona was saying.

"I hate the subterfuge! I cannot bear that you pretend to be something you are not for her."

Heath recognized Neferet's voice and he inched forward. Keeping to the deepest of the shadows, he hugged the wall, being absolutely silent. The voices were coming from the park area, ahead and to his right, and as he moved forward, there was a break in the hedge, obviously an exit, and within the labyrinth Kalona and Neferet came into view. They were standing by a fountain. Heath breathed a shallow sigh of relief. The sound of the cascading water must have been what masked his footsteps. Pressing himself against the cold stone wall, he watched and listened.

"You call it pretense. I call it another point of view," Kalona said.

"Which is why you can lie to her and still seem to be telling the truth," Neferet snapped the words at him.

Kalona shrugged. "Zoey wants truth—so it is truth that I give her."

"Selectively," Neferet said.

"Of course. But do all mortals, vampyre, human, or fledgling, not select their own truths?"

"*Mortals*. You say that as if you are so far removed from us."

"I am immortal, which makes me different. Even from you, though your Tsi Sgili powers are transforming you into something that is close to immortal."

"Yes, but Zoey isn't anything close to immortal. I still believe we should kill her."

"You are a bloodthirsty creature." Kalona laughed. "What would you do, cut off her head and impale her as you did the other two who got in your way?"

"Don't be ridiculous. I wouldn't kill her the same way I did them. It would be too obvious. She could simply meet with an unfortunate accident when she visits Venice in the next day or so."

Heath's heart was pounding so loud he was sure they'd be able to hear him. Neferet had killed Zoey's two professors! And Kalona knew about it *and thought it was funny*. No way would Zo believe there was any good in him after she heard about this.

"No," Kalona was saying, "We will not have to kill Zoey. Soon she will come to me willingly; I've planted the seeds for that. All I need do is wait for them to bloom, and then her powers, which are vast even though she is mortal, will be at my disposal."

"*Our* disposal," Neferet corrected him.

One of Kalona's dark wings swept forward, stroking the side of Neferet's body and causing her to sway toward him. "Of course, my Queen," he murmured before he kissed her.

Heath felt like he was watching porn, but he was trapped there.

He couldn't move. He probably needed to stay until they were actually doing it, and then he could slip away, go to Zoey, and tell her everything he'd overheard.

But Neferet surprised him by pulling away from Kalona. "No. You can't make love to Zoey in her dreams, and then again with your eyes in front of everyone, and expect me to open my body to you. I won't be yours tonight. She is too much between us." Neferet backed away from Kalona. Even Heath was captured by her beauty. Her thick auburn hair was wild around her. The silky stuff that wrapped around her body looked like a second skin, and her boobs were almost totally exposed as she breathed hard and fast. "I know I am not immortal, nor am I Zoey Redbird, but my powers, too, are vast, and you should remember I killed the last male who tried to claim me and her." Neferet whirled around. With a wave of her hand she parted the hedge in front of her and stepped through it, leaving Kalona standing alone and staring after her in the dim clearing.

Heath was getting ready to back slowly away when Kalona's head turned and his amber eyes went straight to where he was standing.

"So, little human, you now have a story to tell my Zoey," he said.

Heath looked into the immortal's eyes and he knew two things beyond any doubt. One was that this creature was going to kill him. The second was that somehow he had to show Zoey the truth before he died. Heath didn't flinch under the creature's stare. Instead he used all the strength of will he'd learned to harness so well on a different kind of battlefield—a football field—and he channeled it through the blood bond of their Imprint, trying to find the element Zoey had the strongest affinity with—spirit. His heart and soul shouted into the night: *Spirit, come to me! Help take my message to Zo! Tell her she has to find me!* Meanwhile his voice calmly told Kalona, "She's not your Zoey."

"Ah, but she is," Kalona said.

Zo! Come to me! Heath's soul cried. "Nah, you don't know my girl."

"Your girl's soul belongs to me and I will not allow Neferet or you or *anyone* to change that." Kalona began walking toward Heath.

Zo! It's you and me, babe! Come to me!

"What is that expression the vampyres use?" Kalona said. "I believe it is 'curiosity killed the cat.' It seems particularly applicable to this situation."

Stark

"I'm an idiot." Stark grumbled to himself as he made his way through the grand entrance to the palace.

"Sir, do you need direction?" asked a warrior who stood just inside.

"Yeah, I need to know where Aphrodite's room is. You know, the human prophetess who came here with us today? Oh, I'm Stark, Warrior to the High Priestess Zoey Redbird."

"We know who you are," the vampyre said. His eyes moved to Stark's red tattoos. "It's all very fascinating."

"Yeah, well, 'fascinating' isn't the word I'd use."

The warrior smiled. "You have not been bound to her long, have you?"

"No. Just a few days."

"It gets better—and worse."

"Thanks. I think." Stark blew out a long breath. Even though Zoey made him crazy, he knew he could never walk away from her again. He was her Warrior. His place, no matter how tough it got, was by her side.

The warrior laughed. "The suite you seek is in the north wing of the palace. Go left here, take the first staircase on your right. On the second floor, that entire suite of rooms has been allotted to your group. You will find your friends there."

"Thanks again." Stark started in the direction the warrior had sent him, walking quickly. He had an itchy feeling on the back of his neck. He hated it when he got that feeling. It meant something was going wrong, and that meant it was a stupid time for him to get pissed at Zoey.

It was just so damn hard. He felt her attraction for Kalona! Why the hell couldn't she see that the guy was bad? There was nothing in him left to save—there probably had never been anything worth saving inside him.

Stark had to convince her that he was right. And to do that he had to stop letting his feelings for her mess with his head. Zoey was a smart girl. He'd talk to her. Calmly. She'd listen to him. From the first time they'd met, before they'd been anything together, she'd listened to him. He knew he could get her to listen again.

Stark climbed the stairs three at a time. The first door to his left was partially open, and he could see into a rich-looking room that had a couple of those couches that were too little and a bunch of uncomfortable chairs—all done up in golds and creams. Like that wouldn't get dirty? He heard the murmur of voices and was just opening the door farther when Zoey's emotions smacked him like a tidal wave.

Fear! Anger! Confusion!

What was going through her head was such a jumbled mess that he couldn't sort out anything except the basest of feelings.

"Stark? What is it?" Darius was there in front of him.

"Zoey!" he managed to rasp. "She's in trouble!" And then the force of it literally made him stagger. He would have fallen had Darius not grabbed him.

"Get a hold of yourself! Where is she?" Darius had him by his shoulders and was shaking him.

Stark looked up to see the worried faces of Zoey's friends all staring at him. He shook his head, trying to think through the terror in his mind. "I can't—I'm—"

"You must! Do not try to think. Just let your instincts take over. A Warrior can always find his lady. Always."

His body was trembling, but Stark nodded, turned, drew three deep breaths and then said one word, "Zoey!"

Her name seemed to echo in the air around him. He concentrated on it—not on the chaos in his mind. He thought only, *Zoey Redbird, my lady.*

And like the words had become a lifeline, they began pulling him forward.

Stark ran.

He could feel Darius and the others at his back. He vaguely saw the surprised look on the warrior's face he'd so recently spoken to, but he ignored everything. He thought only of Zoey and let the strength of his oath draw him to her.

It felt like he was flying. He didn't remember finding the path along the labyrinth, but later he did remember the crunching of stones under his feet as he pulled away from even Darius in his oath-driven speed.

Still he was too late.

If Stark lived for five hundred years he would never forget what he saw when he burst around the corner of the path and into the little clearing. The sight would forever be burned into his soul.

Kalona and Heath were farthest away from him. The two of them were standing in front of the outer wall that enclosed the island and shielded it from the eyes of Venetian humans.

Zoey was closer to him. Just a few yards away, but like him she, too, was running. Stark watched her lift her hands. At the same moment she commanded, "Spirit! Come to me!" Kalona lifted his hands, too, cupping Heath's face almost as if he were caressing him.

Then in one swift, unstoppable movement, the fallen immortal twisted Heath's head, cleanly breaking his neck and killing him instantly.

In a voice torn from her soul, and so filled with anguish Stark hardly recognized her, Zoey screamed, "No!" and threw the glowing ball of spirit at Kalona.

Kalona dropped Heath and whirled around to face her, his expression utterly shocked. The power of the element hit him, hurling him into the air and throwing him over the wall and into the ocean where, with a cry of despair, Kalona's enormous wings lifted him from the water and carried him up and into the cold night.

But Stark didn't give a shit about Kalona or even Heath. It was Zoey he ran to. She lay crumpled on the ground not far from Heath's body. She was facedown, and Stark knew the terrible truth before he reached her. Still, he dropped to his knees and rolled her gently over. Her eyes were open and staring, but vacant.

Except for the sapphire outline of a normal fledgling's Mark, all of her tattoos were gone.

Darius reached them first. He dropped beside Zoey, feeling for a pulse.

"She lives," Darius said. Then he processed what he saw and gasped, "Goddess! Her tattoos." He touched Zoey's face gently. "I don't understand." Shaking his head in confusion, his gaze lit on Heath. "Is the boy—"

"He's dead," Stark said, amazed his voice sounded so normal when everything inside him was screaming.

Aphrodite and Damien ran up.

"Oh, Goddess!" Aphrodite said, crouching beside Zoey's head. "Her tattoos!"

"Zoey!" Damien cried.

Stark heard Jack and the Twins join them. They were crying. But all he could do was pull her more tightly into his arms and hold her close. He had to protect her. He *had to.*

It was Aphrodite whose voice finally penetrated his grief and got through to him.

"Stark! We have to get Zoey back to the palace. Someone there can help her. She's still alive."

Stark met Aphrodite's gaze. "Her body breathes for right now, but that's it."

"What are you talking about? *She's still alive,*" Aphrodite repeated stubbornly.

"Zoey saw Kalona kill Heath and she called spirit to try to stop him, but she was too late to save him." *Just like I was too late to save her,* Stark's mind shrieked. But in the calm voice of a stranger, he continued explaining. "When she threw spirit at Kalona, Zoey knew she was too late, and her soul shattered. I know because I'm bound to her soul and I felt it shatter. Zoey's not here anymore. This is just her empty shell."

Then James Stark, Zoey Redbird's Warrior, bowed his head and began to cry.

EPILOGUE

Zoey

I breathed a long, contented sigh. Peace . . . Seriously, I couldn't remember ever feeling so stress-free. Goddess, it was a gorgeous day. The sun was amazing—all golden and glowy in a sky so birthday-cake-icing blue that it should have hurt my eyes. But it didn't.

Which was kinda weird. Bright sunlight should hurt my eyes.

Huh.

Oh, well. Whatever.

The meadow was totally beautiful. It reminded me of something. I started to try to remember, but decided I didn't want to think that hard. The day was too pretty to think. I just wanted to breathe in the sweet summer air and breathe out all the stupid tension that had been coiled like a slinky inside my body.

The grass was waving around my legs softly, like delicate feathers.

Feathers.

What was it about feathers?

"Nope. No thinking." I smiled as my words became visible, creating sparkly purple patterns in the air.

In front of me was a line of trees that were filled with white flowers that reminded me of snowflakes. The wind brushed gently through their branches, making music on the air that I danced to, skipping and pirouetting through the grove, breathing deeply of the blossoms' sweet scent.

I wondered for a second where I was, but it didn't seem all that important. Or at least not as important as the peace and the music and the dancing.

Then I wondered how I'd gotten here. That stopped me. Okay, well, it didn't really stop me. It just slowed me down.

That's when I heard it. It was a *zing, plop!* sound. It seemed comfortingly familiar, so I followed it through the grove. More blue peeked through the trees, this time it reminded me of topaz or aquamarines. Water.

With a happy little cry I ran out of the trees to the bank of an amazingly clear lake.

Zing, plop!

The sound was coming from around a little bend in the lake's shore, so I followed it, humming my favorite song from *Hairspray* softly to myself.

The dock jutted out onto the lake, perfect for fishing. And, sure enough, there was a guy sitting on the end of the dock, casting out his line with a little *zing* and then a *plop!* as it hit the water.

It was strange. I didn't know who he was, but suddenly a terrible panic intruded on my wonderful, beautiful day. No! I didn't want to see him! I was shaking my head and starting to back away when I stepped on a twig and the *snap* had him turning around.

The big smile on his handsome face vanished when he saw me.

"Zoey!"

Heath's voice did it. My memory rushed back. The sadness knocked me to my knees. He was up and running toward me so that he caught me in his arms as I fell.

"But you don't belong here! You're dead!" I sobbed against his chest.

"Zo, babe, this is the Otherworld. It's not me who doesn't belong here—it's you."

Memory crashed over me, drowning me with despair and darkness and reality as my world shattered, and everything went black.

The End for Now

Stay tuned for more in the next installment of the House of Night

Burned